ESTHER

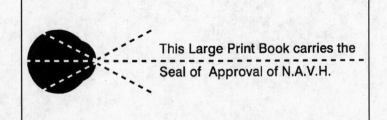

This Large Print Book carries the
Seal of Approval of N.A.V.H.

ESTHER

REBECCA KANNER

THORNDIKE PRESS
A part of Gale, Cengage Learning

GALE
CENGAGE Learning·

Farmington Hills, Mich • San Francisco • New York • Waterville, Maine
Meriden, Conn • Mason, Ohio • Chicago

GALE
CENGAGE Learning

LIBRARY OF CONGRESS CATALOGING-IN-PUBLICATION DATA

Names: Kanner, Rebecca, author.
Title: Esther / by Rebecca Kanner.
Description: Large print edition. | Waterville, Maine : Thorndike Press, 2016. |
    © 2015 | Series: Thorndike press large print Christian fiction
Identifiers: LCCN 2015050116 | ISBN 9781410488848 (hardcover) | ISBN 1410488845
    (hardcover)
Subjects: LCSH: Esther, Queen of Persia—Fiction. | Bible. Esther—History of Biblical
    events—Fiction. | Women in the Bible—Fiction. | Large type books. | GSAFD:
    Bible fiction. | Biographical fiction.
Classification: LCC PS3611.A5495 E85 2016 | DDC 813/.6—dc23
LC record available at http://lccn.loc.gov/2015050116

Published in 2016 by arrangement with Howard Books, an imprint of
Simon & Schuster, Inc.

Printed in Mexico
1 2 3 4 5 6 7 20 19 18 17 16

For Lynn

CONTENTS

CAST OF CHARACTERS 11

Chapter 1: Kidnapped 13
Chapter 2: The Virgins' March 25
Chapter 3: Screaming 33
Chapter 4: Goddess of
       Bullheadedness 36
Chapter 5: The Ride Back 56
Chapter 6: The Market 58
Chapter 7: Vashti 64
Chapter 8: The Vow 81
Chapter 9: The Palace 83
Chapter 10: The Harem 92
Chapter 11: Hegai 105
Chapter 12: The Inspection 110
Chapter 13: Night 115
Chapter 14: Life in the Harem . . . 120
Chapter 15: My New Chambers . . . 141
Chapter 16: Mistress Esther 143

7

Chapter 17: The Women's Court. . . 166

Chapter 18: Lioness. 183

Chapter 19: The Bloody Dagger . . . 192

Chapter 20: Saul's Mistake 203

Chapter 21: Erez 219

Chapter 22: Utanah. 232

Chapter 23: The Approach of My
Night with the King. 252

Chapter 24: Erez, the King, and I . . 264

Chapter 25: Her Majesty. 291

Chapter 26: My Banquet. 304

Chapter 27: In the King's
Chamber 325

Chapter 28: Ruti and Hegai. 339

Chapter 29: My Servant, My
Guard 346

Chapter 30: Heavy Is the Head . . . 358

Chapter 31: The Queen's Men . . . 367

Chapter 32: The Brothers' Blood . . 387

Chapter 33: The King's Soldier . . . 399

Chapter 34: Returns 411

Chapter 35: The King's Bed 422

Chapter 36: Trapped 430

Chapter 37: The Routine. 433

Chapter 38: Dagger Training 440

Chapter 39: Here Lies the Empire . . 454

Chapter 40: The Plot on the
     King's Life 459
Chapter 41: Warning the King. . . . 465
Chapter 42: The Fitful Blade 475
Chapter 43: The Kick 485
Chapter 44: A Crime One Woman
     Commits Against Another . . . 489
Chapter 45: Xerxes'
     Homecoming 499
Chapter 46: The Only Place 505
Chapter 47: The Woman Who
     Walked Beside Me 517
Chapter 48: Haman's Visit to the
     Royal Treasury 520
Chapter 49: Desire 526
Chapter 50: Time Is Servant to
     No One 531
Chapter 51: News of Mordecai . . . 535
Chapter 52: The Edict 539
Chapter 53: Ghosts 543
Chapter 54: The Golden Scepter . . 547
Chapter 55: The First Feast 551
Chapter 56: Friends and Allies . . . 555
Chapter 57: The Second Feast . . . 562
Chapter 58: The King's Dream . . . 573
Chapter 59: Purim 580
Chapter 60: Leave-takings 584

EPILOGUE 587
AUTHOR'S NOTE. 591
ACKNOWLEDGMENTS 595

CAST OF CHARACTERS

Esther: an orphan who is kidnapped and taken to the king's harem

Mordecai: Esther's cousin who takes her in after her parents are killed in a revolt in Babylon

Xerxes: king of Persia

Erez: an Immortal with whom Esther has a complicated relationship

Hegai: the powerful eunuch who takes a liking to Esther

Ruti: Esther's servant

Haman: a high-ranking adviser to the king and enemy of the Jews

Parsha: Haman's firstborn son, one of Esther's tormentors

Dalphon: Haman's second-born son

Halannah: Haman's niece and Xerxes' favorite concubine, she aspires to be queen

Bigthan: one of the many eunuchs who serve in the palace of Shushan

Hathach: a eunuch assigned to Esther, Esther questions whether he serves her or the king

Cyra: Esther's childhood friend

Utanah: the first girl to volunteer to be one of Esther's handmaids, she was suspiciously absent from the harem when the virgins were assigned their places

Opi: a Nubian girl, Esther tries to befriend her

CHAPTER ONE: KIDNAPPED

*Outside the Persian capital city of Shushan,
480 BCE*

They were the night itself. First the darkness and then the blinding light of torches that hid the stars. The whinnying of horses, the crying of a hundred girls, the clashing of swords. The smell of flesh that has traveled a long way through the desert, bringing with it dust and sweat from far-off lands.

I was lying on my straw mattress when I heard the hooves pounding in the distance. It was much too long past the day's end for a merchant's caravan to be traveling upon the road, and the sound was not the slow plodding of oxen, elephants, or camels. It was the hard and fast approach of horses.

My hands started to shake. They did not want to obey me, but mostly they did, clumsily tying my head scarf behind my neck. My feet too were clumsy as I slid them into sandals and wound the straps around

13

my ankles, all the way up to my calves. I pulled them tight. Because I knew. I knew why the hooves came.

Yet I did not run.

I no longer knew what would save me and what would lead to my death. I did not even know if the pounding in my ears was hooves striking the ground or the beating of my own heart. The horses were upon the village — I could smell dust rising from the road.

The door was yanked open and a shadow blocked the light of the stars. It would haunt me until I learned who had cast it. As it approached I heard not only heavy footsteps but also the clanking of armor. The king's soldiers had fallen upon the village. And not just ordinary soldiers, of whom the king had hundreds of thousands, but the king's most elite, highly trained force: Immortals.

A month before, the king had issued a decree that virgins from every province of his empire were to be gathered and brought to the palace at Shushan to serve in his harem. At the news, my cousin, Mordecai, had said, *Soldiers are lazy, they save themselves for great battles. They will take only the girls nearest the palace.* So he had sent me only a day's journey from the heart of Shushan, to a village where a friend of his was willing to let me stay in the tiny servants' quarters behind his hut.

As the Immortal came to hover over me, the rest of my cousin's words rang in my ears: *Though Xerxes is the richest man in the world, he will not feel rich until there is nothing, anywhere, that is not his.* It seemed the shadow was Xerxes himself emerging from my cousin's tales, hungry to add me to his possessions.

"Forgive me," the Immortal said. No two words had ever terrified me so greatly. *Forgive me.* He spoke loudly, as though he spoke not to me but to someone else who was not so near. Perhaps to his god. He pulled me from my straw mattress, threw me over his shoulder, and began walking. My head fell against his armor.

His shoulder pressed up into my belly, making it hard to speak, but still I tried. "Please —" I did not finish — I didn't want the words *do not make me spend the rest of my life as a harem concubine* to exist in the world.

He did not hesitate at the doorway of the hut. He had already asked forgiveness for all he would do.

As we approached the road I could hear girls crying, and I did not want to join my voice to theirs. I did not want to be one of them. I had cried while Xerxes' soldiers quashed the last revolt of Babylon so brutally that for days the city smelled of blood. My tears had not saved my parents.

Instead I felt for the soldier's dagger. My fingers wrapped around it and slid it from his belt. *Lord, let it be me who will need to ask for forgiveness.* I plunged it up the inside of the soldier's tunic sleeve with all my strength.

The dagger was no match for his flesh. It slipped from my hand as if he had knocked it away. I tried again with the most ready weapon I had, one I did not have to grip. I sunk my teeth into his upper left arm. He grunted and threw me to the ground. He was only flesh after all, flesh I could run from. Though first I hastily searched the ground for the dagger. I had grasped it only briefly, yet without it my hands felt unbearably empty. Perhaps, knowing I was about to lose all I had, I could not bear to lose anything more. And for this I will never forgive myself.

What good did I think it would do me? What excuse can I offer?

I was only fourteen. I had made one mistake after another: I should not have put on my head scarf, I should simply have grabbed — not fastened and tied — my sandals. And most of all, I should not have

16

been near Shushan.

The only thing I may have done right, though I did it too late, was run. I ran in the opposite direction of the road and the terrible sound of girls crying.

But I did not go far before learning the terrible strength of men. He yanked me by my tunic and I flew into him so hard the wind was knocked from my lungs. His weight fixed him to the earth as mine did not; the impact did not move him even a hair's width. I knew suddenly that there had never been any use in stealing his dagger and stabbing him, nor in biting him. It was as though I had flown backward into a giant rock face.

As he dragged me toward the road and the pleas of the girls gathered there, I fought to gather enough air to speak. I wanted to tell him my cousin would reward him with gold darics if he would let me go, but my body would give up only enough breath to say, *"Please."*

He did not respond with words. He tightened his arms — one around my ribs and elbows, the other around my neck. If I had not been choking from the soldier's arm I would have choked on the musky earthen smell of men and horses. Sweat old and new, dust, dirt, the frothing around the horses' saddles and bits. As the soldier brought me to stand in the road I could smell all of this but see little — the light of the torches was blinding. Yet for a moment I tried not to close my eyes. I wanted to see the soldiers' faces, hoping to find kindness in one of them.

The arms released me and I stumbled backward, as if the light itself pushed me away. A new shadow came to stand before me. I quickly practiced my lie, practiced not allowing the voice in my head to falter. *Sir, I must humbly tell you that I am already betrothed. My wedding is in two days.*

"Sir," I said. He tied a rope around my wrists so tightly I knew we had passed the point at which we could have pretended I did not want to run away. "I must humbly tell you —"

"You must humbly keep your mouth shut or I will close it for you."

"I am already promised to —"

"Gag her," the soldier ordered. Though he had already tied the rope around my wrists, he did not let go of it.

My eyes were adjusting to the light. The soldier had eyes whose centers were like perfect round drops of honey that have just begun to melt in the sun. Huge, beautiful eyes. He possessed no other remarkable features. Perhaps his eyes had used up all the beauty that one face is allowed. He had a long nose from which the rest of his features receded, as though he had thrust his face too often against the wind. Not even his beard of tight curls could disguise that he had little in the way of a chin.

"My cousin will give you gold coins if you will let me stay here."

He leaned close. I tried to step back, but he yanked me forward by the rope around my wrists. "We will take you," he said, his stale breath hitting my face like something solid, "*and* your cousin's coins."

From behind me a soldier said, "Enough, Parsha." I was relieved to hear someone speaking on my behalf, but I did not like knowing that the soldier who had tied my wrists had a name. It made it harder to hold on to my last hope — that I was having a nightmare, the contents of which would empty back into the night when I awoke. Where would I have come up with the name Parsha? The soldier was not my invention. I leaned away from him.

"You *follow* orders, Erez," Parsha replied. "My brother's orders." Yet he let go of the rope and turned away as I stumbled backward.

The soldier called Erez caught me. My

19

back fell against his chest and his hands steadied me. Perhaps meaning to reassure me, he said, "We only want a hundred of you. When we put you in lines and walk through with torches it will be decided who is plain enough to stay here and who we will bring to the king." He moved on and I had to bear my own weight again, a terrible burden I could not set down.

As the huts were ransacked, the girls on either side of me pressed closer. Whatever stood between the soldiers and the things they wanted was thrown upon the ground. It seemed that the lives we had lived up to that moment were trash to be gotten rid of. Yet the soldiers did us this one kindness. A shower of sandals rained over us like a gift from a Greek god — one who does not halt the terror but sends something to help you through it.

Beside me two girls struggled for the same sandal. The strap broke when neither would let go. Everyone knew that without sandals you could not walk upon the Royal Road once the sun has risen to the top of the sky. Not for long.

When the struggling was over, many girls were left with sandals of different sizes, straps stretched taut over one foot, the other swallowed by leather.

The soldiers had been watching, laughing, but now a few began to argue amongst themselves. I was glad for this, because their shouts drowned out the moans of the men who had been brave enough to fight for their sisters and daughters.

"This is not Athens," Erez said. "You are stealing from the king's own subjects."

A soldier who looked like Parsha replied: "A few of these men tried to stand against us, and for this, they all will pay." His voice was crueler than Parsha's and it overflowed with confidence. He was in charge.

As we were pushed and prodded into lines, I kept my chin down to hide the necklace my mother had given me, a flower of gold foil petals hanging from a plaited gold wire. Crying girls fell against me on either side. When the soldiers began slowly moving through us, girls shrank from the light of their torches. At least, *some* of them shrank away — those without obvious imperfections. A girl beside me stepped boldly toward an approaching torch. Her cheek was deeply gouged, so deeply that with just a little more force behind the knife her tongue might have been visible. Had she pressed the knife to her face herself?

She began to sway upon her feet as though the ground undulated beneath her. I feared she would fall. The torches continued to move through us — illuminating and blinding and then receding to leave us in darkness until the next one came. I saw that the girl with the gash in her cheek was not the only one who was disfigured. Would these girls go free, or would they be punished with a fate worse than living out the rest of their days in a harem?

The soldier who looked like Parsha spoke quietly to some of his men while gesturing at us. Then the soldiers untied the girls with gashes in their cheeks, burns on their necks, missing fingers, and any other obvious injury. The soldiers pushed them away, back toward their huts. Though their wounds hurt my eyes, and surely some would return home to discover a father or brother wounded worse than they were, I wished I were one of them. Why had I not thought to use the soldier's dagger to cut myself? I would have to use my teeth again. *I will bite the side of my lower lip so hard I am too marred to bring to the king's harem,* I decided and brought my teeth down with all my strength.

My cry was so strange it did not seem that it could have come from me. It was loud enough to bring a torch so close that I felt as though the flame licked my cheek. I

22

closed my eyes and watched the spots of blue that floated before me, wondering why the soldier holding the torch was silent. Was he considering whether to keep me for the king or let me go? I had nothing left to offer but what little pride remained to me. "Please let me go."

He hesitated, then so quietly I almost did not hear, said, "I cannot. If any soldier who has seen the beauty of your face catches you going back to your home he will do far worse than bring you to the king's harem."

The voice belonged to Erez. If *he* would not help me, who would? As the torchlight moved on, all hope drained out of me.

Spots of blue continued to float before my eyes. I watched them as I was pulled forward by the rope around my wrists, away from the sounds of the villagers' wailing. Soldiers were yelling at people to stay back. A man ran up beside us, calling to one of the girls, "I will not leave you. I will be beside y—" I heard the crack of a whip and looked back. In the torchlight, I could see the man bent over upon the ground. Farther back I could see the villagers gathered behind us, and soldiers taking water from the village well. Farther still, I could see the outlines of the huts in which we had been sleeping not long before.

23

Tears began to form in my eyes. I quickly turned back to the march. None of what was happening seemed like it could possibly be real.

When the sun finally came up though, I could clearly see the rope around my wrists. I started to cry. I hated myself for it but I could not stop. I was one of a hundred girls being driven like oxen east across the scorching desert plain by Xerxes' soldiers, straight into the rising sun.

CHAPTER TWO:
THE VIRGINS' MARCH

We were being marched single file along the Royal Road, a length of stones laid upon hard-packed earth that stretched from Shushan to the Aegean Sea. My lip throbbed where I had bitten it and my feet soon grew raw in my sandals, but I was careful to keep up my pace. The ropes around our wrists had all been tied to one long rope; if anyone slowed, the rope would yank upon her wrists, burning her skin.

The soldiers were scattered beside us upon horses all the way up the line. The nearest one was at least fifteen cubits in front of me. From the clomping I heard a short distance behind me, I knew they were also at the back of the line.

I wanted to know which one had stolen me from my bed.

I looked for the wound I had inflicted, but the soldiers' tunics covered their arms. There was no way of discovering which one

25

had taken me unless he raised up his hand so I could see where I had bitten him. Still, I could not keep from looking. Though I hated all of the soldiers, I hated him most. The hatred helped me endure the heat and the throbbing of my lip.

Hoofbeats suddenly sounded from the rear. A soldier rode up so close that I could hear the flies buzzing on his horse's flanks and the swishing of the animal's tail.

"You in the red head scarf. Take it off," he ordered me in a voice hoarse from giving commands. It was the soldier who looked like Parsha, but whose tone was crueler and more confident. He had been yelling at the girls to walk faster and following each order with threats of the lash. He had made it known that if a lash fell upon a girl she would no longer be fit for the king's harem, and would instead be given to the soldiers.

"Girl," he said. The girl ahead of me panicked, stumbling in her attempt to move away. The soldier laughed and drew his horse back.

Before she regained her balance and began to slowly plod forward again, I saw the high cheek and proud nose of her profile. She was Yvrit, the butcher's daughter. I had lived in Babylon until my parents were killed, and Yvrit and I had been friends. We looked so similar that people sometimes confused us. Yvrit had admired me and always asked for my advice. She had even wanted to know how to walk and what to say. Though we both worshipped the One God, Yvrit had seemed to worship me most of all. She was moving so slowly that the rope was tugging at her wrists, jerking her forward. I kicked her heel.

"Ow!" Yvrit said, raising her heel up as if it were the road that had kicked her.

"I am sorry, but you must not slow down. There will be time to tend your wounds when we get to the palace."

"Hadassah, is that you?" Yvrit twisted her body to look back at me.

"Hush. Turn around."

The soldier had shifted his attention to the girl behind me. He was yelling, "A drunken old man could walk a straighter line than you." But still he could have heard my true name, and guessed my secret: I was Jewish. My mother had named me Hadassah, as if she had foreseen her own violent death or the march I would one day be forced to make. *Hadassah* meant "myrtle," a plant that only gave off its sweet fragrance when crushed.

"Now I am *Esther,* and you . . . *Cyra.*" *Cyra* was the word for "moon." I was certain that Yvrit wished for the moon to replace the sun as soon as possible. Everyone knew that even scorpions died if they attempted to cross the road during the noonday heat. Though the sun had only risen halfway to the top of the sky, sweat poured down my neck, and my tunic stuck to my body.

"Speak no more — only walk," I said, "no matter if your feet blister or you wish to lie down in the road."

The soldier stopped yelling at the girl behind me. I felt his eyes upon me. "You wish to lie down in the road?"

"No, sir." I was careful to keep all feeling from my voice.

"Then *take off your head scarf.*"

His horse stepped so close that I felt the short, sharp hair of the animal's large flank against my arm. But I would not show this soldier or any other that I was hot and tired and full of fear.

"You can pretend not to hear my words but you will have a harder time pretending not to feel my whip," he said. I glanced up to see if he was reaching for it. It sat untouched upon his hip. He leaned down to look at me. "The people of your village may have thought you beautiful," he said, his eyes moving over me, "but you are no longer in your village."

More hooves pounded up from the rear, driving the soldier's horse ahead of me. "The king wants these girls unharmed, Dalphon," the second soldier said. It was Erez.

"Though this one looks down, her back is too straight," Dalphon replied. "She is too proud for a peasant girl going peacefully to the harem. I want to better see her eyes."

I could have told him I was descended from the great king David, the second king of Israel who had lived some five hundred years before, but then he would know I was a Jew. Besides, however royal my line may have been at one time, it was true that my parents had been closer to peasants than royalty.

"The king does not concern himself with what you want, and neither do I."

I gazed from the corner of my eye. By the butt-spikes of the two men's spears I could see that one was a soldier, one an officer. But not as I had hoped. Erez had only a silver butt-spike. Despite how he had spoken to Dalphon — an officer — he was just a soldier. Except that, unlike any of the other soldiers, he rode a horse so huge it could only be a Nisaean, one of the king's most sacred mounts.

"You are lucky the king likes you, Kitten Tamer, or I would take your tongue. But

Xerxes is no less fickle with soldiers than he is with harem girls. When your valor at Thermopylae is forgotten, I will have you sent to the farthest reaches of the empire."

Erez rode closer to Dalphon. I was glad to see that the closer he came, the smaller Dalphon looked. "You are only an officer because your father is an adviser to the king. You are no more a rightful officer than I a king."

Dalphon's voice no longer overflowed with confidence. "The men are behind me."

"They are behind looting and plundering. You matter little to them."

"I think I will not send you to the farthest reaches of the empire, but to the gallows."

Erez lowered his voice. "You assume your father will always be powerful. But perhaps, Dalphon, it is he who will end up upon the gallows, and you will sway beside him."

I felt a pull upon my wrists. Cyra was stumbling. There was little I could do to help her, except to remain steady as she regained her balance.

Suddenly Dalphon's whip cracked so close beside my face that I felt the air move against my cheek. There was a terrible, wet sound — sharp leather against Cyra's flesh. Cyra let out a scream that was as much surprise as pain, then began to wail.

30

"Walk," I said quietly, "do not think of your flesh but of the palace and the soft cushions and wine that await you."

"She will make a good concubine," Dalphon said, "she will not lie silent beneath a man like some."

I suddenly had the thought that if Dalphon had been the one to storm my parents' hut during the last revolt of Babylon, he would have slit their throats with as little hesitation as the soldier who did it while I watched. I hated him. "How much training did it take to perfect the whipping of defenseless girls?" I said before I could stop myself. "And are there not women who will have you without being forced?"

Dalphon turned to stare at me. This time I did not avoid his eyes. I had been wrong to think that they were just like his twin's. They too were beautiful, but they were not like drops of honey that had just begun to melt. They were big and almond colored, or would be if almonds could contain both sunlight and darkness at once. Why had God given such beauty to someone so cruel? His hand tightened on his whip. "I have clearly not trained enough if a prisoner dares talk back to me."

Erez hit his heels against his horse and hurried to cut Dalphon off. I saw that he carried no whip. He stopped just far enough from me that his horse did not knock me to the ground.

He leaned down toward me, sending a winged figure on a chain around his neck swinging back and forth. *"Quiet."* He had sharp cheekbones, and though most of the other men had beards of tight curls, he had only stubble along his jaw. "You are not a defenseless girl, or any other sort of girl. You are *property* of the king. Unless Dalphon makes you his property first."

He turned and delivered a couple of hard slaps to the flanks of Dalphon's horse. Dalphon looked over his shoulder at me and spat upon the ground. I was afraid he would bring his horse around, but Erez reached out and grabbed the animal's bridle.

As they rode away, I looked beneath where Erez's hair fell a short length from his saffron headband, watching the clasp of the chain he wore bounce lightly against his neck. Across his broad back he carried a bow and a quiver of arrows. Though he had spoken harshly to me, I knew he was the closest thing I had to a protector. But who would watch over him? If the other soldiers ever turned against him, his wicker shield would not be big enough to protect him.

Chapter Three:
Screaming

The sun rose higher overhead and beat upon us without mercy. But the heat wafting up from the road was even more intense than the heat from above. It felt as though we were walking through a great fire that grew hotter as it fed upon our bodies. "I cannot go on," Cyra kept muttering, "I cannot go on."

Her tunic was ripped where Dalphon's whip had hit her. Blood came from the lash upon her neck and back and a blister formed on her right heel. She began to pant.

"Cyra, *Yvrit,* listen to me. *You can bear whatever burning you feel in your feet and the cut upon your back.* Soon we will be in the palace and you can lie upon soft pillows and only rise when slaves lift you."

Cyra's panting quieted but blood continued to flow from her wound. We marched until the sun reached the top of the sky. Then Cyra stopped in her tracks and started

33

screaming.

Dalphon galloped toward us, yelling at her to be silent. She screamed louder and fell to her knees.

The column had come to a stop. Girls were turning back to see what was going on.

"Silence or you will feel my foot upon your throat," Dalphon said. "Get up."

Cyra swayed slightly where she knelt, then collapsed over her folded legs, her head falling hard upon the road. Her long brown hair spilled from her head scarf and lay around her, shining in the sunlight. Though she had fainted, it looked like she was kneeling before Dalphon.

Dalphon jumped off his horse and untied the loop connecting the rope around Cyra's wrists from the line.

"I am her sister," I said. "Let me tend to her."

"No, she will be put to better use lying across the back of my horse — covering him to keep the flies from his flanks."

"A true officer would not bring his king a girl riddled with fly bites," Erez said. He pushed past the other soldiers who had gathered around and jumped off his horse. "You go on," he said to Dalphon. "We will bandage this girl and return her to the line

34

before we reach Shushan."

"Return to your place, soldier," Dalphon said. "Even if you were a physician I would not let you waste time on a girl who is no longer fit for the king."

"I am the soldier the king calls his most trusted. I am going to tend to the damage you have done. If you try to stop me, I will tell the king of how you abused one of the most beautiful girls — one he would not like to be deprived of." Erez quickly untied the rope around my wrists from the main line. He threw Cyra over his shoulder, took hold of his horse's bridle with his free hand, and forced his way through the watching soldiers.

Dalphon pointed at Cyra and yelled loudly enough for everyone to hear. "This one in the blue head scarf will not return to the line. She and any other girl who cannot be quiet and keep pace have fallen from Ahura Mazda's favor and will suffer worse than this march."

I hurried after Erez.

Chapter Four:
Goddess of Bullheadedness

Erez led us to the shade of the nearest palm tree. He set Cyra gently on the ground and turned to me. The sun had pounded the strength from my limbs, and my feet burned in my sandals. But when Erez undid the rope around my wrists, I closed my eyes and let out a long breath. My arms fell limply to my sides.

Erez laughed lightly and I realized that I had sighed aloud. I bowed my head so I would not have to meet his gaze, and then I opened my eyes. Where the sleeves of his tunic ended, his forearms were thick, the veins swollen from the strain and heat of the day. Forgetting my embarrassment, I said, "You do not look like herding girls is all you do."

"I have not trained to be an Immortal since I was seven for *this*."

Immortal. I hated that they called themselves Immortals, as though no one could hurt them and they did not need to heed any laws or perform any kindnesses. They were so proud of their lives and careless with the lives of others. The Immortal who had killed my parents had not even looked at their faces first.

I gazed back to where the girls were being marched away, down the Royal Road to the king. "Perhaps if you had gotten off your horse and joined us you would not feel quite so immortal."

"I replaced a dead *Immortal*. It is the number ten thousand that is immortal, not any of us. As quick as a man dies he is replaced."

Xerxes' forces had recently lost many men in their humiliating defeat to the Greeks at Salamis. Perhaps it was this defeat that made them so cruel. Yet this soldier seemed to have none of the others' cruelty.

"I spoke carelessly. Please forgive me." Before he could respond with either anger or forgiveness, I asked, "Is there water to spare for Cyra?"

The soldiers had been having the girls cup their hands for water, but instead Erez handed his waterskin to me. My tongue was swollen with thirst but I did not drink. As I knelt beside Cyra I drew in my breath at the sight of the blood on the side of her head. I pressed one hand over her wound and used the other to bring the waterskin to her lips. Her mouth filled with water, water which she did not swallow. It ran from the corners of her lips.

"I will try again when she wakes." I wanted, more than I had ever wanted anything, to feel water upon my tongue, but I handed the waterskin back to Erez.

He did not take it. "Have you already forgotten how to drink? Do you need me to hold it for you?"

I hurried the huge waterskin to my lips before Erez could change his mind. The water stung my lip where my teeth had tried to open it, but still, it tasted better than any sweet wine ever had.

While I drank, Erez took off his bow and quiver and set them on the ground. When his hands were free again, I gave the waterskin back to him. It was much lighter than when he had given it to me.

"I am sorry," I said. "I —"

Before I could tell him I was parched, he interrupted, "You are right to quench your thirst while you can. Dalphon did not think to bring enough water for the march. Or did not care to." Erez had only a small sip and then turned away to fasten the waterskin back to the saddle of his horse.

It was not easy to hate him, except that from behind I could not see his face, only that he wore the same uniform as all the other Immortals, including the one who had killed my parents. His tunic was a shade of saffron so rich that not even a layer of grime could fully dull it, and his calves looked like small, dust-covered boulders. He turned around and saw me staring.

My cheeks felt as though they had burst into flame.

Erez fastened his eyes upon me and then did something surprising: he laughed. Not lightly like before, but fully, his body shaking with the force of his sudden happiness. Without the serious expression he usually wore, he looked no more than nineteen, five years older than me. I feared he was laughing at me.

"There is no reason for happiness."

"You underestimate yourself," he replied.

I do not think that is possible. I could not forgive myself for standing back, sobbing uselessly, while my parents were killed. If I did not save Cyra now, I would have three deaths on my conscience. I looked down at her with even greater urgency. "I have to bandage Cyra before too much blood has spilled from her. She is parched and will not survive the loss of any more."

"What would you have me do to help?" Erez asked.

"Bring us home."

"That is where we are taking you — home. A much better home than the one you came from. Have you not seen the palace at Shushan?"

I had seen it many times, walked in its massive shadow when I went to the market. Once a woman entered the harem she was never seen outside the palace again. How could Erez believe this was better than the home I came from? I ignored his question and said, "Then there is nothing more you can do. Would you be kind enough to look away? I will have to take off Cyra's head scarf to see to her wounds."

He inclined his head in a slight nod and turned to tend his horse.

I tore swathes from the bottom of my tunic and bandaged Cyra's head and back. At the sound of the fabric tearing Erez cocked his head, but he did not turn around. Cyra's brow was dry as parchment, and sometimes she gasped for air. When I put my hand over her heart it fluttered fast and weak against my palm. I told her she would be well soon. I do not know if she heard me.

Erez had taken the saddle off his horse

and was letting the huge animal drink water from his cupped palm. "May I turn around now?"

He did not need to ask, just as he had not needed to turn around, and just as he had not needed to help us in the first place. But he had.

"Yes," I said. "Thank you for the kindness you have shown us." His kindness gave me courage to ask, "How can the king allow this march?" I looked down at Cyra. "What if this is his future queen?"

"He will never know of this girl or any of the others who have been bloodied by the lash."

"Where will they go?"

"Dalphon."

"She will be a wife of Dalphon?"

"Not a wife, and not just Dalphon."

"I do not believe you." But as the words left my mouth I knew they were no longer true.

He stepped away from his horse and came to crouch in front of me so that his eyes were level with mine. I dropped my gaze to the winged man that rested at the base of his throat. I watched the words moving beneath his skin, flickering up through his neck to his lips. "The most beautiful must be careful not to look up or slow their steps.

41

And *never* talk back to any of the soldiers, especially not Dalphon or his brothers."

"You are one to talk."

He stood abruptly. "I said not to talk back to *any* of the soldiers."

I was shocked that I had said something so foolish. Surely soldiers had killed people for less. "I am sorry," I said. "Please forgive me."

"Forgiveness is not something I am good at."

"I will give you no more need." This time I hoped he would see the flush that had come over my face and know I was ashamed.

He did not look at me and I could see by the tightness of his jaw that he was angry. I felt flustered whenever he gazed at me directly, but I found that I also did not like when he would not look at me at all.

"May I try the water once more?" I asked.

He held it out without looking at me.

Again the water filled Cyra's mouth and ran from the corners. "Cyra," I said. If she did not wake and drink she would not be able to go on. How dare she not fight with all her strength? How dare she move closer to death in my arms?

I thought of my mother bleeding upon the floor and how I would not let her go until life flowed back into her eyes, and she moved her gaze from whatever far-off place she was staring up at and onto me. That was what scared me the most, more than the blood: I was there and she did not look at me. If I could just get her eyes on me she would have to wake up because *I am still here Mother you cannot leave.*

Wake up!

But she did not move her eyes. The sight had gone out of them when I most desperately needed her to see me. *Mother, please, tell me what to do.* I had stayed with her while Xerxes' soldiers continued to storm the city. I had taken her cooling hand in my own, trying to figure out where life went when it left. *I will find it, I will put it back.* I had to put it back if I were going to go on, because the hut was not my true home. She was.

And now Cyra too was leaving me. I put my free hand to my brow as though to wipe away a bead of sweat. I was trying to hide my despair, but I knew I had failed when I heard Erez take a deep breath. He leaned down and placed his calloused hand on mine. I had the urge to pull my hand away and also the urge to turn it over and hold on to him. But instead I sat completely still, feeling the kindness of his touch and the pounding of my heart. Then he gently pulled my hand from my brow. "She is not your sister," he said. "And she is dying."

My hand began to tremble and he took the waterskin from me.

"It is best," he said. "Dalphon would have made her life worse than death. We will bring her to the palace and I will ask the king to set her upon the dakhma." The dakhma, or tower of silence, was a high, wide platform open to the sky. Corpses were left there to be eaten by vultures. The bones were then put into a pit at its base.

"You would leave her upon the dakhma *while she lives*?"

"No, we will leave her upon it as she is about to be." He straightened. "Come now."

"How easily you give up. But you have probably seen a hundred people die."

"A hundred? I have seen many more than that die in a single battle."

"If it pains you to see men die, perhaps you should not have become a soldier."

"I am an *Immortal,* not a soldier. And it is not of my choosing."

"You were forced?"

He was silent. I knew I had angered him again. Still, I believed he would not rush us back to the line if he thought there was hope for Cyra. Her head lay in my lap. I moved

44

my leg slightly. "Ehhhh . . . ," Cyra murmured.

"See how she stirs? She says my name."

"Your name is unusual."

"It is Esther. She is too parched to say it fully."

Erez gazed at me and then at Cyra. "Perhaps I counted her among the dead too hastily, *Ehhhh*sther." He raised one eyebrow. "But I do not think so."

I had no argument except my resolve. *"Please."*

He flinched only slightly, but still I saw it. Hearing me say "please" pained him. "Being a soldier has taught me to do what I am told without thinking too deeply about it. You will learn the same lesson as a harem girl, or you will suffer."

I wanted to delay our return to the line as long as possible. "Will you tell me of how you came to be an Immortal?"

"Esther." He looked at me with such seriousness that I was not certain I wanted him to go on. "It is likely that you will never, from this day forth, have your way again. But I will grant you this one request, if you agree to accept your new life as soon as I have answered your question."

I agreed and he told me of a panther who mauled a girl in his village twelve years before. He had killed it with a single arrow, and that had sealed his fate as an Immortal. Word of his skill traveled and the king's men had come for him shortly after. He had been seven years old.

"If you killed her, why does Dalphon call you 'Kitten Tamer' instead of 'Kitten Killer'?"

"There is only one way to truly tame anything wild."

I hoped he was wrong. It was said that lions were kept as pets in the palace.

"Every hunter knows this is true and all men are hunters of one kind or another," Erez said. "You would do well to pretend you are not so wild as you are."

I willed myself not to blush again. I swallowed without meaning to and coughed from the dryness in my throat. "Have you gotten word to your parents since you were taken to train? Do they know you are well?"

"Their village was wiped out by plague."

I surprised myself by saying, "I am sorry, Erez. I am an orphan too."

"I know."

Did he mock me? "I do not see how that is possible."

"You are too independent for a girl your age —"

"I am *fourteen*."

"— and too stubborn. It is why I fear for you."

"For me, but not Cyra? Perhaps you were made an Immortal so you could save people."

"Do not be foolish, I was trained to take lives, I do not know how to give them back. Your friend's life has already been taken. It was the king's — just as yours and mine are — and now it is Ahura Mazda's. He will watch over her. Do not ask me to change fate. Not even a king could do it, and I am only a soldier."

"*Only?* Do you not see how lucky you are? I would gladly trade places with you. The king favors you, you have the most beautiful horse I have ever seen, and you have traveled parts of the world I never will. Not now."

"I have seen the world, but not as I would have liked to. I see its beauty only as I diminish it. I saw the great temple of Athens as I sacked and burned it. And I have done many things worse, including" — he gestured to where the line of girls had disappeared down the road — "this."

"What do you wish for yourself instead?"

"This is a cruel question, because it does not matter. I only know what I do not wish to do anymore — bloody the earth for the

47

sake of expanding Xerxes' empire. I do not hate the Greeks who revolt against him because they do not want to be slaves. I hate that I do not have a true home. I hate that I have rarely known the same woman twice. If I had any children they were probably flushed from their mothers' wombs with herbs or worse."

I tried to show nothing in my face. I did not like to think of the women Erez had known, but I did not want to seem a naïve child. "Then why have you done all of these things?"

"I regret almost everything I have done since drawing back the bow and killing the panther. Yet all that I did for Persia I would do again, if Xerxes commanded. I have been training for most of my life to do exactly as I am doing. If this — being an Immortal — is to be my life, my wish is that I be an officer instead of a common soldier. The cruelest among us have risen to the top and they are eager to spread their misery everywhere they go. As a common soldier I can do little to stop them."

"I had hoped you were an officer. I know you would be a good one." He had said "Xerxes" as casually as though he spoke of a friend or uncle. "Have you ever spoken to the king?"

"I have spoken to him without beginning or ending each sentence with 'Your Majesty.' He cannot trust his own brothers but he can trust a man who fights for him. Each of the six years of his reign he has recalled me to one of his four palaces to ride and hunt with him."

"Then you have his ear. If we bring Cyra back you can ask him —"

"His ear is full. Enough talk of your friend. You must turn your thinking to your own life. It is yourself for whom you should fear."

"I am not afraid," I lied. "I am Esther, named after Ishtar: goddess of love, fertility, war, and . . ." I could not bring myself to say "sex." Erez's hand upon mine was as close as I had come.

"If there were a goddess of bullheadedness that would suit you better."

I moved out from under Cyra and set her head gently upon the ground. I stood to try to take the water from Erez. "If there is even the tiniest crumb of hope for her, how can we not help her?"

"I will show you how." He tied the water to the saddle and moved to walk around me, toward Cyra. He was going to take her back to the march.

My heart beat wildly as I stepped into his

path. "I will not go."

"Then I will retie your hands and throw you both over the back of my horse."

He reached for my wrists but I stepped away and yanked my head scarf off. His eyes widened. My hair was long and dark and spoken of throughout the market after one day when my scarf had come undone. Though I could feel that I was blushing yet again, I stood tall and lifted my chin. I began tearing the scarf into long strips.

"Foolish girl," he said. "Put your scarf back on. Do you know nothing of soldiers? In war you learn that whatever you see and can take is yours."

"Cyra's bandages have soaked through. I must change them."

For a moment he looked at me with a mixture of anger and sadness. Then his face seemed to draw closed. "You would have had a hard time in the king's harem," he said. "You would not have been wise enough to hide your insolence. The king's favorite — Dalphon and Parsha's cousin, Halannah, is famous for breaking the spirits of even the most willful girls. And the eunuchs would have helped her by pouring endless Haoma wine down your throat to drown your stubbornness." He came half a step toward me and it took all of my strength

50

not to back away. *"But you will like being one of the soldiers' concubines even less.* Perhaps that is the fate you deserve though. Very well." He turned away.

I told myself that he spoke in anger and his words were untrue.

Without meaning to, I began to pray.

When I finished securing Cyra's new bandages, I became aware of Erez's gaze upon me. He had turned around without me noticing. I swallowed the rest of my prayer.

"I see, much too clearly," he said, looking down at my naked face and hair, "how dangerous this is for you. You would do better to have some sense."

"I must do this," I said. I shook Cyra. Her eyes remained closed and her head limp. I shook her with greater force and whispered her given name into her ear. *"Yvrit. Wake up."*

"Her fate is in the hands of Ahura Mazda. Shaking her will not wrest it from his grasp."

"I have learned not to leave the fates of those I love to God."

"Did I not just see you praying?"

"Perhaps I was only talking quietly."

"You were not that quiet."

Though I was angry at God, sometimes I still found myself praying to Him. "I pray in the vain hope that He is listening," I said.

Erez looked as though he wished to say something more but instead he bowed his head and reached behind his neck. His tunic sleeves started to fall down his arms and he quickly lowered his hands. He used his right hand to turn the chain around and bring the clasp in front of him, beneath his chin. "Unclasp this," he said.

To get a good grip on the clasp I had to come close to Erez. My hands began to tremble. I wanted to both step away from him and to tuck my head into the cradle of his neck. I did neither. I was careful not to touch him as I tried to open the clasp. It was slippery with sweat; a few times it slid out from between my fingers before I finally undid it.

He took his eyes from my face and looked down at the small silver man with wings that hung from the chain I now held in my hand. It was a Faravahar, symbol of the Zoroastrian religion. I lowered it into his palm. He squeezed it gently, then looked back up at me. "Wear this."

I knew by the way he had gazed at it that it was of great value to him.

"I cannot accept it."

"I am a soldier, of the ten thousand Immortals, and I order you to take it."

"For what purpose?"

"So that no one besides me knows that you are Jewish."

"I am not —"

"Then you are the only non-Jew I know who prays in Hebrew. If you make it through this march, you will have to learn to whisper more quietly. Eunuchs can hear a moth flap its wings from half a palace away."

"I will not even move my lips next time I pray." I realized I did not fear that Erez would reveal my secret to anyone. I trusted him.

"Please turn around," he said, and I obeyed.

He brought the chain over my head and lowered it until the winged man rested on my chest, right below the rosette of my mother's necklace. I tried to keep my breathing steady and I willed my hands not to shake as I lifted my hair so he could fasten his chain around my neck. He did not immediately take his fingertips from my skin. Somehow, though I was hot, the warmth of his flesh against mine was not unpleasant.

No man who is not my husband ought to touch me this way, and this man is not only a stranger but also a gentile. It should not feel good to be touched by him.

53

I stepped away, my heart stuttering in my chest. The Faravahar rested heavily upon my breast. Could this figurine of a false god keep me safer than the One God? *And what will the One God think if He sees this around my neck?*

I turned to face him. "Thank you, Erez." I reached back and undid my mother's rosette necklace. "Will you also take this, and give it to a man in Shushan? I want him to know I am well."

Erez narrowed his eyes. "What man is this?"

"Mordecai. I live — I *used* to live — with him. When he heard that the king was gathering virgins he sent me from the heart of Shushan. He thought I would be safer outside the palace city."

"Mordecai the Jew? The one who keeps the king's accounts?"

"He is my cousin. Before my father died, he asked Mordecai to watch over me."

"I will make certain he gets it." Erez dropped the necklace into his pocket. "And now we must return to the line." He went to Cyra. Instead of swooping her up he knelt beside her. He put a hand beneath her nostrils and then put his head to her heart.

"Esther," he said, turning to face me, "you

54

must be strong. Though you did all you could to save her, your friend is gone."

Chapter Five:
The Ride Back

Erez took Cyra's head scarf and spread the blood upon it, turning it from blue to an uneven purple. "It is a girl in a blue head scarf who Dalphon said would not return to the line," he said. "You will wear this one."

He did not mention retying my wrists together and I did not remind him.

I tried not to cry as he put Cyra over the back of his horse. His words echoed in my head. *You must be strong, you must be strong, you must be strong . . .*

"Ride with us," he said.

"How will I do that?"

He repositioned his bow and arrows so they hung from his shoulder instead of across his back and held out his hand. I only hesitated for an instant before grasping it. His hand was steady and it felt good to hold it. "You will have to sit sidesaddle," Erez said. "To maintain your . . . proof of virtue."

There was not much room between him

and where Cyra lay across the horse's flanks. He shifted forward so I could squeeze into the saddle behind him.

I had never ridden on a horse, and I had never been so close to a man. I pressed my side against him to steady myself, and at the horse's first unsteady step I put an arm around his waist. My heart was beating so hard I was afraid he might feel it through his armor. With the other hand I held on to Cyra.

I wanted to beg him to turn around and return Cyra and me to the village. But I knew it would do no good to beg. I was going to the palace, and Cyra was going to the dakhma.

Please God, do not place so much suffering before me again, unless You have given me the power to stop it.

CHAPTER SIX:
THE MARKET

I cannot go on had been Cyra's refrain. When I slid down from Erez's horse and was tied again to the line, Cyra's words walked with me in her place. I finally knew how she felt. I wanted to be strong, but it takes strength to hold on to hope, and her death had left me little. *How could I have let her die?*

Before we reached Shushan the sole of my left sandal ripped. *Perhaps this is how I will die, from a torn sandal.* My foot grew so hot that several times I almost dropped to my knees. When I heard the market not far ahead, I did not know whether to be over-joyed or to despair. We had entered Shushan. If I squinted up over the market square, I would see the king's huge palace looming just beyond it.

It would not be much farther.

Voices boomed in the market square. Mordecai had often said that no deal was made in fewer than two hundred words, and that the best merchants' voices could travel half a day's journey in front of them. If a merchant could not send his voice through a crowd he would not survive in the capital. His only hope would be to peddle his wares from village to village.

While I had always hated how my ears rung after going to the market, at that moment I would gladly welcome the ringing if only I could return home with it, and wait, as I had each day, for Mordecai to come back from the palace to eat the food I had prepared for him. Peeling pomegranates, chopping figs, kneading bread, milking the goat and cleaning his pen now seemed like great pleasures. I thought longingly of my almond honey cakes. Dipped in rosewater syrup they were Mordecai's favorite dessert. I envied the girl who had made a batch a few days before, as though she were someone other than me.

As the march got closer to the market, I kept my head down. I could hear merchants shouting the praises of their wares:

"Look here!" a man with a Nubian accent yelled. "Genuine ivory combs adorned with ostrich feathers! Priceless treasures, yet I will give them away for two sigloi each."

"You will give them away if the price is

right, eh?" a local merchant asked. "I have vases like those in the palace — handles decorated with winged ibex — for only a few more sigloi than those *genuine* ivory combs."

"Who should spend his sigloi on vases when right here I have beaded curtains that will make every woman who enters a room beautiful?" a man with an Indian accent called out. "Men, string them from one wall to the other and turn your hut into a palace with many rooms. Women, hang them in your huts, and you will receive all of your husband's love, and gifts even more valuable than that."

"I will sell you what no other vendor will," another merchant yelled. "I offer you courage and long life. Look here! A saber engraved with a man hunting a giant tiger. The length will give you the reach of a god and valor beyond measure."

I had been looking at a trail of blood in front of me, where one of the girls' feet was losing a battle against the ground. But when I heard the sound of cart wheels, I glanced up. Canopies of bright red, indigo, and gold streamed behind the merchants' wooden stalls as they made way for the march. *Will I never see any of this again?* I knew that the only women allowed out of the palace were the ones who became concubines to the king's army and traveled behind the soldiers.

If I could run, it would be a short journey to Mordecai's hut.

Can I run? I had taken so much for granted. Only a few days ago, before Mordecai sent me out to the country, I had been in the market. I had sifted absently through pomegranates, wild plums, and cherries whose juices I had never yearned for as deeply as I did now.

Now I was returning as a captive.

Except that I had decided I could not allow the chance at freedom to pass me by, even if the chance was small and the price for failure steep. The only way I would know if I could run was to push off the ground and see what came of it.

The rope scratched my flesh as I forced it over my knuckles and down the length of my fingers. I draped it over my wrists.

Most of the soldiers had ridden to the front to clear the marketplace — I did not hear more than a few horses in back of the line. As soon as we got to the emptied market I would run. I would force my bloody feet to carry me through the merchants, past the modest mud huts beyond, and finally to the row of larger huts made of glazed bricks where I had lived with

Mordecai. The Immortals' horses would be too large to follow.

I looked to the side of the road, let the rope drop, and pushed off the ground.

I had only taken a few steps when I stumbled and fell onto my hip. Even before I looked up I felt eyes piling on top of me. I pulled my head scarf down to hide as much of my face as possible and stood. My feet still burned and now my hip burned as well. Perhaps I could not run, but if I could quickly walk into the merchants and lose myself among them I might still find my way home.

A horse rode up next to me and my head scarf was yanked from my head. Parsha's huge honey-colored eyes stared down at me. "A mouse is small but runs quickly. An elephant moves slowly but is not easily brought down. I was hoping you would be like some combination of these, but that after much chase I would bring you down anyway." He affected a sigh. "You are a great disappointment. You have left me bored and I will not forgive you for it. Now you will walk uncovered through this crowd, tied to the back of my horse."

I could no longer keep the despair from my voice. "Why?" If I were not so parched I knew that tears would have streamed down my naked face. *"Why would you do such a thing to me?"*

"Because I am Parshandatha, firstborn of the empire's foremost adviser and nobleman Haman, and I can."

If I'd had a dagger in my hand, I would have summoned the strength to plunge it into his heart. I felt the power of my hatred. It gave me strength. "If you are firstborn, why is it *Dalphon* who is an officer?"

"Because he was quicker to take up the spear of a fallen officer than I. And this is as it should be. The officer is the man everyone's eyes are upon. But me, born only one moment sooner than Dalphon, I always do exactly as I please." He turned the head scarf over in his palm and held it out to me. "And now it will please me to give this back to you."

When I reached for it he ripped it in two and let it fall to the ground.

"My father did not rid the empire of Queen Vashti so that a peasant could be installed in her place. My cousin Halannah will be queen. If not, the girl who thwarts her will suffer more than anyone has ever suffered before."

CHAPTER SEVEN: VASHTI

Queen Vashti has committed an offense not only against Your Majesty but also against all the officials and against all the peoples in all the provinces of King [Xerxes]. For the queen's behavior will make all wives despise their husbands.
— Book of Esther 1:16, 17

Only a few weeks before I was kidnapped by the soldiers, Mordecai had told me of the feast king Xerxes held in the third year of his reign — the one that led to Vashti's exile. He had been teaching me to read, and he had brought home a scroll of parchment from the palace. We each held one side open upon the high table where Mordecai usually pored over numbers late into the night.

In the middle of a sentence I was reading, a long number-filled sentence about taxes collected from the eastern provinces, Mordecai let go of the scroll. It coiled away from his hand like a snake that has been poked with a sharp stick.

"Hadassah," he said quietly. He did something he had done only a few times before: he looked directly at me. He was a head taller than me, but because he stooped, his eyes were level with mine. They were shiny in the glow of the oil lamp that sat upon the table.

"There is a terrible story I must tell you. All the more terrible because it is true. It is more important for you to know than any palace record you will find upon a scroll."

He was twenty-four, only ten years older than me, but people often assumed he was my father. Indeed this is how I thought of him. I assumed he thought of me as a daughter.

He had been the king's accountant from a young age, and possessed none of the fancifulness of youth. He had a close-cropped beard in the Persian fashion. His brown eyes were small and tired from looking all day at numbers. His lips were perpetually pursed in thought, thoughts he never shared.

Every once in a while, though, he did like to tell a good tale. But this one seemed to stick in his throat. "I do not like to burden you," he said.

I gently pushed the scroll aside, out of Mordecai's reach, so he would not be able to resume our lesson. "If you do not continue I will be burdened by thoughts of what is too terrible for you to tell me."

"A couple of years ago, Xerxes feasted all the power of Persia and Media, the nobles and princes of the provinces, for one hundred eighty days. I was amongst these men, but I was not one of them."

"Because you are a Jew?"

Mordecai flinched. We did not speak of our religion, even when we were alone. I was not sure why, as it seemed everyone already knew he was a Jew. In fact, in the marketplace he was referred to as "Mordecai the Jew."

He continued, "Because they were merrier and more drunk than those responsible for a kingdom should be. They drank wine out of golden vessels until they passed out upon beds of silver and gold. Each time they woke they resumed their drinking with even greater zeal than before.

"The banquet was a celebration of the king's abundant riches of food — meat from over twenty different animals, wines from every province. The men enjoyed all of it while girls from across the empire danced for them. Girls barely older than you, Hadassah."

I flushed.

"After this banquet he held another one for seven days in the palace garden, and all the men of the palace, high and low alike, attended. Again girls danced for them. The girls' hips and the naked flesh of their stomachs helped build the men's appetites for the women the king provided them. But they could not quell the men's appetite for the sight of the queen. On the seventh day, a cry came from one of the gold couches, 'Vashti!' Soon others joined their voices to the first man's, and their unified cry was so great that the alabaster columns seemed to shake with their desire.

"She was the most prized of all the king's possessions, and every man suddenly realized that it was, after all, her that he had come to see."

I had heard of her legendary beauty. She was a Chaldean renowned for an abundance of womanly assets divided by a small waist. Her beauty was spoken of by men and women alike. Sometimes men who were caught trying to sneak into the palace confessed they had been attempting to catch a glimpse of her. Occasionally Xerxes allowed one of them to see her before hanging him upon the gallows.

"The heart of the king was soaked with wine," Mordecai went on, "and when his adviser, Haman, bent to his ear and suggested the queen not only come before the entire banquet but come before them in only her crown, he could barely get the words out before the king clapped his hands together and cried 'Yes!' "

Mordecai was prone to exaggeration, but I did not interrupt to ask if he had been close enough to the king to hear this. I wanted him to continue telling the story.

"As though the idea had been his own, Xerxes commanded Haman and his six other chamberlains, 'Bring me my queen, naked but for her crown. My subjects will see that a man who possesses such a perfect vessel is one worth fighting for.' "

Knowing what came of this fighting, I could not help but groan inwardly at Xerxes' words. The Persians had lost many men and all except a few crumbs of their pride to the Greeks.

"But not one of the seven chamberlains the king sent to Vashti could rouse her from the silken cushions upon which she reclined with the noblemen's wives. The women too were feasting, and when the chamberlains appeared the women did not set down their goblets.

" 'The king has sent us,' Haman said.

"It is said that at this, Vashti seemed to sober. She set down her goblet and inclined her head at the courtier she hated more than any other.

" 'He commands you to appear before the banquet.'

" 'Get my crown and my purple robe at once,' she ordered one of her handmaids.

" 'You will not need your robe,' Haman said.

" 'Out of respect for the king, I, his queen — and also *yours* — will appear in my royal robe.'

" 'He does not want you to wear your robe.'

" 'Then where is the robe he would like me to wear?'

" 'He does not want you to wear a robe, or anything else, other than your crown. Not even sandals.' "

Only slaves did not wear sandals.

"She did not raise an eyebrow or react in any way. 'No,' she said, and picked up her goblet again.

"The chamberlains beside Haman pleaded with her. 'Your life, beautiful queen,' one cried, 'is the king's, and he will take it if you do not obey.' It was actually his own life that he was pleading for. The chamberlains thought the king was too proud of Vashti's beauty to harm her, but that they themselves, no matter how close to the king they were, could be replaced. All of them, except Haman. Or perhaps he too worried, but he did not let his worry overshadow his ambition. Because surely he wanted the queen to refuse the king's request, and that was why he had suggested it.

"So he must have been happy when Queen Vashti could not be swayed by the chamberlains' pleading. It wounded her that the king would ask her to parade naked except for her crown in front of a room of drunken men. 'The king has many concubines; I am not one of them' she said.

"Upon hearing this, the chamberlains had a litter brought forth to carry Vashti into the banquet, so she could enter like a queen and not a concubine. But when they ordered servants to lift her onto it, she held out her hand to stop them. 'Tell my husband that I cannot come to his banquet, while entertaining my own.'

"Neither the chamberlains nor the noblemen's wives could reason with her.

" 'If it please Your Majesty,' one of the chamberlains said, 'let me go to the king and beg for your modesty, so that you could wear sandals and a beaded scarf across your hips.'

" 'I will not beg for what is rightfully mine.'

" 'Your Majesty —'

" 'Go now.'

" 'But —'

" *'Now.'* "

"Surely people could sympathize with her position," I interrupted. What woman would want to be paraded naked in front of a thousand men?

"Perhaps they could have, if they had not been so bent on war. Vashti's grandfather Nebuchadnezzar was killed by Cyrus. This murder was a teacher to her, just as I am to you. It taught her that no victory is great enough to completely wipe away the losses of war."

"Nebuchadnezzar destroyed our temple and started the Babylonian Captivity of our people. Should not we be glad Cyrus killed him for us?" I asked. Every Jew knew that a few decades before, when Xerxes' grandfather Cyrus was king, he had issued a decree permitting Jews to go back to their homelands. Fifty thousand Jews had returned to Jerusalem. "We are too often at war already."

"Cyrus has rightly earned the love of our

people. I know war is necessary, I wish only to tell you that we as Jews do not make war without reason, and we do not glorify it. Vashti was like us in this way, and believed the king's expansion of his empire was not reason enough to justify the many lives that would be lost. She was smart and strong-willed enough to suspect that the king was asking her to come before the men naked because he hoped to win their support for an attack upon the Greeks. The men who write history will hate her for this. To a man with a quill in his hand, murder, war, and heartbreak make far better subjects than peace."

"Do not you usually hold a quill, cousin?"

"Yes, and I do not write of peace. I write down the taxes collected from the peoples who pay for luxuries they will never experience. They will never be invited to the palace to lie upon beds of silver and gold and share in the exotic wines and meat they pay for."

I should not have asked him a question. He was always unhappy about one injustice or another. "What happened to Vashti?"

"When the chamberlains returned without her, it was silent for the first time since the wine had started to flow seven days earlier. As Haman put his lips near the king's ear, you could have heard a feather floating to the floor. Those closest to the king say that even through the screen they could see his face grow the same red as the sun setting upon the desert sand. They heard his golden goblet break upon the marble floor."

"But a golden goblet does not break so easily."

"The tale men fashion is as important as what really happened. Until many years have passed. And then it is more important."

Is this the lesson he means for me to learn? I could not think of what else I was supposed to glean from this strange tale. It seemed to have nothing at all to do with me.

"Haman pounced upon this opportunity that he had so cleverly made for himself. He could finally rid the palace of the voice that spoke most loudly against the war. He had a maiden niece whose beauty rivaled Vashti's — a girl who was as hungry for war as a general.

"He whispered in the king's ear, 'Listen now to their silence. It is louder than a hundred women screaming. When they learn that Vashti will not come before them, all these men will lose respect not only for you but for your war as well — the war that will make you the greatest king the world has ever known.'

"He paused and looked out at the crowd. 'Your Majesty,' he said urgently, 'I can see that already they are losing respect for you, just as Vashti has. They stare unflinchingly at a man they should not dare to look at directly.' He put his lips so close to the king's ear that they were almost touching it. 'You must punish Vashti in such a way that they tremble before you once again.'

"The other chamberlains expected that upon these words the king would recoil. But he did not draw his ear away from Haman's lips.

"Haman saw that victory was within reach, and that he must seize it before the king emerged from his goblets. The only way to know he had truly gotten rid of Vashti would be to see her swaying upon the gallows. But he could see that first he must appeal to the king's pride, make it swell larger than his love for his queen.

" 'Word of this will spread to every woman in the empire' he told the king. 'Vashti's disobedience will feed each wife's own insolence, and every husband's resentment of you.

" 'But a royal decree will set your kingdom to rights. A decree meant for every person in the land. Though your subjects are mostly lowborn men who spend their days growing and harvesting barley and sesame, who cultivate palm trees, who are shepherds, potters, and craftsmen, *we will make each feel like a king.* For should not every man be a king to his wife? First we will tell your subjects that what has happened with Vashti has not happened to you alone, but to all men. What man has not had a woman linger too long in carrying out the tasks he has commanded her to perform? Bringing his dinner, beating the dust from his rugs, weaving the tunics and blankets needed for the next season?

" *'Women will dethrone us all with their contemptuous laughter, every one of them, if we let Vashti's slight pass.*

" 'But!' Haman cried, delighted already by the words he was about to speak, 'we will place a royal foot upon women's backs, bending them so that they bow to men once again. The decree will be sent out to each people in their own language. It will begin: *All wives shall give to their husbands honor, both to great and small.* It will be a letter of husbands' superiority and rule over their wives. We will tell each scribe that if a *single word* is altered he will see his reflection for only the briefest moment in the swords of the king's soldiers.'

"Haman did not mention that the number of men in the empire who could read was even less than the number who will live to fifty years."

I was impatient for Mordecai to come to whatever lesson he wished to impart. But he continued, "The Greeks have more men who can read, and therefore, more men who think deeply. They know what has come before, so that they can build upon it. They will build higher than we will. This is how they continue to advance, and how they will pass us by in learning if not in numbers."

"Is this the lesson I must learn? That reading is important?" I was tired of my cousin's grim pronouncements about the empire.

"You know it is the Persians' practice to deliberate upon affairs of weight when they are drunk; and then on the morrow, when they are sober, the decision to which they came the night before is put before them by the master of the house in which it was made; and if it is then approved of, they act on it; if not, they set it aside. Yet, long before the day ended and the king had emerged from his cups, Vashti was gone. The very next day he mourned the loss of his queen. He had no remorse about the decree though. Hadassah" — he took a deep breath — "you are not one of the king's subjects.

Men are the king's subjects. Women are the subjects of men."

It was true I never saw a woman selling wares in the marketplace anymore. Persian women had enjoyed status that Greek women never could have imagined. They could own property and engage in trade as freely as men. But that was before the decree was issued the year before. "Am I your subject?"

"You are not my subject. The decree has taught me . . ." He cleared his throat. "The decree has taught me how deeply I care for you. I know this because the thought of the empire's foot upon the backs of women angers me more now that you have come to live with me. My love for you has started to make me wish the world were kinder."

I felt my face flush. We had never before spoken of any affection for each other. "Was Vashti exiled or executed?" I asked quickly.

"If she was ever executed it was done in secret, for she did not end up upon the gallows. I believe Xerxes could not stomach the thought of his queen's lifeless flesh being eaten by vultures, her eyes picked out and loosed on the world so that he would feel them, always, upon him."

"You spoke to him?"

"It is not my place to speak to him of

anything but numbers. I listened. When the feast was over he called me to him to find out what taxes had been collected while he was in his goblets. His eyes were unfocused as I spoke until suddenly he said, 'Haman advises me to send soldiers to bring Vashti back from the place to which I have sent her. He says that it is too dangerous for her to be free. She will spread false tales about the palace, the empire. About me. I told him she is the mother of my heir, Artaxerxes, whom I have hidden away. I cannot kill her.' "

He stopped for a moment to catch his breath, before continuing, "Haman could not have liked to hear this. But he knew that at least he would have his war. The war we have just lost, the one that has cost the empire half its glory.

"Hadassah, whose fault is this war?"

"Haman's."

"No, it is Xerxes'. A ruler's most important task is figuring out who to trust. Xerxes is both aggressive and uncertain. He is strong-bodied but his heart is weak. His reign will not end well. I only pray he does not bring the whole empire down with him."

"Now I know this story is not true cousin, for you do not pray."

He half-smiled. This was half a smile more

than I was accustomed to seeing on his face. "It is true, I do not pray," he said. "But a few times I have thought of what this king will do to the empire and been tempted. I hope our God is more powerful than the king's and Haman's gods, and more wise."

I had not prayed much either, not since God let my parents die. "Does Xerxes miss his queen?" I asked.

He looked at me in surprise. "Ah! I knew I had left something out. I was in the palace when the feast ended, and the king came out of his goblets and remembered that he had sent his queen away. His belly that had been so full of wine now filled with misery. It grew so heavy that it dragged him from his throne. Yet his agony became larger still, pressing against his bowels, his lungs, his heart. He let out a terrible wail that could be heard throughout the palace. It did not sound human. All of his misery birthed from him in that wail."

Though Xerxes seemed impetuous and weak, I could not help but feel sad for him.

"I fear this misery is his *true* heir," Mordecai said, "and soon it shall rule the empire."

I thought of Mordecai's tale as I watched the son of the king's cruelest and most ambitious adviser place a rope around my wrists and tie it with a bowline knot. Parsha smelled like he had not taken a wet cloth to his neck and underarms in many days of journeying beneath the pounding sun. His nails scratched my already raw skin as he hooked his fingers over the rope and pulled me to stand. I was glad for my cousin's long hours in the palace, hours that did not allow him to be out in the road except very early and very late. I did not want him to see me at the mercy of a soldier. He might blame himself for not sending me farther from the city.

Parsha got back on his horse, and the rope tugged upon my wrists. I began to march.

Chapter Eight: The Vow

I did not raise my eyes from the ground. I felt alone except for the Faravahar against my breast. I hoped that if God were watching, He would not look at the Faravahar, but at all of our suffering, and that He would bring it to an end. An end other than death.

Just when the humiliation seemed too great to bear, my feet went out from under me and my knees and elbows opened upon the road. Because I had torn off strips of my tunic to bandage Cyra, it was too short to shield my legs.

"You brought this upon yourself," Parsha called down to me. "You are lucky this is your only punishment for trying to escape."

After I managed to rise to my feet again, I felt a calloused hand gently squeeze my shoulder. I knew by the Nisaean horse that had ridden up beside me that it was Erez's hand. The kindness of his touch diminished my anger and brought me more pain than my burning knees or the rope around my wrists. I wanted only to be angry. If I allowed myself to feel sadness — for Cyra, my parents, my own future — I might not have the strength to go on.

I do not yet know how to run on bloodied feet, but I will learn. And then, one day, I will find a way to have Dalphon and Parsha killed. Them and the man who pulled me from my bed and forced me into this nightmare.

CHAPTER NINE:
THE PALACE

It filled me with shame that men I had bargained with only days before watched as I was marched behind Parsha's horse. Each day Mordecai had dropped silver coins into my palm and sent me to the market to choose lamb and goat meat, jars of honey and fresh goats' milk. I had freely haggled with men from all over the empire. Now I was conscious not only of the rope around my wrists but also of my sweat-soaked tunic. It was ragged at the bottom where I had ripped off strips to bandage Cyra's wounds, and my bloodied knees were as naked as my head. Humiliation kept my gaze lowered upon the hooves of Parsha's horse.

On the ground lay evidence of the haste with which the market had closed. I stepped over a broken pitcher but could not avoid some smashed dates that stuck to the bottom of my sandals and to my left foot where the sandal had worn through. I saw swathes of yellow and blue silk that only yesterday would have seemed like treasures too good to leave behind.

I also saw, out of the corner of my eye, that Erez had stopped to subdue a man who must have been the father of one of the virgins. The man was screaming, "She is only twelve!"

"Then she is the king's twelve-year-old."

"She is betrothed!"

"And she will be fatherless if you do not turn around and quietly walk away."

I remembered what Erez had said: *I regret almost everything I have done since drawing back the bow and killing the panther. Yet all that I did for Persia I would do again.*

One of the merchants gathered along the side of the road waiting for the market to reopen said, "*These* are the prettiest virgins in the empire?"

I recognized the voice. It was Arshan the rug seller. He had sold me four crimson rugs and had his sons carry them to Mordecai's hut for me. The rugs now hung on the walls of what had been my home.

I did not let my shame keep me from turning to glare at him. *It has been a long walk, you soulless boar.* Arshan must have felt my eyes upon him, because he looked back at me, and whatever it was he saw silenced him. Did he recognize me? Would he talk about me with the other merchants, with neighbors, with Mordecai, who would now have to come to the market himself each day until he took on a servant?

Erez rode up beside me again and leaned down with a piece of purple silk. I did not have to ask him what to do with it. I lowered my head and clumsily tied the fabric over my hair with my bound hands, pulling it low on my brow as though it were possible to hide.

Ahead something was starting to block out the sun. I looked up just enough to see the girls ahead of me leaving the sunlight and moving into a shadow — the shadow of a giant stone arch.

In my haste to escape the merciless sun, I overtook Parsha. He pressed his foot against my back — not hard enough to push me over but just enough to let me know he could. He dropped the rope. "Watch this one!" I heard him call to another soldier.

I had seen Xerxes' palace many times. It was said that at least half the world's gold was housed inside, and it looked like no small amount was on the outside either. I would never again mistake the oddly colored sphinx, winged griffins, and bulls for decorations; they were a warning: *the gold and power of this palace are many thousand times greater than you.* Golden lions that had looked regal and graceful when I had gone to market each day now gazed upon me with scorn.

I gathered up the rope that hung from my wrists and pitched myself into the shadow of the arch as though the darkness had arms to catch me.

A hundred stairs loomed before me. By the tenth step I understood that the heat had penetrated my bones and the marrow inside them had caught fire and turned to ashes. What blood had not evaporated from my body seemed to have crusted in my veins.

And yet I continued to climb until finally I stood panting, with the others, in the colossal doorway to the king's gatehouse.

I was filled with a terrified awe. The hallway in front of me was wide enough for fifty men to walk through side by side. I knew that I was going to disappear down that hallway. Soon only the king's servants would see me, unless one day the king himself deigned to look at me. I would spend my days in the maze of rooms at the southern side of the palace, waiting for him to want me.

My fears came back to me like blades I

had somehow managed to swallow but now felt tearing my stomach. The fear I'd had in the marketplace, that someone would see me, was replaced by the fear that no one outside of the palace would ever see me again. I wanted to turn around and scream at the merchants, even the one I had just glared at, "Look at me — at my eyes, my hair!" No husband would ever see them now.

I thought suddenly of Erez and how his eyes had widened when I'd yanked off my head scarf. He was still in the world, somewhere behind me. Maybe I had seen the last of him. But maybe I had not. Thinking of him gave me the strength to walk through the gatehouse without glancing at any of the rooms along each side of me. I put one foot in front of the other until I emerged into daylight again. I ignored the heat. I had decided I would ignore as many horrible things as possible. I would live if I could, I would fight if I had to, I would do whatever was necessary in order to hold on to my life no matter how much I would not like it.

We were herded around the northeast corner of the palace, through the doorway of a court larger than some villages. As I gazed around I had a wonderful realization: *Parsha and Dalphon could never raise a whip here. There are too many treasures.* Xerxes had not foregone the opportunity to display his victory over the Greeks. White stone men with no tunics on — spoils from Athens — stood all around. Beyond them, colorful statues of soldiers with spears were posted at even intervals along the perimeter of the room. I was startled when one of them coughed. Though the soldiers were as still as Greek statues, they were men, men who might cough at the dust we brought from the road or run after me should I try to escape. Despite the size of the room, I knew I was trapped.

I looked to the heavens, hoping for some sort of sign. Columns higher than twenty men held up a ceiling made of stone. I could not suppress a vision of it crashing down and crushing us the way the winemaker crushed grapes beneath his feet.

Dalphon's voice came from somewhere ahead of me, ordering the soldiers to untie the girls from the line. A soldier looked suspiciously at the rope I held in my hand. But he undid the bowline knot around my wrists and took it from me without a word.

"Come up here where we can see you," Dalphon ordered us.

Parsha was suddenly beside me. "Did you not hear my little brother?"

My feet and legs were too tired from climbing up the stairs for me to shuffle any faster. I expected Parsha to prod me with his hand or foot as he had done before. I braced myself for the kick, but it did not come.

Instead he said, "Slowing your steps will not stop time."

I smiled despite the aching in my body. "You cannot touch me here."

"I told you I do what I want." But he did not sound as confident as he had outside the palace.

I looked him full in the face, unafraid of him for the first time. My mother had once told me: *Be careful what you say, Hadassah. Being unkind drains the beauty from a person's eyes.* When I looked at Parsha's huge honey-colored eyes I could see that she had lied to me. "Farewell, Parsha," I said.

"Maybe not. My cousin Halannah is the king's favorite, and she will skin you like a lamb being readied for a stew. We will see how the king likes you then. Perhaps you will end up in our barracks and we will come to know each other better."

He laughed, and then, mercifully, fell back.

There were many more girls in the hall than there had been on the march. At least two hundred girls were ahead of me. There were girls from Ecbatana, Persepolis, Sardis, Nineveh, and Memphis, and a few other girls who must have naively visited Shushan at precisely the wrong time, or perhaps their families had heard of the royal decree and sent their girls here in the hopes they might be queen. The king would have his pick. It seemed many more girls were crying now than on the march. Perhaps they had not had the energy to cry then.

Little men walked amongst us. If they pointed at a girl, the soldiers separated her from the group. I looked at these girls, trying to figure out why they were being set apart. When I saw a girl with pale, desert-colored skin tuck her chin to her shoulder to hide a dark mole, I understood that I did not want any of the little men to point at me. The girl raised a hand to hide her face but it was too late. A little man pointed at her and a soldier directed her to another group of girls and a life that I would not have wished upon anyone.

One of the little men looked at me. When he walked on I took a deep breath. I could no longer tell what was greater — my fear, my anger, or my despair. *What sort of man would have so many girls torn from their homes for what little time he could spend with them?* I easily answered my question: *a king.*

Already I hated him.

I desperately wanted to see a kind face. I turned back, hoping to see Erez. There were several soldiers, but none of them was him. Where had he gone? I reached my hand up and pressed the winged man Erez had given me hard against my chest. I was trying to make an imprint in case, like everything else, it was about to be taken from me.

Chapter Ten:
The Harem

We were herded south through the palace, and then down a long hall with no windows. I peeked over my shoulder at the slaves who followed us. They pushed towels over the floor with their backsides high in the air, wiping away the dust, sweat, and blood we left behind. We were led right and left and left and right and right and . . . I lost track. *I will never be able to find my way out.*

I put my hand over my nose to keep out the stomach-churning blend of scents — roses, cloves, mimosa mixed with essence of musk, sandalwood, myrrh, and balsam. We had come to the door of the harem court.

The soldiers turned and started to walk back in the direction we had come, and the little men took their places. These men looked us over differently than the soldiers had — carefully, without seeming to want to get any closer. They wore robes of fine linen richly dyed with emerald green, deep blue, and crimson. Robes with perfectly groomed fringes. None had even the slightest hint of a mustache or beard, and no hair poked out from beneath their tall white turbans. They were bejeweled like the daughters of wealthy men. Chains and rings of silver and gold gleamed in the lamplight.

A small, chubby one in a crimson robe saw me staring. His head was too big for his body, and his belly pressed against his robe with the immovable hardness of a boulder. I was surprised when he came toward me, and even more surprised when he lifted his hand and I realized he was going to touch me. I did not know if I should let him. *Am I permitted to stop him?* Before I could decide he continued past.

Then I felt a slap upon my rear. "Time to wash the filth off!"

His voice was as high as a girl's. *Eunuchs,* I thought with no small amount of relief. I no longer cared about the smell wafting under the door from the harem. *We are safe now.*

The eunuchs waited until the soldiers had disappeared down the hall. Then two of the less richly adorned eunuchs — eunuchs who wore only white — labored to open the heavy doors. I could not see inside. The smoke from the incense burning within was too thick.

The eunuch in the crimson robe who had slapped my rear strode to the entrance and cleared his throat as he turned to face us. "I am Bigthan, second in command to the head eunuch, Hegai." He said Hegai as though choking on a piece of tough meat. "When we reach the harem court, do not move from the entrance until you are taken to the baths. If you set foot inside, the whole room will have to be purified and the pool drained. And you will be sent to the soldiers.

"When you return from the baths you will be assigned to a section of the harem. Once you have gone in to the king you will be in the concubines' section of this room. Until then, the most beautiful virgins will be hidden in the back to keep them from sight. The least pleasing will be in front, closest to the entrance. Now come."

I wondered which section I would be assigned to. My hair was beautiful, but it was covered. Was it the pieces that fell out of my head scarf that often caused people to stare when I walked past? Or was it the way I walked? *Be careful,* my mother had said. *Your hips move as though melted honey were sloshing back and forth inside you. Wherever you go, men's eyes follow.*

We were herded down a wide staircase

that led to a huge square room with a sunken pool in the center. The incense was not so thick here. Rugs even more elaborate than those upon Mordecai's walls circled the pool.

I became aware that scattered upon the rugs and on pillows along the perimeter of the room women sat staring out at us. Their eyes, hundreds of them, raked over us.

One of the women stood. She had skin as white as ivory and huge brown eyes heavily lined with kohl. I felt the other women's eyes slide off of us in order to follow her as she walked toward us.

The closer she came the more colors I saw in the braids piled on top of her head. Crimson and royal purple streaks. I did not know if her hair had been dyed with henna or if lengths of silk were woven in. She was tall already, and the braids added as much to her height as a second head. She wore just a thin gauze robe and through it I could see a small waist and breasts that bounced heavily against her chest. All the women wore similar robes. I had been both happy and embarrassed when my own breasts began to push up against my tunic two years before. I could see that whatever embarrassment this woman might've once had was long gone. She looked like she was of noble blood, born in the palace or one like it. How else could she have skin even whiter than the eunuchs'?

She smiled at us. "Girls always come to the harem with big eyes. They make you beautiful despite the matted hair poking from your head scarves and the masks of dust over your features. But Egypt's gifts of opium will make your eyes small. The bigger and more terror-filled your eyes are now, the smaller they will become." She turned to Bigthan. "Right, girl?"

He remained still, like an animal who knows that if he moves he will be pounced upon.

"I am the king's favorite and you will answer me or I will have the rest of your appendages cut off. Right, *girl*?"

When the eunuch still did not reply, she tossed her wine at him. Her goblet clattered to the floor. I watched the eunuch's face, willing him to defy her in some way, however small. A raised eyebrow, a sidelong look.

"Your big head must contain only a small brain if you think I cannot make you regret that there is still life in your fat little body," she said.

Bigthan did not reach down to clean his robe where the wine had hit him. His face was nearly the same crimson as his robe.

"Yes, Mistress Halannah."

My stomach tightened. *Halannah, Parsha's cousin.*

She returned her gaze to us. "The more afraid you are," she said, "the more you will like the opium." The virgins were starting to shift away from her. She narrowed her eyes at a girl directly in front her. "You do not back away like the others. Do you think you are brave?" The girl did not answer. Halannah raised a henna-tipped finger high into the air, sending thick gold bracelets clanking from her wrist all the way to the meaty flesh of her upper arm. Then she brought her nail plunging down to stab at the girl's forehead. The girl screamed and stumbled backward. I expected a eunuch to rush to her aid, but none came forth.

"Already this one can hardly stand upon her own feet," Halannah said of the girl. "What will she be like after a goblet of wine?" She turned to Bigthan. "This batch of girls is even uglier and more useless than the last. Why have you not sent more of them to the soldiers? I will have to do this myself." She looked at us once again. "Who volunteers?"

Silence.

"Soon you will volunteer each other. You have no friends."

Though she spoke to all the girls, it was me she looked at. She came closer. "Hegai will be here shortly to soften your flesh, perfume your skin, and most important, to rid your bodies of souls. Platters of dates, honey, Haoma wine, opium. You will go numb and be glad for it. You will feel only hatred for each other. You will gladly kill the girl beside you for a golden goblet full of wine, a jewel from the king, or for no reason at all. Of this I am as certain as I am that the sun will rise in the East, and that we will not see it."

I did not allow myself to cower as she came to stand only a few cubits from me. She smelled of wine. Her eyes moved over my body. *You create a hundred moments in the first one,* my mother had told me after some girls had teased me one day at the well. *Do not let them see that their words have any effect on you and they will stop wasting them.*

"Your feet have lost their prettiness to the road," she said. "And your hands are even more worn." She hit her rings against my fingers. I jerked my hand away but then let it fall back against my side as though it did not hurt. "You have washed bowls in boiling water and have probably lost most of the feeling in your hands." She looked to my legs. "How unfortunate. The blood upon your knees does not mask their roughness. You have spent a great part of your life kneeling." Her gaze returned to my face. "Are there no trees where you are from? Are you kept outside with the goats, beneath the sun?"

My goat. A loss I had not yet thought of.

"Your skin is not fair like mine or any of the girls the king calls to his bed more than once. He does not like dark flesh."

Then Halannah yanked off my head scarf, the one Erez gave me, and went silent. I let her search for something cruel to say, something to undo the beauty of my hair. But she said nothing and this gave me courage.

"I have been told that my hair is the richest brown in all the world," I said. "Even the shyest boy will gaze upon it and forget his shyness for a moment."

A great hot breath gushed from Halannah's nostrils and she grabbed at my chest with her fingers. It was modest compared to hers, but still there was plenty to grab onto. I did not allow myself to flinch. Instead I hit her hand away. She laughed and pinched my hip, then reached around to grab my backside. "This tiny morsel is not enough to sate a man's appetite. The king will only want you once, or perhaps less."

Once. A fate worse than death, to spend my days growing old in this room as an unwanted woman. Except that I had seen no old women other than servants.

Halannah took her hand from my backside and looked over her shoulder at Bigthan. "Girl," she called to him. I stepped away from her, relieved. I just wanted her to go back the way she had come, getting smaller and smaller until I could tell myself she was not so huge as she seemed.

Instead she turned back and reached for my face. To keep her from grabbing my chin I lowered my head to my chest. Her reach was so great she did not even have to step toward me to press her nail against my chin. "This insolent peasant gazes down but stands upright. She is fearful but stubborn. It is your job to break her," Halannah told Bigthan. Then she took a deep breath and sighed loudly. "Yet I will be a little disappointed when you do." She was so much like her cousin Parsha that it seemed I had not escaped him after all.

With that Halannah pushed me. I fell hard upon my tailbone and a jolt went up my spine.

"Clumsy," Halannah said. She turned and began to walk back to the pool. As though I could be discarded as easily as a piece of trash. I felt my face flush.

"It is your breath I stumbled away from," I called, rising to my feet. "I have never smelled a rotting vineyard before."

Halannah turned back. Instead of lashing out at me, she gently asked, "How old are you?"

I thought I should lie to her, not just about my age but about everything. Give her nothing to use against me. But for some reason I told the truth.

"Fourteen."

"So old." She shook her head sadly. "None have wanted you for a wife and now it is too late."

"There was no man worthy of me in Shushan, Babylon, or anywhere in between," I said. In truth I did not know why Mordecai had not found a husband for me.

"Let us see," Halannah said, coming toward me, "how pretty you are with lines of blood across your peasant face." She raised her hand over my head and her bracelets jangled down her arm. As her nails descended toward my face I caught her wrist, squeezed, and turned her arm out to the side so that she stumbled sideways, screaming. I let go and she fell to the floor, her goblet clattering across the marble.

Her braid was so heavy she could not pick her head up. She remained on her hands and knees with her head pointed straight at the floor. She reached blindly for the frayed hem of my tunic.

She bunched it in her hands and pulled with all her weight.

I felt my tunic cut into the back of my neck. I hurried to hold on to it but still I heard a tear and then I was standing half-naked in front of the whole harem. The women broke into laughter. As I tried to pull my torn tunic around me, I felt Halannah's nails and then the warmth of my own blood on my stomach. Her neck was still bent by the weight of her braid and it seemed a demon was upon me as she clawed her way up my body. Her braid was so tight that winding snake-shaped lines of scalp were visible, fringed by tiny flakes of skin. She was about to tower over me and perhaps rake my face.

"Forgive me," I said, and drove my knee into her stomach.

She fell sideways and let out a garbled scream. I backed away, remembering what my mother had told me. *A wounded animal is the most dangerous. You may wish to help, but do not be foolish enough to do so.*

"*No one* but the king is allowed to touch

me," Halannah said, though she allowed a eunuch to hold her braid and help her rise to her feet. "Especially not some low-born vermin-ridden girl." She pointed a finger with my blood under the nail at me. "Once the servants have tended to my flesh I will tend to yours. The only difficulty will be watching to make sure you do not take your own life. It is *mine.*"

I held my torn tunic tightly around me and lifted my chin. "I am not here by accident. When God wants me He will take me Himself."

At that Halannah threw a goblet at me. I was impressed by her strength if not her aim. The goblet struck one of the girls in the chest, but by then it was empty. Only a girl beside Halannah had been hit with the wine — her and the pool.

"Ahura Mazda," Bigthan cried. He called to the other eunuchs, "Drain the pool and refill it quickly, before Hegai arrives."

As soon as the words left the eunuch's mouth, a rotund man in royal purple with a tall white turban entered. He towered above the four other eunuchs who attended him. They stayed back as he came to stand before us.

A lioness in a jewelled collar and gold

anklets walked beside him. She was un-
chained.

CHAPTER ELEVEN: HEGAI

Though I clutched my tunic tightly around me, as I stared into the lioness's eyes I felt as naked as a cut of lamb hanging in the butcher's stall. Her eyes were shiny black rocks, unreadable. She yawned, revealing four long fangs.

Hegai smiled, almost sadly, as girls shuffled backward. "Do not panic, it will excite her. She had only a small portion of the wildebeest she killed yesterday and has not eaten since. She will soon be hungry again."

"Feed her as much as you like," Halannah said. "One day she will still crave the abundant flesh of a fat man. Or whatever is left of a man inside that gaudy robe."

Hegai raised his palm up and the lioness sat back upon her haunches. She yawned again, perhaps enjoying the effect upon us. She seemed more regal than any human queen.

A serving woman walked into the room

with a pitcher. She passed close enough to the four eunuchs behind Hegai for me to see that she was at least a head taller than all of them. Hegai was not tall, he had just surrounded himself with smaller eunuchs.

He gazed at us one by one. "As you may have heard, I am Hegai." His tone suggested that he was recognized and spoken of over all the provinces. "I will teach you to please the king."

"*You* will teach them to please the king?" Halannah cried. "That is like a man with no hands teaching a child to be a great swordsman."

Without looking at Halannah, Hegai said, "Any who disobey me will not stay here."

He did not threaten that we would go to the soldiers. Perhaps too much relief shone in my face. Hegai's gaze fell upon me. I did not know if it would be disrespectful to meet his eyes, or not to. I remembered what Erez had told me about hiding my wildness. I dropped my eyes to the marble floor and bowed slightly — just enough that no one could argue that I hadn't, or that I had.

Hegai laughed, delighted. "You may mistake me for the king, but Halannah has spoken true. I cannot enjoy you as he will. Yet you will find I am far more demanding. You are wise to show me respect." His gaze moved over the girls. "Almost all of you will spend one night with the king, and the rest of your days with women and eunuchs."

The lioness yawned again, this time roaring loudly as she did so. A golden vase sitting along the edge of the room trembled slightly.

"Take off your clothes and follow the servants to the baths," Hegai said. When we did not immediately do as he had commanded, he continued, "Do not flatter yourselves that you have anything worthy of even the slightest crumb of modesty. The king has many palaces and you are in the greatest of them — the greatest palace the world has ever known. You are filthy and underfed. You have lice or you had them once, perhaps 'once' for your whole lives. You have stepped on floors covered in filth, dust, dung, and the footprints of diseased children who have since died. If the king saw you now he would ask the soldiers to gather another batch."

Servants began prodding us and pulling at our clothes. The gray of the tiles was quickly covered by a sea of blue, purple, green, and yellow as scarves and tunics fell to the floor. The girls were now a mass of flesh, some of it sand colored, some of it the color of clay, and some the color of soft wet earth. They looked like one shifting, trembling throng.

I let everything I wore fall to the floor, except the necklace Erez had given me, which I hid in my mouth. I needed one thing in the world that was mine. It tasted of the road, something I thought I would never walk upon again.

Hegai ordered the servants to bring wine. "This will ease what is to come," he said. "You are going to be in a beauty contest, one that will take a year of preparation and will determine your fate."

Do I want to win? And if so, who will tell me how? I did not know what kings were like. Other than what Mordecai had told me, all I knew of Xerxes were the exaggerations spread at the market square: He was the tallest man in the world, the most beautiful, the strongest. Few people ever actually saw him. He sat behind a screen whenever he dined with his officials, and he invited only a handful of people a year to come closer. To go in to see him without being invited was a crime punishable by death.

As we were prodded into different rooms containing tubs of washing water, I had to pass by the she-lion. If a girl quickened her pace or knocked into another girl in an attempt to leave a wide berth, the she-lion's tail began to lash back and forth. She was huge. Even her paws. "If you show fear she is more likely to attack you," Hegai said. "Animals cannot tell the difference between fear and aggression." I looked only at the goblet a servant handed me as I took slow, steady steps away from the beast.

Instead of sating my thirst, drinking seemed to increase it. I drank deeply, being careful to keep the Faravahar safely tucked into my cheek, and then I held my goblet out for the nearest servant woman to refill. The sweetness traveled down my throat, through my chest, and filled my belly.

A new lightness was flooding my head and somehow expanding even though already it seemed to fill my whole skull. Around this blissful glow, I saw the smoke rising up over the harem courtyard. A little part of me knew I should be sad, that something irrevocable and terrible was happening. Our clothes were being burned. Unless one of the other girls had hidden something as I had, none of them had anything left. As I entered the baths I moved my tongue against the Faravahar. *I must never lose this, or I will have nothing.*

CHAPTER TWELVE:
THE INSPECTION

Perhaps to distract us from the smoke, a servant said, "These baths rival the late king Darius's at Persepolis. You will be as clean as polished marble soon." She gently placed a hand upon my back and steered me toward a long line of bronze washing tubs. Before I could stop her, the woman took the goblet from my hand and helped me into the bathtub. "Just rest," she said, putting a hand on my shoulder and pressing me back.

I tried to resist. I wanted my goblet. But I also wanted to conceal my private places, and so I did not move my hands from where they covered me.

"Even with all the wine you have drunk you feel the need to cover yourself? You must dispense with thinking of your body as your own."

Without meaning to, I started to pray.

The servant pressed her hand over my

mouth. *"Hush. Do not speak aloud of God. Just lie still."* She knelt beside me and began scrubbing my neck with washing powder and a rough cloth.

After a moment she put down the cloth and pressed a calloused fingertip next to my eye. *"No tears."* I had not realized I was crying. The servant gently lifted a lock of hair out of the way so she could clearly see my face. The wine had not caused me to forget that touch is the purest testimony of a person's feelings. Hers was gentle.

"There is no cause for tears, your cuts will heal in time. As for Halannah, it is true that she is the king's favorite, but she will never be queen. If Xerxes meant to make her queen he would have done so already. After learning that he was rounding up all the virgins and would take a queen from among them, Halannah drank up the harem wine and great quantities of opium tea. She did not eat for many days.

"She will spend the rest of her youth as a wine-soaked harem girl. When the king is done with her she will be a servant to the new, younger harem girls. She will clean the chamber pots just as I do now. One day she may even clean your chamber pot."

It took me a moment to realize that the servant thought I was crying about my cuts or Halannah, and not all that I had lost. She had forgotten everything outside the palace walls.

"Until then, though, you will have to be careful. She does not like you. If you do not win Hegai's favor and secure his protection, it will not be safe for you to sleep." She pressed the cloth so hard against my neck that my breath stopped. "Look at me."

Her skin was wrinkled and thin. The bridge of her nose was slightly crooked, as though long ago it had been broken and no one had attended to it. Her eyes were hooded and sad.

"I did not please the eunuch in charge at the time I was brought here. He gave me to the soldiers, and beneath them I grew old. It took no more than a few years of that rough life to put bitterness in my heart and then it made its way onto my tongue. Not even the toughest soldier can withstand a woman who mocks him with laughter. Now I will spend the rest of my days as a servant."

"I am sorry, mistress."

"I am a slave. Do not call me mistress."

"I do not know what to call you."

"I was born Ruti, but now I am 'woman' or 'servant.' Do not seem too familiar with me." She shoved my goblet into my hand so hard that wine splashed over the edge and onto my stomach. "And stop crying. It is not yet time to pity yourself. You still have a chance."

I kept the Faravahar against my cheek as I drank. I thought of Erez's kind eyes, and the strength in his arms when he had helped me onto his horse.

"There is the little smile that will win Hegai's favor," Ruti said as she gently patted my hand.

After she had scrubbed me from head to toe she told me to stand. She looked at me for a moment before she pressed a towel over my body. "The scratches upon your skin will heal. You are clean as a baby, and beautiful enough to be a queen."

The floor seemed to undulate beneath me. Still I was strengthened by her faith in me. "Thank you."

Next I was escorted to another room that held only a table with a large pillow on it.

"Think of palm trees, a soft breeze, the wine you have drunk and the wine you will drink soon," Ruti whispered in my ear. She pushed me back onto the pillow. Wine sloshed down my arm, but when Ruti tried to take the goblet I tightened my fingers around it. If they were going to clean my teeth I would need a place to hide the winged man.

After hot wax was used to remove all the hair from my body, Hegai's own attendant eunuchs gathered around the table and Hegai himself came to stand near my feet. I sat up to look for his she-lion. I was relieved to see that Hegai had not brought her. Ruti took both of my hands in her own.

"Lean back and close your eyes."

I did as she ordered and soon felt fingers upon my thighs. Ruti held my hands tighter and I pressed the Faravahar hard against the inside of my cheek. I pressed until I tasted blood, so I could focus only on the pain in my mouth.

Ruti yelled at one of the eunuchs, "Not so hard! You will ruin her for the king!"

I could no longer raise my head. Each part of me had become unaccountably heavy.

Finally Hegai announced, "She is untouched." This seemed a strange thing to say, as I had never been touched so much in my life. "Bring her to the king's harem."

"*Carry her,* you mean," someone muttered. And then I could no longer keep hold of my goblet. I heard it clatter onto the marble floor, and then I heard nothing.

CHAPTER THIRTEEN: NIGHT

I woke in the dark. A lamp burned somewhere nearby, giving off just enough light
for me to see a ceiling that was not the
simple flat expanse of clay that had been
above my straw mattress in Mordecai's hut.
It was so high above me that I had to squint
to see that it was made of polished blue and
red stone. The walls were full of bulls, lions,
and winged men.

The day before came back to me and my
heart started to pound so hard that I could
not get enough air. With my tongue I felt
for the Faravahar. My cheek was full of cuts
and nothing else. I groped in the darkness
beside me, hoping the winged man had
fallen onto the mattress.

My eyes were beginning to adjust to the
darkness. It was an uneven darkness. One
piece was blacker than the rest. It sat beside
me.

I screamed and it folded over me as if my

voice had woken it. Hair, necklaces, and breasts swayed above me. Fingers lightly touched my thigh.

I slapped at the hands with all my strength as they yanked my tunic up.

"Hit me again, peasant, and I will not be so gentle." It was Halannah's voice.

Had Halannah taken my Faravahar? I swallowed back the bile rising into my throat. "What do you want?"

"That is a foolish question. Does a man with only one jewel wonder why he is being robbed?"

I knew the Faravahar was not the jewel Halannah spoke of. I turned my head to the side and vomited.

"You do not make this pleasant," Halannah said. Her fingers dug into my legs and she yanked one of them to the side.

I looked up in time to see another, smaller woman-shape of darkness come up behind Halannah. The shadow-woman brought something down upon Halannah's head and Halannah let out a startled cry and fell on top of me.

"Out, *demoness*!" Ruti cried, throwing the pitcher to the ground and knocking Halannah off me.

"What goes on here?" Bigthan asked as he rushed in.

"What kind of guard are you, who does not protect the girls Hegai has instructed you to watch over?" Ruti gazed at his wrists in the light of the oil lamp he held. *"One paid with a portion of the trinkets Halannah is given."*

Now I could see other girls and another eunuch hurrying toward us. I did not want anyone to know of Halannah's hand upon my thigh and also I was afraid for Ruti.

"Halannah came running toward me with a pitcher," I said to Bigthan, "but she fell before she could hit me with it. You can see she has vomited here. Ruti came to clean up Halannah's mess."

"Your tale was believable until you said Halannah vomited. Her body has not wished to rid itself of wine since shortly after she arrived here three years ago."

"She owes you no explanation," Ruti cried. "Take this demoness from here before I decide to tell Hegai of your corruption."

Once we were alone Ruti knelt to clean the floor. The room was not whirling quite so violently as before so I tried to help. Ruti waved me away. "But it is my fault," I said. "I drank too much wine."

"You will get used to the wine. Or you will lose your treasure."

"Please do not call it my treasure."

"Halannah was trying to ruin you for the king and she will try again."

I knew this, but hearing it aloud caused me to cringe.

"Stop that, or you will become wrinkled before meeting the king," Ruti said. "You need every drop of beauty you possess for your night with him."

I knew it was childish to pity myself, but still I said, "If my beauty is the reason I am here, it has done me little good."

"Do not pretend you do not cherish your face. Like all foolish girls I am sure you dreamed of a good marriage. Whatever boy you might have desired in your village no longer exists. Nothing outside the palace walls does — not even this." Ruti held up the Faravahar. I reached for it, but Ruti moved it out of reach.

"*God* does not exist?" I asked.

She did not respond.

"Please, it is important to me."

"It should not be. Do not waste another moment thinking of this trinket. All your thoughts must go toward your survival." She dropped the Faravahar into her tunic pocket. "Your beauty will not save itself."

When my strength returned I would find a way to get it back.

"After I clean your face, I will pick and

whiten your teeth, then give you a rinse that you should use whenever Hegai might enter the harem. You must win his favor. He can protect you better than I can."

"How will I win his favor?"

"By making him feel like something he can never be again. A man."

I waited for Ruti to explain, but instead she said, "You are too alone. I will not always be able to rush in and hit the drunken demoness on the head."

"Why did you protect me? Halannah will surely take revenge upon you."

"What can she do to me? Take away my beauty? Take away my freedom? I do not even remember what it is like outside these walls and I have no children to take care of me. All I have is my life and now, a reason for it."

I suspected that if Ruti truly was loyal there was a reason for it that she hid from me. And yet I was somehow certain that she really did care for me, or for something she hoped to gain from me, and I wanted to help her as much as she had helped me. "I hope I *am* made queen, so I can give you a life worthy of all you deserve."

She laughed. "Well, if you are going to be queen, I would prefer much more than that."

Chapter Fourteen:
Life in the Harem

In the morning, an old woman massaged oil of myrrh into my skin. I was both thankful and unnerved to see that she wore the expression of someone performing a menial task with which she has long ago grown bored. I did not close my eyes, even when my hair was soaked with olive oil and wound in a warm towel.

Ruti explained that I would undergo skin softening and hair treatments for the next six months. "During your second six months of treatments we will more thoroughly cover you in perfumes and cosmetics."

When the old woman told me to turn my head so she could apply perfume behind my ears, I pretended I did not hear her. I needed to keep watch for Halannah. Perfume was also dabbed between my breasts, and in my private places. I wound my fingers tightly together to keep from knocking the servant's hands away.

I closed my eyes only briefly as my face was powdered and my eyes were ringed with kohl. Then I resumed my vigil over the entrance to the baths as pomegranate juice was rubbed into my cheeks and lips, and my hair was brushed with ivory combs and styled high on top of my head. I understood why Halannah kept her head straight upon her neck. I would have to get used to the added weight.

When I stood up with my hands covering me, Ruti sighed impatiently but wrapped me in a large swath of thin gauze identical to those the women of the harem wore. I felt no less naked than I had without it. Unlike other Persians, the women of the harem did not wear undergarments.

"Is there not a robe to wear over this . . ." I did not know what to call it.

Ruti wrapped two more swaths of gauze around the first. They floated behind me as Bigthan led me toward the harem room and my new place among the virgins. Even before we entered, I heard the women's voices bouncing against the marble; it sounded like the room itself was speaking.

As soon as we stepped inside, the noise faded to echoes and then disappeared. Hundreds of kohl-ringed eyes turned to stare at me. The day before there had been space for the concubines to be scattered throughout the room, each woman on her own cushion. Now the room was divided into two separate sections left and right: one for concubines and one for virgins. Most of the concubines and all of the virgins had to share cushions.

There are so many, I thought. Each one of them seemed to be looking at me. *Are all these eyes that look upon me now unkind, or do all eyes heavily lined with kohl look so merciless? Do my own eyes make me look as capable of cruelty as all of these?*

Maybe word of the struggle with Halannah the night before had already made its way through the harem. No one spoke or invited me to come near. Perhaps Halannah had not lied when she said that there is no such thing as a friend in the harem.

Bigthan stopped near the entrance. It was where Hegai had said the least beautiful virgins would be kept in case the security of the harem was breached. But around me were girls who could not possibly be the least attractive among us.

I turned to Bigthan. "Certainly these girls are not —"

"Hegai is fickle, as you will soon learn. Now he has decided the most beautiful virgins should be where he will see them each time he enters. If anything happens to you or the others he will lose his position." He could not suppress a little smile.

"Sit next to Bhagwanti." He gestured at an Indian girl.

"I am flattered that I am thought one of the most attractive," I said, "but I would prefer to be farther back."

"Your preferences are not important."

"Surely I should not be in the same place as Halannah. Is not the front of the harem where she is kept?"

"Halannah is not kept."

With that he went back toward the baths, to fetch the next girl and show her the small spot where she was to live out the rest of her days. Before disappearing through the entrance to the harem he looked over his shoulder and spoke to me loudly enough for everyone to hear. "Sit down. You do not hold your wine well and you are less likely to hurt yourself if you are already on the floor."

From the silk cushion where she lay, Bhagwanti raised one of her perfectly drawn eyebrows. "Are not your feet tired? Sit down before you draw any more attention to us." Without waiting for me to respond she turned her body away from me.

The first meal we were served was lamb's

meat cooked with dates and plums, and sugared almonds for dessert. And of course wine. I hesitated. Was the lamb before me slaughtered according to Jewish dietary law — a quick, deep stroke across the throat with a perfectly sharpened blade? Was it drained of all blood? Was it prepared in a kitchen that kept meat apart from milk, cheese, and yogurt? I was certain that the answer to at least one of these questions was no. But Bigthan was looking at me. And I had broken our dietary laws already. The day before I had drunk grape wine prepared by gentiles. I had drunk so much of it that it had overcome me.

Without moving my lips or making a sound I implored God, *Please forgive me.*

I tried not to taste the meat as I chewed it, as though that might lessen my sin. The other girls spoke of the food before us and of the beauty treatments we had received. If any began to speak of their families or where she was from, a eunuch told her to eat lest she be too reedy, boyish, or chicken-legged for the king. Kohl ran down the face of a girl who cried loudly beside me.

"One of you will be queen," Bigthan said, "but this one has little chance. There is none less desirable than the girl who dares cry with the riches of the palace kitchens spread before her."

Not long after our first meal, I heard Bigthan shout, "Opi! Get back." Out of the corner of my eye I watched a tall Nubian girl walk toward the pool. *"Return to the rear of the harem before Hegai sees you here."*
Instead the girl sat by the pool, not far from me. She dangled her toe over the water.
"None are to touch it," Bigthan said.
Opi did not lower her foot to touch the water. But neither did she take it back.
The eunuch said, "I will get someone larger than myself to put you where you belong."
She appeared not to hear his threat, but I suspected that she stayed close to the pool to torment him. My heart expanded in my chest. *Her.* The cruelty we had been subjected to had not shamed or broken her. Just the opposite, it seemed.
Before I could approach her, the girl yawned and returned to the back of the harem.

It was painful to eat all that the eunuchs insisted upon. I had never before wondered at the skin of my stomach, how thick it was and how far it could be stretched before it tore. I could not help imagining the food piling higher and higher inside me, dates and pastries and salted meats filling my lungs, my throat. Suffocating me. After the third meal, I ran behind the screen to the chamber pot and vomited. The relief was so great I began to cry.

After the fifth meal, the concubines began talking amongst themselves, but loudly enough for everyone to hear.

A woman with a voice as high-pitched as a eunuch's said, "Halannah has not returned. Perhaps someone else will be called in to the king tonight." I rose up on my cushion to look at her. Her face was almost perfectly round. She looked like a large child.

"*Someone*, yes. But the king never bothered to learn your name — Nabat, is it? — so how could he call for you?"

"You think he remembered *yours*?" Nabat said.

"He called for me twice."

"Perhaps he told Hegai 'My councils tire me and I have not laughed for many days. Bring me the old woman with two different breasts.' "

More women's voices joined these, yelling out similar insults, until it seemed all the women must have misshapen, tiny, or otherwise hideous breasts along with hips too small or large for the king's pleasure.

The eunuchs did not stop the arguing. A few barely stifled their smiles or laughter. To a plump woman deriding another woman for her thinness, a eunuch said, "But, Armaiti, look how much flesh this little bird has added to her bones since she first flitted into the harem."

"It does not matter how much she eats now," Armaiti said, "the king will never know. He will only know the twisted vine he found beneath him once, which was one time too many for his taste."

The woman retorted, "You were as fat as you are now when you went in to him. So what is your excuse for not being called back, Armaiti?"

"I am sure my name is on his tongue, and my body shall soon follow."

A third woman laughed so wildly the bracelets on her arms jangled. "He will need more than his tongue to hold *you* up."

I remembered what I had heard in the market after going to live with Mordecai in Shushan. Each woman in the king's harem got to pick out jewelry from the harem collection to wear when she went in to the king. If he liked her he would let her keep one piece. I now saw the cruelty of this.

Every woman was reminded day and night that the king did not love her as much as he loved another woman. Every woman except Halannah. The day before I had marveled at how much jewelry she wore. She was so heavily weighted with the king's affection for her that she would not be able to jump if a mouse ran through the harem.

There was only one adornment that I truly longed to feel against my skin, and the king could not give it to me. Only Ruti could.

"His big chest must contain a huge heart. He calls you in to him out of pity," Armaiti, the large woman, said to the woman with many bracelets on her arm.

The once-thin woman cried out, "And is that why *you* grope my breasts at night — *pity*?"

"Oh, was that you? I only meant to search near my mattress for some grapes I dropped. When my hand felt how they had turned to raisins I did not want them anymore."

It was a relief when Hegai came in to announce who the king wanted that night, or would have been if the she-lion had not been with him. The women went silent as he stepped into the harem entrance, his purple robe more lustrous and splendid than anything the women wore, his tall white turban towering over the four smaller eunuchs who attended him. The lioness also wore a purple robe. It was draped over her back like a cape, and it fell around her as she sat upon the floor. She waited patiently while Hegai's eyes sifted through us as carefully as if it were he and not the king who chose a woman for the evening. I do not know why he looked at virgins too, when we were not going to see the king until we had completed a year of beauty treatments. He frowned at the crying girl and sniffed as if he could smell her from where he stood more than twenty cubits away.

Then he looked at me. "My eyes are tired little flower, come closer."

Slowly, I rose and walked toward him. My legs grew weak as I came within ten cubits of the she-beast.

"Stop. If you come any closer I will not be able to see all of you at once." His voice was high but his eyes moving over me made me wonder if he truly was without his manhood. "I have seen enough women to know when I am not seeing as much of one as usual. You are wearing too many robes."

I grabbed the third robe I wore and started to pull it over my head.

"No. At least there is one girl in the harem who is still a mystery."

"You are kind to let me keep my robes,

my lord."

"I do not allow you to keep it for your pleasure, but for mine. Return to your place."

Bigthan mumbled, "Before he changes his mind."

As I returned to my cushion a few of the women looked at me with eyes so narrow they were smaller than the thick lines of kohl with which they were lined.

"Now what did I come here for? Oh yes, a vessel for the king." Hegai sighed, as if the king's choice seemed unfortunate to him. "Nabat."

Some of the women jeered. More than one began to cry.

Nabat called attention to her many bracelets by reaching up to touch her nose ring so that they jangled as she walked toward Hegai. When she came near her gaze flittered over me and then she batted her eyelashes at Hegai. She was unfazed by the lioness. "To the Jewelry Box!" she cried.

No one imagined that she would never return to the harem.

That night as Ruti pressed a damp cloth to my skin she told me that someone like Halannah had ruined her for the king. "When I went in to Darius he would not have me. He sent me instead to the soldiers. That was twenty-nine years ago."

I tried not to show my surprise. Ruti looked old enough to be a great-grandmother.

"Halannah comes to each pretty new virgin. Few make it to the king unbroken. And so the king believes there are no beautiful virgins left in his empire. He thinks only plain girls are pure."

She squeezed my arm with her bony fingers. "If you do not show him he is wrong, he will seek younger and younger girls, until he finds the purity he desires."

"How old were you?"

She let go of my arm. "Too young to imagine what was to come and too old not to have known better: fourteen. My family tried to discourage the soldiers from taking me by telling them I was even younger. Surely they regret this. It sealed my fate."

"Soldiers are the most ruthless of all creatures," I said. "I wish God had never made them."

"No, Halannah is worse than a soldier. It did not take war to make her cruel."

"And the king?"

"He does not know anything his advisers do not tell him. He looks like a strong man, but at his core he is weak. You must rescue yourself. Do not be fooled by the treatments you receive and delicacies at your fingertips: you and the other virgins are not truly being taken care of. You are the most endangered creatures within these walls. You have something of great value and no way to protect it. But if you band together perhaps you can —"

"I have *many* things of great value." I could not help but think of Erez. Did he also believe a tiny piece of flesh was a girl's greatest attribute? If I mattered to him at all, would I still after my night with the king?

"Your purity *and* your strong spirit are more important than anything else, and you must spend this year before you go in to the king preserving them. You will find that in the harem you have to hide anything you wish to keep."

"A tiny bit of flesh is not more important than my face or my words or my thoughts."

"*Look* at me, girl."

The anger building inside me turned on her as I looked at her heavily lined face and tired eyes. Why had she allowed so many bad things to happen to her? But her eyes upon mine were so full of concern for me that I could not maintain my anger. It drained out of me, leaving me weak. "Ruti, there is one thing that will give me the strength for all that is to come."

Before I could ask for my Faravahar, she said, "You will have to *earn* the return of your necklace. Now, you had best get back to the harem. I would tell you to get some rest, but you will have to earn that as well."

I lay awake in the virgin sleeping quarters all night, clutching a narrow vase with all my strength, switching it from hand to hand whenever my fingers grew tired.

By morning my eyes burned and my hands ached. I was exhausted. I had to make friends before night if I wished to sleep.

When I entered the harem room I saw the Nubian girl sitting by the pool. As I approached her, I tried to recall the Nubian words that the ivory, ebony, and gold merchants had spoken amongst themselves in the marketplace.

"I speak Persian," the girl said in Persian, "and Aramaic," she said in Aramaic. "But if you are going to ask me to move away from the pool then I do not understand any language."

"I had not planned to ask for anything but your friendship."

"My mother told me never to befriend the first person who approaches you in a room.

That person is desperate."

"We are all desperate right now but not all of us know it."

The girl looked at me for the first time. "If I do not know I am desperate, then I am not."

"We are in danger. But less if we band together."

She was not moved by my words. She returned her gaze to the pool.

I tried again, "You speak beautifully. But surely these are not your native languages."

"My father was an archer in the king's army and my mother and I followed him across the empire, from battle to battle." She had lit up a little when she said "my father."

"Was he brave?" I asked.

"The bravest. He spilled so much blood upon the earth that at sunset you can see the pink glow of the path we took through the empire, where the sand is red beneath the top layer. He was more accurate with a bow and arrow than most men are with a dagger. But one of his fellow archers was not."

I sat down to comfort her. She leaned away until I retreated a couple of cubits.

"When he died my mother and I were taken here to be servants. She was overjoyed that I was chosen for the harem. That was only a few months ago."

Speaking of her mother had caused Opi's chin to jut like a sword held in front of something fragile. "Do you sit by the pool to think of her?" I asked.

"No. I sit by the pool because I have been parched my whole life and here is all the water I have not been able to drink. I come from deserts no girl of Shushan" — she looked briefly at me — "could survive. Not even the toughest Persian soldiers can live in the land where I was born. Have you never heard that when Cambyses was king he marched a large army toward Nubia to punish our king for insurrection? His men ran out of supplies in the barren deserts of Nubia and got so hungry that they started to eat one another."

Opi seemed to like my discomfort. She continued, "Cambyses hurried what was left of his army home."

"Still I do not understand why you sit by the pool. We cannot drink this water."

"I know." Opi tipped her goblet up and drained it, then held it out for a servant to refill. But no servant came; they would not serve a girl outside her place.

She did not lean away as I came closer in order to pour what was left in my goblet into hers. "You should not be kept in the back of the harem," I said.

She ignored my flattery and instead examined my face. "You did not sleep last night."

"I am afraid Halannah will harm me if I cannot see her coming."

"And if you can?" Opi asked, but did not wait for an answer. "She thinks I am no threat and will not bother me."

"So you can sleep, despite the spirits wandering through the harem?" I asked.

"I only know of one spirit wandering through the harem. Queen Vashti's slaves were dismissed along with her. But my mother was not among them. Xerxes had a fondness for her."

"Why?"

"You think the king does not enjoy dark flesh as much as any other?"

My cheeks flushed. Halannah had criticized my skin for not being fair enough for the king, and I had taken her words to heart. "Forgive me. It was a foolish question."

"The king is not swayed by anyone else's tastes."

Though this is not what I had heard of the king, I said, "You speak true."

Opi was not deceived. "Unlike you." She tilted her head a little to one side, as if considering whether or not to continue. I tried not to appear eager. I feigned interest in my newly cleaned nails until finally she spoke again, this time more quietly than before. "My mother told me that Vashti disappeared before the soldiers came for her. No one could find her. The eunuchs and servants secretly searched, afraid that the king would kill them for not watching over her more carefully. When they could not find her they decided to tell the king she had gone to Chaldea.

"My mother was certain that Vashti never left the palace. She believed Vashti stayed here, so she could be near her son. After taking her own life."

I reached up to touch the Faravahar around my neck. When I found it was not there, still I did not drop my hand. "What part of the palace is your mother in?" I asked.

"The dakhma. Vashti or her spirit murdered my mother out of jealousy. She was found with no face. There were *no cuts, no sign of injury.* Yet she had no mouth, no nose, no eyes."

"You saw her?"

"I see her often, in dreams. She warns me to cover myself at night, so when Vashti's spirit flies over the harem, she will not see the daughter of the servant whom the king loved."

"What do you cover yourself with?"

"I curl my body into a fist and cover myself with a pillow."

"Tonight you can put your head on top of a pillow instead. I will watch over you if you will watch over me tomorrow night."

Opi did not answer and I did not want to appear too desperate. I returned to my cushion to let her consider my offer. When my goblet was refilled with wine I did not object. I tipped it to my lips and thought suddenly of Erez holding the animal skin of water out to me and refusing to take it back until I had drunk from it.

I continued to think of Erez through the morning. Thoughts of him, combined with the wine, were like tiny windows letting sunlight into a dungeon. The sounds of the harem — women laughing and talking, and underneath it whispering and crying — faded. I was once again seeing Erez's dark eyes and then the chain bouncing against his neck as he rode away and then I myself was on the back of his horse with my arms wrapped around him.

I was awakened from my daydreaming not by a noise but by a sudden silence. I raised my right hand in front of my face and caught a blade in my palm. The pain was so great that I thought it could not be real.

Halannah let go of the blade, grabbed my hair and yanked my head back. Her other hand drew into a claw. I could see that her nails were filed into sharp points and that she was going to rake them over my face.

I slammed my left fist into her stomach.

She screamed and doubled over. The eunuchs surrounded her, all except one, who brought me more pain than Halannah had: he pulled the knife from my palm. Another pressed cotton to my skin to hold back the blood that was rushing toward the new opening.

It seemed my childhood was leaving me through that cut, that Halannah had opened me to what I could become. I felt strong. Even with my eyes closed, I had somehow known my enemy was coming as clearly as if I had seen her. Though I was bleeding, she was the one hurt. I could hear it in her cries, which were jagged and high.

I could be queen, I thought.

"Do not touch me," Halannah yelled at the eunuchs. "Xerxes cares nothing for this peasant, he cares only for me and I could make him hang all of you."

"You do not make him do anything." It was Hegai, and he had come without his she-beast. "You are not one of his advisers, you are not his mother, and you are not a woman he will make queen." He turned to some servants and gestured at Halannah and me. "Tend these two," he said irritably. "Do not spare our best wine. Go to the kitchens and tell them I have ordered it."

His eyes caught on mine and he studied me carefully for a moment. Then he looked away, toward two of his servants, and waved his hand back at me. "Do not bring this one back here."

CHAPTER FIFTEEN:
MY NEW CHAMBERS

As eunuchs prodded and then pushed me from the room, I thought I heard cheers. *Do the women cheer because I am being cast out?* I did not cry. If I were going to the soldiers I hoped I would shut my eyes against my tears and only let them out in the dark.

Someone forced me down upon a table piled with thick cushions. I did not know where I was. It was a simple tiled room with about ten tables. The table beside me was full of towels, bottles, and silver instruments.

Ruti came to stand near me. She tipped a goblet up to my lips while an Egyptian physician cleaned my palm. He applied a salve that burned worse than the blade Halannah had used. When I screamed the physician turned to Ruti. "Poppy tea."

The tea was bitter but Ruti whispered in my ear, "It will take the pain from you."

141

Still, my palm felt as if it were being divided by fire over and over again.

And then I felt nothing.

I dreamed I watched a silver blade enter my palm and emerge from the other side a beautiful shade of crimson.

I woke on a soft mattress, with a servant in attendance on either side of me and Bigthan standing at the foot of the bed. My palm was bandaged. Ruti was gone, but I could feel the Faravahar against my chest.

I looked beyond the servants to see where I was. Colorful wall hangings surrounded me on three sides, golden vases decorated each corner, and statues of lush, nearly naked women looked vacantly from all along the edges of the room. Against one wall was a curtain.

"Where am I?"

"Your new chambers," Bigthan replied.

I stared at him to see if he would laugh or sneer at his jest but instead he bowed his head slightly, and added, "Mistress Esther."

CHAPTER SIXTEEN: MISTRESS ESTHER

The next time I entered the harem it was behind Hegai. I was only briefly rejoining the virgins in order to pick seven handmaids from among them.

The women looked at me with curiosity, taking in my rich crimson robe, the bangles of silver and gold upon my wrists, and my carefully arranged hair. Two servants had spent the entire afternoon putting it into a hundred small braids which were then woven higher and higher, each one piled upon another, all except those that were twisted together and wound in a circle around my head like a crown.

Hegai told the women, "Seven maids will tend Ishtar in her chambers." A few women gasped to hear Hegai call me Ishtar. "They will enjoy the sweet white wines of Jerusalem, the rich reds of Sardis, and the poppies of Egypt. Musicians will play for them whenever they wish, day or night.

"And each will owe thanks for her new life to Halannah. If it were not for Halannah, we would not have to move Ishtar to a place where her offerings can be kept safe, and we would not have to give her seven handmaidens. Handmaidens who will enjoy the pleasures of her new status with her."

The only person more surprised by my new position than the women of the harem was me.

Hegai had come to see me shortly after I had awoken from the poppy tea and Bigthan had called me "Mistress Esther." My mouth was nearly as dry as it had been on the march. I would learn that this was one of the effects of poppy tea. Out of the corner of my eye I had seen his purple robe and tall white turban. I had almost fallen off the mattress rushing to stand with my head bowed before him. I had ignored the pain in my palm.

From beneath my lashes I had watched him gazing upon me. "Ishtar," he said.

I glanced up to see whom he spoke of. Perhaps it appeared to him that I was answering to my name.

He had several servants with him and he signaled to one of them. A gold plate was placed over my palm to hide the bandages. It was held in place with gold chains.

Though it was awkward and made it hard to move my hand, Hegai commanded the servants to fasten it tightly. As if he could see my thoughts, Hegai had told me, "It is not supposed to be comfortable."

I bowed my head again. It seemed the safest thing to do with the head eunuch.

"Halannah threatens my position by making it look as though I do not properly examine girls or preserve their innocence once they are here," Hegai said. "You have stood stronger than anyone else against Halannah. I have battled her by myself for years, knowing I could never win."

He came to stand not more than a couple cubits from me. Servants rushed to put a stool before him. He stepped onto it and placed a soft finger under my chin, raising my face not all the way up, but just enough so my eyes were level with his. "Until now."

Up close I could see that his eyes were a light, saffron-speckled shade of brown. Below each was a dark bag of purple flesh, not so unlike the purple of his robe. The intensity with which he gazed at me made me want to step backward, away from him, but also to stand up straighter and meet his gaze with one just as forceful. I did not allow myself to move a hair's width in any direction.

"The women cheered for you, Ishtar." He ignored the surprise on my face. "I will help you win the king's love, and you will repay me by helping to protect the harem. I do not want to send another broken vessel to the king. Watching over virgins is the one thing I have been tasked with, and as often as I have succeeded, I have failed." His voice deepened so that he almost sounded like a normal man, causing me to wonder again if he were truly a eunuch. "You want to help them, do you not?"

"Yes, my lord."

"Then you must listen carefully. You are no longer a child. You cannot just do whatever you would like."

"But I would *like* to help them."

"You have a strong spirit, but if you do not control it, it will destroy you. The first thing you must always do is think before you speak or act, or you will lose your chance to do good. Even when you think you are not watched you must be careful of what you say. There are a hundred unkept secrets for each of the many peepholes in the palace.

"Second, do not waste time trying to convince yourself that everything you do springs from pure and selfless goodness. And certainly do not waste mine. I cannot tolerate girlish silliness. Whatever path you take to save a child from a burning hut does not matter so long as the child ends up safe in your arms. Think like someone cruel — cruel people think clearly. They are completely focused on their goal and they do not waste time on remorse."

He turned my head from side to side.

I must confuse him, or he would not study me each time we meet.

"Do you waste time on remorse?" he asked. "That is something Ishtar would not do."

I did not want to tell him of my parents. Still, he had asked me a question and I had to think of some response. But he quickly dismissed whatever I was going to say. "Do not tell me of it. It does not matter."

I pressed my chin down hard against his finger. *It does matter.*

He laughed. "Without my she-beast here you are a fierce little dragon, just like Halannah. You have the fire within you that the king has come to enjoy. But it is a precarious task to enchant a king. You will have to learn to appear fierce and submissive at the same time. That is the task of womanhood, and you must master it while you are still a girl."

I was still pressing my chin down against

his finger. He dropped his hand and my chin fell to my chest. "If you fail in this — after all I intend to do for you — I will throw you back into the harem and allow Halannah to torture you as much as she desires. This will be no small amount."

He continued to study my face.

"I see you do not tremble at this. At least, not that I can see. Perhaps instead I will cover you in the blood of a wildebeest and leave you alone with my cat."

"Do you wish her to develop a taste for human flesh?" I asked.

"Do you wish her to develop a taste for human flesh, *my lord.*"

"My l—"

He had already turned and begun to walk from the room. "Come," he said.

And now I stood looking out over all the women, some of whose eyes were filling with hatred for me, and some of whom looked at me with admiration.

"Choose your seven, Ishtar," Hegai ordered.

I had told Opi I would watch over her, and I would, whether she liked it or not.

"Opi."

Opi did not rise from where she sat by the pool. My hand began to throb more violently beneath the gold plate. To distract the women from Opi's insolence, I quickly chose another. I pointed at the girl who had cried loudly beside me at our first meal. If any girl needed rescuing, it was she. She began to cry harder. Bhagwanti looked at the crying girl with disgust. Perhaps she scorned the crying girl because she herself would welcome being my maid. I pointed to her. She turned her disgusted gaze upon me.

Not one of the three girls rose from her cushion. Another girl, one I did not recognize, stood and bowed. "I am Utanah of Shushan, and I would be honored to be your humble servant." As soon as the words left her mouth other girls rushed to stand and offer themselves as handmaidens as well.

I looked to Hegai. His eyes were narrowed upon Utanah, but he offered no counsel. I chose her and three others. One girl with a broken lip, one who stuttered as she declared her loyalty to me, and one whose body looked more like a boy's than a woman's. I hoped these girls would be grateful, and pay for their gratitude in devotion.

I turned back toward the entrance of the harem, as though confident they would follow, and left the huge room with Hegai. A beaded curtain had been strung across the doorway of my new chambers so no one could sneak up on me. I was relieved to hear the beads continuing to rustle against each other for a couple of moments after I entered, long enough that seven girls could have followed me.

I went to the table crowded with bowls of fruit and platters of dates and honeyed almonds. They were like the fruits in the main harem room, except larger, completely without blemish, and as shiny as though they had been polished to just short of bursting. I took some grapes and reclined upon the silken cushions. "This is ours. You have only to ask and these devoted women" — I gestured to the three servants who stood around the room — "will rush to bring you whatever you desire."

The crying girl fell upon the nearest cushion and continued to cry. The four who had asked to be handmaidens also made their way to the cushions. They looked around, taking in the colorful wall hangings, golden vases, and statues of plump, bare-breasted women.

Bhagwanti came to survey the food, then sniffed and sat down without taking anything.

Opi did not look around and she did not

come farther into the room. She stood by the doorway, as if she might sneak away.

"Opi," I said, "we are not confined here. We can still relax in the harem room."

"I am glad my mother is not alive to see that I have been made into a servant for a harem girl."

"You are not a servant. You will not wash clothes, fetch salves, clean, or stand by with wine waiting to refill my goblet. You will do only simple tasks, dress me —"

"If you told me right now to come rub your feet, could I refuse?"

The other girls were looking on. Though the word felt like a rock almost too big to spit from my mouth, I forced it from my lips. "No."

Utanah knelt before me and bowed her head. Her dark brown hair fell over the sides of her face. Her eyelashes were so long I could clearly see each one despite the heavy lining of kohl around her eyes. I wondered why such a beautiful girl had not been with Bhagwanti, the crying girl, and me in the first group of girls. "Mistress, what do you wish me to do for you? I am yours."

"Right now all I wish is for you to enjoy this" — I gestured to the bowls of fruits and platters of dates and honeyed almonds —

"and recline with me to listen to the musicians."

"Oh!" The crying girl looked up. "I was afraid I would never hear an oud or harp again."

One of the servants pulled back a curtain to reveal a screen. The outlines of the men with ouds, harps, flutes, and a drum sat unmoving, as if waiting for something. After a moment I realized they waited for my command.

To reward Utanah for her loyalty, I turned to her. "What would you like to hear?"

"I would like to hear whatever you would like to hear, mistress."

"Play whatever song is at your fingertips," I told the musicians.

It was a happy song they played. I could see the quick plucking motions of the oud player's hands and the long strokes of the harpist's. The crying girl had stopped crying, but tears flowed from a couple of the other girls' eyes. Even Opi seemed moved. She stayed by the entrance but cocked her head to one side, listening.

Utanah kept beckoning the servants to refill our goblets. I wondered if I should be the one to do this, but I said nothing. I continued to drink; I was enjoying the girls' company and each drink dulled the pain in my palm a little more.

When Utanah started to sing everyone joined in. We drank all the wine, and I sent to the kitchens for more. "Just leave the pitchers. You are dismissed," I told the servants when they returned. We drank until we fell asleep to our own crying, singing, and laughter.

I woke to a shout: "Do not move, lizard." It was Opi's voice.

In the light of the lantern high up on the wall, I could make out Utanah standing over me with a cushion. When she saw my eyes open she lowered the cushion and said, "I was watching over my mistress. Your safety is my greatest concern. I took the cushion from this conniving Nubian before she could smother you."

Opi spoke from where she had rushed up beside Utanah. "If I held that cushion you would not have been able to take it from me."

Utanah ignored her. "She is not faithful like me, she is bitter and full of treachery."

I yanked the cushion from Utanah's hands. "You are dismissed. Hegai will decide what to do with you."

The girl's mouth twitched. "Mistress . . ."

I waited, but she did not go on. I flung

153

back the curtain. Bigthan stood outside the door.

"Are not you the one who is supposed to protect me?" Before he could answer, I continued, "Escort Utanah to a guarded cell, and tell Hegai that his loyal servant humbly requests an audience with him."

Utanah did not protest as she was taken away.

While I waited to hear from Hegai the mood in my chambers was somber. I wondered if I would ever again be able to safely close my eyes. The crying girl was still overfull with wine. She laughed and cried and laughed and cried until I told her to be silent. Then she only cried.

When the servants returned, the girls did not eat much from the platters of dates and almonds or drink the honeyed milk that was offered. I forced myself to eat and act unafraid. Mordecai had told me that a ruler's greatest task is figuring out who to trust. So far only Ruti and Opi could be trusted.

Opi had returned to standing by the door. "Thank you," I told her. "Your action is worth far more than any empty show of loyalty."

"It is usually the ones who smile the biggest who mean to do you harm," the crying girl said.

Opi continued to gaze at the side wall, as if she could not bear to see the girls she was trapped with for the next year. "With me they do not have to smile," she said.

"Perhaps they do not wish to do you harm."

"And this is the biggest insult of all. Everyone thinks I am too foreign and ugly to win the king. You yourself do not believe my mother was the king's mistress."

The other girls looked to see my reaction to this insolence. The girl with a cut lip gazed at me with something no one had ever gazed at me with before: fear.

I forced a smile. "Everyone may return to the harem. All but Opi."

Once they left I walked toward Opi, trying to intercept her gaze. "I do believe you."

She turned her head to avoid eye contact. "You are polite. And I do not mean this as a compliment."

"Because you saved my life, I will allow you one moment of insolence, though you are wrong. If I were polite, Halannah would not have tried to destroy my face and we would not be here now."

"You are too polite *to me*. I do not like it. You never know what someone who is polite is thinking, you must puzzle over it all the time you are with them. I prefer the girls who spit at my feet. They leave me free to think of my father, what a strong and agile archer he was, and of my mother, who was so beautiful it almost hurt to look at her. Vashti's spirit killed her, but if Vashti had not done it, some other woman would have."

"I will not try any longer to talk you out of your anger. Think of all you have lost if it helps you."

"Nothing helps me."

"I'll help you if I can."

"I will not trust you. This way if you do not follow through I will not be wounded by it, if you do I will be happy for a moment. But likely I will never know what you would do, because I do not think you will be queen."

"In front of the others you will treat me as though I am."

It was the first time I had spoken harshly to her. She looked me in the eye for only long enough to say, "Yes, *mistress.*"

"When I am queen, you will be able to sit by the pool all day and no one will glare at you or spit at your feet unless they wish to be made into a kitchen servant. I will not forget the debt I owe you."

Opi turned away and held up her goblet

for a servant to refill.

"You may stay as long as you like," I said, "but you are free to return to the harem if you wish."

She drank two goblets of wine in quick succession and left without another word.

I had some wine and thought of the person who brought me the most joy: Erez. When Bigthan entered he looked at my chest, frowned, and said only, "Mistress," before turning to leave. I realized my hand was wrapped around the Faravahar. I tucked it back under my robe, dropped my arm to my side, and rose to follow Bigthan down the hall, through a massive marble doorway, and into chambers that made my own seem a hovel.

Hegai sat on a throne with a golden headrest to match the gold on his fingers. The throne was so large he looked like a child. His feet did not touch the ground, and I could see now that his purple robe was too big. It was gathered partly in his lap and sat limply on either side of him. His she-beast sat beside him wearing only a crown of flowers. Her nostrils flared as I entered the room.

I bowed my head slightly to Hegai, without completely taking my eyes off the beast, and said, "Your humble servant is grateful for an audience."

"What do you desire, child?" Hegai asked.

"One of my maids wanted to smother me and would have been successful if another of them had not stopped her. I ask that this girl be sent somewhere she cannot harm me. Perhaps to the kitchens."

"The kitchens. Have you ever been in a kitchen, Ishtar?"

"Of course, my l—"

"Then you must know that food is prepared there. If I do as you suggest, the only choice about your life left to you will be how it ends: by poison or starvation."

I was not thinking like a queen, or even a clever maid. "Please forgive my foolishness. I trust in your wisdom to find the best place for the girl."

"She will stay with you. There you can best watch her."

"And she me!" I quickly bowed my head and added, "My lord."

"You must learn to be amongst those who wish you ill."

"Is this why you keep a lioness with you? My lord."

"You are doing well here with her. I can hardly see how afraid you are, except that you have not taken a full breath since entering these chambers. Know that the higher you rise the more enemies you will have. Every one of them chained only as my cat is, by fear. If you are chosen as queen, many will want you dead before you conceive."

"But Vashti's son Artaxerxes will succeed. She was queen and her son is the rightful heir to the throne. It is rumored that Xerxes has him hidden somewhere."

"You are not as quick as I had hoped. The rules of ascension are loose and this remains in peoples' minds. Surely you know that Xerxes is not Darius's oldest son, he's the oldest son of Darius's favorite wife, Atossa. Besides, Artaxerxes' whereabouts are a great mystery. If he is in the palace, without Vashti here to protect him, his life will be short. Especially with the king being a man more easily swayed than the leaves of a palm in a strong wind." He looked carefully at me. "Perhaps you do not know this about him? If so, you are the only one. Everyone wants their own daughter or sister whispering in his ear. The king's advisers brought Vashti down because she was the one whispering in his ear and she did not favor war."

"I do not have anything to whisper in his ear, my lord."

"You are lucky you are fair to look upon." Perhaps it was the sternness of his voice that brought the beast to all fours. "Or I would not allow your ignorance to go unpunished."

I was not sure how I had erred but he seemed to be waiting for some response from me so I said, "I will not doubt you again, my lord."

Hegai raised his palm, as though lifting something, and the lioness sat down again. "Not aloud. But take care you do not doubt me in your mind either. I see through your skin as easily as I see through the robes of the other women. You have no royal blood yet you do not think yourself a peasant."

Though I was descended from the great king David, I spoke true when I told Hegai, "I was born little more than a peasant, my lord."

"You will realize this like never before if you are made queen. Only then will you know how cruelly this can be used against you."

"I have been called peasant many times in the last few days."

"And yet you do not think yourself one of the girls here, peasant or royal."

What he said was true. I had not felt that I was like everybody else since my parents were killed. I was an orphan.

"By your unwillingness to show the least amount of fear and by the uprightness of your spine I can see that you are not an ordinary girl," he said. "But I must tell you: you are not yet royal in rank or disposition. Do not forget your forms of address, and take the rebellion from your face. Your mouth does not sneer, yet if I looked only at your eyes I would not know it. Pretend you are looking down at your feet —"

"But does not one naturally move in the direction in which she looks?"

"Pretend you are looking down at your feet instead of directly up to where you wish to be stationed. When you are with me or the king, look up with your head down, peeking through your eyelashes. The fewer people know where you wish to go, the fewer who will try to stop you."

"I do not wish to be *stationed.* I wish to be of use. I have already been docile and" — my voice faltered slightly — "this was of no help to anyone."

"Do not cry. Every tear takes a drop of your beauty with it. Besides, it annoys me. The first ten girls you see crying you take pity upon. Each one after that makes you hate all girls a little more."

"I have heard that girls are not the only ones who cry, my lord."

"Unfortunately this is true. It is rumored that Xerxes himself cries. One of his guards said so before he was put upon the gallows for it."

Though I suspected what his answer would be, I asked anyway, "For what does he cry, my lord?"

"Vashti."

In the silence that followed she seemed to fill the room.

After a moment, he continued, "I hope this will be to our advantage. You have the same eyes as she had, and after a year of wine and honeyed dates, your body too will be like hers. You are as fierce as Halannah, but you are not as fierce as Vashti. This is for the best. You move with the same pride peeking through a shell of subservience, but Vashti's shell cracked, and that is why Xerxes' advisers turned against her. She should have hidden her influence over the king better, made him think he had decided against the war himself. Your ideas must seem to be his ideas if they are to survive. You will have to find a way to make him think it is his idea to banish Halannah."

I started to ask him how I could do this, but he cut me off. "I know you will be smarter than Vashti. You will *hold your tongue* until you are perfectly positioned to use it. Do not use it to senselessly lash your enemies, they will learn to see you coming.

162

They will move out of reach. Do not let your feelings be known. It is never safe to do so — there are too many peepholes to keep track of. And do not say what you are going to do, that way no one can argue against it."

"Yes, my lord."

"Now tell me, as future queen, what is to be done with Utanah?"

I thought of Nabat, and how the jangling of her bracelets announced her. "Would my lord be generous enough to give Utanah bracelets for her wrists and ankles with bells upon them that clang together at her slightest movement? Bracelets that cannot be taken off?"

"You are starting to think like a queen. I will adorn her with bronze and silver and it will be fitted so tight to her skin that she will not ever have to be concerned about it coming loose. I will have her sent back to your chamber so you can deliver this good news to her in front of your other maids, who can learn by her example."

He dismissed me, but as I was leaving he called out, "Do you remember this maid from your first day at the palace?"

"No, my lord."

"Neither do I."

Before I could ask him where Utanah had

come from he raised his hand to keep me from speaking. "You may go."

"But my l—"

"You may go."

When I returned to my chamber I recalled all my maids besides Utanah from the harem room. I wanted Utanah to have to enter alone, with everyone's eyes upon her.

"Mistress," she said as she entered, "you called for me."

I did not invite her to sit down. I gazed beneath her thick eyelashes. "Gentle Utanah, I am blessed by Ahura Mazda to have you in my service. You are devout and I wish to reward you for watching over me this past night. You will be given many bracelets of bronze and silver. They will wind tightly around your wrists, ankles, and neck."

Utanah's smile shook a little at the edges.

"Each bracelet will be adorned with bells that will sing for us whenever you move, a joyous song to announce my loyal servant."

"Thank you, mistress. You are fair and kind and I will serve you with all my heart and body."

"Yes, you will." I held my hand out. When Utanah neared I lowered it so she had to bow deeply to put her lips upon it.

"Now you must go at once," I said. "I have picked out some bracelets for you and Bigthan will take you to the forge."

Her eyes widened at the word "forge" and I was overcome with pity for her. But I did not show it. "Do not delay," I commanded. "The forge's fire grows hotter each moment."

CHAPTER SEVENTEEN:
THE WOMEN'S COURT

And Mordecai walked every day before the court of the women's house, to know how Esther did, and what should become of her.

— Book of Esther 2:11

My maids were loyal and agreeable after that. All but Opi, who never seemed to come all the way into the room. She would stop just inside the door, but I know her head and heart did not come even that far. It pained me to see her so unhappy. Nearly every day I ordered her to go to the harem where she could sit by the pool.

The other person I did not see as much as I would have liked was Ruti. On the second day that Ruti did not come to my chamber, I asked Bigthan if she was unwell. He told me she had been assigned to serve the virgins in the back of the harem. I tried to keep the panic from my voice. "Please tell

Hegai that I would like an audience with him."

"He may grant you an audience but he will not grant your request," Bigthan said.

When I went in to Hegai's chamber I bowed my head, forced a little smile, and looked up at him.

"That is the smile the king will like," Hegai said. "Save it for him." I had never before seen him in such a dark mood. I thought that perhaps I should save my request for another day. But I missed Ruti too greatly.

"My gracious lord, thank you for granting me an audience."

"A brief one. There are more important matters than whatever it is you have come to see me about. The king is ever concerned with attempts on his life and lately he has become more suspicious. I wish it were Halannah instead of Nabat that I could have sent to him last night. After he took Nabat and closed his eyes to sleep, he dreamed he was drowning. When he woke his face felt scratched. He gazed into his polished copper mirror and thought that his nose was angled to one side, as though a pillow had been pressed hard against his face. He looked back at his bed and noticed that Nabat was on his left side, instead of the right, where she had been the night before." Hegai sighed. "He has given me the task of making her disappear and has instructed me to root out any in the harem with whom she kept company."

"And will you do this, my lord?"

"I am here and not upon the gallows, so that is a foolish question. I will not bring forth any girls who Nabat was close to, but no words will save Nabat herself."

My tongue felt heavy in my mouth and my palm throbbed as though it were being squeezed by a hand much stronger than my own.

"Do not stand there looking as though you are wetting yourself. Make your request."

"If it please my lord, I would like Ruti to attend me in my chamber."

"It does not please me. That one's mouth is twisted in bitterness and you must believe me — I have been here over twenty years — ugliness can spread from one woman to the next. It is why we keep the most beautiful together. Some girls think that by standing near a maiden who is not fair she herself will look fairer in comparison. She soon finds her own mouth has grown small and wrinkled from frowning."

"Ple—"

"You are dismissed."

"No, my l—"

"You are dismissed."

I had not told my maidens why I went to see Hegai and none was bold enough to ask when I reentered my chambers. While the beaded curtain rustled behind me I took a moment to look at the crying girl. She loved listening to the musicians. Sometimes she even smiled. If she had smiled very wide when she first came to the harem she would not have been assigned to the front section with the most beautiful virgins. She was missing two teeth. Still, she was much pleasanter to look upon when she smiled.

"Mistress, may I comb your hair?" she asked.

"Yes, and talk to me, so that I might forget myself for a little while. Tell me why you cry."

She gently ran an ivory comb through my hair then put it in tiny braids as she told me of her life as a henna artist. Her father was a quick-fisted man who had punished every mistake and rewarded any good she did with a blow.

She lost her teeth after one of the wives of an Egyptian dignitary did not wait for the henna on the backs of her hands to dry before putting her shawl on. The henna smudged and the woman screamed at her so loudly that her father was awakened from a drunken stupor. The dignitary's wife demanded her siglos back. The girl's father came out of the hut and said, "Here, this should give you as much satisfaction as your coins," and punched his daughter in the face.

"I have been crying ever since one of his blows cost me two teeth," she told me. "But I think I am done with sadness. You have given me a better life than I could have imagined."

Her real name was Mena but everyone took to calling her Crier. Her happiness spread to my handmaidens. Except Utanah. She cringed at the clanking of bells every time she moved. She had become very still.

Despite the contagiousness of Crier's happiness, over the next few months I worried that with all the time the girls spent idly within my chambers they might grow bored and turn upon each other and me. Sometimes I sensed that they were forcing their courtesies. I kept reminding them that they had far greater privileges than the other virgins.

"Is there anything at all that you desire?" I often asked.

They requested things I could easily

procure: instruments we had not heard before, delicacies from distant provinces, until one day Crier answered, "Mistress, I would love to see the sun again. And people walking past. And birds! I want to sit in the gardens we have heard so much about."

If I asked Hegai for the privilege of sitting in the garden and he did not grant it, the fear I had instilled in them by sending Uta-nah to the forge might be lost. I took a long, slow drink from my goblet while I thought through all of the things I could tell them. I longed for Ruti. *How can I talk them out of their desire?* I wanted to ask her.

I pictured her speaking as she usually had, through her worried little frown. *You cannot. A better question to ask yourself is how you can flatter Hegai like he has never been flattered before. He is bored and his pride is great. Relieve his boredom and feed his pride and he will give you whatever you want.*

I had come to understand that in the palace nothing was given freely. Debts and favors owed were as carefully accounted for as the king's coin. Mordecai would have drowned in ledgers if he had to keep track of the transactions of the harem.

Hegai liked the hands of virgins and concubines alike to massage the knots from his small shoulders and wash the sweat from his feet. Virgins who had been full of fear and bashful at taking their clothes off when they first entered the baths danced so seductively for Hegai that I wondered if they remembered that he had been cut. They filled him with a desire that climaxed in the gift of a trinket of bronze or silver or a privilege which would set a girl above the others in the harem.

But I knew that for a privilege as great as sitting in the garden, simple flattery would not be enough. I could not think of anything that would be worthy of such a reward. *I will allow my maids to choose the pathway to Hegai's favor, so that if our request is denied, I will not be to blame. Not completely.*

"How shall we please Hegai, so he will grant us this privilege?" I asked.

The next day I instructed Bigthan to tell Hegai that I requested an audience with him.

"What is this?" Hegai asked when my maids and I entered his chambers.

"My lord." I bowed and then raised my arms over my head, so that my sleeves fell away from them. Crier had painted Hegai's face on the undersides of my wrists and hands, including on the gold plate. When I kept my arm straight and tilted back my

172

hand it looked as though he were talking. As I did this my maids began to sing.

"Bold and strong, big of heart and deft of hand, one man rules the harem with the grace of a god. Robe of royal purple, turban of the purest white, he is just and fair and the beloved of every maiden."

I tried not to cringe as they sang, but only to tilt back my hands and smile. I knew that if Hegai was the one counseling me in this silly affair he would tell me it did not matter what I actually felt. It only mattered what I appeared to feel. I fought to keep Hegai's frown from pulling down upon the corners of my smile. After the last note left the maidens' mouths, we fell to our knees and bowed our heads to the floor. There was silence. I peeked up at Hegai. He was staring at us as though we had laid a pile of horse dung at his feet.

"Do you think I sing my own praises? Do you think I sing like a bunch of girls?" he asked me.

"No, my lord, but they are all I have. We have been practicing for many days." It was exactly the sort of lie I knew he would have encouraged me to tell, had he been counseling me in how to sway someone above my station.

"I have not been honored so foolishly in

all my years as keeper of the women." He tilted his head slightly, examining me. "What reward do you wish for this strange display?"

"To sit in the court of the women's house."

"I hope you do not think to escape, little flower. There is only one escape."

"I do not wish to leave you, my lord. Not by any route." It was true. I did not wish to die. I had discovered when I thwarted Halannah's attack that I would not give up without a fight.

"Those words from your lips are a welcome sound at least. I will do something foolish and grant your wish."

We had to don veils and wear heavy robes when we sat in the court, because officials often walked past, and sometimes soldiers. "The king likes for other men to see what he keeps for himself," Hegai had told me. "But he does not want them to see all of it." I thought of Vashti and perhaps he did too. "Not usually."

So we sat in the shade of cypress trees, looking out over the bright paradise before us. The courtyard was full of fruit trees and fountains, statues of beautiful women, and the singing of little birds emboldened by the prohibition against harming anything in

174

the garden. A tiny yellow canary flew low overhead and perched on a jasmine branch not more than five cubits from me. Hundreds, perhaps thousands, of tulips, hyacinths, narcissuses, and crocuses swelled upon their stems. Bees buzzed around the bright flowers, and a peacock strutted tirelessly back and forth. It was almost unbearably lovely, but also, unbearably lonely, because I could not see my maidens' faces and their voices were muted by their veils. We were completely covered but for our eyes.

Bigthan and another eunuch, Teresh, stood watch on either side of us while servants fanned us and refilled our goblets after each sip we took. We watched people walking to and from the west gate. Sometimes we sang.

One day an envoy from Nubia walked through the courtyard with two lionesses. The beasts were chained and followed by two men with great glistening muscles who carried whips. One man's whip was short and the other man's was so long he wore it coiled around a metal sleeve. Hegai later told me the Nubian had brought the lionesses as a gift to Xerxes, to try to improve the uneasy peace between Nubia and the capital.

■ ■ ■ ■

I recognized my cousin the instant I saw him walking alone across the court. The maids and I had eaten our last meal and the sun was lowering itself to the ground. Mordecai was leaving the palace. I knew it was him by the stoop of his shoulders, as though the ledgers he pored over were still in front of him.

I longed for the time when I had waited each day for him to come home and put his kind eyes on the floor I had swept, the pillows I had plumped, and the food I had prepared for him. I wanted to run and embrace him — something I regretted not doing when I'd had the chance.

Mordecai was so caught up in his thoughts that he walked by without noticing me.

The next night I brought two servants bearing platters of dates and honeyed almonds. I did not bring my maids with me and I did not recline on silk cushions. Instead I sat alone upon the marble tiles surrounding the courtyard. This was strange enough that surely Mordecai would look more carefully at me.

As Mordecai's stooped shoulders and bowed head came into view I beckoned both servants near. Abruptly I stood up, knocking over one of the platters. The plate of almonds clattered onto the tiles.

"Oh, I am sorry," I cried loudly enough for Mordecai to hear me through my veil. I waved my hands at the mess, my robe fanning out like wings on either side of me. "Please get all of this out of my sight." The woman who had borne the almonds knelt. I turned to the other servant. "Help remove this mess from the courtyard — both of you, *hurry* — and return with something else, I do not care what. Now *go.*"

Once they had left I turned back toward Mordecai. He had come to a complete stop and he stared openly at me. He smiled, and his smile was sadder than any frown.

I started to walk toward him but came to a halt when some dignitaries bearing gifts for the king entered the courtyard.

"Mistress Esther," I heard Bigthan say as he rushed up behind me.

I did not wish to put Mordecai in any danger, and so I turned away from him. "Escort me back to my chamber," I told Bigthan. "I am confused with wine."

The sadness of Mordecai's smile kept me awake that night. Though it was not true, I wanted to tell him I was safe.

The next night I sat farther out in the

177

court, not more than a couple horse lengths from where important officials walked past.

This time Mordecai's gaze searched before him as he approached. He slowed when he saw me. I sang, *"I have found favor with Hegai. I am happy in the courtyard, happy in the palace, happy in my chamber. All who know me treat me well. When I am hungry there is more food than ten men could eat, when I am thirsty there is wine. When I am tired I sleep soundly on a mattress full of feathers. Perhaps one day I will be queen, but already, I think I am queen enough. I want for nothing."*

I did not say: *Except to embrace you, and return to our home. I mourn for a husband I will never have, and a soldier I have no right to think of.*

Mordecai seemed to know my song was not complete. He had come to a stop.

"God rains blessings down upon me."

"Esther," he whispered harshly, as if he were giving an order. "*Ahura Mazda* rains blessings down upon you."

To reassure him that I had not revealed my religion, I lifted Erez's necklace up out of my robe. Mordecai stepped back, as though I had struck him.

Heat seared up my neck, into my cheeks. I looked pointedly at the tight curls of his close-cropped beard. "It is a disguise no more false than yours, and less elaborate."

He did not answer, and my anger mounted. *The meals I prepared in accordance with the dietary laws were your only connection to our people, yet you look at me with disapproval for wearing a trinket about my neck?* I thought suddenly of my mother's rosette. "Did the soldier Erez give you my mother's necklace?"

"Yes," he said. I waited for him to pull it from the pocket of his robe.

"It is safely kept," he said.

"What does an accountant want with a girl of the king's harem?" Bigthan yelled as he came up behind me. "All that will come of looking upon her too long is a new and final home for you upon the gallows. *Move along.* The day's accounting is done and there is no more use for you."

Mordecai gave no sign that he had heard Bigthan's threat. He remained where he was, staring down at me as though I were a mirage that might disappear if he stopped concentrating on it. I did not want him to be suspected of taking an interest in a girl of the king's harem. I turned away.

I lay awake again that night. The outside world had faded over the four months I had been in the palace. Seeing Mordecai had brought it back. I wondered about his life.

Had he taken in a servant to keep his home? A wife?

The past lay all around me in the dark — the hustle and shouting of merchants, the slow plodding of donkeys weighted down with rugs and other goods, the sounds of children laughing, cries and yelling coming from inside the many huts packed closely together through the city, the feel of the bread I kneaded, the warmth of the goat as I milked her, the curiosity with which she watched as I cleaned her pen. I thought also of Yvrit — long before she was Cyra — calling my name as I led us through a maze of legs, through the colorful market we were not supposed to go to.

A sudden ache took hold of my chest. *Mother.*

No matter how many legs and hips and protruding bellies I ran past, and how lost I might have gotten, I always knew which direction would lead me back to her, toward her worry and then her happiness, emotions that were twin sisters, one prettier than the other but both born of the same source: her love for me.

Even her anger was welcome. "I have told you *too many times! Do not* go running off to town!" She was rarely angry, and so it seemed to me she had become angry because her worry was too big to be contained in only one emotion. Her worry was a shawl that seemed to protect me even when she was not near. As I ran through the market, stomped at the flies that surrounded the butcher's stall, snuck up to the well to throw pebbles in and hear them hit against the rock on their way to the water below, I knew she thought of me, and her thoughts of me would shield me from harm. Cuts and scrapes did not trouble me, because they troubled her. She watched me and would not let anything hurt me.

Once she died, I had to start worrying about myself. I was sad, but I did not mourn. To mourn is to wade through the sadness in order to get to the other side. I was afraid my mother would not be there. As she had kept me safe with her worry, I kept her near with my sadness.

Even while I lay in my bed I felt myself lunge for her.

Mother.

Mother.

Over the next month, Mordecai and I continued to see each other in the courtyard. I looked forward to these meetings but also dreaded them. We could not speak freely. Each day, before I quickly looked away from him, I could not help but notice something strange in his eyes. A look he had not had before, as though something was trying to break loose inside him while he fought to hold it still.

But we have never truly spoken freely, I thought. *Why should it bother me now?*

In a dream I saw him. Like Opi's mother he had no lips, and also like her, he was on the dakhma. Yet his eyes seemed to see, and they looked at me with great disappointment.

I awoke with the answer to my question. *Because he wants to tell me something.*

After this I touched my ear each time I saw him. But he did not speak to me. And though the dream came nightly, one day Mordecai himself came no more.

Chapter Eighteen: Lioness

Ten months after arriving at the palace I was awakened from my nightmares by the sounds of people shouting and statues crashing upon the floor. I knew I must rise and hide more quickly than I had ten months before, when the Immortal had come to snatch me from my bed.

All my maids except Opi, who was with the other women in the harem room, were on their feet, ready to run but unsure in which direction to go.

They did not get the chance to decide. Two palace guards burst into our chamber. "Do not move," one of them said while the other tried to steady the beaded curtain that rustled behind them. "If you run you will bring the beast. Stay where you are and be silent. She will have to maul us before she can touch you."

"Which beast?" one of the girls asked.

"The one that belongs to the fat, prideful

little eunuch who will soon sway upon the gallows."

If Hegai ended up upon the gallows I may as well follow. Halannah would find a way to have me sent to the soldiers.

"Are there only two of you to guard us?" Utanah cried.

Their silence was answer enough.

Statues continued to smash upon marble tile, and women continued to cry out.

"You are becoming more valuable with each scream," one of the guards said. "Soon you may be each other's only competition for the king. That is, you, and the new virgins we will have to round up."

"What will happen to Hegai's lioness?" Crier asked.

The crashing and running came closer. The guard gestured for us to get behind the screen. *"Hurry."*

Utanah took measured steps, her bells barely jingling. But in the other girls' haste to get behind the screen they knocked it over and fell down upon each other. Crier screamed.

"Quiet, your cries will summon the beast!" I said. But no one heard me over the screaming. Screaming which was quickly drowned out by a roar.

I turned back to see the guards running

toward me, away from the lioness. Blood dripped from the many spears stuck in her hide. Her paws too were red with blood. She bounded so close that I could see only her. She roared, and the roar took up all of her face. She had black gums and yellow fangs. Pink drool dripped from her jaw.

She leapt upon a guard and he went down next to me. With trembling hands, I grabbed hold of one of the spears in her side and tried to take it out so I could thrust it into her throat. But the spear did not move, except when the lioness raised her fangs from the guard and turned to me. Her bloody tongue slapped from side to side as she flung her head back and forth.

Crier screamed at me to run and then hit the lioness with a silver pitcher. The beast turned and fell upon her. Soon all I could see of my friend's face was blood. More guards had come up behind the lioness and one thrust a spear into the top of her spine. Another jumped upon her and reached low to slice her neck open with a short sword. Torrents of blood gushed from the beast's throat as she tried to roar one last time. She choked, and then her body convulsed. After a moment she went limp.

I rushed to push the lioness off Crier. But my hands only sunk into the loose, warm flesh of the beast, and did not move her. Blood streamed over my favorite hand-maiden.

"Help her," I screamed as I was pushed away by guards who surrounded the beast, some of them continuing to stab her though she was already dead. I tried to shove one aside to get to Crier but I was pushed away again.

"The beast is gone, but my friend is still alive," I cried. "We need a physician."

No one heard me. I ran for Hegai's chamber. In the corridor I almost tripped over a guard whose face was marked by four deep red stripes.

He was not the only guard slumped upon the floor in the corridor. I wanted to get a physician for Crier before they were busy tending other people mauled in the attack.

I burst into Hegai's chamber to find him too upon the floor. He knelt with his forehead almost touching the tile. I saw no blood.

"My lord," I said. He did not move even a hair's width. *"My lord."*

"Child, you are speaking to a dead man."

"My friend is hurt, she needs a physician."

"I cannot protect you any longer."

"Surely you did not set the she-lion free."

"You are wiser than you used to be, but

186

not yet wise enough to know that it does not matter. The king sees conspirators and assassins in every shadow. He is no longer governed by reason."

"But why would you be suspected of releasing your she-beast? You have more cause to keep her from running loose through the palace than anyone."

"You had best listen more closely, little flower. I only have so many words left and I do not want to waste them. My life is over."

I started to protest, but he interrupted. "Do not despair. You do not need me."

"I have never needed anyone so badly as I need you. If you believe that a peasant can be queen so should you believe that you will survive this."

"I do believe you can become queen, even without me. But know that after Halannah there will be other enemies. The higher you climb the smarter and more ruthless your enemies will be. As you can see."

"Are you speaking of whoever released your lioness?"

"I do not know for certain who did it. Bigthan wants my position. Halannah wishes I were not already a eunuch so she could castrate me herself. But perhaps someone more important than these two had a hand in this. Halannah's uncle, Haman, cannot be happy that I am helping you become queen instead of her.

"Never forget, little flower, the hierarchy is a vine that grows more thorns at the top."

I needed him to look up, into my eyes, so I could plead with him not to give up. "Your words are muffled, my lord."

"There are people who will want you dead even more than Halannah does. You must learn the ways of court unless you wish to die soon after becoming queen."

I moved closer to him. I planned to throw myself down on my knees and beg.

"They will protest because you have no royal blood. They will say you were not a maid. Men and boys will come forward to confess that they had you when you were still a girl. They will risk their lives, but their families make them do it for riches, to repay debts or for promise of advancement. Everyone wants their sister or daughter to be queen. Witnesses will say they saw you robbing the feeble, the blind, the old, the sick."

His head tilted up ever so slightly. "Do not come any closer."

I started to apologize, but he cut me off. "And do not look scared when the king or anyone else tells you of an accusation against you. Laugh. It is the safest sound you can make besides 'Yes, my king.' Never forget for a moment that all these problems are better than the ones Halannah will give you if you fail to become queen."

"But without you I will not have to worry about any of this. Without you I may as well leave this room and go directly to the soldiers' barracks."

"You will become queen if you heed this advice, which is more important than anything else I have told you: when you are taken in to see the king make certain he sees your hair and face, even if you have to take your veil off without being invited to."

I understood how desperate the situation must be for him to advise me to do something so dangerous. In which case I needed him even more than I had thought. "If anyone can fight his way out of this, Hegai, it is you. Suspicion is not enough to remove you from the king's favor." I fell upon my knees in front of him, and this is when I saw that he held a sword with both hands. The point was against his stomach. He took a deep breath and extended his arms to better position the sword for a hard plunge.

"Stop," I commanded, throwing the little man onto his side and knocking his sword away. I yelled for the guards, not realizing men were already rushing toward us. We were yanked apart and I felt arms wrap

tightly around me. Another guard held Hegai.

"Your time is up, little girl," one of them
told him.

"Step back and I will end it then," Hegai
said. He was not begging. It sounded like
an order and for a moment it seemed the
guard was going to follow it.

But then he grunted and said, "Be silent.
Your games are for women."

The arms of the guard who held me
loosened for a second and I broke free and
ran toward the corridor. I tripped over a
body slumped on the floor.

"Please," I begged as the guard grabbed
me once again, "my friend needs a physician. She saved me from the lioness."

"The one who died with her head in the
lion's mouth?"

"No, she is still alive."

The guard turned me to face him, and his
tone softened. "Your friend is a hero, unlike
many who have trained their whole lives to
be heroes — most especially the men who
were supposed to guard you. No one will
acknowledge that she died bravely, but you
will know: she valued your life more than
her own. Often the most heroic do not live
long."

He brought me back to the virgins' sleeping chamber. "Your chamber is only a lioness's grave now," he told me. "Your friend has been taken away."

One of my maids was near the door. Without meeting her eyes I asked, "Crier?"

She whispered so quietly I almost did not hear her. "No."

CHAPTER NINETEEN:
THE BLOODY DAGGER

Bigthan came for me the next morning. I did not ask where we were going. As we neared Hegai's former chamber my feet grew heavy. It would be hard to see another man sitting on Hegai's throne, but I knew I must make a good impression. *The man does not matter, but to the throne I must show respect.*

I heard my ally's voice before I saw him. "My most humble servant," Hegai said to Bigthan as we entered. My heart swelled. Hegai sitting regally upon his throne was the most welcome sight in the world.

I did not permit myself to cringe at a strange odor that hung in the air. Hegai's face glistened with sweat and the bags beneath his eyes were swollen larger than the day before, but his eyes themselves were calm.

He held out his hand for Bigthan to kiss, and my happiness fell away.

"My lord!" I cried.

"Wait your turn," Hegai jested.

Each of the fingers of his left hand was shortened by a knuckle. He wore no bandages yet he did not bleed. The strange smell was that of flesh that has been sealed with heat.

Bigthan pursed his lips so hard that his mouth disappeared as he lowered his head to Hegai's freshly cauterized hand. He kept them pressed together even after he rose. Hegai waved him away with the maimed hand and Bigthan shuffled backward, nearly tripping on his crimson robe as he hurried from the room.

I could not keep my gaze from Hegai's hand.

"You are wise not to ask your question directly." A bead of sweat rolled down his face. His cheeks were so flushed that they nearly matched the robe of the eunuch who had just rushed away. The drop of sweat caught for a second on the end of his chin, then fell onto the large shelf of his belly.

"Does it hurt?" I asked.

He leaned toward me. I thought he might chastise me for asking such a foolish question. But then his mouth collapsed at the corners. "Child." He took a wobbly breath. *"I cannot tell you how much it hurts."*

I wanted to comfort him, to tell him I was sorry for what had happened to him and that I wished I could have somehow prevented it. I knelt in front of him and placed a hand on his robe where it covered his knee.

"Is there anything you wish me to do to help you?" I asked.

"Yes. Do not forget your place, *nor mine.* Take your hand from my knee."

I yanked my arm back as though he had bitten it. "Forgive me, my lord."

"If you touch the king without being asked you will have committed a crime punishable by death. Even when you are queen."

When I am queen. Only moments before I had thought I might go to the soldiers. But I would not go to the soldiers, I would go to the throne if I could. I knew I must do whatever Hegai advised. "Does not the king *want* to be touched?"

"He wants what he has not already had. You will have to be new each night."

I moved back to look at him more fully. His eyes were not playful. They narrowed at me, as if to pin me in place so I could not draw back any farther. "You asked if you could do anything to help me. Did you ask on a whim? Will you forget to return the favors I have bestowed upon you?"

194

I opened my mouth to speak, but he did not give me the opportunity.

"Because there is only one thing you can do to help me, and that is to become queen and whisper to the king of Halannah's atrocities in the harem, and how he is the only man powerful, kind, and wise enough to stop her. It may take more than one night, and so you must be new as many times as it takes."

"Who whispered in his ear that he should take the tips of your fingers?"

"The most melodious whisperer of all."

"I do not know who this is."

"Yes you do."

"Why would *you* ask the king to take your own fingertips?"

"I took them myself, before he could decide that he wanted more."

"My lord, I do not understand."

"And I have little faith you will figure it out, so I will just tell you."

Despite that Hegai continued to sweat, and drew in only jagged breaths, light shone in his eyes as he spoke. "When the guards dragged me to the king's chamber I took note of their daggers, but I did not make a move toward them."

I remembered how I had slipped a dagger from the Immortal who yanked me from my bed. Still, I asked, "How would you have taken one?"

"Very easily. Distract with one hand and take with the other."

Without meaning to, I again looked at his shortened fingers.

"Yes," he said, "something I will no longer be able to do."

"Forgive me, my lord."

"I have better things to do. Do not waste your pity upon me, I will not waste forgiveness on you. Shall I continue, or do you want to tire me with girlish silliness?" Without waiting for an answer, he went on. "Xerxes sat upon his throne, surrounded by a few of the most despicable men in the empire, including Haman."

"Have you discovered if he is responsible for" — I struggled to find words that would not hurt or offend him — "your lioness?"

"Yes. He had someone fill my lioness with wine and then provoke her. Unfortunately we are not yet in a position to deal with him. Now be silent so I can continue my story."

I pressed my lips together and bowed my head to listen.

"The guards stood close to me on either side," Hegai said, "as if I might wish to harm the king. Haman turned to Xerxes. 'This rebel set his lioness free with a finger that wears your own ring. I am not surprised. I suspect it was he who bid the concubine Nabat to smother you.'

" 'Your highness,' I said, 'king of all the provinces from India to Nubia, I am your loyal servant. I had no part in the tragedy last night, except that I did not keep watch over my pet as I should have.'

" 'Lions are not so wild as most people believe,' Xerxes said. 'They are never indiscriminate and unplanned in their attacks. When my men marched to Greece, lions came at night and attacked neither man nor beast, except for our camels. So it is strange that your lioness, who is given more meat than any man, killed soldier and harem girl alike.'

" 'You are wise, my king. My lioness would not have arbitrarily attacked, except for the wine someone gave her. The Egyptian physicians who examined my beast smelled it upon her breath.'

"I thought the wine on my poor cat's breath might save me," Hegai told me. "I do not drink wine, and neither did she. Not willingly. My pet and I were of one mind. One alert mind." His face held nearly as much sadness as it had when he was going to take his life. "But the king's eyes were like stones. His arms gripped his throne so hard as he looked upon me that the veins of his hands grew fat as worms. 'I did not bid you to speak,' he said.

"I knew he was thinking, as always, of himself, and how I had cost him men, and some of his pride. I did not give him time to decide what to do with me. I grabbed a dagger from the guard beside me and put it to my own throat.

"The guard moved to stop me, but Haman said, 'Let him.'

"This angered the king. My life is his, not Haman's. 'Hegai,' the king said, 'take the blade from your throat.' "

"I lowered it, but I did not give it to the guard who reached for it. I spread my hand wide across the tiles I knelt upon. Instead of proclaiming my loyalty with pretty, hollow words, I pressed the dagger just above the knuckle of my littlest finger. I put my full weight upon it and bit my tongue to keep from crying out. But my flesh would not give way. I summoned all my strength and strength I did not have. I cut off the tip of my finger. After one I did not stop. I only paused to look up and see that the king was not satisfied, and then I took another. *It is this or worse,* I told myself so that I would not hesitate despite the agony searing my flesh. A red river rushed from the new, abrupt ends of my two fingers. Again the king did not seem satisfied. After this one I did not pause to look up. I went on to the next one and then arrived at my pointer finger. That one hurt more than all the rest combined. Without a second's hesitation, I raised the blade up over my thumb. I could not keep from thinking that if I lost my thumb I would be even less a man than I am now. Yet I knew I could not take time to think about it, because then Xerxes too would have time to think. He may have considered having me sway upon the gallows, but he was not yet certain, so he reacted as I had hoped. 'It is enough,' he cried out. 'Four fingers is enough. I command you, *no more.*' "

I was holding the Faravahar as I listened to Hegai, tightly pressing my fingertips against it to reassure myself they were still there.

"And then afterward," he continued, "how could he ask for me to be more severely punished when it was he who had stopped me in front of all his chamberlains? What is the lesson here?"

"Forgive me, I do not know."

"That you should never go into a meeting uncertain. And so, little flower, what is it you want?"

"It is you who called me here."

"Do not go into a meeting uncertain, even a meeting you did not arrange. Think what it is you want, what is your plan, because from now on you must always have one."

"I want to hear your tale."

"And I want to tell it, so you would be wiser to act as though listening is a favor you are bestowing upon me. I ask again: What do you want *that I do not want to give you*? You do not need to waste time trying to get the things you will already be given. You can only call upon so many favors."

I bowed my head. "Yes, my lord."

"You are playing at a game that still does not come naturally to you. You truly are lucky I did not die." He fell silent, and after a moment I looked up at him. "And I am lucky you did not let me, though it is unwise of me to say so. But I wonder if perhaps your innocence is a game, and you are wiser than you seem."

"I am not fit to play any game with you, my lord." I realized that I did not know if my words were fully true. He was teaching me many things, including how to charm and fool someone, perhaps even him. I feared that there would come a time when I did not even know I was doing this.

Because I knew it would delight him, I

added, "Not yet."

He laughed. "You enchant me. It is hard to focus on my story with you undulating back and forth between innocence and boldness. I feel almost as though I never trembled beneath the knife in my youth."

I tried to stop the blood from surging into my cheeks, but I had only learned to control my words, my blood still did as it wished.

"Now tell me, why did Xerxes stop me and order me back to my chamber?"

"Because he knows you would never loose your lioness upon the palace."

He frowned, and — too late to take it back — I heard the ridiculousness of my answer. It was too obvious. He did not give me a second chance. "I knelt upon the floor in front of Xerxes," he said, "as you are now kneeling before me. But I did not sit motionless. I moved too quickly, and this caused our king more unease than he could withstand. Because I was the one wielding the knife he panicked, though I doubt he knew why. He was not in control. He wanted only for everything to stop for a moment so he could think. But once he stopped me he could not let anyone know he had done so because of his confusion. Kings are not supposed to be confused. But our king is easily confused. He could not think with me there

— strange and bleeding upon the tiles — and so he dismissed me.

"And now here I am. All but four tiny pieces of me and my pride."

"But you acted courageously, my lord. Why does your pride suffer?"

"Because I was not alert when someone gave my pet wine and provoked her. Because I could not stop her once I woke to her roaring. Because I have fallen in the king's esteem and am now maintaining my position only because he would feel foolish admitting that four fingertips is not enough. Because after I dropped the bloody dagger upon the tiles, the king spat upon the floor beside his throne, and said, 'Some eunuchs are like women — careless, cruel, and disobedient. Even many of my soldiers cannot be trusted. I will bring *real* men — men who have fought for me — to guard the palace.' "

Hegai hesitated. I bit my tongue to keep from commanding or begging him to go on. "He was speaking not of common soldiers, little flower. He was speaking of men upon whom I have little influence — the most inhuman of all creatures: Immortals."

CHAPTER TWENTY:
SAUL'S MISTAKE

I dreamed of hooves pounding closer through the night and of the blinding light of torches. I heard horses whinnying, girls crying, and the clashing of swords. Then I heard the worst sound of all, the sound of armor clanking as a soldier came to yank me from my bed.

The only comfort when I awoke, gasping in a pool of my own sweat, was the thought that perhaps Erez would be among the Immortals recalled to the palace.

One night my dream was especially vivid and in the morning I awoke to find the palace swarming with soldiers. They lined each room and corridor like relief carvings that had stepped out of the wall to watch us more closely. I knew by their saffron uniforms decorated with tiny stars that they were Immortals. They were silent and unmoving but for their eyes, which followed us as we walked past.

I knew I should keep my head lowered and not gaze at any of the soldiers directly, but I could not keep from looking for Erez. My heart rose into my throat as I thought of him. What would I say if we met again? *Thank you for your kindness, it has sustained me? Often I wake up with my hand wrapped around the Faravahar?*

"Soldiers have bigger appetites than ordinary men," Bigthan grumbled. "The king is putting both eunuchs and virgins in danger."

He and another eunuch were escorting my maids and me from our chamber to the baths. He jumped when one of the Immortals standing against the wall just ahead of us said, "Do not flatter yourself that you are in any danger, you castrated little peacock."

The wall was overcrowded with men. Parsha stood slightly in front of the others, as if he had inserted himself among them and did not truly belong. He was not an unwelcome sight. If Parsha had been recalled to the palace, Erez might have as well. Parsha moved his gaze from Bigthan unto me. "But your eunuch is half right about who is in danger, and the Hunter is not here to protect you."

I held my head high as I walked past, trying to hide my disappointment.

Though soldiers were not allowed in the baths, I did not want to disrobe. They were too near. *And they will always be too near now.* We had grown so used to being bathed that we were no longer self-conscious. We usually talked, laughed, and drank in the baths as if we were safely in my chambers. But on this day, there was no laughter. I overheard the handmaiden who'd had a broken lip when we arrived in the palace whisper, "He is so handsome." I did not know which Immortal she spoke of, but I feared it was Parsha. I was glad when no other maid spoke up to agree with her.

For once Bigthan showed some kindness. He did not force me to disrobe.

After he had escorted us back to our chamber, I requested an audience with Hegai. I wanted Ruti back. I would charm and beg and cry if I needed to.

When I entered Hegai's chambers that evening, I did so with my head bowed and fell upon my knees before him.

"My l—"

"Little flower," he interrupted. "I have been thinking too much about you." I looked up into his eyes and immediately regretted it. I did not like the intensity of his gaze. "My affection increases even when you are not near. It has grown so that . . ."

I was relieved that he let his voice trail off before finishing his thought. He continued, "I realized when the tip of my sword was against my belly and you came to my chamber that I liked you more than I have liked any harem girl before you. Though I thought I would not live to benefit from it, still I wanted to help make certain you became queen." He looked carefully at my face. I must not have hidden my discomfort at his words as well as I had hoped. He laughed lightly. "Or perhaps I only wished to help you because Halannah would be hurt by your rise to Xerxes' side. Yes, that is where my desire must have come from."

I was grateful that he had undercut his declaration of feeling for me. I wished he could also take back his gaze.

"Affection for people is weakness," he said, "and weakness must be hidden. Surely you know that by now."

Maybe I would have believed this except for all the times that thoughts of Erez had lifted me out of my despair. "Yes, my lord," I said.

"Rise. You are here because you want something. Because you saved me, I will grant it to you."

"You are generous, my lord, but I have only a humble request. One of Haman's sons has returned to the palace, and perhaps the other one will follow. These men are my enemies. They will not be pleased to see that I have won your favor and that we have our eye upon the crown. With these men so close, I must have an ally with me at all times. All I ask for is Ruti."

"A servant. How we love our servants! They tell us what we want to hear and seem to live only for us. We think they are more loyal to us than themselves."

All I have is my life and now, a reason for it, Ruti had said. I did not know why she was devoted to me, but I was certain that she was.

"With each other we must preen and strut about, but our servants see us with our hair undone, with no clothes . . . They see us when we sleep. You can be fooled into thinking they have no schemes of their own, no desires but yours. You can feel too safe. Ruti wasted no time in securing herself to you. Keep your eyes open."

"I will, my lord."

"Even while she washes your hair and puts kohl around your eyes?"

"Yes, my lord."

"And when you sleep?"

"I will sleep lightly."

"Not as lightly as I. I will return her to you, if you promise to consider carefully before listening to her counsel. She was not born into servitude. She made her way there herself."

"But cannot one learn from her mistakes?"

"She knows one wrong path, but there are many. You would grow old ruling out one by one all the paths that lead down instead of up."

"Do not fear for me. My ears are empty but for the voice of your counsel," I lied.

He laughed. "Go before I can no longer control my desire for you."

I hope he is what he seems, I thought as I hurried from his chamber.

"Ishtar!" he called before I reached the door. "How long have you been in the harem?"

"Ten months, my lord."

"Do you know what this means?"

There had been almost a hundred virgins rounded up along with me, and I had heard that the king was often at his palace in Persepolis, working to finish the construction that Darius had begun, so I had not thought I would have my night with the king exactly one year after entering the harem.

"Be ready in two months," Hegai said.

208

■ ■ ■ ■

When Ruti came into my chambers that night, I dismissed my maids and embraced her so tightly that she gasped. We talked until morning as I told her everything that had happened while we were apart.

"Two months is not so many," she said. "You have won Hegai's favor, but Hegai has lost the king's. You will have to win the king on your own."

I did not want to hear this. "I am suddenly very tired, Ruti. I wish to sleep."

"Not *all* on your own. I will help you." She gently pinched my hip. "As will all the meats, nuts, and dates you can consume in the next two months."

The next night I went to the Women's Courtyard for the first time since learning that Immortals would be returning to the palace. A group of them glanced at me on their way to enter the palace through the Western Gate, but not for very long. I wore many layers of loose robes and a veil with only a small slit for my eyes.

I had come to the courtyard hoping to see my cousin, and I was not disappointed. Whatever business had kept him away, or perhaps just a desire to avoid me, had ended. "Mordecai," I called through my veil when I saw him. And then I could not stop my feet from carrying me toward him.

"Do not come any closer," he said sharply. I stopped. "Forgive me for my foolishness, cousin."

"You have done nothing for which you need to be forgiven, Hadas— Esther. I just do not want anyone seeing a virgin of the harem speaking again to the king's accountant."

I wanted to throw my arms around him. Without Cyra, Mordecai was the only one at the palace who knew who I really was. He was the only one who had known my mother.

"But I will speak to you secretly," Mordecai said. "Sit by that cypress over there, and do not look at me."

Once I was sitting he turned slightly away from me, took a deep breath and looked at the ledger in his hand. "I am glad all is well with this," he said, as if to himself. "It is important for these numbers to find favor with the king, in case they are needed soon. Discontent rises amongst certain accounts, and ones' own numbers may be threatened. The mistake Saul made over five hundred years ago will come to cost us all we have."

"Cousin," I whispered, "I am at an utter loss as to your meaning."

He glanced at Ruti, to indicate he could say no more with the woman close enough to hear. Because of my veil, I had not noticed her come up beside me.

"There is no one I trust here more than her," I assured him.

"You must become queen. The fate of all our people depends upon it," he said.

That night I tried to make sense of Mordecai's words. But by morning I still did not understand who was threatening our people. Why had Mordecai mentioned Saul, and was the Saul he mentioned *King* Saul? I considered the possibility that even those I had trusted — my maids, Hegai, and even Ruti — could be somehow linked to whatever danger Mordecai was trying to warn me of.

As she bathed me, it seemed that Ruti wanted to tell me something. But just when I thought she was going to speak she pressed her lips together. I knew she had kept some secret from me for as long as we had known each other. Had I been wrong to trust her?

"Did you sleep well, Ruti?"

We were alone in my chambers, and it occurred to me that Ruti was the only one who would not disturb the beads in the doorway if she wanted to lay her hands on me at night. She had slept upon the floor so that anyone who came in would have to step over her.

"Probably better than you," Ruti said, "but no." She lowered her voice. "I do not trust the eunuch who guards your door. Eunuchs cannot sympathize with girls, they sympathize only with promises of jewels or power. Halannah's family can provide this."

I watched her carefully. "But you do not care for jewels?" I asked lightly.

"No jewel will bring back the life I could have led had I found favor in the harem."

That evening I could find out nothing more from Mordecai because Bigthan's gaze upon me did not waver. I feared he suspected something.

The next night, and for several more after that, Mordecai did not appear. When he finally walked through the courtyard again, I could barely keep myself from calling out to him. But I forced my tongue to remain still. He did not wish to bring attention upon himself. His back was stooped as usual, but he kept gazing behind him.

"Did you think about what I have said?" he asked as he neared the cypress tree.

"Yes, but it has done me little good. I am as confused by it now as I was when the words came from your lips."

Without warning, Mordecai nodded almost imperceptibly and continued toward the Western Gate.

Bigthan startled me. "The Jew lingers too long." My veil, which kept me safely hidden from the soldiers, also made it hard for me to tell when someone approached. Bigthan came around in front of me and gazed up into the slit in my veil. "This is quite dangerous for him. Also, for you. What is it worth to you that I not tell the king?"

If I bribed him it would be plain that I had something to hide. But perhaps it was plain already. I reached inside my robe and pulled out one of the silver bracelets that Hegai had given me when he had made me Mistress Esther.

As I returned to my chambers I felt a strangeness in my belly. I did not know if the sensation was due to nerves or elation. I had never bribed someone before, yet it had been surprisingly easy.

"Mistress," Ruti said that evening in my chambers. "I cannot let you go on wondering what Mordecai was trying to tell you. It may be hard to believe from looking at me

— but we are related."

"Then it is strange my mother never spoke of you."

"We are not first kin, but some of my blood is in your veins, and some of yours in mine." I allowed her to draw me to sit beside her. "I must tell you what Mordecai does not have the privacy to."

"He does not know of this . . . relation?"

"I have been keeping it secret, waiting for a time such as this. He spoke of Saul, the first king of our people over five hundred years ago."

"*Our* people?"

She began to sing. *"Sh'ma Yis-ra-eil, A-do-nai E-lo-hei-nu, A-do-nai E-chad."*

I knew I should not seem to know the meaning of the Hebrew prayer, in case Ruti had only learned it to trick me into admitting I was Jewish, but it brought back memories of my mother singing quietly into my ear in the mornings when she had woken me with it: *Hear, O Israel, the Lord is our God, the Lord is One.*

No one had sung me the Sh'ma since then. As I listened I felt like a five-year-old girl again. I wanted my mother. I pressed my lips together to try to stop their trembling. *I wish you were here, Mother. I need you.*

"You have to trust someone," Ruti said.

"No, I do *not*."

"You are right. I meant you have to trust someone or go mad."

"Forgive me. I am tired and confused. Please tell me the meaning of Mordecai's words."

"Do you remember the Amalekites?"

"Mordecai told me of them. They attacked us as we fled from Egypt."

"Yes, and they did not attack from the front. They attacked from behind, taking out the old, the sick, children, and anyone whose pace had slowed beneath the force of the sun."

"Why were the weakest left to fend for themselves? Were there no warriors watching over them?"

"No, that was one of the lessons that only the Amalekites were brutal enough to teach us. I think perhaps it is from them that we learned we must watch over each other more carefully. Later, Saul successfully made war upon them. But he did not kill Agag, the Amalekite king, as God commanded. Instead he took him prisoner. Samuel, a soldier in Saul's army, came upon the king lying with his queen. He killed the Amalekite king, saying, 'As your sword bereaved women, so will your mother be bereaved among women.' But he left Agag's wife alive. She ran away, careful not to jostle Agag's seed within her. The seed of our enemies."

"Our God wanted *her* killed too?"

"All gods are gods of war, our God and all of the false gods people have invented. That is the only kind. Think of the goddess whose name you have taken: goddess of love, fertility, *and war.*"

"Is there no other kind of god?"

"What good would that be? And tell me, are not you too thinking of vengeance?"

I could not deny that I wanted Parsha, Dalphon, Haman, and whatever Immortal had pulled me from my bed to suffer.

"Do not be squeamish," Ruti said. "It is our nature, we are made in His image. Besides, with warring tribes, often only one people can survive. That is the case now. Though the war with the Amalekites is no longer visible to us, still it is raging in Persia, in plots and schemes and vows. We must correct Saul's mistake."

I stood from my cushions and began to pace. Was I wise and courageous enough for whatever this task entailed?

"Take heart, mistress. We are strong — our enemies have kept us that way. They are the secret of our strength. We would not

216

have to be strong if they were not always rising up from every direction, thirsty for the blood of Israel. Without them we would not know that we can rise up again after any attack, no matter how brutal. But I fear we have met an enemy too big to defeat with strength alone. We will need wisdom and cunning to survive. Haman is descended from Agag. He is hateful and greedy. Suddenly there are rumblings that he is looking for a way to convince the king to allow him and his kin to annihilate us and take all of our possessions.

"Xerxes is no Cyrus. He will not help us if it does not serve his own interest." She put her finger under my chin and turned my face toward hers. "You must win him and quickly become more valuable to him than Haman's council and all the riches he would receive were he to allow Haman to annihilate us."

Though she had not directly asked a question, she waited for some response.

I remembered riding back to the line, holding on to Cyra's lifeless body. I had asked God not to place so much suffering before me again unless He gave me the power to stop it. Had He heard my plea?

I knew I could not say no. "Yes," I said, feeling a huge weight falling down upon my shoulders, "I will win him and save our people."

That night I had trouble sleeping, and for the next few days I could not bring myself to eat more than a few almonds or dates.

One morning as Ruti bathed me, I said, "How can I make the king love me?"

"If you wish for the king to love you, do not be sad. Your sadness is starting to bring your bones up from your flesh. Just as it will take the womanliness from your form, so too will it ruin your face. Make yourself smile. You must trick yourself into believing you are happy."

Perhaps she would not have said this if she knew how I would trick myself. There was only one thing left in the world that allowed me to forget my cares for a moment: thinking of Erez.

Chapter Twenty-One:
Erez

Exactly one month before my night with the king, I saw Erez. I set my goblet down with a hand that shook so violently wine splashed over the rim, onto the cushion I sat upon. I shifted backward until I was leaning against the column behind me. The column supported the courtyard roof, so perhaps it could also support me while my heart beat too hard for me to know what to do.

I had been waiting in vain for Mordecai every day, but any thought of my cousin fled when Erez appeared. His face looked thinner than before. His cheeks were sharper, and he had deep hollows beneath his eyes. Yet he was the most welcome sight in all the world.

He was coming from the Western Gate, walking toward the inner courtyard on the other side of the Women's Courtyard. But he was not coming alone. I heard voices —

rough, irreverent and loose — soldiers' voices. I grabbed the cushion and my wine and hurried behind the column.

Parsha's voice rang out across the courtyard. "The king likes you so well, perhaps you should join his harem. Then he can call upon you nightly and you will not have to wear armor in his presence. You will be clothed in nothing but perfume."

I peeked around the column and saw Erez casting a look back over his shoulder. "It is not I who need perfume, Parsha," Erez said, reminding me of how foul Parsha had smelled when he had secured a rope around my wrists so he could pull me behind his horse.

One of the men looked about, as if he had lost something. "What has become of the maidens we brought the king? Surely there must be some he has tired of. Will he not allow us to add a few of them to our own collection of concubines?"

"It is amazing how you never tire of yourself," Erez said. "You are among the least interesting of all the creatures the gods have created."

Parsha laughed. "Even the most willful woman does not so desperately protest against a man's natural desires. When my father convinces the king of the great benefit to the empire, we will go on a mission that will be over almost as soon as it is undertaken. Men and riches lie unguarded throughout the land, wasted on a people who are loyal only to themselves. A people who do not bow down to any but their one god. Each of us will be richer when it is over."

I looked to Ruti, who stood holding a pitcher of wine in the doorway to the courtyard. I could see by the blood draining from her face that she too had heard Parsha's words. "We will have more women in one night than some of you have had in a lifetime," he continued, "and many times more than you have had, Erez."

I pushed with my feet to adjust my position on the cushion so that as the Immortals advanced I would still be on the opposite side of the column from them, hidden.

I remembered the goblet too late.

It clattered against the column. I held my breath, afraid that any movement might draw the Immortals' gazes to me. Bigthan was afraid of them, and I knew he would not come to my aid, but Ruti might rush from the doorway to fetch up the goblet. I hated to think of how the Immortals might treat an old serving woman if they found her on her hands and knees in the court-yard.

When Ruti did not come, and the soldiers continued talking amongst themselves, I thought that perhaps no one had heard the goblet clatter upon the tiles. I peeked around the column.

Parsha and the other Immortals continued walking toward the inner courtyard. All except Erez, who was squinting in my direction.

I did not give myself time to think better of it — I reached my hand up to my neck to lift the Faravahar out from under my robe and set it against my chest. It was small, and in any case it was not unusual for someone to wear a Faravahar, yet Erez looked into the slit of my veil, at my eyes. He came to a halt.

The Immortal behind Erez stumbled off to the side of the path, onto some polished stones, to avoid crashing into Erez. The others slowed to laugh at the soldier.

Erez took a deep breath and started walking again. But he stole a couple of glances back at me, and he did not move as quickly as before.

"Have your sandals filled with rocks to make you walk so slow? Or are you suddenly shy of your master?" Parsha asked.

"He is your master as well," Erez said.

"But I do not serve him as you do, without promise of anything in return. You will march to your death —"

"I can think of no better way."

"— sooner than later."

Though he walked slowly he did not stop, and soon I watched him disappear into the inner courtyard.

Ruti's voice came from behind me. "They have gone to guard the king, and will not be out again tonight." I turned to look at her, and she moved her gaze from where Erez had disappeared to my face. "Soldiers should not be able to put a girl who hopes to be queen in such a trance."

That night my heartbeat seemed to quicken with each new thought. I was filled with a strange, fearful elation at seeing Erez. But the elation was diminished by fear that Haman might somehow successfully convince the king to kill the Jews. I was angry at Xerxes himself for giving power to a person as serpentine as Haman. How could an intelligent king possibly trust in the counsel of such a man? And yet, Erez was loyal to this king.

Soldiers were never taught to read, so it

would do no good to write Erez a note. But perhaps just the sight of me could compel him to think of my people and how he might help us. After my bath, when I told Ruti where we were going, she said, "What foolishness is this?"

"A foolishness that might save our people. Parsha may speak again of his father's plans while crossing the courtyard, and so that is where we must be." I did not mention Erez.

"If Parsha sees you, your veil will not save you from his cruelty."

"He would not touch what belongs to the king."

"The king will not restrain them while he is so full of fear for his own life. He believes they are the best guards in the empire. Do not think they will leave you alone because you are the king's. The king cares more for them than for you, and you are not yet in a position to change that."

I sat behind the column where I had hidden the day before, ignoring the irritated look from Bigthan. Ruti had made me promise to eat all I could, so I forced lamb, dates, and honey past the lump in my throat. I used wine to help it into my belly.

After the sun had climbed to the top of the sky, Ruti came and stood next to me. This time I heard her approach. "Mistress, surely you will have to go to the baths again if you sit out here much longer. The perfumes of roses and almonds I massaged into your skin have probably been carried away by the breeze." She dropped her voice to a whisper, "And I do not think being here is a good idea. If you are degraded or soiled in any way, we are ruined."

"I will not go now. I am relaxing in the fresh air."

"You do not seem very relaxed. I am worried for your neck because of how you keep craning it around this column."

"Ruti, please return to the doorway. After you refill my goblet."

"Very well. I will get you more meat and nuts as well. We must continue to bring forth a woman's softness from your flesh. The king is not Greek. He does not want a little boy in his bed."

I knew that some Persian men lay with eunuchs or boys, but I had not heard this of Xerxes. I ate as much as I could. Despite Ruti's constant complaining that I was too thin, my body had grown as soft and lush as those of the concubines. Perhaps the king had not yet made me a woman, but I looked like one. I felt the confidence that comes from taking up more space in the world.

When the sun was almost directly overhead, Erez walked into the Women's Courtyard from the inner courtyard. He looked to where I sat and nearly came to a halt.

"Have you seen a ghost, Erez? One of the men you killed come to pull your intestines out your nostrils and feed them back to you?"

Another said, "That is why all but the most foolish soldier will only kill from a great distance or by thrusting a dagger into a man's back, so the man will not lurk in this world looking for the face of the soldier who killed him. But it is too late for you, Erez. You may as well start giving away your possessions. No, excuse me, I forgot. You have none."

While the men laughed, Erez and I stared at each other, neither of us smiling. There was a hardness in his eyes that scared me. He appeared to have fallen into a trance. Who was it he saw — an ally, an enemy? Me, or someone else?

And then something did come across his eyes. Sadness. It is what the hardness had hidden.

When the other Immortals caught up to Erez the hardness returned. He hurried to try to get in front of them as they continued on the path.

Parsha paused to see what had caused

Erez to slow his pace. His eyes fell upon me. "This is what brings you to a halt?" He came toward me, trampling the tulips, hyacinths, narcissuses, and crocuses that lay between us. Erez hurried after him but the other soldiers blocked him. I smelled the stale stench of Parsha's unwashed skin as he bent to look at me. He came so close that his face was all I could see. His lips were chapped and he had pockmarks on his cheeks and jaw. His eyes were cold except for a cruel, playful glint.

"Is it not hot in there, maiden? I think I can see your breath coming through the little slit in your sack. Take it off. We will tell no one."

Ruti came rushing up beside me. "This is your future queen, *soldier.*"

He stood so that he towered over Ruti. "Or a girl who will have the honor of following in our train with the other concubines."

I was surprised to hear Bigthan yell, "Get away from her! I will tell the king!" He did not come near, though. This made Parsha laugh.

He turned and went back along the path of trampled flowers. I saw that Erez had pushed through the other soldiers and that he was coming toward us. He stepped into

Parsha's path. Perhaps to preserve his dignity, Parsha did not avoid Erez completely as he stepped around him. He threw his shoulder into Erez's. Instead of moving Erez from the path, this only caused Parsha himself to stumble. Erez watched without emotion as Parsha righted himself and continued walking away as though nothing had happened. He and the other soldiers walked toward the Western Gate and then disappeared through it, leaving Erez behind.

Erez's face was flushed and cords stood out in his neck. Still, I was going to ask him if he would find out all he could of Haman's plans. And I wanted to ask him if he had missed me. But his dark eyes were not full of affection or even kindness. He narrowed them so severely at me that I saw only the blacks of his irises.

"We need your hel—"

"You should find a different place to spend your days," he said.

I could not have responded even if he had given me the chance. He didn't. He turned and walked away. I watched his broad back get smaller and smaller and then disappear through the Western Gate.

That night, as on so many others, I did not sleep. I had hoped there might be some way, besides making the king fall in love with me, to save my people. What if the king did not like me, much less love me? If Erez, the one man who I thought cared for me the way a man cares for a woman, did not wish to see me, how could I expect the king to choose me from among hundreds of girls?

But perhaps Erez did care for me. Perhaps he was lying awake, or standing guard somewhere, thinking of me, and wishing he had spoken more gently. Perhaps he was even thinking of how he might learn more of Haman's plot so he could tell me of it.

The next day I went back to the courtyard and returned to the same spot behind the column that I had sat in the day before.

My heart leapt when he came by himself, walking quickly from the inner courtyard. But as he continued without slowing his pace I knew he did not want to see me.

"Is that the same sack as yesterday?" I heard Parsha call from where he must have just entered the courtyard. I did not look at him. I watched Erez approach with his eyes directly ahead of him.

Do not ignore me. Did you not give me your Faravahar because you cared for me?

He passed not more than ten cubits in front of me. I kept my eyes upon him, willing him to look back. He was almost to the Western Gate.

"I promise I will try not to recoil if you take off your sack," Parsha said from what sounded like not more than a few cubits away.

My heart swelled as Erez turned around and began walking toward Parsha. Was he returning to make certain Parsha did not harm me? I did not get to find out.

Parsha continued, "I have not seen anything truly interesting since Erez slaughtered a child and blood poured from the boy's eyes."

Erez stopped.

From the corner of the slit in my veil I saw that Parsha had begun walking again, and that the other Immortals followed. Erez remained as still as a stone as he waited for them to pass.

My heart ached for him. I hoped that he would look at me again. I would use my eyes to tell him that surely God had forgiven him.

But when the footsteps of the other Immortals could no longer be heard, he turned around and walked from the courtyard.

Perhaps helping my people would free him from the shadows that have fallen over his face.

I continued to wait for him each day, and watched as he walked past. He did not look at me, except every once in a while, so briefly I hardly saw into his eyes. I could not read the darkness there. He seemed to be flinching from something. Perhaps the memory of the boy. Perhaps from me.

Though I knew that he would not stop to talk, and he would not acknowledge me, I could not keep from going to the courtyard each day and waiting for him to walk by, gaze trained like an arrow, unwavering, upon his destination.

CHAPTER TWENTY-TWO: UTANAH

When only three weeks remained until my night with the king, the cut in my palm began to burn so hot that during the night I woke to my own screams. It had never been able to heal all the way, and I had reopened it a few days before. The golden plate that covered it now felt many times too small. I tried to tear it off, but this was a task too great for only one hand.

"What goes on here?" Ruti said as she came near. "I thought surely someone was trying to slice your throat open." She unlatched the chain and stepped back. "Oh."

I had never before seen her step away from any task. I looked at my palm in the low light of the oil lamps. The bandage the physician had applied a few days earlier was stuck to my palm with blood and something else. Something sticky and yellow. I yanked the bandage off, as if to allow the pain to escape.

"No," Ruti cried. "Do not look!"

I was stunned by the pain. My head burst into flames, and my body flew in all directions at once.

Something was spilled down my chin and finally I heard Ruti telling me to drink. When I had finished the goblet of wine she held to my lips, she said, "I will get you a physician and some poppy tea, but first you must promise me you will not look at your hand."

It was too late. The cut and the skin around it were red, brown, and yellow, and raised up as though something was being birthed from my palm. Something that smelled both sour and sickly sweet.

After what felt like many years Ruti returned with the tea and a physician. I drank the tea in two choking gulps while a salve was applied to my palm. It felt as though I had just pressed my hand into the center of the sun.

"The wine will cover your pain until the physician has drained it away."

It was a poor cover. At that moment I did not care that I might lose my hand. If cutting it off would stop the pain, I would have welcomed the blade. I do not know if it was the wine or the tea or the pain that finally allowed me to pass into a deep sleep.

The physician came to look at my palm twice a day. He said it could not be kept under the golden plate all the time. And so I had a reason to send my handmaidens away. I needed to let the ugliest piece of myself breathe, unseen, in my chambers.

"You are lucky you did not lose your hand," Ruti told me whenever I was about to complain of the pain. She had come to know my suffering too well. She kept refilling my goblet. "At least we are putting some flesh upon your bones."

One morning, during the brief time I allowed my handmaidens to be with me in my chamber, Opi looked at me. Her eyes, which were usually cold, filled with pity. "Mistress, do not forget you promised me that when you are queen, I will be able to sit by the pool all day and no one will glare at me as though he wants to spit upon my feet. Not unless he wishes to be made into a kitchen servant." When I did not respond, Opi tilted her head a little and said, "I have noticed that I am no longer the thirstiest among us."

"Do not worry for me. I am merely tired. I have not paid attention to how many times my goblet has been refilled." My palm itched and I wished to take off the golden plate. I gestured at the beaded curtain my handmaidens had recently come in through and told them, "You may return to the harem."

No one moved. The girl whose body had looked more like a boy's than a woman's when she first became a handmaiden said, "Mistress, we would rather not return to the harem room. The concubines tell us terrible stories of what awaits us during our night with the king."

Another girl, the one who'd had a broken lip when I made her a handmaiden, said, "It is true, mistress. They tell us of pain and humiliation. They say that any child conceived during such a night will be horribly deformed or even kill us as it is being birthed."

I too feared lying with the king, and what might come afterward for me and my people. But I was tired of being a girl. No matter how painful my night with the king was, at least afterward I would no longer be categorized by a tiny length of unbroken flesh. I would be a woman, free of the fear which overtook me whenever I heard a sound in the night — the fear that Halannah had come to take what she had not been able to the first time. Free to think of things that were truly important.

"The concubines tell tales for their own amusement," I said, grateful that I had managed not to run into Halannah for many months. "Do not listen. The king will not harm a girl of his own harem."

"We have heard stories of him. How he cut off the heads of his own men because the bridge they built was smashed by a storm," the girl continued.

"I have just told you not to listen to the concu—"

"It is eunuchs who have told us this," Opi said. "They have also told us of a man whose five sons went on the campaign with Xerxes to Sardis. He asked Xerxes to release one of his sons from service to take care of him in his old age. To punish the man for asking, Xerxes took the man's oldest son, cut him in half, and put half on either side of the road so all his army could march between the man's most beloved son."

I wished I could unhear this tale. I did not doubt that it was true. "Opi, do not speak to me without the proper form of address."

"And, *mistress*," Opi continued, "we have noticed that Nabat never returned from her last night with the king."

"Perhaps the king was pleased with her

and has given her chambers of her own."

"If so, he has not given her any handmaidens to serve her. No one else is missing."

"Not everyone can be as blessed as I am."

"No, mistress," Opi said, "they cannot."

I forced a smile and I told them all would be well and that they were dismissed. "Except Utanah. You will stay here with me."

When the other girls had left I asked Utanah about a mark I had seen between the clicking bells that hung from her neck. She looked as though she had just been sentenced to a slow death upon the gallows.

"It is nothing, mistress."

"Your lies have become less heroic. I am surprised you do not say that Opi gave it to you while you were trying to defend me."

Utanah pressed her lips together.

I looked to Ruti. She inclined her head toward the beaded curtain. "Very well, Utanah," I said, "you may go."

"I have seen her in the baths," Ruti said after Utanah had left and the beads had stopped rustling. "It is not only her neck that is bruised."

"Tomorrow I will take my bath when she takes hers."

I woke the next morning to hands shaking my shoulders. "Mistress," Ruti said, "it is time to observe your handmaiden."

As Ruti and I entered the baths, I saw the girls stealing glances at each other. Their gazes scurried over each other's flesh like little mice looking to make off with something before they were caught. I was surprised at how plump they were. Over the past few moons I had only half-noticed them eating greater quantities of meat and sweets and drinking as much wine as they could without falling down or otherwise marring their bodies. Hegai had told us, "The king wishes to make the first mark upon each girl's body. Each of you should go in to him as fair and unscathed as you were the moment you were born. As if the midwife took you from your mother, washed you, and put you high upon a shelf so you would go untouched by the world until you are put before the king." Though the agony in my palm had lessened, there would always be a scar. I tried not to think of what the king would do with me if he saw it.

Utanah did not glance openly at me but I knew she watched me. I too had perfected the palace skill of looking at something without seeming to, and so I could see that Utanah wore a cape of colorful bruises upon her back.

"I have never seen anything like it," Ruti

whispered in my ear as she ran a cloth over my shoulder. "It is like a painting. The artist is cruel, but the painting he has produced is one of the most beautiful I have ever seen."

"Who is the artist? Does no one care?"

"Who is there to care? Utanah has lost favor with Hegai, and even if she had not, his favor with the king is uncertain. Everyone is looking after their own interests. Few possess the courage to see someone else's suffering."

"I hope I will never be so cowardly that I do not see a coat of bruises upon another woman's skin."

"This is my hope for you too, though there is little you can do for anyone now. I only worry about the bruises upon Utanah because whoever put them there may wish to do even worse to you."

When I was done with my bath I went to stand, dripping, over Utanah.

"It is not nothing," I said.

She seemed to shrink inside her skin. "It is nothing I can speak of, mistress."

"Come to my chambers when you are done bathing."

When Utanah arrived, I told Ruti to wait in the hall. Ruti started to protest, "Mis—"

"Thank you, Ruti, for watching over me so diligently. But I am awake and not overfull with wine, so I will guard myself now."

Ruti gave me a look before she left. *Do what you must to save yourself. Our people's survival depends upon it.* I was reclining on my mattress, surrounded by all the food Ruti was pushing upon me to "more fully bring forth the lush woman hiding behind the little girl." My body had begun to feel like a weight too heavy to carry very far. My thighs rubbed against each other beneath my robe when I walked. The skin chafed, despite all the lotions and oils Ruti applied to my skin.

I picked up a platter of dates and set them on the floor. "Utanah," I said as warmly as I could with the memory of her standing over me grasping a cushion tightly in her hands still fresh in my mind. I gestured to the place I had just cleared upon my own mattress. "Join me."

Utanah sat uneasily beside me.

"Does it pain you?" I asked her.

"What, mistress?"

"Does it pain you to walk and to sit and to breathe with the injury someone has done you?"

She did not answer.

"Does it pain y—"

"No. I am in no pain, mistress."

"Perhaps I would admire your easy ability to lie more if I were not the one being lied to."

Utanah took a breath, as if to speak, but instead she pressed her lips together and dropped her gaze to the floor.

"Who has done this to you?"

"Please."

"Do you not jingle enough as you walk? I am certain we could find more bells."

I would not have known that she had heard me except for the lines that appeared in her forehead.

"The skin beneath your jewelry must be growing quite strange. I wonder what color it will be when the jewelry is removed the night you go in to see the king." I lowered my head to peer more closely at her. Her lips were trembling. I placed my left hand on her shoulder. "I promise to help you."

Now Utanah did look at me, without moving her head.

"I will do all I can," I said.

"Mistress, there is nothing you can do."

"Let me try."

"It is you who needs help."

I took my hand from Utanah's shoulder. "Very well."

I called for Bigthan, then told Utanah, "I have heard of women's skin growing around their bracelets and necklaces, until the only way to remove the jewelry is to also remove the surrounding flesh." Without pausing I turned to Bigthan, who had just come to stand in front of me.

"Take Utanah to the welder."

Bigthan's eyes brightened. He was happy to get away from Ruti for a while.

Utanah did not move from my mattress.

"Come," Bigthan said impatiently.

I turned away, so Utanah would not know how desperately I hoped I would not have to carry through with my threat.

The bells of her necklace and bracelets jangled as she dropped to her knees near my feet. "Mistress. There is no need. I will tell you all you wish to know."

I hesitated, as though I were not sure I would give her another chance, then sighed. "Bigthan, I will likely call you back shortly, but for now you can return to standing guard outside the door."

When the beads had stopped rustling after him, Utanah said, "I wish I had not taken up a cushion and held it above you, mistress. But I hope you will believe me that I could not bring myself to press it to your face."

"You held it up over my head even after

Opi's yelling woke me. Did you wish to be caught?"

"If I were not caught I would have suffered far worse than these" — she looked at her bracelets — "gifts."

"At whose hands?"

She hesitated, and I turned toward the door as if I were going to call to Bigthan. "Haman."

"How did he find his way into the harem to ask you?"

"He is the one who placed me and a couple of others in the harem. But I am the only one you chose to be a handmaiden."

She told me she was from Shushan, and was the oldest of three sisters. Her parents owned half a league of land, two hundred sheep, and had no sons. Haman had promised them that if they gave two of their daughters to the king's harem, the remaining girl would marry one of his sons. Haman swore his son would not sell the land.

"Why would your family have any need of Haman's son? There are women who own land."

"There are also women who have lost their land, and since the king's edict this has been more common. My parents did not wish to risk it. Haman looked us over himself. We thought he would want to take the prettiest for his son, but we were wrong. My littlest sister was mauled by one of the war dogs from India that Xerxes prizes so highly. The dog was badly wounded and the army must have lost track of it. It took my sister's left eye before my father managed to put it out of its misery.

"My littlest sister is the one Haman chose for his son. Me and my other sister are the ones he chose for the harem. He said we were to do as Halannah instructed. I thought we would be handmaidens to her."

"Your sis—"

"Will you help her if you can?"

"Where is she?"

"Halannah keeps her close and tells me she will have a back like mine if I do not do what she instructs. She asked me to smother you. After I was caught, the other maidens gossiped about it in the harem and Halannah thought I had tried to do as she instructed."

"But you could not bring yourself to harm me?"

"I cannot bring myself to believe Haman and Halannah. If they are so good to those that help them, where are all these loyal girls? Why must they recruit new ones? Haman and Halannah will have me beaten, but, for now, they will not send me to the soldiers. They think I might still do as they have asked. Which they have much reason to believe. After all, Haman's third oldest son, Aspatha, has my younger sister. I suspect her back hurts more than mine."

I did the only thing I could think of to ease her pain. I poured us some wine. She did not object to me serving her.

"Now that I have told you, I have no choice but to hope you are made queen, so you will help me as you have promised."

"I will do whatever I can. So you had best tell me of any plans Haman and Halannah have for me. I can help you better if I am alive."

I called Bigthan and Ruti in. To Bigthan, I said, "Take Utanah to the welder and have all these collars removed, then escort her back to my chambers."

"Mistress," Ruti said when they left, "I think it is unwise to call her back here."

"I must see the damage I have done."

Ruti took my left hand in both of her own. "Do not forget that you are the one who will have to save our people. Even now Haman may be convincing the king to murder every Jew in the empire. Y—"

"What have you heard?"

"Nothing yet. But we must prepare. Leaving marks upon a girl who tried to smother

245

you is a small price to pay for the safety of our people. You will surely have to make sacrifices much greater."

When Utanah returned her face was the color of ashes. I tried to speak but felt as though my tongue was too big. Any bond between us had been broken along with her shackles. She had a collar of darkness about her neck and bracelets of tender blue around her wrists. But her ankles were the worst. The skin was red and hardened, with patches of dead, flaking flesh.

I wanted to look away but I forced my gaze to remain steady. The words "forgive me" had gathered in my throat, but from the corner of my eye I saw Ruti looking at me. "We are allowed to wear whatever jewels we like when we go into the king," I said. "You can pile them one on top of the other until all these marks are hidden."

"And if he wants me completely naked, mistress?"

"There are some jewels that are not easy to take off. But this time you will only wear them for one night, and they will not have bells."

The color did not return to Utanah's cheeks. "You are dismissed," I told her. To Ruti I said, "More wine."

■ ■ ■ ■

I could not drink away the image of Utanah's skin. The visions woke me in the night
and caused my palm to throb as violently as
though my heart itself beat inside my hand.

When I told Hegai about the danger Utanah was in and asked how we might help
her, he ordered that a gash be painted across
my neck, and told me that I would walk into
the harem room with it. "For Utanah's
sake," he said. "I will announce only that
she has been given other duties. They will
have to wonder: the kitchen, the soldiers'
barracks, or is she even now one of the girls
who follow on foot behind the soldiers
crossing the empire? She will be kept apart
from the other virgins until her night with
the king."

Hegai called a meeting of all the virgins,
servants, and eunuchs. He did not dismiss
the concubines. He had told me to arrive a
few moments late, so everyone would see
me. But perhaps that had not been necessary.

As soon as I stepped into the room girls
turned to look at me. A hush fell over the
room as I went to sit beside the pool. I knew
the horror of what I had done to Utanah

showed upon my face. "Mistress," Opi said, "Utanah may have failed in taking your life, but you do not look like you realize it."

I hardly heard her over a strange "oo-oo-ooo-aaa-aaa-aaa" that suddenly rang out from the front of the room. Hegai entered the harem. Instead of the lioness he had a little carob-colored monkey perched on one shoulder, its black toes curling down over his royal purple robe. The animal was dressed to match, and had a gold necklace and bracelets, which he was pulling on as if they were toys. The only part of Hegai's costume that the monkey did not share was the many rings on Hegai's remaining fingers. He was holding on to Hegai's head.

Hegai pried the monkey off and handed it to one of the other eunuchs who he then ordered to leave the room. Though he did not allow his face to frown, little lines appeared around his mouth as the animal's noises echoed in the hall.

He looked over the harem and swept his hands to either side, sending his tunic flowing out around him. "There is one less girl among you. Some of you that remain have schemes that will get you sent to the soldiers before you have a chance to win the favor of the king. I will not warn you again. I have many eyes among you, and those who are plotting or are otherwise at the call of evil will disappear. Perhaps from this very room, perhaps from the baths, perhaps in the middle of the night. You are always watched."

At that, he turned and left. The silence may have gone on for some time, if a laugh had not come from the back of the room. "He is without his manhood in more ways than one," Halannah said. She was walking toward the front of the room. Toward me. "He could no more make a girl disappear due to suspicion than cause the water in this pool to boil just by gazing upon it. His eyes are weaker and far fewer than mine."

I stood up from the tiled floor beside the pool and turned to face her. Her sneer stole much but not all of her beauty. "You will never be queen, Halannah," I said, "not even if you were to send every last one of us to the soldiers. Xerxes may like you beneath him, but he does not want you beside him."

Halannah looked down at me. The sneer had fallen away and left her beautiful, though not so beautiful I could not hear the sharp rattle of anger beneath the forced cheer of her laugh. It had been so many months since I had seen Halannah that I had forgotten the power of her dark eyes, eggshell-white skin, and towering height.

Her earlobes were elongated by a pair of heavy gold rosettes; she had not fallen in the king's favor.

This huge, powerful woman still wishes me dead.

Perhaps Halannah was struck by me as well. She could not keep the smile on her face, even as she turned from me and said, "This silly peasant knows nothing of womanhood. She will cry like any other virgin. The worst night of your lives awaits. The first time the king has you, you will pray for death to take you before he is done. *Do not think to anger or betray me, or I will whet his appetite for the worst ways a man can have a woman.*"

"We have survived marching here," I said, "and not seeing our families for over eleven months, and listening to your grating laughter whenever you are scared or angry and wish to hide it. We will survive a night with the king."

She turned back to me but continued speaking loudly enough for everyone to hear. "Some have not. I told the king about their waywardness — the impurity, the stench, the men who had been there before him. I have rid this harem of more girls than Hegai has."

"You have sent your own informers to the

soldiers as often as you have sent your enemies." I was not entirely certain if this was true, but I said it all the same, because I was completely certain of one thing: "You are the enemy of every woman and girl in this room."

"No, only you and anyone who helps you." She stepped closer, so she was no more than a few hands' widths from me. "That is a strange wound upon your neck. Some seems to have rubbed off on that ugly chain you wear."

"That is the thing about blood, Halannah. It spreads."

Chapter Twenty-Three:
The Approach of My Night
with the King

Despite what I had said to Halannah, my courage wavered as my night with the king drew near. I tried not to think of what would take place, and whether I would win the king's favor, and what would happen afterward to me or to my people. Ruti told me that each of my handmaidens had already been called in to the king, and reassured me that Utanah had not had to take off the bracelets around her wrists and ankles or the thick necklace she had worn when she went to him. Each of the others was allowed to keep at least one of the things she had chosen from the harem jewelry before going in to see the king. Except Opi. She was allowed to keep everything. I was grateful for their good fortune and full of hope for my own night with the king. Perhaps he was in a good and generous mood, and it would not be as painful as some of my imaginings.

When my night with the king loomed only seven days away, I asked Ruti, "Were they happy afterward?"

She hesitated. "They were happy with their new jewels."

"More wine, please."

Ruti did not rush to fill the goblet lying sideways on the tiles where I had dropped it earlier, before passing into darkness. "God chooses cowards to be brave, barren women to give birth to prophets, passionate men to be patient, and a man who stutters to command his people through the desert. So it is not surprising that He has chosen a drunken girl who pouts and sulks like a child to save our people."

"Sometimes I wish our peoples' survival did not depend upon me. Sometimes I am afraid."

"Of course you are. Do you expect that you should always be happy? That everything you want will magically appear before you without any effort? If you are to be a woman, you must leave such childish notions behind."

"At times I wish I had saved Cyra's life instead of my own."

"Did you do everything you could for her?"

"I was afraid to hurt her, so perhaps I did

not kick her hard enough to keep her alert and marching quickly."

"If you did not do all you could, then you did hurt her. Doing what you must is not often pretty. Sometimes you must make a mess, anger someone, be thought cruel. Do not shy away from whatever must be done."

"I will try."

When I awoke, Ruti was there, kneeling beside my bed. I was about to ask her what she was doing when I realized: *she is praying.* Her right hand was over her eyes and — very quietly — she sang the Sh'ma:

"Hear, O Israel, the Lord is our God, the Lord is One. Blessed be the name of the glory of His kingdom forever and ever.

"You shall love the Lord your God with all your heart, with all your soul, and with all your might. And these words which I command you today shall be upon your heart. You shall teach them thoroughly to your children, and you shall speak of them when you sit in your house and when you walk on the road, when you lie down and when you rise."

I remembered the feel of my mother's hand caressing my back as she had sung this to me each morning.

"You shall bind them as a sign upon your hand, and they shall be for a reminder be-

tween your eyes. And you shall write them upon the doorposts of your house and upon your gates."

"But we cannot write them anywhere," I interrupted Ruti, "or someone might know us for what we are."

"Do not be so literal, child. You will not appreciate all the songs and poetry you are about to inspire." My sadness must have shown on my face. "What troubles you?" Ruti asked.

I could not tell her the truth: I hated what I had done to Utanah, I hated that my people were in danger and that their survival might depend upon me, and I hated that the man I most wanted to inspire did not seem on the verge of poetry. He did not seem to care what I did, so long as I left him alone. Instead of answering I reached for my goblet.

The next two days I did not go to the courtyard. I did not want to watch Erez walking past without stopping.

"You must eat, and then I will go with you to the courtyard," Ruti said.

"My head aches, besides, why would I want to go to the courtyard?"

"Yesterday there was an Immortal who looked long upon the column you sit by."

"How do you know?" I could not keep the eagerness from my voice.

"I went there, vainly hoping Mordecai would come and ask me to convey some message to you which might inspire you to rise from this mattress, or that Parsha would reveal something of his father's plan."

"And what of this Immortal you speak of?"

"He walked by but his eyes did not move as quickly as the rest of him. His breath caught in his throat when he saw you were not there. I am certain it was not the first time you have caused him great pain."

"Then why did he not acknowledge me all the times I sat waiting for him to look at me?"

"Did you not just hear what I said? Because it hurts him to look at you. Only someone he loves could cause him as much pain as you have."

The throbbing in my head suddenly did not seem so great. "Why did you not tell me this earlier?"

"Because no good can come of you longing for a man you can never have, except if it gives you a reason to get out of bed and keeps you from ruining your face by frowning. Nothing will compel the king to get rid of a girl more quickly than sadness."

I wondered what Erez would think of my new body. It had been hidden by my veil and robes every time he walked through the courtyard. Would he like how the food and wine had caused my face to fill out and my breasts to grow so heavy that I felt their weight shifting as I walked? Sometimes in bed I ran my hands over myself to see what it would feel like to touch me. I was careful not to go near the ache between my thighs.

After the king has had me I will not have to be so careful. I will be able to touch myself as deeply as I desire.

My own hands were not the ones I truly longed for though.

"To the courtyard," I told Ruti.

As Erez walked by, dark eyes trained upon his destination, I silently repeated Ruti's words, *Only someone he loves could cause him as much pain as you have.*

"You must rest tonight," Ruti said the night before I was to go in to the king. "Tomorrow, hopefully, you will not get to."

"You had just as well tell me to hurl an ox ten cubits into the air with my littlest finger."

"At least think good thoughts. Good thoughts make you pretty, dark ones make you old."

I looked away from Ruti, so she would not see what I was thinking. "Yes," she said, "old like me. But tonight I am going to think only good thoughts in my old head, because I know that in two days you will be queen."

I waited for her to add something such as "*If* you do all I have said." Instead she sat down next to me and rubbed my back as my mother used to do.

"I will try to make it so. Whether I am queen or not though, I know that after I go in to the king everything will be different. I will no longer wonder what it might be like to be with a man."

"You will not know this tomorrow either. He is not a man, he is a king. You will do whatever he asks of you and expect nothing in return — not kindness, not gentleness —" Ruti stopped suddenly. She took a deep breath and dropped her chin. "Forgive me, child. I no longer seem to know how to care for someone other than to caution and instruct them."

"You have done nothing for which you must seek forgiveness, Ruti. I do not always like your words, but I prefer them to silence."

"It will likely be over so quickly you will hardly know anything has happened except for the pain."

"Hegai says I must bleed."

"You do not need to bleed, but the king must think you have. We will paint your left hand with henna and you can brush it on the blanket beneath your hips. Other than that all you have to do is smile, compliment him, be humble, subservient. He will see what everyone else does: you are the most beautiful virgin in the palace."

"You flatter me, Ruti, and I am grateful for it. Thank you."

That night, it was not only fear that kept me from falling asleep. A tiny bead of hope was loose in my chest. If Xerxes found me beautiful enough to be queen, I might save some of the harem from going to the soldiers, and help my people survive the reign of one more foreign king.

But if I were not made queen . . . I hated to think of myself as a harem concubine — one of many women fighting for the king's attention and gifts, worrying each time more virgins joined the harem — *will this one be my replacement?* A girl with my features, but new. Something I would never be again.

When Ruti heard me tossing upon my mattress she said, "I told you, you must rest tonight."

"How am I to rest when one night will determine my fate, and perhaps that of our people?"

"Maybe you could pray, Your Highness."

Your Highness echoed in my head for a moment before I realized she was speaking to me.

Preparations for my night with the king began that morning. Ruti stood over the servants as they bathed me with rosewater and rubbed almond oil into my skin. She oversaw them as they applied pomegranate to my cheeks and lips and kohl around my eyes. We could not be certain the king would ever see any of me besides my eyes, but each feature was attended to as if the king would study it carefully. As I thought of the king and all the evil that he allowed to take place not only in his empire but also in one of his own palaces, I could not stop a refrain from running through my head: *I do not want his hands on me. I do not want his hands on me.*

After Ruti dismissed the other servants she looked carefully at me. "Quit crumpling your brow, I can see your thoughts."

I tried to relax my face, but this only seemed to make it worse.

"It will not be hard to please him. He cares nothing about you but only about how you make him feel. Do you make him feel strong and powerful? Do you make him feel that he is the smartest man in the empire and the most majestic — more king than any king who has come before?"

"How do I do all this?"

"Open your eyes wide when you see him, as if struck by his beauty. Then bow your head. He is used to subservience. But do not forget to smile shyly, as if delighted to be in his presence. When he touches you with his hands or even just his breath, look as though you have just tasted the finest wine. Whatever he offers you, you must thank him profusely for it. If the wine tastes like the urine of an old mule, still you will thank him."

I was given a lighter meal than usual. When I looked questioningly at it, Ruti said, "You should be plump already — it is too late to make you more pleasing. Tonight it is better that all the food you have eaten does not grumble within you. You only have one night — and perhaps not even that long — to win the king."

I could not manage to eat more than a few grapes anyway.

The beads rustled as Hegai walked in unannounced.

I quickly stood. Before I could even say

"my lord," he said, "I have come to look at you."

"And how do you find me, my lord?"

"Wanting."

Ruti stiffened. "I have overseen her bathing, cosmetics, and perfume myself, my lord."

"Was I incorrect in thinking you had lived in the palace thirty years?"

"About that, you were not incorrect."

"Did you not see Vashti?" he asked.

"Many times."

"You may have looked upon her but obviously you did not truly see her. Pomegranate juice was applied so heavily to her lips and cheeks that I sometimes wished to take a bite out of them. Her eyes were ringed not with black kohl but with blue azurite."

"Does the king wish to bring back the queen he *exiled*?"

"We both know his pride would not allow that. Yet, he wishes she were with him still."

The truth of this registered upon Ruti's face. "But I do not know where to find this blue."

"I am not surprised. Luckily I have brought some."

Before he left my chamber, Hegai said, "You will wear a head scarf and veil tonight. You must take your veil off at the soonest opportunity. We cannot risk the king taking you in a hurry without seeing all of your beauty."

"My lord, will he not be angered by my boldness?"

"Perhaps. But that is one of many risks you will have to take. All the other girls seemed conquered even before he took them — all but Vashti. Be bold and meek in turns. Be a puzzle he wishes to solve. Do not adorn yourself with jewelry. This will get his attention. Tell him jewels are not what you want — you want nothing except to be queen — *his* queen. Look him in the eye when you tell him this. Speak with the confidence of a woman whose neck could support the weight of a crown."

There was so much to remember. I thought about Hegai's many instructions as I was being escorted to the king's chambers and decided I was going to take a risk much more dangerous than removing my scarf. I was going to do what no other girl would dare to do: deny the king.

Chapter Twenty-Four:
Erez, the King, and I

Esther was taken to King [Xerxes] . . . in the seventh year of his reign.
— Book of Esther 2:16

Immortals stood on either side of the doors to the king's bedchamber. One leaned against the wall, half asleep. The other stood rigidly in the glow of an oil lamp a couple of cubits over his shoulder. I looked at the hollows of his eyes, his strong nose, the wide bones of his cheeks, his hard jaw . . . *Erez*. My heart rose into my throat.

Bigthan was escorting me to the king's chambers, urging me forward. "Thank you," I told him, waving my hand to dismiss him. He started to protest that he needed to see me safely inside, but I interrupted, "You will regret this disobedience when I am queen." I spoke loudly enough that he would hear me through my veil even though I was not looking at him. I could not take my eyes off Erez, who stood only a few cubits in front of me. Soon I heard Bigthan's footsteps retreating down the hall.

Erez slowly turned his head toward me. When our eyes met I reached into my robe and pulled the Faravahar out. His pulse became visible in his neck.

He moved his gaze over my robe and head scarf. "I am glad to see you have the favor of someone important," he said quietly. "Hopefully someone who will keep you safe, not just expensively clothed. Your head scarf is the richest I have seen."

"I had one I liked better," I said, my veil rustling against my lips. I was thinking of the one he had given me after Parsha ripped mine in half. "It was burned along with everything else worn to the palace."

"Yes, I saw the smoke rising from the courtyard. I am sorry."

I had never been able to look him in the eye comfortably unless I was speaking sharply to him, and I had never been able to be near him without feeling like I was restless inside my skin. My words to him had always been confused little attacks and retreats. But I no longer wanted to retreat, even though my heart beat too fast in my chest, and my lungs were full of air that would not allow me to breathe it. *I wish it was your bed I was going to.*

"I do not desire what awaits me behind those doors," I said.

His eyes hardened and he drew himself up taller. "Do not bring the king's wrath upon yourself. I do not want to stand guard while you are with him, but that does not matter, it is my duty. It would not be called duty if it were what I wanted. It is time for you to go and do yours."

Though I knew he had spoken out of concern for me, his words stung. I took my eyes from his face and turned toward the doors I had to walk through.

His voice was gentler, but no less fervent, as he said, "I hope that the next time I see you I have to bow."

Without looking at it, he hit the king's door with the back of his fist.

I put the Faravahar back inside my robe and walked as I had done on the march. *Do not think, do not feel. Just keep moving forward.* Still, I could not drive away the thought that as hard as it was to see Erez on my way in to the king, it would be harder to see him on my way out.

I took a deep breath as I reached the doors. *I will do as I must to leave these chambers a queen.* From inside, the door opened.

The room before me was huge. My quarters, and even Hegai's, were mouse holes in comparison. It was lit by only a few oil lamps along the walls. By their light I could see that the room was full of women. Statues, like those in my own chamber. They wore only colorful veils and bracelets and necklaces of gold. Surely the Greeks would be furious to see their statues in Eastern garb.

In the center of the room was a huge bed. It was veiled more splendidly than any woman, stone or flesh. Scarves of purple, blue, red, green, and yellow hung down from a thick golden frame. Did the king await me there?

I turned to see the soldier or eunuch who had opened the door. A man taller than the tallest man I had ever seen, and as broad as two regular men, stared down at me. *Xerxes.* He wore a robe of purple silk and his hands were weighted with gold rings. His beard was made up of thick dark curls that shone with oil. He almost completely blocked the light of the oil lamp behind him. My anxiety grew as I looked at him. It seemed hard to believe that this man worried for his safety.

His eyes widened as he gazed at me, reminding me that Ruti had instructed me to open my own eyes as wide as possible. Ruti had not needed to. I was certain my eyes — which were all he could see of me — were as wide as his.

"Welcome," Xerxes said. His voice sounded as though it came up through a long echoing chamber to reach his throat.

I dropped to my knees. "Your Majesty."

"Hegai told me of the great beauty he would bring me tonight. Do not deprive me. Stand. I am not done gazing upon you."

My knees trembled as I stood. With only his gaze and a slight movement of his head he directed me to a lamp upon the wall.

He closed the door and turned back to me. He did not hold food of any kind or a goblet, but as he came within a hand's width of me I smelled spice and wine. Though it was late and the room was not warm, he was sweating. And it seemed to me there was another smell too, one I did not like, and so I did not breathe deeply: the smell of death, the blood of all those he'd had killed.

I had to act quickly, before he tried to take me without fully seeing my face. As I raised my hands the gold chain fastening the plate over my palm trembled against my flesh. Before I could take off my veil and head scarf myself, Xerxes saw what I meant to do and reached out a hand so massive that I could see nothing else for an instant. I felt a whoosh of air against my lips.

He drew in his breath and let my veil and head scarf float from his hand to the marble tile. His mouth opened but no sound came out. The smell of spices grew stronger.

I did something forbidden and looked him in the eye. "I hope you are pleased. I have been preparing for this night a long time, Your Majesty."

He considered me for a moment, a moment in which I tried to show no fear. Instead of scolding me for my boldness, he said, "Your eyes look wiser than they should. Tell me something of yourself. Which province are you from?"

Ruti had told me not to mention Babylon, because of the last rebellion Xerxes had put down there, the one in which my parents had been killed. I dropped my eyes so he could not see any sadness in them as I answered, "Shushan, Your Highness."

"Little Shushan, look up again so I can see your eyes."

I tilted my head up, though not enough for him, it seemed. His rings clinked together as he put his hand beneath my chin and jerked it upward. My flesh was caught between two of the rings. I tried not to wince or show any emotion, but still, heat spread through my chest, all the way to my face.

He took his hand away. "My horse's nostrils do not flare half so wide as yours."

"Would you have a horse with no spirit, Majesty?"

I could not tell from his smile whether he was angry or amused. "Since taking the throne that is the only kind of girl I have had. It is how they are sent to me." His tone softened. "What is it that angers you, little Shushan?"

"I am upset I was not able to bring you any gift, my king."

"What gift would you have brought me?" he asked quickly.

He does not want to give me any time to conjure something up. But I do not need any. Almost as quickly as the question was asked, I found an answer, one I thought Hegai would like: "A scroll of the finest papyrus, my king. Your subjects could fill it with praises to you. When you conquer a new land the defeated ruler could be made to sign it. When you ride through your loyal provinces your servants could gather and press the flowers thrown at you within. I would have written your name in it in the finest ink."

"You know how to write?"

Perhaps I could have used more time after all. It was too late to lie. "Yes, Your Highness."

He touched my cheek. His was not the flesh of an idle noble but that of a soldier. Despite the roughness of his skin, this time his touch was gentle. "You are smarter than most girls. Which means you are also more dangerous. And yet your voice soothes me, unlike those of my advisers, which will not often leave my ears. Not even to let me sleep. It has been a long time since I have slept deeply."

His hand trailed down my face. I hoped that he was going to let it fall away from me. Instead, his fingertips lightly brushed my neck. My flesh started to hum all the way down to the soles of my feet. It was not altogether unpleasant. In fact it was not at all unpleasant. "But I will not mind going without sleep tonight," he said.

I felt my cheeks flush. Ruti and the other servants touched me every morning in the baths, but this touch was different. This touch was not an end to itself. It was only a beginning. Despite myself, I tilted my head, better exposing my neck to his hand.

Xerxes' fingers stiffened, his nails pressing against my skin. Then he exhaled very slowly, and I understood that the rigidness in his fingers was restraint. But his restraint was fleeting. He moved his hand lower and squeezed me through my robe.

I had to do as I had planned. I could not give in to him, not yet. Lying with the king had not yet made any of the girls queen. I stumbled backward.

He frowned as though he had hit upon some gristle in a piece of meat he was eating, but quickly regained his composure. "Are you still saddened about the book you could not bring me?" he mocked.

"I do not want to be known by a stranger, even one who is a king."

He dropped his hand back to his side. "So you wish to be a kitchen servant?"

I meant to be bold and confident like Vashti, and to speak always to some purpose, as Hegai had taught me. But I could not keep the pain and anger from my voice as I replied, "Until a year ago, I had always thought I would have a husband to love me."

"And you might still."

Before I could think of a reply he indicated a table near his bed on which sat a large silver pitcher and two golden goblets. "Come. Pour us some wine."

"Very good, my king." I hurried to pour the wine, deeply inhaling the sweet smell. The king's words filled me with hope. *And you might still.*

"Do not be cautious, I am thirsty. Fill our goblets so that it is hard to carry them without spilling. I must make use of the servants who clean my chambers each morning or they will grow bored." I filled the goblets so high that wine sloshed over the brim of one of them.

I did not hear him moving around, but the light in the room suddenly grew brighter. He no longer blocked the oil lamp near the door. I held my breath as I turned around.

He was reclining upon some cushions, watching me. Hegai had told me if the king was not truly interested in me he would take me immediately and send me away, to the concubines' harem. Since his night with Nabat, he often wanted only guards around him while he slept. I walked toward the cushions, not knowing whether I was about to be yanked down to the floor or merely looked at some more while the king quenched his thirst for wine.

I tried to hand him a goblet, but he said, "Set it down."

Did he want his hands free so he could reach for me? Have me and forget me? I extended my arm to set the goblet close to him — close enough that the sight and smell of it might be more enticing to him than my flesh.

He still had not asked my name. "Recline with me upon these cushions and tell me something more of yourself," he said.

Ruti had told me that the king would not care much about me, so I had not made up anything about myself to tell him.

I sat just out of reach. "I was born fifteen years ago in Shushan."

"Tell me something I do not already know."

"My king, I was born in Shushan and lived there my whole life. I am quite ordinary, my life does not compare to yours. I would be honored to hear of your great valor and many victories."

"If I found my own voice soothing I would talk myself to sleep each evening and also during the day, when my advisers somehow seem to have more opinions between them than bodies." He took a drink and I quickly took the opportunity to do the same. "What is your father's trade?"

I could not reveal that my true father was killed when Xerxes put down the last revolt of Babylon, and neither could I tell him that Mordecai, his own accountant, was the closest thing he had left me to a father. But for some reason I did tell him my father was an accountant, quickly adding, "for a number of merchants. There is little else to tell, Your Majesty."

"Or little else you wish to tell me." His eyes traveled over my body. "In which case we are done talking."

He was lying upon his side, facing me, and now he leaned closer. I pushed backward upon my cushion, out of his reach. "My king, if you take me before I know you it will be as though I was taken merely by a king. But if you tell me something of yourself, and then have me, I will say I was taken by the great king Xerxes."

A glint came into his eyes, and again I was uncertain whether he was angry or amused.

I continued, "I will find a way to get the blank scroll I wished to give you, and —"

"I have a palace full of scribes already, and besides my tales do not soothe. I am the most powerful man in the world and the world is not at peace."

I looked away in order to hide what I was thinking. *It is not at peace because you wish always to rule more than you do.*

He leaned so close that I could feel his breath through the thin material of my robe. "Do not turn away from me, little Shushan. I do not usually waste time talking to women other than my mother. If you are not grateful I will stop."

He was so near that I thought when I turned back our faces might touch. But then his breath was no longer warm against my shoulder. He had pulled back for some reason, perhaps to look at me. I widened my eyes and turned quickly to him so that my hair fanned around my face.

He took a moment to study me, then he reached out and wound a lock of my hair around his finger. "There is something about you that holds me in its grasp. Hegai has told me that the more he looks at you the less he knows. The way he speaks of you makes me wonder if he regrets that he is no longer truly a man."

He smiled at something he saw in my face. "If I were to spit upon my hand and rub the pomegranate from your cheek, I think I would find that you are blushing now."

"I have been blushing since first seeing you, Your Majesty."

He ignored my flattery and asked, "Did you mean to inspire that sort of love in a eunuch, the sort of love that makes him speak dangerously enough to sway upon the gallows? Or perhaps he only pretends to feel this way about you to make certain I do not overlook your beauty. He thinks he is responsible for it — that it is his greatest work. I do not fault him for wanting to make certain it does not go unnoticed or unrewarded."

He pulled lightly upon the lock of my hair that was wrapped around his finger and then released it. "Lay back."

I did as he commanded and he leaned over me, his eyes not more than a hand's width from mine. My heart beat hard against my chest and I held my breath. With as much concentration as a blind man would have, he touched my temple, my cheek, and then my lips.

"I think it is both of these things. He is proud of who he has made you, in love with his own work." His breath smelled so strongly of wine that I felt I was drinking as he spoke.

"That is the way I feel when I sack a great city. It is my greatest work. Some may not think a sacked city is beautiful, but when I destroy it and take its treasures, that is when it is most beautiful to me. Poor Hegai must give his treasures away. His only hope is that I might value the things I take from him, not just throw them into a caravan with all the others."

I had not realized that I would have to fight not only his body but also my own. Though his words frightened me, it took strength not to arch up against him.

"He has reason to be proud," Xerxes said. "Your skin is soft and unblemished, and carries the musky smell of a garden after it rains. I will not know until I have had you and the morning light shines upon your face what you look like beneath the mask of powders and juices you wear, but your cosmetics are without flaw. Hegai cannot take credit for all of your beauty though. Servants can put perfume, powder, and paint upon a girl, but they cannot put fire in her eyes."

His lips were so close to mine I could feel his breath upon them. I feared my body would invite him closer without my permission. I turned my face away and began to cough. The king sat up and told me to sit up as well. He handed me my wine goblet.

"Thank you, Your Majesty. You are as kind as you are brave."

"And yet you looked away a few moments ago when I told you I rule a world that is not at peace. As though you think me cruel."

Though he had not asked a question he seemed to be waiting for an answer. When I did not offer one he asked, "Do you blame me for the unrest?"

"Your Great Majesty, I was only nervous, please forgive —"

He waved his hand at whatever I was going to say. I noticed that the muscles of his arm were nearly as large as my head, and also, that the spicy smell of him no longer bothered me.

"I want peace as much as any maiden — as much as you," he said. "But it does not spring up like a cypress. It must be fought for. The world will not know peace until it belongs to me. Until the empire extends heavenward to god and the sun cannot illuminate anything beyond the boundaries of what is mine. I will make the whole earth one country or I will destroy it."

I tried to hide my dismay, but still Xerxes must have seen it. "How can I leave any part of a world so beautiful to be ruled by mere men, and how can I leave mere men uncertain of their mortality?" he asked.

I remembered what my handmaidens had told me of Xerxes beheading his own engineers whose bridges were smashed in a storm and cutting one of his subjects in half so his army could march between the man's torso and legs. And I was reminded of my own parents' death at Xerxes' soldiers' hands.

"The Greeks think that they are of a higher breed, more intelligent, more perfect because of their learning and their creation of laws that govern all of their men. As if all men are equal just because they have no king to rule over them. I have no choice but to fight them. If they defeat me in one war I must wage another."

He narrowed his eyes at me and half-smiled. "I am not surprised to see you flinch. Women are the only creatures upon the earth who do not like battle. And yet they enjoy its spoils more than all others. Do not you enjoy the gold, papyrus, linen, grain, and poppies from Egypt?"

"Yes, Your Majesty," I said. I could see now that his half smile was full of both sadness and amusement. I was determined not to flinch again. I looked closely at him — surely more closely than one should look at the most powerful man in the world. A man so at peace with war. There was something I could not read behind the amusement on his face. "The Egyptian physicians that I ordered to serve in my palaces are the finest in the world. We are less mortal because I crushed the Egyptians and took what I wanted."

I blushed so hotly that he would not need to spit in his hand and rub my cheek to see it beneath my cosmetics. I did not give in to the urge to look away. "You are truly a wise ruler. A great king is admired for his conquests, but loved for his gifts to the people."

Xerxes raised an eyebrow. Instead of responding he took a long drink, perhaps to give me permission to do the same. He waited to set his own goblet down until I had placed mine back upon the marble floor. As I withdrew my fingers the empty goblet teetered. More quickly than I could have reached out to steady it myself, Xerxes leaned over me and caught it in his massive hand.

I did not think to say thank you. I did not think to say anything at all. His head was near my legs and he did not raise it. I had never imagined that I might one day gaze down upon a king. From my vantage point above him I could see his long lashes beneath his prominent brow and the slight bump on the bridge of his nose. He lowered his head farther and kissed my knee through my robe. When it began to shake he placed a hand upon it. His hand was heavy enough, and the force with which he pressed great enough, that my knee was stilled.

Beads of sweat began to run from beneath my arms. "My king, please let me get you more refreshment."

"Me only? Are you going to fill only my goblet?"

"If that would please you."

"Fill both goblets and let neither be for only one of us. It would please me to watch you drink from my goblet." He took his hand from my knee and immediately my leg began to shake again. I moved carefully to the table where the silver pitcher sat and filled the goblets all the way, knowing I would spill the wine at the slightest misstep. When I turned back, Xerxes' eyes were tight upon my hips.

"Come," he said. "I have more than enough words to fill your scroll. When you have heard my tale I will no longer be a stranger to you. So hurry."

I must gather my wits. People have put their faith in me. "You do me a great honor, my king. I have no scroll, but I will write your words upon my soul."

Even from across the room I could see Xerxes again raise one of his great eyebrows. "Hegai was only to send me one girl but instead he has sent two. One who is silent and full of thoughts she wishes to keep hidden, and one who is bold and never lacks for a more flattering way to say what she has said already. All girls must flatter a king, but only the most beautiful are allowed to be bold. You are lucky for your large eyes and the strange light within them. Otherwise I would grow bored hearing you repeat not only your own words but those of hundreds of girls who have come before."

I walked toward him. "Please forgive me if I have given offense, Your Majesty. I have never been in the presence of any noble, much less a king."

"Perhaps you will not be so shy once I have told you of my victories and defeats."

I stumbled and a few drops of wine spilled onto my feet. I hoped none of the henna would be washed from my skin.

"Yes, I have lost battles. I can say this, because I will not lose the war." His eyes moved over my body. "Sit, or my desire for you will not wait."

I lowered myself down upon the cushions just out of Xerxes' reach. There I listened in silence to all he said. I suspected that he was speaking not to me but to his exiled queen, telling her of the war she warned him against, the men he lost, the valor of some and treachery of others. He told her how he had more men than could be counted in one day, and that of all these men he trusted almost none.

"I had so many men in my army that there was not a single head of cattle or stalk of grain left in any town I passed through from Asia to Greece. My naval fleet was so large that there was no harbor big enough for us to take refuge in a storm. I did not count my men until Doriscus. I packed ten thousand men as close together as grains of sand and drew a circle around them on the ground. Then the first men were dismissed and the next ten thousand placed into the circle. We did this over and over again. It took two days to move all of my men into and out of the circle, until finally one million, seven hundred and ten thousand men were counted.

"Of these, do you know how many I trust with my life?" He did not wait for me to answer. "Any man can seem brave as he wins a war. That is no feat. There is only one true test of a man's loyalty: how he fights for you when he knows you will lose.

"Outside my chambers stands a man who cares less for his life than for my honor. He battled hard though he knew victory would not be ours. If I instructed him to drive his own sword into his belly he would not need to think any last thoughts or say anything by which to be remembered. He would not need to take a final breath. His hands would be steady and the task would be over in one thrust. This is the type of loyalty a king should have."

The faraway look left Xerxes' eyes; he watched me carefully. He set his goblet down and reached for my hands but stopped before clasping them.

"A queen too must be loyal; her fate is tied to her king's. If he has riches she too will have riches, if he has a happy kingdom, she too will be happy. If any harm should come to him, it will inevitably come to her as well."

I softened toward him for the first time since entering his chamber. It could not be easy to be suspicious of everyone around you. He did not even trust himself: "I think you would be a worthy queen," he said, "but I have been told I am not a good judge of character."

My heart began to pound so hard it shook my entire body. Was the most powerful man in the world truly considering whether to make me his queen? I slid off the cushions, onto my knees. "My king, whatever you ask of me, I shall do it without hesitation."

"Then do not look at the floor as you profess your loyalty."

I was so near to him that his eyes seemed huge. Despite all he had seen and done, they held as much hope as a child's.

"I am yours to command, great king. No sooner will I know your desire than I will fulfill it."

"I do not even know your name, but I

believe you."

"Esther, Your Majesty."

He leaned forward and reached for me with both hands. He pushed my hair back from my face. " 'Ishtar' is fitting. You are stronger than all the girls who have come before you and more lovely than any mortal woman could be. Perhaps you are the one I have been searching for." I was still kneeling before him. He looked deeper into my eyes. "Do you not wonder why I say perhaps?"

"I am too stunned to wonder anything, Your Majesty."

"You appear humble for one so beautiful. Yet you shun the riches I have acquired for the glory of the empire, in favor of only the strange plate of gold you wear upon your hand. Why did you not take the opportunity Ahura Mazda provided you to dress yourself in jewels before coming to my chambers?"

"I have a wound I did not want you to see."

"If you did not want me to see it why did you not adorn yourself in whatever gold you could, so this piece would not stand out? You must know that in the morning I often make a gift of the jewels that a girl has worn."

"That was not the opportunity I wanted."

"You want to be queen."

"I want to be *your* queen. I had hoped my loyalty would stand out."

He looked at my palm. "Show me."

Was he checking to see if the wound was too ugly for a queen? "It is hard to unclasp with only one hand, Your Highness."

The plate was held in place by chains whose clasps met on the back of my hand. They seemed to grow tinier as his large hands came near. His nails lightly brushed my skin as he easily unclasped one chain and then the other. The plate fell away from my palm. He placed it beyond my grasp so that my hand lay naked between us. He turned my palm upward. His eyes slowly traced the reddish blue and purple skin that had stopped Halannah's blade before it reached my face. "The best soldiers bear scars. They are badges of honor." He pressed lightly upon it. "This skin is stronger now."

His fingers tracing my scar felt even better than his fingers tracing the curve of my cheekbone had. A strange feeling spread through my stomach and chest and gathered around my heart. I felt that perhaps I could love him.

"I will have my physicians called in tomorrow. I will make certain they are using the finest salves and giving you all the poppy tea you need."

"Thank you, my king. I do not know what I have done to deserve your kindness but I will return it many times over if given the chance."

"There are many things I will have you do for me." He let go of my palm. "I will think of them until we meet again."

He saw my body respond to his words and reached out to touch me through the thin material of my robe. My heart seemed to beat not only beneath his hand upon my chest but lower still.

"First I am going to have the finest jewels in the empire gathered together. I want to see you in them and nothing else."

Could he feel the flesh beneath his hand trembling?

He continued, "Then I will take you. You will be goddess of my eyes, my hands, and my heart."

He withdrew his hand and I knelt so low that my head almost touched his feet. "Thank you, my king."

"I prefer to be thanked by deeds instead of words. Words are fleeting. Rise." As I returned to my feet he said, "There will be a banquet for you unlike any you have ever seen." I had not seen even one, but it did not seem a good time to mention this. "I will show the empire the one creature in all the world who is as beautiful as the queen they convinced me to send away.

"You will come back tonight, as queen from India to Nubia, queen over a hundred and twenty-seven provinces. Queen of Persia."

I felt as though I no longer inhabited my body. Was I dreaming? Was I ill? Without meaning to, I touched my robe where it rested over the Faravahar that lay against my chest. *Erez.* I quickly dropped my hand to my side. It was not a good time to think of Erez. In fact, it would never again be a good time to think of Erez. I found my voice and concentrated on Xerxes' rich brown eyes. "Queen of the great king Xerxes."

We shared a goblet of wine in celebration. He insisted I have the last few drops, and then he instructed me to go knock three times on the door to summon the Immortals and numerous chamber attendants who waited on him each morning.

I held my breath. I wanted very badly to see Erez, and I wanted very badly to never see him again. I felt guilty at how my flesh had hummed when Xerxes touched me. I was relieved and disappointed when the door opened and Erez did not appear. Two Immortals I had never seen entered, followed by four eunuchs with silk towels over

289

their shoulders who wheeled in a basin made of gold. Three more servants followed with platters of bread, fruit, and honey, another with a pitcher of wine so sweet I could smell it. After this came about twenty musicians, three girls with bells on their wrists and ankles, and another girl with a large fan of date palm leaves. Xerxes waited to speak until they had arranged the tub in front of him and gathered to wait for his command. "I do not need any of this. I will not wash the perfume of my new queen from my skin."

The two Immortals, seven servants, four girls, and many musicians stared at me.

"I am going to take my rest now," Xerxes said. "You are all dismissed."

To me he said, "Go and prepare for tonight. Prepare for your first night as queen."

I held my breath once more as I left Xerxes' chamber.

"I am queen," I told myself. *I am queen.*

Chapter Twenty-Five: Her Majesty

Parsha stood just outside the king's chamber. He moved his gaze over my hair, which was still piled atop my head, and then to the cosmetics undisturbed upon my eyes and cheeks. He sniffed at me like a dog, and a smirk spread across his face.

"I see the king does not want another foolish girl," he said quietly. "Not even for a night."

"You would do well to keep your words sweet, Parsha, or you will soon be eating them."

"My father sent Halannah to sate the king's hunger yesterday," he said quietly. "*She* has never left these chambers without some sign of the king's touch."

I did not like the thought of the king lying with Halannah, but if she had satisfied him enough that he was able to go all night without touching me as deeply as he wanted to, then she had helped make me queen.

I heard someone rushing up behind me. "I am to take you to the queen's chambers, Your Majesty, and to serve as one of your personal escort."

Parsha's beautiful eyes were not so beautiful as they bulged from their sockets. His mouth twitched but no words came out. He made a sound like that of an animal surprised by an arrow in its flank.

I smiled and turned to the Immortal who had spoken. One of his eyes was brown, the other green. I could read no emotion upon his face. Behind him were five more Immortals I had never seen. "I must go first to my former chambers to gather my things," I told him.

"The king has seen to it, Your Majesty."

"And my servant?"

"I do not know."

I was not certain whether I should send him back to the king to find out, and I did not want to seem uncertain in front of Parsha. "I am eager to see my chambers," I said, turning away from the king's door.

It was strange to move through the palace surrounded by Immortals — two in front of me, one on either side, and two following close behind. Xerxes was tall enough that he could easily see over his escorts' heads, but my own escort took up much of my view.

As we neared my new chambers my regret at not asking the king if Ruti could continue her service to me grew. But when I entered the receiving room with two of my escort, Ruti was waiting. She fell to her knees upon the beautiful crimson, green, blue, and gold rug beneath her and laughed more happily than I had heard anyone laugh since I had arrived at the palace. "It is much more comfortable to kneel in this chamber than anywhere else I have been, my queen. This is the greatest moment of my life. I have already pledged myself to you, but I will do so again now. You will be the greatest queen Persia has ever known, and I will be beside you until my dying day."

"Leave us," I told my escort. When they were gone I dropped to my knees in front of Ruti and we wrapped our arms around each other.

"Our matriarch Sarah lived for one hundred and twenty-seven years," Ruti whispered, "and you rule over one hundred twenty-seven provinces. Surely this is no coincidence."

I pulled back to look at her.

"You have risen higher than any other woman in the world, and this can only be for one great purpose," she said, grabbing my hands. "To save our people. Our God has not deserted us."

"Perhaps He has not." I slid one of my hands out from hers and looked around the room. "Though I cannot quite believe that I am queen, when I behold the table long enough to seat at least thirty guests and the golden reliefs of lions and ibex, I know that by some miracle I am."

"Your wealth will sway many people to our cause, if you use it wisely. But" — she squeezed my hand — "we can think about that later. Let us take another moment to breathe in the joy of this occasion."

It was not long before we heard arguing coming from outside the receiving room. "You cannot go in." It was the voice of the Immortal with one brown eye and one green eye.

"I am the keeper of the women. And of a few guards as well. I have more men in my employ than you have saved or even killed. Move from my path."

"You are no longer the keeper of *this* woman, little man."

I rushed to open the door. "My lord!" To assuage his pride, I said, "I have been waiting for you."

As he fell to his knees and bowed his head

I realized I was no longer expected to call him "my lord." His voice, however, was not so humble as his posture. "Your Highness, I have had to wait to see you as well."

I turned to the Immortal with different-colored eyes. "Thank you for your vigilance, but Hegai may be granted full access to my chambers."

"Yes, Your Majesty." The Immortal bowed his head only slightly. *Not as much as he should,* I thought.

It was odd to walk before Hegai, but after the Immortal's halfhearted show of respect I was careful not to give him reason to think I was anything less than queen. Hegai followed me into the receiving room. I marveled at it once again. It was nearly as luxurious as the king's. I took off my sandals and pressed my feet into the rug. I saw that just as in the rest of the palace there were gazelles, griffins, and archers. The perimeter of the huge room was lined with fat satin cushions. Silk curtains, which hung from thick golden rods, were tied back to reveal a set of heavy doors. Ruti hurried to open them, and light flooded the room. I walked toward it, and stepped out onto the balcony. I looked down upon trees whose fruits I could almost taste: sour cherry, pomegranate, apple, fig.

Next I explored the wardrobe connected to my chambers. "An attendant will be brought to care for your robes," Hegai said.

I felt guilty gazing at the exiled queen's things. *Will I ever be able to think of all this as mine?* Chests of scarves and jewels extended from one end of the wardrobe to the other. Shelves of gem-encrusted leather sandals took up all of one wall. More than a hundred fine robes of different materials — linen, silk, and velvet — hung from hooks all around me. In a chest at the back I found veils of every color, almost none without gems or gold of some kind. I was certain I was looking at the vastest wardrobe in all the world. Which of these veils would Vashti have worn? I picked up one that was purple and had a band of gold coins. I brought it to my nose, searching for a sign of the exiled queen. Any physical trace of her had been erased. Only the king's desire for her kept her spirit inside the palace walls.

When I was done marveling at my new quarters I turned to Hegai. "Thank you for all of this. I will share these riches with you and Ruti."

"Do I look like I am wanting for riches?" Perhaps he was unhappy that I had not addressed him with "my lord."

"I know you are wealthy beyond measure,

I only wanted to express my thanks. We have done what we set out to do."

"What we set out to do was reform the harem. Our struggle has only just begun."

I turned away from him. I wanted a moment in which the only thing everyone wanted to do was celebrate our victory.

"May we sit, Your Highness." His voice did not get higher at the end of his words — he was not asking. *And why shouldn't he give me an order? He has brought us here, after all,* I told myself. But this did not rid me of my irritation.

"Ruti, some refreshment please." To honor Hegai, I said, "The finest."

"Nothing less ever again, Your Majesty." Ruti bowed low and went to the kitchens.

Hegai did not make small talk and he did not wait for the wine. "New queen, do not let this splendor make you forget all I have told you: if you are not sharper than your enemies you will be assassinated."

I sighed. There was no way to avoid a conversation with Hegai.

"The greater portion of being sharp is figuring out who they are," he said, "but you will never be fully certain."

"I am most certain of the one I have not met yet."

"Yes. What you are not certain of is who

takes Haman's coins and whispers secrets in his ear. But I have faith you will soon know. Tonight you will meet the two men who rule the empire."

"Does not *the king* rule?"

"Yes, he and Haman. You will meet the *true* king for the first time, the king as he is when he stands at the head of his empire. He will not seem to you to be the same king you met last night. It is no longer you that he will be concerned with. He will introduce you to Haman in the hopes that Haman will be impressed by his choice of queen. Pretend you know nothing of his cruelty and appear delighted to meet him."

"I do not know that I can do this very convincingly."

"You must try. You can see more when watching a man who does not know he is watched."

A man. My enemies would no longer be only women. Even before Xerxes' edict about husbands' superiority over their wives, men had always been more powerful than women, even men who were not powerful over other men. Shepherds, metal smiths and armorers — makers of all things copper and bronze — moneylenders, men who sold wares at the market — a year ago I was less powerful than any one of these.

Now I would have to maneuver my way around the most powerful men in the world.

"Everyone in the palace has ambitions. Every adviser wants to be a top official; every top official wants to be king. Xerxes is always in danger, and hence, little queen, you are as well. If he is assassinated you will be taken by the one who ascends the throne. Or killed. Even if you manage to survive and find favor with the new king, your children will be murdered."

"How can I keep watch over Xerxes?"

"That will be difficult. You need eyes and ears that can only be gotten through promises and gold. Yet Xerxes should not find you greedy or know you desire anything but him. You must be the sort of queen a king wishes to rain gifts upon."

"And if one of the men I have bribed —"

"Brought into your service."

"If one of the men I have brought into my service should tell me of a plot against Xerxes, am I to tell him, and if so, how?"

"Anyone who goes in to see him uninvited is subject to death."

"I must wait until he calls for me?"

"In that situation it will be your life or his that is in danger. You will get to decide."

"But if he is assassinated I may be too, so both our lives are in jeopardy."

"Then you have your answer."

When Ruti came with the wine I almost cried with relief that I would no longer be alone with Hegai. Perhaps I should not have told the Immortal at the door that Hegai was to be granted full access to my chambers.

"Speaking of your enemies, it is almost time for the banquet in your honor," Hegai said.

"Let us celebrate first amongst ourselves."

Hegai did not protest aloud when I invited Ruti to drink with me. It would have been cruel to expect me to drink alone on such a momentous occasion. But the look he gave me was not one of approval. Still, the mood turned festive again. Ruti and I went back to marveling at the vast luxury of my new chambers until there was a knock.

"A messenger from the king," one of my personal escorts announced. "Send him in."

When the door opened I saw that the messenger had two guards of his own. He fell to his knees in front of me and bowed his head. "Your Majesty, I bring your crown." He held it up to me on a cushion of purple silk.

I did not need to bite down upon it to know it was pure gold. It was decorated with jewels of purple, green, and red.

"Does not the king want to place it upon his new queen's head at the banquet?" Ruti asked. The messenger looked up, no doubt surprised to be questioned by a servant. I wondered too if he had noticed the second goblet in the room, the one Ruti had quickly set down when I invited the messenger in. It was not a secret that Hegai did not drink wine.

"He does not want his guests to see her as anything but a queen," Hegai said.

Xerxes is afraid I will seem a peasant.

I did not want the messenger to see me crowned by a servant and the keeper of the women. As soon as Ruti carefully took the pillow from him, I said, "You may go." I did not like how he looked about the room as he left. If the king were present, the messenger would have left quickly, his eyes upon the path he would take from the room and nothing else.

"It is fitting that you two who have helped me become queen should now put the crown upon my head."

Hegai snatched the crown from the pillow Ruti held and raised it over my head. "From now on you must always carry yourself as though you have never coughed dust from beating a rug, stumbled beneath the weight of a jug of water carried home from the well, or bent your back to scrub a floor."

I wondered how he knew the tasks of a peasant girl. But I did not wonder long. I bowed my head and closed my eyes as he lowered the crown down upon my head.

It seemed to me that I felt it when four knees hit the floor at my feet — a reverberation that traveled all the way up my spine. I took a long breath. *God, you have placed this crown upon my head. Now please help me bear its weight.*

I raised my head up slowly. The crown was heavier than it looked. I would have to be careful not to make any sudden movements or I would send it crashing to the floor.

"Your Majesty," Hegai said, "you are exquisite. When I look at you I see that Ahura Mazda himself has put this crown upon your head."

"Thank you, I am very blessed. Will you be at the banquet?"

"No. You must keep your own counsel tonight, my queen." I tried to look disappointed. But I also felt a little seed of happiness sprouting in my chest. I did not allow myself to smile until he was gone.

While Ruti helped me get dressed I stared at myself in a large slab of polished copper. The golden crown shone upon my thick

dark hair as if it were meant for me.
"I am ready to be queen," I said.

Chapter Twenty-Six: My Banquet

My heart drummed inside my chest as I approached the noise of the banquet hall. Despite my escort, my crown, and the gold and gems that weighed upon my neck, arms, and ankles, I could not help but feel small. The last time I was in the large banquet hall I had just been kidnapped and brought to the palace with numerous other girls, only one of whom would be queen. As I stood in front of it with a crown upon my head, the room seemed just as large as it had then.

My eyes were drawn up toward the ceiling, which was held by six rows of six columns, each higher than twenty men. Even with the deafening clamor of people laughing and yelling, and even through the haze my veil cast over everything, as I gazed up the room felt empty except for the rams' heads at the top of each column that seemed a warning to all those who dwelled within the palace walls: do not challenge the powers that reside here.

I did not want to seem as impressed as I was, so I quickly lowered my gaze from the ceiling while keeping my chin up. The hall was big enough to host ten thousand guests, not counting the many more who could sit in the balconies. It was filled with more color, shouting, and excitement than even the marketplace had been. Voices echoed, seeming to come from everywhere at once. Princes from all over the empire, along with their attendants, crowded around tables near the dais where the king sat waiting for me. Because Xerxes was Ahura Mazda's representative ruler on earth, he was kept away from the view of his subjects, except for formal audiences. He sat behind a screen through which nothing but his silhouette was visible — a giant figure elevated upon a stone platform, a huge goblet his only company as he waited for his new wife. *We are not so unalike, my king.* I felt the reassuring pressure of the Faravahar against my chest. *I too am hiding.*

I stretched my spine as tall as possible and entered the banquet hall. The king stood and his subjects' voices died as they quickly did the same. In the silence that followed, the room seemed to grow larger. I kept my

305

head high for the thousands of eyes that watched as I made the long journey to my new husband.

Before I reached the elevated platform I saw the table of Immortals. The king's favorites were celebrating like royal sons, drinking without armor on. They sat at one of the tables close to the king's screen. Parsha was among them, and also, Erez. He looked as though all but his body was elsewhere. His broad shoulders were hunched, and I could not help but wonder what he was thinking.

He turned and looked through my veil, right into my eyes. I was certain he saw me more clearly than anyone else in the room. I took a deep breath and forced myself to look away, back toward the stone dais. Servants hurried up on either side of me so that I would not trip on the three stone stairs I had to climb to stand with the king. Hegai had told me not to approach. *Bow and wait to be summoned to come behind the screen.* As soon as I was on the dais, though, Xerxes stepped out from behind the screen to meet me. "My queen has returned."

"Your Majesty," I said. In my haste to bow the crown slid from my head. He rushed forward to catch it. It looked small in his huge hand. He frowned down at me. "I see you have not chosen any of Vashti's former attendants. Your servants too must learn to fasten your crown so tightly to your head that nothing can move it.

Nothing but your own advisers. Or is not this the same crown they took from Vashti?

As he continued to stare at me his eyes softened again, and the corners of his mouth lifted. "My queen," he murmured.

Besides the rings upon his hands he wore only a white tunic and his crown. His thick arms and legs were oiled so that they glistened like those of a man who has just come from the battlefield. When he leaned toward me and bowed, he was still taller than I was. But not so tall I could not discern the three-cornered hat of the man behind him. The man stood closer to the king than any of the king's own escort, and this is how I knew that he was Haman. I leaned slightly to the side so I could look at the father of my enemies and now, also, my own enemy.

Long hair, straightened and slick with olive oil, hung down past his shoulders. His narrow eyes were ringed with kohl. They gazed at me with contempt.

I thought I heard grumbling from the crowd as the king remained bowed to me for an unusually long time.

Finally he rose, taking my hand in his own and turning me toward the guests. He reached his other hand across his large chest, and there was a whoosh of air upon my face as he lifted up my veil. *"My queen!"* he shouted to the crowd.

I opened my eyes as wide as I could and smiled. Thousands of eyes fell upon my face. I wanted to touch the Faravahar, but I knew this would seem odd to the many onlookers and perhaps to Xerxes himself. Instead I concentrated on the feel of the chain weighing slightly upon the back of my neck, and the winged man resting against my chest.

"The most beautiful woman from India to Nubia," Xerxes announced, his voice booming out into the banquet hall. "Bow down to the new queen."

In a great mass they bowed. But even as they did, I could see that many did not bow so low that they had to take their eyes off me.

As I looked over the crowd, I saw my cousin gazing up at me with an expression I had never seen upon his face. He was smiling, and there was a light in his eyes that was visible even from far away. *He is proud of me.*

As the mass rose up, someone called out,

"From what line is she descended?"

The words seemed to hit Mordecai directly in the face. His smile fell away.

How I wished I could cry out, *King David, the greatest king who ever walked upon the earth.*

Xerxes let go of my veil and it floated back down between the crowd and me, casting a haze over everything once again. I did not welcome the barrier. I wanted to see clearly enough to know who my enemies were. "I command the man who just spoke to come to the front of the room!" the king cried.

There was neither sound nor movement anywhere within the great hall. I looked to the back of the crowd, at a sea of faces whose features I could not discern.

"Send the traitor up before I decide to punish not only him but every one of you as well."

"It was this man!" someone cried, and soon the crowd was pushing an Indian man toward the front of the room.

"Your Majesty," the man said as he fell to his knees before the dais. "Those words were not mine."

His voice was not that of the man who had demanded to know what line I was descended from. I looked to the king. From his furrowed brow it appeared he knew this too. Haman stepped forward. "Guards! Seize him!"

Two of Xerxes' own personal guards rushed from beside the throne to grab the man and yank him to his feet. Xerxes did nothing to stop them from dragging the man away.

"Your Majesty," I said quietly, "this man does not speak in the same voice as the traitor."

"Halt!" Xerxes commanded his guards so quickly it seemed he was trying to recover the time that had elapsed since Haman's command. "Did *I* order you to seize this man? Release him."

One of the guards holding the man gave him a hard shove that sent him once again to his knees. But at least he was free. I looked back at Haman, and it was as though neither space nor my veil lay between us, and all our thoughts were visible. He would have been happy to wrap his heavily ringed fingers around my neck. I remembered what Hegai had said, about how I should be friends with my enemies. But the smile that came across my face could not possibly be free of the pleasure I felt at keeping Haman from killing an innocent man.

"Send up the true utterer of the vile words without haste or ten of you — Shushan and

Nubian alike — will meet your fates upon the gallows," Xerxes called.

Shoving broke out in the back of the hall. "Ungrateful Nubians!" a man cried out. "The lions you brought for the king are not even fine enough to make a peasant's rug and no tamer than the one that killed a hundred of His Majesty's palace soldiers. It is no surprise you seek to challenge him by criticizing his queen."

The exaggeration of how many men Hegai's beast had killed made me wonder what sort of exaggerations about me people would spread. I imagined Hegai saying, *If there is a rumor you do not like, spread a better one.*

Haman had sidled up to the king. He whispered, loudly enough for me to hear, "I hope this unrest over the queen's peasant roots will pass, Your Majesty, before it diminishes you in the eyes of the world and strengthens the Greeks' position against you so much that your subjects cannot be rallied to your cause."

A Nubian man was sent up to the front of the crowd. The king did not wait to hear his voice. Before I could protest, the king ordered that he be taken away. "Now that we have done with that, let the feast begin!" he cried.

Cheering erupted in the hall.

I was standing on one side of Xerxes and Haman was on the other. Xerxes turned first toward Haman and then toward me. "My queen, meet the empire's first adviser and nobleman, Haman."

I waited for Haman to bow to me. Instead he stood taller. He too seemed to be waiting. Finally he said, "But you may call me 'my lord.'"

I did not tilt my head up to look at him. "I am certain I will come up with something better."

His jaw tightened but he kept a little smile on his face. Why did Xerxes not command him to bow to me? I tried to keep the fear from my voice as I addressed Haman again. "Do you not bow to your king's bride, at her own banquet" — suddenly I thought of what I would call him — "loyal *subject*?"

A tiny smile appeared on the king's face at my words.

Haman's bow was only a slight tilt of his head — a tilt no greater than a man would need to spit upon the floor.

But it satisfied Xerxes. He clapped his hands together and said, "Come, let us enjoy this feast!"

As I sat with the king at his low table on the dais, I fought to keep from glancing at

Erez through the screen. He seemed interested in neither food nor drink. Lavish courses of ostrich and other exotic meats were accompanied by wines from every province. Erez let each of them pass before him untouched.

After the third course, musicians entered the banquet hall playing a slow, undulating melody which signaled that dancers were not far behind. When the girls did not immediately appear, the guests looked toward the hall's entrance. Xerxes finished the wine in his goblet and then he too looked. He had drunk at least two pitchers of wine. Abruptly he stood and knocked the screen from the dais. The guests at the table below screamed and jumped away.

"Remove this from my banquet hall!" Xerxes yelled at their shocked faces. I could see now that they were Egyptian. "Tonight all shall look upon my queen Ishtar's beauty, while mortal girls dance for us."

As girls flooded the hall, men cheered and called out among themselves and to the dancers, saying things that made my face flush first with embarrassment and then with anger. I put my hand on the Faravahar beneath my robe and kept my eyes fastened upon my wine while the girls danced. Until I heard Erez's voice:

"I am tired of your crudeness and even more tired of watching you grab at every girl within reach. Think of your mothers and sisters."

I looked out at the drunken, laughing Immortals. Erez's eyes were narrowed upon Parsha's hand as it seized at the ankles of the girl dancing on their table. The girl's smile shook upon her face as she attempted to dance out of Parsha's reach. "You have had one of these 'sisters' plenty of times," Parsha told Erez.

"I have had as many as I ever will."

"Did you have one that you could not wash off?" asked a huge Immortal whose neck was a series of flesh rolls. By the crude way he stared at the girl dancing before him I feared she would feel his full weight later in the evening.

"You are even less fun than you used to be," Parsha said, wrapping his fingers tightly around the girl's leg.

"What is fun for you is dishonorable to me," Erez said, yanking Parsha's hand off the girl and slamming it upon the table.

Parsha cried out. The girl fell and clumsily rushed away.

The huge Immortal stood up and the other Immortals followed. The men beside Erez grabbed him. "Are you so brave that it takes five of you to bring down one man?" Erez asked.

I looked to Xerxes. Surely he would stop the men from harming his favorite and most loyal soldier. But Xerxes watched with amusement, as if it were a performance. "My king," I began.

He waved a hand to dismiss whatever I might say. "They are restless because they have been confined to the palace too long. Tonight, in celebration of you, my queen, I will let them battle each other."

This is how your most elite, highly trained force is allowed to act in front of the empire's noblemen? People were standing up from their tables to watch. Using the two men holding him to support his weight, Erez kicked Parsha in the stomach. Parsha grunted and doubled over. I begged God to keep him from rising, but he rose up almost immediately, causing the crowd to break into wild, bloodthirsty cheering. Parsha wound his right arm back, turning his torso so far that I thought perhaps he would not be able to aim his fist precisely enough to hit Erez. But his knuckles soared toward Erez's face and met with his cheek, driving a strange sound from Erez's lips or nose, I do not know which.

I wanted to scream. As queen, shouldn't I

be able to stop this? Help him the way he had helped me? But I knew that the men's numbers and the wine made them so bold that they would not listen to me. My only hope was to convince the king to stop it.

Parsha slapped Erez with the back of his hand, knocking his face to the other side.

"My king," I began again, this time more urgently.

"Hush, little queen," he said without looking at me.

"But, Your Majest—"

He turned his head toward me without taking his eyes off his favorite Immortals. "You must learn to keep silent in matters you do not understand."

"But one of your favorite Immortals is being beaten to death right before our eyes."

"This is nothing to him. If he could not overcome this pitiful attack he would not be my favorite."

Each time Parsha drove a fist into Erez's face or torso, I felt it in my own flesh. Tears formed in the corners of my eyes. I knew I could not let them fall, or they would smear my cosmetics. I pressed my veil close to my face with a trembling hand.

The Immortals were not content to merely pummel Erez. They called him self-righteous, impotent, a man too proud to know his true place, a man unworthy of the title Immortal, unworthy even of being called a man. Then they released him into a bloody pile upon the floor.

"You are barely more alive than the last man to hang from the gallows," Parsha said. "You are a dead man, as you have been since first making an enemy of my brother."

I looked to the king again. Surely now he would intervene. But his face registered nothing except the same amusement he'd had since the beating had begun. He leaned close and whispered, "Watch how he will let them beat him until he is so bruised and bloody no one thinks he can rise up to defend himself, and then he will throw this pack of dogs off his back as easily as a horse swishes its tail to remove a fly from its flank."

Erez stood, wincing slightly. His tunic was torn and it hung from his shoulder by only a few threads. In one quick motion he reached back for the table and raised it up over his head. Goblets of wine and platters of meat, fruit, and bread crashed to the floor. People at surrounding tables jumped up and moved back a few steps, but they did not run away. They did not want to miss the fight.

In the instant before Erez swung the table

at the three men who surrounded him, I saw a scar on the back of his arm. Two half ovals of little pink lines. The sort of bite marks the man who had stolen me from my bed would have.

Parsha backed up enough to avoid being hit as Erez swung the table, but there was a horrifying slap as the table crashed into the other two Immortals. Erez lifted the table again, and again the scar stared out at me. My own scar began to throb beneath the gold plate. I knew Erez would not have taken — *kidnapped* — a girl from her bed and put her in the hands of the very soldiers who now sought to drive the life from his flesh. But the harder I stared, the darker Erez's scar grew.

He suddenly looked at his arm and then up at me. He lowered the table to hide the scar, but he must have known it was too late.

The other Immortals took the opportunity to set upon him, driving him to the floor.

I looked away. *Whoever is being set upon now is not the man I cared for. And perhaps he does not truly care for me either, and only gave me the necklace because he felt guilty for destroying my life and taking me from my home, not because he thought me beautiful. Maybe this same guilt is what keeps him from defending himself.*

Still, it hurt to hear the sound of fists meeting flesh. I wanted to press my palms to my ears but I could not. I slowly turned my gaze back to where he lay on the floor. He was thrashing so violently that the other Immortals were having a hard time keeping hold of him. The huge Immortal, whose neck was a series of flesh rolls, fell upon Erez's legs, allowing Parsha to get ahold of Erez's ankle.

Erez's torso shot up and there was a sudden flash of movement toward the huge man. As Erez withdrew his dagger from the man's neck I heard a gurgling sound and then the man fell forward, already dead.

"My king," I cried. "Surely you cannot want to watch your best soldiers fight to the death!"

Erez used the body to shield himself as the other Immortals set upon him once again.

"Soon your corpse will rot in pieces," Parsha said, "each more fly covered than the next."

"Enough!" Xerxes cried. "My finest soldier should fight no more tonight — he must save his strength to battle for the empire. The best wines and as many dancing girls as desired for my Immortals." He said nothing of the huge Immortal who lay facedown upon the marble floor in a pool of his own blood. "And virgins from my own harem!"

The king snapped his fingers at two servants standing near the entrance to the hall and they hurried to carry out his orders. My heart broke for the virgins and, I had to admit, for myself. Erez's scar hurt me worse than my own. The Immortal I had cared for was not my ally or protector after all.

I hate him, I told myself.

Yet I glanced up to make sure he was not near death. Defending himself against the other Immortals did not look like it had been as easy as it is for a horse to swish his tail and remove a fly. He was standing now, but he swayed upon his feet, his face swollen grotesquely, blood pouring from his nose.

Exactly what he deserves, I told myself. Even so, I felt as though a cold hand crawled up my spine as I saw how Haman glared at him.

The king finally seemed to realize that Erez was injured. "And Egypt's finest physician!" he added. He looked impatiently down at the Egyptians whom the screen had fallen upon. As if they were moving too slowly, he said, "Is not this physician already among us here in the palace, or must I dispatch you to return home and fetch him?"

A small Egyptian man pressed a swath of Erez's own ripped tunic to his nose and, with the help of another Egyptian, began to lead him from the room. Erez looked at me, wincing at some pain as he turned his neck. Looking back caused my new hatred of him to waver. I knew only anger could keep me strong, so I gazed away. He was leaning so heavily upon the physician that from the corner of my eye I saw the small man stumble.

Xerxes had turned his attention back to the wine and food that continued to pour forth from the kitchens. He urged me to take some sugared date plums from a tray a servant held before us.

"Are you not hungry, my queen?" Xerxes asked. "Why do you not lift your veil and delight in all that has been brought for you?"

"I am only nervous for tonight, Your Highness."

He smiled. "I would not want you any other way."

My stomach hurt so badly I feared that if I stood and began walking I would not be able to keep down the little I had consumed. *I must forget about Erez, and think of my people.* I had to focus on what needed to happen next. And after that I would again focus on what came next. That is what I would do — *all* I would do, and all I would think of — from now on. Putting one foot in front of the other, concentrating on my feet as though each step took the full force of my will, which sometimes it might.

After the banquet, will we go to the king's chambers, or am I to go to my own chambers and wait for him to call for me? And if we do go directly to his chambers, am I to walk beside him or behind him?

"Let us retire to my chambers," Xerxes said after the platters of meats, fruits, dates, sugared pistachios, and pastries had been cleared. He rose, and everyone in the great hall quickly followed. "We will leave you to enjoy all the best that the empire has to offer," he told his guests. Then he smiled down at me. "*Almost* all of it."

Without waiting for a reaction from me he moved toward the stairs that led from the dais. His escort quickly took their places around him and my own escort hurried to take their places as well. I followed my husband toward the entrance to the hall.

"May the king have many strong sons," someone cried out.

"To the strength of the king's seed!"

"May the queen's womb flow with milk and honey enough to please the king and keep him at his task until she brings forth a son!"

"A son with a warrior's strength and a lion's heart!"

"With eyes keener than a bird of prey!"

I imagined this son the crowd was making: huge-muscled arms and legs, beady eyes, and a bloody lion's heart beating within his chest. I imagined him growing in my belly. Was this truly the sort of son Xerxes would plant in my womb? And would this son fill the emptiness spreading through me? It was an emptiness where the loss of my parents and Cyra had eaten away at me. If I did not stay angry enough at Erez, he too might add to the hollowness inside me.

I could not allow the crowd to know my unhappiness. I raised my left arm up and waved. Cheering erupted in the hall. But not only cheering. "Peasant!" a man shouted. He did not shout loudly, but still, I heard him.

I turned my head to the right and looked out over the crowd. My gaze fell upon a man whose sneer was replaced by fear as I lifted my veil. *Do not think I will not have you put upon the gallows. I am no longer a little*

323

girl. Today I was made queen of the most powerful empire the world has ever known. The only reason I do not have you seized and punished is that the king did not hear your insult and I will not trouble him now.

The man took one step back, then another, before turning and running. People jumped away from him as if from a venomous snake. The crowd had quieted, and there was fear in some of the eyes that stared back at me. It was not an unwelcome sight. I felt my strength growing with each pair of frightened eyes I looked into.

I turned back in the direction I was going. I imagined that Ruti was near. *At least,* Ruti whispered, *he did not call you* Jew.

Thank you, Ruti, I thought as the procession reached the entrance to the banquet hall. I was eager to leave the hall behind, along with the Faravahar. *I am going to the bed of the most powerful man in the world, and this time I am going as his queen. Perhaps tomorrow I will carry the next king in my belly.*

I was not going to be a stupid girl anymore.

I unclasped Erez's chain from behind my neck and let it fall to the floor as I stepped from the room.

Chapter Twenty-Seven: In the King's Chamber

As I went for the first time to my marriage bed, six guards surrounded me. Two in front, two in back, and one on either side. The guards were strangers to me, and I did not trust them to shield me from all the people who would try to snatch away the crown that had just been placed upon my head.

They suddenly came to a halt. One of the soldiers of Xerxes' escort came to speak to one of mine. "The king would like you to walk beside him," the soldier said. I nodded and we continued away from the banquet hall until we were beside Xerxes.

The king looked down from where he towered above me. "Little Ishtar," he said, holding out his elbow.

I had worn the crown less than a day, but already, it had changed me. My spine seemed to rise up to meet it. I was not without fear, but I now knew that even when I was afraid I could stand as tall as the proudest soldier. I had faced down the man who had cried "peasant" as I left the banquet hall, and the crowd had stared back at me with fear. My back felt so strong I knew that no one could bend it, no one but the king. Despite my fear of what was to come, my hand was steady as I placed it upon his arm. I knew a queen's hand should always be steady, unless the king wished for it to tremble.

His flesh was slippery from the oil upon it, but I managed to keep hold of him as we walked to his chambers. I noticed some of the red henna from my fingertips mixing with the oil upon his skin. He too looked at his arm, and then at me.

The lust in his eyes, combined with his size, his mood swings, his drunkenness, and the thought of what was to come made my heart race. He was taller, broader, and more godlike than any man I had seen. There was more muscle in the arm I held than in the whole body of some men. He was so large that perhaps the One God would not see me lying beneath his huge, uncircumcised body.

He smiled. "You will never again want for anything, however big or small."

I felt my heart open to him — not fully,

but a tiny crack that perhaps time could enlarge.

The procession came to an abrupt halt outside his chambers, and I nearly stumbled into the soldier in front of me. He quickly stepped aside. "Forgive me, Your Highness," he said. I kept my eyes lowered as I entered Xerxes' chambers for the second time. I had decided I must in turns appear timid and strong with the king. He was not yet certain who I was, and so long as that were true he would not grow tired of me.

The king dismissed the guards and attendants, and before the door was fully closed behind the last servant he raised up my veil and kissed every surface of my face. When he pulled back to look at me, I began, "My king, there is something I must speak with you abou—"

He pressed his lips to mine so quickly that he ate my last word and the breath I had used to speak it. I had never been kissed and I did not know what to do. Yet, seemingly of their own accord, my lips parted. The king held my head in his huge hands so he could kiss me more deeply. He kissed me until I gasped for air. Then he pulled my hair against his nose, inhaled, and said, "Your beauty is proof that Ahura Mazda watches over me still." He walked me backward until I was against the wall.

I no longer felt my emptiness. I felt only those parts of myself that the king was touching, and my back, which was tightly pressed against the wall. His sweat smelled of wine and salted meat, and unlike the previous night I did not wish to shield myself from it. Despite my robe and Xerxes' tunic, I could feel the warm breath and blood moving through him.

Without meaning to, I arched. Even as I pressed upward I felt as though I was falling backward. Something stronger than my fear was overtaking me.

He continued to hold tightly to me with one hand while he moved the other between our bodies. He roughly touched me through my robe as he moved his mouth down to my neck, and then I felt the front of my robe being parted. Lips touched the bare skin of my chest. He ran one finger down the center of my stomach and all the blood in my body rushed after it.

I knew I was supposed to talk to the king about Halannah, but I no longer wanted to mention her. I wanted nothing between Xerxes and me.

The hand that was not pressing between my legs took hold of my robe and yanked it from my body.

He abruptly released me and stepped back. His gaze was so intent upon my flesh that it felt as though he were trying to take something from it, and the longer he looked, the more he wanted to take. His eyes, usually a deep brown, had grown so dark I could not tell where his pupils ended and his irises began.

When he came toward me my heart jumped in my chest. I felt more naked than I ever had before. More naked than when the other maidens and I had first arrived and been commanded to strip off everything, even our jewelry. More naked than when I was bathed by servants in front of the other girls and any eunuchs who cared to watch.

Xerxes reached inside his tunic and pulled out a chain. For an instant I feared it was Erez's necklace, the one I had just unhooked from my neck and dropped onto the marble tile of the banquet hall. Instead it was a chain with the eight-pointed star of Ishtar. The king opened it and held it in front of my neck. The star came toward me until it was so near it appeared there were two stars, then it disappeared beneath my chin and I felt it fall against my chest.

I bowed my head so Xerxes could fasten the chain behind my neck, and my eyes fell upon his tunic where it covered his stomach. Lower yet, I could see his arousal. I wondered if Xerxes could feel the heat in my cheeks even without touching my face.

His fingers brushing against my neck felt so good I wanted to press my cheek to his stomach, despite what loomed below. Before I could fall against him though, he took his hands from me and then nothing touched my flesh except the chain weighing lightly around the back of my neck and the crown upon my head.

I would not be recklessly bold but also I would not be passive and silent like hundreds of girls who had been in his chambers before me. "How do you find me, husband?"

He did not answer right away. *Is he memorizing me as I am now because I will never be this fresh and beautiful again?* I willed my legs not to shake. I imagined they were stone pillars like those in the banquet hall. If those pillars could hold a roof so heavy that the first time I had seen it I feared it would crash down upon me, surely my own legs could hold me.

Finally, he said, "You are a perfect picture of how a queen should wear a crown."

He bent down and lifted me off my feet in one smooth motion that made me feel both small and great at the same time. He was more than twice as big as me, yet he had bowed to pick me up. As he carried me to his bed, he kept his eyes upon mine. Without looking at the scarves of purple, blue, red, green, and yellow that hung from the thick golden frame above, he pushed them aside and set me down in front of him.

Instead of calling in a servant to unpin my crown from my hair, Xerxes did it himself, as deftly as though he had done it many times before. He placed it carefully on a table beside the bed.

"Lay back." There was a strain, something different in his voice. He had been patient the night before, but now we were on a path from which there was no turning back. I opened my eyes and watched him peel his tunic over his head, then I gasped and squeezed my eyes shut again. My courage had fled at the strange sight of him. I knew he came to kneel between my knees by how the mattress sunk beneath his weight. My blood halted inside my veins. I wanted to press my legs tightly together. I wished I had drunk more wine. I wished I had lost consciousness.

"Do not be afraid," he said. He touched me again, until once more my blood rushed toward his hand. "Open your eyes, my little queen." He raised his face up away from mine so we could look at each other. I had never looked at any man so close. His pupils were huge, his mouth seemed big enough to swallow me, his breath covered my whole face. And then he was done waiting.

I did not yield easily, but Xerxes did not yield either. I remembered what Halannah had said: "The first time the king has you, you will pray for death to take you before he is done." But then my body responded and we moved more easily together. Still, I was uncertain whether I was in agony or ecstasy for most of it, and then, all too soon and not soon enough, it was over.

Xerxes rolled onto his back and called for wine. My heart beat wildly. I could still feel the heat where his body had pressed against my own. *The king, my husband.* I had been made a queen and a woman all in one day.

I am no longer Hadassah, a girl who stood by in silence while her parents were killed.

I hoped that neither the servants nor the king would glance at me until I had a chance to use the powder I had brought for my face and had taken a cloth to my damp flesh. I wanted to appear no less than a queen.

Two servants entered with a pitcher that had a handle in the shape of a lion's tail, as well as goblets and a tray of sugared pistachios. The king motioned for the servants to set the wine and nuts down and then he waved them from the room. Though I desired almost nothing more than the warmth of wine traveling down to my belly, I did not want him looking too closely at me when I was unkempt. Without waiting for permission, I reached to the floor for my robe and grabbed the powder Hegai had given me. "Your Majesty, please excuse me," I said as I hurried behind the chamber pot screen to make myself presentable.

When I returned to the king's bed with the wine he did not look at me. "You have dropped our son into the chamber pot."

I felt as though the air had been knocked from my chest. Perhaps God did not want a gentile's seed in my belly after all and that is why I had suddenly been overcome with the urge to get up. No, it was my own stupidity. I wanted to fall to my knees and beg forgiveness, but any sudden movement might further aggravate the king or cast out what was left of the child the king had tried to plant. "Please forgive me, Your Majesty."

Without responding he rolled away from me, onto his side, and fell into a fitful sleep. I watched his huge back, thinking of how he had exiled Vashti for refusing to appear naked before his banquet, and wondering if

I too had just committed an offense that would cost me his favor.

When he awoke he was not too unhappy to reach for me again. Afterward, I did not get up. I tried not to worry about how I might appear to him. There was only one thing that could bring us truly together. I pulled my knees into my chest and prayed. *A son. Please send me a son.*

Until then I would make do with what I could. "My king," I said, "I do not want to jostle your seed. Will you hand me my goblet?"

He reached across my body to retrieve the goblet from the little table beside me, and placed it into my hand. His arms were so long that he easily grabbed his own without moving away from me. I raised my goblet.

"To our son!" I said hopefully.

"To our son," he said, "and the future of the empire."

We drank and coupled until the king was too drunk to continue either one. Though I wanted a son I almost cried with relief when Xerxes had had his fill of me. My body ached so deeply that I was afraid it would ache forever.

I fought the urge to rush behind the chamber screen with the powder and a damp cloth. I told myself that he was too overfull with wine to notice that I no longer looked like the goddess Ishtar. *When I carry his son I will appear beautiful to him even when my cosmetics have worn off and I lie in a pool of his sweat.*

"My love," I said, "there is something I must ask you."

"Do not pretend to seek my permission if you *must* ask."

I was uncertain if I should go on, but I did, because I had no way of knowing when he might call upon me again. Vashti was said to have sometimes gone over a month without seeing him. Xerxes had four palaces and hundreds of girls at each one.

"There is a great evil that all virgins in your harem face, and many do not come away from it unscathed. Their maidens' seal is broken by someone besides you, my king."

"Who would risk the wrath of Ahura Mazda to take what is rightfully mine?"

I made sure to keep my voice steady as I said the name of his favorite concubine. "Halannah." I watched his face. It showed nothing.

"I will see to this," he said, "but now I must rest."

I pulled my knees into my chest and lay that way — unmoving — all night, willing the king's seed to take root in my womb. I did not run behind the screen to make myself presentable until morning. Afterward I waited for the king to awaken.

"Thank you, my king," I said as soon as he opened his eyes.

He did not need time to rouse himself — he awoke alert, as finished with sleep as he must have been with each harem girl in the morning. He turned so that his huge chest rose up beside me like a wall. "And I thank Ahura Mazda, little Shushan. In giving me such a beautiful queen, he shows me that from this moment on he will give me only good things." He traced his fingertips along the curves of my body, then spread his hand so that it stretched across my whole stomach. "The Greeks will wish they had already lost to me, compared to how they will lose now."

I hoped he would not be foolish enough to attack the Greeks again, but I would worry about that later. "And I hope the evil-doer in your harem will be equally as sorry as the Greeks."

He looked confused for an instant, but then his brow relaxed. "Yes. I will put a stop to this evil immediately."

"Thank you, Your Majesty. You are truly a great and benevolent king. I am even more proud to be your queen today than I was yesterday."

"There is much to enjoy, my queen," he said, then yelled "enter!" Servants rushed in to prop us up in the king's huge bed with thick cushions. All the attendants I had seen the morning before paraded into the king's chamber once again: two Immortals from the king's escort, four eunuchs with silk towels over their shoulders who wheeled in a basin made of gold, three more servants with platters of bread, fruit, and honey, another with a pitcher of sweet-smelling wine. After this came about twenty musicians, three girls with bells on their wrists and ankles, and another girl with a large fan of date palm leaves. Two of the servants fastened my crown to my hair.

"My queen, I would have you bathed in my own basin of gold while I look upon your great beauty and give thanks to Ahura Mazda."

I did not wish for anyone to see my naked body and whatever marks or swelling might show upon my thighs, but also I could not plainly refuse the king's wishes as Queen Vashti had done. "You are too gracious, my king. On this morning I thought to be bathed in the herbs my servant has been procuring in order to hasten your seed to my womb. But I will bathe for you instead.

337

I want only to please you."

He regarded me carefully, and it seemed one eyebrow was on the verge of rising, but he did not risk the son he might have planted during the night.

"Go now, to soak in your servant's herbs. You will bathe for me another time."

He kissed me so sweetly, and for so long, that I could not tell whether he loved me or we were not going to see each other again for a long time.

CHAPTER TWENTY-EIGHT: RUTI AND HEGAI

As I stepped from Xerxes' chambers and saw the Immortals standing guard, I could not keep from thinking of Erez. "Hurry," I said to my escort as they led me back to my chambers and the wine that awaited me there. I hoped it might ease the new ache in my body.

As soon as I entered my chambers, Ruti said, "Tell me all, my queen." She quickly added, "If it please you."

I would have been happy to see her but for my exhaustion and the many questions I knew she would ask. "While we are in the baths, Ruti."

The Queen's Baths were as large as the women's baths, but instead of a long line of bronze washing tubs, they contained only one large golden basin. When Ruti asked me how the evening had gone, I did not lie. "I think it went well, but I cannot be certain."

Ruti stopped moving the damp cloth along my arm. "How is it you do not know, my queen? Were you overfull with wine?"

I placed a hand, the one that did not hold my goblet, onto my belly. "Time will tell whether something good has come of it."

The heaviness fell from Ruti's face. The way her emotions swung wildly up and down at only a few words reminded me that everything I did now was important. The crown was much heavier than it looked.

She put the hand that was not holding the cloth on top of mine. "He will be Jewish, whether anyone knows this or not."

Not even he will know. The thought filled me with sadness, but I knew I would do all I could to protect my son, even conceal his true identity from him. I did not want to burden him with a secret he might not be able to keep.

"Xerxes is the most powerful man in all the world," Ruti continued, "yet his seed is not half so strong as what is inside us. Xerxes will not be able to take the One God out of his son's blood." She squeezed my hand. "And what of Halannah's cruelty in the harem?"

"The king said it would be dealt with."

Ruti dropped the damp cloth and clapped her hands together as it made a slapping sound upon the tiles. "You have done what no other person has been able to. Hashem has guided you to this great moment. Perhaps He will guide you to many more."

"First I hope he will guide me to a deep and dreamless sleep."

Not long after I had returned to my chambers, God granted my wish.

I awoke to find Ruti staring down at me. "Hegai is here to see you."

"Help me dress and I will go to him."

"You are the queen. He has come to you."

"How long has he been waiting?"

"You are queen, how long he has been waiting is not your concern. It also is not your concern that he is furious."

"Because he had to wait?"

"He was angry before he had to wait. But yes, now he is furious." Ruti was not able to fully suppress a smile.

"Oh, Ruti."

When Ruti opened the door Hegai burst into my chambers. His cheeks were red with rage. He ran the fingers of his complete hand over the stubs of his shortened hand. "What did you tell the king of my harem?"

"Surely you mean '*Your Majesty,* what did you tell the king of *his* harem?' "

"It is you who have forgotten yourself.

Two days ago you were a harem girl with the special privileges *I* granted you. Today you are a girl who has been queen *for one day,* and that is how you are spoken of. Tomorrow you will be known as the girl who has been queen *for two days.* You will not be only 'queen' for at least a year."

"I will not allow anyone to give me less than my proper due. Because you have helped make me queen, you honor not only me but also yourself as well when you address me properly."

"*Your Majesty,* Bigthan has been removed from the harem and put instead at the king's gate. Halannah remains."

Ruti exhaled as though she had been punched in the belly.

"I do not understand," I said. "I did not mention Bigthan. Only Halannah."

"Was the king overfull with wine when you spoke to him?" Ruti asked. Without waiting for me to continue, she said, "You waited too long to make your request. His tolerance is not so great as yours is now."

The crown which was so heavy upon my head seemed to be invisible to them. If my own servants did not pay homage to the crown, how was I to expect anyone else to? Before I could reprimand Ruti for speaking disrespectfully to her new queen, Hegai said, "*Your Majesty* would be wise to think more and drink less. Hopefully the king will call for you again this evening. If not I will send the most unattractive of all the harem girls to him."

I stared at him. "*You* will send whoever you choose? He does not care who you send him?"

"Sometimes he asks for a virgin, but usually he says 'One is as good as another.' Except for one woman who he has asked for by name many times."

I thought of Halannah's many bracelets, necklaces, and earrings. I remembered her earlobes elongated by a pair of heavy gold rosettes. The king had given her a fortune, and now I knew that she was the only harem woman he truly lusted for or perhaps even loved. It felt as though a handful of rocks had just been dropped into my stomach.

"I did not tell you because I did not want you to lose courage," Hegai said. "But now you must know your enemy's strength so you are prepared. It does not appear you were ready for your task last night. It takes more than a crown upon your head to be a queen."

I knew a true queen was one who outsmarted her enemies and did great things for her people. But in the meantime I could dole out punishments and rewards to remind them of who I was. "I am your queen and you will give me my proper due or you will no longer have my ear."

Hegai looked like he might say something, but he swallowed it.

"Up until now you have served me well," I said, "and I wish to reward you for it."

I turned first to Hegai. "I know you have as many riches as a man could want, but I wish at least one of them was from me. Is there nothing you desire?"

"There is only one gift you can give me."

"Yes, removing Halannah from the king's harem. Very well. If you have nothing more to tell me, you may go."

Though he left, the disapproving look he gave me seemed to linger.

Ruti was more easily won over. When I told her to pick whatever she liked from the wardrobe, her eyes widened like a child's. Once she had made her selections, I spoke to the wardrobe attendant. I spoke firmly so that she would not dare to look strangely at me as I ordered her to have clothes for a queen made into a servant's dress-up things. Ruti would not be able to wear her new robe and head scarf outside of my chambers, but this did not seem to dampen her happiness, just as my failure to get Halannah removed from the harem no longer dampened it. She twirled before me with a surprising grace that had been hidden in her sack-like garb. The gem-encrusted purple robe she had chosen brought out hints of green in her brown eyes.

"It is a good color for you," I said.

"Thank you, Your Majesty. I feel as though I am floating."

She looked like she was floating too. Happiness had lifted some of the creases from her face, and I could see that she had once been beautiful.

Even with all the mistakes I have made, and whatever is to come while I am finding my way, at least there will always be this moment in which Ruti seems as light as though she never cleaned a single chamber pot or suffered beneath a multitude of soldiers.

All because of a robe and a head scarf. *If only everyone could be so easily won over.*

CHAPTER TWENTY-NINE: MY SERVANT, MY GUARD

I had risen as high in the world as a woman could, yet the afternoon following my night with the king I had the same thought as the lowest girl of the harem: *Will the king call me to him tonight?* By the last meal of the day I knew he would not.

"It is a blessing from Hashem," Ruti said. "You look terrible."

But surely it was not a blessing from Hashem when the king did not call for me the next night, or the one after.

After the third night that the king did not call for me, Ruti returned from the servants' quarters with news. The king had spent the last two nights with Halannah and had called her to him once again. "But, my chil— *queen,* I have been instructed to keep track of your monthly bleeding. Surely this instruction comes down from the king himself. It is likely he does not call you to him because he does not wish to risk disturbing the new life in your belly."

"How long will this go on?" I realized what a foolish question this was as soon as the words left my mouth.

"Hopefully nine months."

When I bled a few days later, Ruti tried to hide her disappointment. "Well, now you will have a chance to see the king again," she said, "and make your request before he is overfull with wine."

As soon as my time of bleeding had passed word was sent to the king. He did not call upon me that night either. Even in sleep I could not escape a thought: *Is he punishing me for getting up after the first time he lay with me?*

I awoke to a familiar voice screaming for me to hide. Then came a wet, sinewy sound. Flesh being opened with a sharp blade. There was a cry that hurt me as much as if it were my own flesh being torn. Though the voice was distorted by pain, I knew it was Ruti's.

I shifted my feet off the cushions, but when I tried to stand my foot came down upon a goblet that lay on the tile.

"Hurry — hi —" Ruti choked and went silent. I knew I needed to obey her command and hide. But it was too late. Someone fell upon me, straddling my chest and taking hold of my hair. I put my hands up to protect my neck.

Footsteps — not the light flying footsteps of assassins but the heavy footsteps of soldiers — rushed closer. The soldiers' torchlight reached me before they did. I saw that my attacker was all in black, his face hidden by a mask. In his hand — the one that did not hold my hair — was a knife. It was exactly as it had been when Halannah attacked me. I raised my right hand just in time to catch the knife as it came rushing down toward my neck. The knife point hit the gold plate, bending back my wrist and then sliding off to strike the tile beside my head.

Soldiers were upon us — five of them — dragging the man off of me. I shuffled back away from them and stood up. A sixth soldier rushed up behind them. Parsha. "I am sorry," my attacker stammered when he saw Parsha. Before he could say more, Parsha grabbed him by the hair, bent his head back, and slit his throat.

Bodies lay all around us: two of my servants, the two Immortals who stood guard inside my chambers, and two men in dark tunics and no sandals, like the man who had attacked me. "Who has sent you?" I asked him. *"Who has sent you to kill me?"* But it was too late. The man was choking and making horrible gurgling noises.

Three soldiers carried the bodies of the attackers from my chambers. The bodies bounced against their backs, blood pouring unevenly down the soldiers' legs.

I heard Ruti choking and noticed blood pooling upon the marble tiles around her head.

"My servant," I cried. "She must be tended at once!"

I stumbled past Parsha, to where Ruti lay upon the floor. The blood poured from a long wound upon her face, some into her own mouth. I turned Ruti's head to the side so she would not choke to death, my hand nearly slipping from her face because of the blood gushing down it.

"Have you not tended to each other in battle?" I yelled at the remaining soldiers, who I now saw were Immortals. I wondered where the Immortals who stood guard outside my chambers were. The ones before me did not follow my command with any urgency. One pulled Ruti's back up against his chest and pressed his fists into her stomach until she threw up blood.

I stood and grabbed Ruti's shaking hands.

She flinched and I quickly let go of the one which was cut. My surviving servants reentered my chambers and one immediately rushed over with a cloth and began to wipe my hands. I grabbed the cloth from her and pressed it to Ruti's face. "Can you not see with your own eyes who is injured?" I asked the servant. I knew from looking at her face that she was ashamed she had run away. She moved to hold the cloth against Ruti's face while keeping her gaze low.

"You will be cared for by the best physicians," I promised Ruti as she gazed at me out of huge, terrified eyes. "And when you are well again you will be elevated to the highest position I can make for you."

I instructed one Immortal to rush Ruti to the physicians' chambers. He threw her over his shoulder like a captive, ignoring the servant who tried to keep the cloth pressed to her face.

"No!" I yelled at him. "In your *arms,* as you would carry your own child, with a servant to stop the blood flowing from her face."

The Immortal pulled Ruti back over his shoulder. I had to bite my lip to keep from crying at the sight of her bleeding face. I ordered two additional servants to see to it that Ruti was brought to the physicians, and then report back to me. They looked at me incredulously. They were not accustomed to reporting on Immortals. "Go!" I said.

As the Immortal who held Ruti disappeared through the doorway, one of the other Immortals looked at me and muttered, *"Child."*

Did he truly think I could not hear him? I remembered Hegai's words: "It takes more than a crown upon your head to be a queen."

Parsha had wandered deeper into my chambers, and he was looking around with what seemed to me to be too much care. I could not think of any good reason for him to be memorizing the layout of my chambers. He turned and gazed at me with more scorn than I would have thought could fit on just one face. He was standing near my bed, and this unsettled me almost as much as if he were within arm's reach of me. "Are you surprised no man has thrown himself behind your cause? Only one man is fool enough, and he is not here. Men do not willingly give up their lives for a girl who has temporarily fooled a king into believing she is worthy of him."

"If you spoke for an entire army you would not need to send men sneaking into my chambers to kill me."

"Another woman will occupy this bed soon," he said quietly.

"Seize this traitor," I commanded the two remaining Immortals.

One of them began laughing. The third did not meet my eye nor do as I had commanded. He followed Parsha, advancing farther into my chambers. He stopped to pick up the goblet that lay overturned and empty upon the marble tiles next to the cushions I had fallen asleep on. He smirked. "So it is as we have heard," he said to the other Immortals. As though I was not there. As though I was not queen.

I fought to keep the distress from my voice. "The king will hear of this."

"He seems to have desired only one night with you, and you cannot approach him uninvited unless you wish to die," Parsha said. "By the time you see him again you will probably have forgotten this slight, buried it beneath all the other slights you are certain to receive each day you play at being queen."

I looked about for an ally. The servants stared at the floor or busied themselves with small tasks. One hurried to wipe the tiles where my goblet had lain.

I knew there was only one threat that would send Parsha hurrying from my chambers. An offense the king would not hesitate to put a man upon the gallows for. I approached him and stood so that not even a cubit separated us. He did not smell as terrible as he had on the march, but still there was an unpleasant odor about him, something both bitter and sour at the same time. "Get out now," I whispered, "or I will tell the king you sought to take what he has claimed for himself. Even if I have to risk my life to do so."

Parsha considered me a moment. "Your life is worth little now," he said, "and so I believe you."

He brushed past me as he left my chambers, taking the remaining two Immortals with him.

In addition to the two Immortals who had died in my chambers, two of the four Immortals who stood guard outside my chambers had died of the injuries they had sustained when they were set upon by the five men who had come for me. The two Immortal guards who had not died were being tended to by the physicians. Of the five assassins, the two who had not made it into my chambers had not given up their secrets, and they were all dead now. Perhaps Parsha had made certain of that. This is what Hegai told me after he entered my chambers without knocking.

"Have I no guards?" I had demanded when he stepped in unannounced. I was studying the new dent in the plate over my palm in the daylight that had just begun to peek under the balcony doors. I had not dared open those doors or any others. The servants I had sent with Ruti had returned to report that she had indeed made it safely to the physicians. I had sent one of them back for news of Ruti's condition and the other to bring word of the attack to the king. I was pacing while I awaited their return.

"Unless you find eunuchs to be suitable defenders, then yes, you are unguarded."

"This cannot be true. If it were I would not still be alive."

"Seven of my own men are outside your door. Soldiers will soon take their place." He smiled sadly at his own jest.

"Some wine for my guest," I told one of my servants, in my distress forgetting that Hegai did not drink wine.

"I desire privacy," Hegai said, "and nothing more."

I instructed my servants to wait outside the door. Hegai did not speak until it had been closed behind them.

"You have survived an attack of Immortals. When I was informed of the attack upon you I had one of my men follow the attackers' bodies as they were carried from your chambers. They have the cuts and calluses of archers. While all Immortals must have some skill with a bow and arrow, these Immortals specialized in it. Haman, or whoever hired them, did not get the best men for the task. I suspect Haman is involved because Dalphon does not seem to have reported any men missing from the ranks."

When I wrapped my arms around myself Hegai gave me a look that told me he liked this gesture no more than he liked crying. I dropped my hands to my sides and assumed a more regal posture.

"Do not think this is an attack only upon you, little queen. It is also the king who is attacked. There are always those who desire the king's position. The king's own army could mutiny if incited. Surely some ambitious noble would be happy to spread word that choosing you proves Xerxes is unfit and that the tides have turned against the king. Perhaps he will whisper that this is the decline of the empire." Before I could ask him what he had heard, he said, "I do not know if this is already happening. The only things I do know are that you should not hold out hope for Ruti and that you are in great danger."

"Ruti was alive when she was taken from my chambers, and if she was properly tended to she is alive now," I said. Before he could respond heavy footsteps sounded toward my door. Hegai did not have to tell me to hide. I rushed to my wardrobe and hid there until Hegai came calling for me.

"You are guarded by whole men again, my queen. Four of them will escort you to the king. He has sent for you."

I started toward the door of my chamber but Hegai stopped me. "You may want to refresh your cosmetics, Your Majesty. And do not forget your crown."

When Hegai opened the door a few moments later there were four Immortals I had never seen before standing guard. Erez was not among them. I was reminded that I had one less ally than I thought I did the week before. Or two, if Ruti did not recover.

"Take me to my husband," I told the Immortals.

Hegai fell in behind me. *If I am only to have one ally, I am glad it is the most cunning man in the palace.*

A servant rushed to kneel before me. Despite Hegai's words from a few moments before, I was flooded with hope for Ruti.

"Yes? Speak."

"Your Majesty, the physicians have tended to Ruti and she is resting."

"She will recover?"

"Yes, Your Highness." Though the servant went silent after this, I could hear that there was more. Something the servant was afraid to say.

"Fully?"

"She will be deeply scarred, Your Majesty. Her face . . ."

"It is her mind and her strength which concern me." *Without them she will not survive here, and the attacker will have taken from her what he meant to take from me.*

"The king awaits, Your Highness," Hegai quietly reminded me.

Chapter Thirty:
Heavy Is the Head

I resisted the urge to look frantically about as we made our way to the throne room. Perhaps no one would know how closely I listened if I kept my head straight and my face expressionless.

I must see from the corners of my eyes and with my ears. I must act as though nothing has happened.

We stopped in front of the guards who stood before the entrance to the throne room. If they resented me the way Parsha and some of the other Immortals did, the only way to deal with them was to make them love or fear me and I did not have time to make them love me. "My husband awaits," I told them in a voice that would have caused a dead man to rise up and do as I commanded. The guards stepped aside and the doors were opened. Though I was queen, and though I had been summoned, I was not allowed in the throne room until the king held out his scepter to me. Only the king's advisers were permitted to enter freely.

I held my head high as I was announced by one of the king's eunuchs. I wanted the king to know his queen was strong, even in the face of danger. Strong enough to bear the son who would rule the empire Xerxes was building for him.

Xerxes himself appeared far from strong. He sat — huge and fragile-looking — upon his throne. He stared down from the slightly elevated platform upon which his throne was mounted, his head lowered and hair falling forward from his crown. His face was half-hidden from me. Advisers crowded around him, Haman closest of all. Behind them was a sparkling backdrop of treasures that did not seem worth the burden of ruling a kingdom.

If I looked only at Xerxes, shutting everyone else out and letting my eyes blur the crown from his head, he was a large man weighed down by his thoughts. When I let everything come into focus again, I saw that he was weighed down not by his own thoughts but by theirs, and by the crown upon his head.

I wished I could pluck him out from the circle of advisers and just for a moment lift away the crown. If he were not king, what sort of man would he be? How would he speak to me? How would he touch me?

Haman smiled slightly as Xerxes continued to stare down at the floor. The king did not seem to hear that I had been announced. I stood tall, struggling to keep my fear from making its way onto my face. Finally he heaved a great sigh. He held his scepter out to welcome me before using it to wave the circle of advisers away. He still had not glanced up.

My escort stepped aside to make way for the king's advisers to exit. Haman lingered, not looking at me directly. I knew he was aware of me because he moved into my path and turned away from me, trying to claim the king for himself. But he was not large enough to completely block my view of my husband.

Still without looking up, the king waved his scepter at Haman. As Haman stepped back I watched him just barely stifle an indignant huff or grunt of some kind. He narrowed his already narrow, kohl-ringed eyes at me on his way out, passing much closer than any man should come to a queen. Almost as close as his son had come to me not long before.

I rushed forward to fall upon my knees

before my husband. I hoped he would order me to stand and come closer so he could wrap his huge arms around me and tell me he would do anything to keep me safe.

"Rise," he said. I peeked up from beneath my eyelashes. My cosmetics had been wasted. His gaze was still weighted to the floor as he said, "I know the old woman is precious to you, and so I had two of my most trusted advisers check on her. There is no longer a place for her among your servants."

Are you certain you have two trustworthy advisers, and do you believe Haman is among them?

"King — *husband,* I stand before you now because of Ruti's loyalty and courage. Ruti saved my life." I put the slightest emphasis on Ruti, hoping to make it more difficult for him to think of her as only "old woman."

He still did not look at my face. I had the terrible thought that maybe he wished the assassins had been successful so he could choose another queen. Halannah, perhaps. "She is too scarred. The palace's servants are the finest. You are not a girl newly risen from peasantry who must take whatever old woman is nearest."

"Please, Your Maj—"

"No!" His head jerked up and suddenly he

was shouting. "She will be a reminder that people wish you dead, that they do not respect my choice of queen. That they do not respect or fear *me*."

My heart beat wildly in my chest, but I did not step back or soften my words. "You are king, anyone can see that. Ahura Mazda has made you larger than other men so that you might easily rule over them. But no king is without enemies. Will not all see your strength when you show them how your choice of queen has survived an attack? How weak your enemy and how vigilant Ahura Mazda's watch over you must be if a mere servant was able to thwart three men?"

He gazed directly into my eyes, and this time his voice was so calm it frightened me. "Six of my own men died, little Shushan."

I held myself rigid so I would not recoil at this news. Hegai had only told me that four had died. I would have to find out what had happened to the others. "If they died, without first stopping the attack, then they were unworthy of their position. Ahura Mazda has rid you of them. Just as many of your bravest men have been scarred battling for you, so my servant was scarred in battle for me, a battle she fought bravely, even though she must have known she might lose."

Keeping his eyes upon mine, he lifted his chin so high that he stared down at me as though he towered twenty cubits over me. There was great sadness upon his huge face. I imagined what I would tell Ruti of this moment if I saw her again. *It is hard to see a great king so sad — it feels as though the whole world must be sad.*

After a moment, he lowered his head again and said, "She will stay with you. But she will always wear a scarf that can be pulled up to shield our eyes from the sight of her."

"Thank you, my gentle and generous king." I fell again to my knees. I put my forehead upon the floor and stayed bowed before him while tears of relief pooled beneath my eyes. The crown was tightly fastened to my hair, and though I felt the pull of its weight, it did not slip.

"She will carry two daggers," he said. "One in a belt for all to see, and one in a sheath beneath her tunic."

Does he not have trained men to protect me? I looked up at him. "Very well, my king. And which soldiers will watch over your queen now that some have proven unworthy of the task?"

"Many of my men are not suited to palace life. They are not on their guard as they should be. They think their enemies will always wear the uniform of a foreign army. My finest soldier would not have allowed *any* man who came near your chambers to live. Not even one in the same saffron uniform that he wears. His arrows have landed in a hundred men's hearts — more perhaps, and I have seen him kill, with his bare hands, a Greek soldier a whole man larger than himself. He has held a fellow Immortal's hand to a flame for trying to keep the spoils of war for himself. He is more loyal to me than any dog to his master."

I dropped my eyes back to the floor so the king would not see me wince. I knew he spoke of Erez. Though I hated Erez, I also hated for him to be compared to a dog.

"He is training to battle once again for the empire," Xerxes continued. "But perhaps the true battle is here."

I felt a sudden ache in my palm where my scar had slowly pulled my flesh tight beneath the gold plate. I had lost the ability to move my right hand freely. When the plate was taken off at night it felt rigid and weak. I told myself that all my weakness was contained in my palm, leaving the rest of me strengthened for whatever sort of battle I must fight. Was the makeup of my escort a battle I should join? Was it worthy of whatever capital I had left with the king? My husband and a stranger. I looked back up at him. I did not have the right words, I had only the truth and it would not do: *Please do not send Erez to guard me. I loved him until I found out he was the one who tore me from my bed and forced me on the journey that ended here, with me becoming the hated queen of a weak man.*

Xerxes continued, "He will kill anyone foolish enough to stand against the empire, from outside, or from within."

Not me, but the empire. Soldiers did not belong to women, or children, or to the people who raised them. They did not belong even to themselves. A soldier belonged first to the king, then to the second highest-ranking man, then the third, then the fourth . . . Erez would always be the king's man, even if he did not like the king or the duties the king had given him. He would be the king's man because that is who he had trained to be since he was seven.

Even if I were not the queen or a girl of the harem, Erez would never have been mine.

"Return to your chambers," Xerxes ordered. "Your servant will be returned to you when my physician thinks it is time. I will carefully consider which soldiers will be entrusted with your safety, and if my finest will be among them."

CHAPTER THIRTY-ONE: THE QUEEN'S MEN

As I walked back to my chambers, a single thought walked with me:

I am going to die.

My feet dragged along the tile, growing heavier with each step.

I am going to die too soon.

I was unlike many in the palace. I was unlike Erez. I did not think of myself as the king's, or the empire's. Once my parents were killed I was my own. I remembered standing on the steps at the end of the march, wondering if anyone outside of the palace would ever see me again. I had known that however obscure and miserable my life was, still I would fight for it. And perhaps I had already known that I would need to.

I no longer had any reason not to fight. If I did nothing and allowed Parsha and the other soldiers to threaten and disrespect me, I would be killed. If I fought back they might kill me, or they might come to fear and respect me.

As I walked toward what was likely my death, I told myself that even if I failed in keeping assassins from my body my legacy was mine to make. I would take away the power of time to bury me. All I had to do was put my name upon peoples' tongues, a place from which Haman could not remove it by sending men with daggers through the dark.

I will not die before they kill me and when they do take my life they will do so with great shame.

I would no longer be critical of the king's desire to expand the empire. Whether it was right or wrong, I understood it. I would tell the Immortals I respected their valor, that if they killed me they were also killing a queen who wished to see them victorious. I would tell them I wanted for them what I wanted for myself: to be bigger than only my time upon the earth.

I would make them kill me or lay down their swords at my feet.

When we arrived at my chambers, I ordered the four men who were my temporary escort to walk with me into the Women's Court-yard. Once there I instructed them to take me east through the courtyards in the center of the palace — the Women's Courtyard, the inner courtyard, and the central courtyard. Surely they thought this strange, but they obeyed my commands.

Before we got to the outer courtyard, my escort slowed. We could hear soldiers training — clashing swords, an officer yelling commands, the whoosh of arrows.

One of the two guards who walked in front of me turned back. "Your Majesty, this is the military courtyard."

I narrowed my eyes at him. If he were to disrespect me by suggesting another route I would not make it easy for him.

"There is surely another way to get wherever we are going, Your Majesty."

We had walked all the way across the palace. There was no mistaking that this was our destination. "Do you wish to be dismissed so you can slink back to my chambers?" I asked.

"No, Your Maj—"

"Then you dare to suggest that the king would want the woman he has chosen from among hundreds to creep along the edges of the palace?"

His gaze dropped to the floor. "Your Majesty, please forgive me if I have given offense."

"I will forgive you. Once."

I checked to make sure my crown was still tightly fastened to my hair. *If someone wants it he will have to take my whole head.* I took a deep breath, pushed past the guard, and walked through the western entrance and into the noise of the military court.

It was a huge open courtyard, almost as large as the banquet hall. Hundreds of common soldiers were packed up against the northernmost wall, where they sharpened their spears and daggers and sparred lightly. Those were not the men I was concerned with. The Immortals, though there were fewer of them, were spread over most of the courtyard. Some practiced hand-to-hand combat, the others held bows with arrows pointed toward five huge bull's-eyes along the southern edge of the court. When a few of them noticed me in the entranceway, their arrows slackened in their bows. Two men turned and bowed to me, but they quickly stood again when they saw that no one else did the same. Not even the slaves lined up behind the Immortals bowed to me.

Only a few have noticed me, I could turn back now. My humiliation would be far less than if the whole court sees me and does not bow. But I could not turn back. This was likely to be my last chance to speak to them.

"Release," an officer cried from about eighty cubits to the right of me along the western wall. He stood beside the front row of archers.

A flock of arrows flew up with a *whoosh*. They hovered overhead for an instant, casting a shadow over the court. Then they fell as fast as stones. They made countless little thuds as they hit the targets on the southern wall, the wall I had started walking toward.

As my escort rushed to take up their places around me, Immortals looked to see what the commotion was. Some murmured as they watched me walk, but none bowed. The officer remained standing to the side of the first row of Immortals, directly in my path.

"Load." I recognized his voice. "Pull." It was that of the man most responsible for Yvrit's death. "Release!" he cried.

I walked toward Dalphon, fighting not to let each line of unbowed soldiers I walked past puncture my dignity more deeply than the last. My escort stopped when they reached him. He did not acknowledge us. "The queen," the guard who had suggested we take another route through the palace announced.

"The king surely does not want a woman

here," Dalphon said.

I moved to the front of my escort. "I am no mere woman. I am *queen.*"

"A queen does not interrupt the empire's most elite soldiers as they train to enlarge the kingdom," he said.

One of the archers called out, "Peasant for fourteen years, queen for a handful of days." His voice too was familiar.

"And no more!" someone called out.

"No more!" another man echoed.

I looked at the archers and saw Parsha sneering at me. I knew he had been the first to call out. I turned back toward Dalphon. He would not touch me in front of so many men. I walked past him toward the southern wall.

"*Load!*" Dalphon called from behind me.

My escort did not assume their places around me again. Perhaps Dalphon was not letting them pass. I did not check. I would appear weak if I looked back, and besides, I told myself, it did not matter if they were with me. *In fact, it is better that they are not.*

I passed all the men and moved into the empty space over which their arrows would fly. A space not meant for anyone except the slaves who would pull the Immortals' arrows from the targets and collect the fallen ones from the ground.

I was walking out in front of the hundreds of men in the military court.

"*Pull,*" Dalphon shouted.

I had almost reached the front southwestern corner of the court, where I would turn left so that I could walk east along the wall lined with targets.

"*Release,*" Dalphon ordered.

Whoosh.

The hall filled with the sound of vibrating bowstrings for an instant as the arrows hovered overhead. I braced myself for the sharp pierce of an arrowhead in my back. I suppressed the urge to cover my head or to glance up. I gazed instead upon the nearest target. I watched the arrows hit with quick, crisp thuds. I watched their tails quiver and go still.

I had not been hit.

The beat of my heart was so loud it provided a rhythm for me to march to. Every four beats of my heart equaled a step. *1-2-3-4 step. 1-2-3-4 step.* I continued until I reached the front southwestern corner of the court. I turned left, and began walking east along the wall lined with targets, the first of which was not more than twenty-five cubits away.

"Load . . . pull . . . *release!*" Dalphon said again, and again arrows rose up into

373

the air, blocking out the sun. While darkness hovered over the courtyard I prayed,
God please guide their arrows.

Again I was not hit.

I kept walking toward the first target.
When I was not more than six cubits from
it, once more Dalphon cried, "Load!"

Do not think, do not feel. Just keep going.

"Pull."

Time slowed. I tried not to think about
how long a man could hold an arrow pulled
in his bow before his arms began to tremble.
Still I could not help but watch them from
the corner of my eye. Arm muscles bulged
where sleeves had fallen back. *God, please
keep them strong, let their grasps upon their
bows not waver.*

My whole body was shaking now. But I
had to continue and so I did, holding my
breath as I walked in front of the first target.
I thought I could hear the men's arrows
quivering in their bows, but I did not allow
my pace to slow. I kept putting one foot in
front of the other until I reached the middle
target.

*God, harden my flesh so that nothing can
puncture it. Let nothing enter me from now on
but Your strength.*

"Release!"

This whoosh of arrows was not so great as

the others, it did not completely block out the sun. I closed my eyes. *I will not cower. If I die now I will be the Queen Who Died Bravely.* Air rushed across my face. I remembered Xerxes reaching out a hand so massive that I could see nothing else for an instant and then the rush of air against my lips as he tore my veil from my face to look at me for the first time. *Goodbye, my king.*

Three arrows thudded in quick succession, one on top of the other *thud thud thud.* Then there was only quivering — in front, behind, and above me. I waited for an arrow to enter my body. But the only movement was the quivering of the arrows that had hit the target around me.

I opened my eyes and reached for the end of an arrow's shaft not more than a cubit in front of my eyes. It went still as I wrapped my hand around it. I took a deep breath, pulled it from the target, and turned to face the men. Their arrows slackened in their bows and almost unanimously they lowered their arms.

I stepped out in front of the arrows around me. "I am your queen," I cried loudly enough for my voice to be heard throughout the hall.

Hundreds of unbowed soldiers stood before me. All except Parsha had lowered their arms, even the Immortals whose targets were fifty cubits to my right and left, but not a single one bowed.

"I am your queen," I cried again.

My voice echoed through the court so that I heard it even after I spoke. Some of the men shifted their weight uneasily, perhaps unsure if they should bow. They seemed to be looking around from the corners of their eyes, waiting for someone else to be the first. Soon the awe I had inspired would fade away. But whether they bowed or not, they would know my voice. I would give each man who would try to kill me, and especially the one who succeeded, a new name: *coward.*

"Last night, men no more skilled than boys and with not half so much honor killed six of you in order to break into my bed-chamber and take my life. They too were Immortals. My old faithful servant stopped them."

This did not seem to go over well with the Immortals. There was some muttering, and in some of their eyes I saw a deadening, a wall forming again between us. I knew I must make clear that I did not wish to insult any of them except the ones who wished me harm. But also I would not try to ap-pease them. I did not need their love. Their fear was enough.

"You cowards who want me dead, will you not kill me now?"

No one spoke but some of their eyes grew wider. I saw approval and even awe in some of them. The thing I most feared was no longer trapped in my head, the secret thought we all shared would no longer be the center of each silence. I let the silence enlarge my words until they filled the entire courtyard. I tried to breathe normally as I looked from one pair of eyes to another. I was certain that no man whose gaze locked for an instant with mine would find it easy to kill me.

I waited to speak again until I had given the men enough time to see that it was Dalphon and Parsha who I had fastened my gaze upon. "I was chosen by Xerxes, who was chosen by Ahura Mazda." I took my gaze from Dalphon's stony face and looked again at the other Immortals who stood unbowed before me. "You who will do the bidding of cowards and come to kill me in the night, you are thieves. The one you wish to steal from is none other than Ahura Mazda himself. Your true crime is not against me, or Xerxes. It is against god.

"So think before you choose who to ally yourself with: a man who hires others to do

what he knows he would be a fool to under-
take, or the most powerful man in the world
and the god who made him such. For those
who choose foolishly, the gallows will be a
relief that will not come as quickly as
desired. Ahura Mazda has put me here and
no man will suffer lightly for going against
him."

There was commotion along the western
wall where my guard was being held up by
Dalphon's refusal to step aside. My escort
pushed past Dalphon, and he stumbled
back against the western wall. No one
rushed to his aid.

"Even if you take my body you will not
take me from this palace. Ahura Mazda has
put me here and if you do not believe it,
then kill me now and watch how I will haunt
you."

Dalphon glared at me from eyes as narrow as his father's. I did not glare back.
Only those who are afraid of losing, or who
have lost already, narrow their eyes like that.

"Kill me!" I yelled. "Make me stronger.
Free my spirit to follow you through all your
days so I can rain upon all the happiness
you would ever have known. Free me — *take
away my limits!*"

I raised the arrow up over my head and
extended my arms out to include the whole

room. "Or greet me as your queen. It is not yet too late."

No one bowed but I did not lower my arms even though they shook slightly. I lifted my chin. I would not take back my call to them. I looked hardest at those Immortals in the first row who could not see that no one else bowed. They did not stand so tall as the others. I hoped they would bow beneath the weight of my gaze.

There was movement within the ranks as one Immortal pushed through the others and limped out in front of them.

Erez.

His face was black and blue, his ear mangled. His dark eyes stared into mine as though trying to tell me something. Perhaps the same thing he had said before pulling me from my bed, *Forgive me.*

He came to where I stood in front of the target. He knelt stiffly, setting his bow and arrow at my feet.

It hurt to look at Erez, but I did not look away. He knew that many of the men behind him would have been happy to put an arrow in his back, yet, still, he knelt before me.

The four men of my guard followed Erez's lead. They knelt where they were along the western wall of the courtyard, keeping their eyes upon the other soldiers, still on guard for me.

I stood tall and looked harder at the Immortals in the front line. I focused my gaze upon their faces as if memorizing each feature in order to tell the king.

They began to kneel — first one, then another, then many at once. Soon the entire first row of Immortals was kneeling, and then the Immortals in the second row, and the third, and the fourth. One after another, like a great wave. This sight was accompanied by a lovely sound that was so quiet I had to concentrate hard to hear it: bows and arrows being laid upon the ground.

Parsha did not kneel, and neither did the men around him. Dalphon, also, stood tall, and with his gaze kept some of the other Immortals from kneeling. I addressed the men around the brothers. "The king will need to know of this" — I moved my eyes over each man who still stood — "treason."

The word *treason* brought the men to their knees. Only Parsha and Dalphon still stood.

Soon the other men started to shift around, growing agitated at having to remain kneeling while the twins refused. For an instant I wondered if I should tell all the men to rise, as though Parsha and Dalphon were too unimportant to concern myself with, or if I should let them all wait while their resentment at the brothers grew. I waited. I wanted to see an entire room kneeling before me.

"Two men stand while all others kneel. Two men" — I pointed the arrow at Dalphon and Parsha, then made a sweeping motion across the room — "keep *hundreds* upon their knees."

There was grumbling from among the ranks of Immortals and even from the common soldiers. I was uncertain whether it was the brothers or me who caused the men to grumble, but I suspected it was not me.

I looked again at Dalphon and then at Parsha. Though they remained upright, they were silent. Perhaps afraid to say something blatantly treasonous. Their silence enlarged my courage.

God, thank You for not allowing me to back down.

Dalphon turned and walked from the court. Parsha stumbled through the men kneeling beside him and followed his brother from the court.

I addressed the men. "You are the best warriors in the world, and I will tell the king I have seen this for myself. You are the great king Xerxes' warriors. And now, mine as well. Rise."

The men — all of them — rose, armor clanking, and looked at me expectantly. I noticed Erez wince as he used his hand to help push himself to his feet. I could not dwell upon this. The men had just knelt for me, and surely this made them uncomfortable, and they wished for me to reassure them that I was worthy. I would give them what I had come to give them, enough of a story for them to fashion a legend from.

"I am not so unlike you. I too learned to live without parents too soon. Even while they lived, I woke up in a hut with no servant but myself, I used my hands for work. I slept sometimes with a belly that rumbled from hunger and went to market knowing I needed more than my sigloi could buy.

"Perhaps this is not what you wish to hear from a queen. I had hoped you would be happy to see a girl of humble origins ascend to the highest position in the world that a woman can occupy. But perhaps you do not want to give your lives for a woman who has been as lowly as some of you once were. Perhaps you want to fight for people who are closer to gods than men.

"And this you will do when you fight for me."

I walked toward them until I could clearly see their eyes and discern their lips through their beards, still I looked closer. I looked at their scars. One man was missing half of his nose, another was missing an eye. One man had a plate over his hand and I wondered how he could hold a bow. My gaze lingered on him a moment. Maybe I could hold a bow too.

"It is you who brought me to the king's harem, the place from which the king chose me. I did not want to be here any more than you wished for me to be. But now that I am here" — I looked at Erez — "I know it is where I belong. With your help, Ahura Mazda put me here."

That is as close as I would come to telling Erez I forgave him. His dark eyes had not always held the warmth for me that I wished for, but they had always held something better: strength. I saw that he wanted, just as badly as he had outside the king's bedchambers the first time I entered them, to give me that strength. I would show him that I was no longer a girl.

I did not falter as I said, "I am named after Ishtar: goddess of love, fertility, war, and sex. I am crafted in her image. My body is mortal, but my soul is invincible.

"As are yours. The sons of the empire,

including those I will bear soon, will know of your valor. Before mothers send them to their dreams each night, they will be reminded of your struggle at Thermopylae and how you triumphed. We will tell them of your valor at those Greek cities you have conquered and those you will conquer yet."

There were grunts of approval at my prophesying.

"You were born at this time and in the places you came from so you could be part of history. You will be written of in the hearts of maidens. Boys will dream of one day being like you. Elders will tell tales of you and scribes will capture them. You will live forever in the hearts, dreams, and scrolls of Persia. As long as men populate the earth, you shall live." I was speaking now as much to myself as to them. "You will never die."

A cheer went up from the men.

I looked at Erez. "You have shown yourself a leader of men here today, and the king will hear of it." I moved my gaze onto the men. "The king will also hear of the officer who committed treason by not bowing to his queen." I stared for a moment at the men who had stood around Parsha and Dalphon, the men who had been the last to kneel. "He will also hear of those who foolishly fired arrows while their immortal queen walked before them.

"This better man" — I pointed to Erez — "will command here today. Go back to preparing to enlarge the empire. The scribes will not wait for you to be victorious before they write history."

I was queen, I did not need to look to Erez for a response. But before I could stop them my eyes sought his. He bowed his head slightly, and then lifted it not as high as another man might have — not as high as Parsha, Dalphon, or their father — just so it was level with mine. "It is an honor, Your Majesty."

Even with a feeling of power still coursing through my veins at my seeming imperviousness to the men's arrows, I was not able to do all I wished. I could not say "thank you" aloud. I could not even look grateful.

I threw the arrow up into the air above the men with strength I had not known I possessed. The man who caught it kept it raised up above his head and cheered even louder than the others. I turned toward the southern exit. "My chambers," I said when my guard rushed up around me.

As I left the men, I felt the weight of my crown. But I also felt the strength of my neck, and the power of the men's awe. I would not have to support the crown's weight all on my own anymore. Hundreds of men would help to keep it balanced atop my head.

CHAPTER THIRTY-TWO: THE BROTHERS' BLOOD

It was not long after I returned to my chambers that the king called for me. I knew he must have spies, and I hoped it was these men, and not Dalphon or Parsha, who had told him of my visit to the military court.

I could not read his expression when I entered the throne room. His eyes were as wide as I had ever seen them. I was relieved that he no longer looked sad, but I did not like that Haman was the adviser who stood closest to him.

To everyone but me, the king said, "Leave us."

I had just stood between hundreds of men and the targets their arrows were trained upon. There at least I had been able to see where the danger might come from. I felt certain Haman had filled the king's ear with things that could do me as much harm as any arrow.

He did not leave, and I realized the king's

order had not included him. The adviser's face was red, though not red enough to hide tiny bright patches of crimson — hives.

"What urge is strong enough to propel a queen into a military court filled with armed men?" Xerxes asked.

"The urge to make you proud, my king. If I am to be assassinated, first I will show the men the full force of the little Ishtar you have chosen to be their queen. If assassins will not kill me there, if they must creep through the night" — I looked briefly at Haman — "then my death will be more of a defeat than a victory for them. The true victory, my king, shall be ours."

Haman's breathing was audible now, jagged.

"Why did you send Haman's sons from the court?"

"They would not kneel."

"You are not kneeling either."

I crossed the space between us and dropped to both knees. "I am always kneeling for you, my love. I am kneeling whenever we are in the same room, and every time you are mentioned, and whenever I think of you."

"Who is it that mentions me, and what is said?"

"I ask how to please you."

"You must not have asked if standing before my men would please me. You stood where a king would stand."

"I stood there for you, for your choice of queen. I stood there to honor and defend you, Your Majesty."

"You think I need to be defended from my own men?"

"From some of them."

"And which are these?"

I had already been bolder than Hegai would have liked, so I did not say what I wished to, *The one beside you and his sons, men you should not allow within striking distance of you.* Instead, I said, "I am not wise enough to know, my king."

"Rise," he said. Then, without taking his eyes from mine, he shouted to men I could not see, "Bring forth the traitors."

From behind a screen, four common soldiers dragged out two men naked but for the blood that coated most of their bodies. "When Haman heard of his sons' traitorous disobedience, he ordered that they be stripped of their uniforms and whipped."

Hegai had not lied when he said the hierarchy is a vine that grows thornier the higher you climb. Still it was hard to believe that Haman would sacrifice his own sons to gain influence with the king. I could not tell if they were alive. When Xerxes commanded the soldiers to release them, neither Dalphon nor Parsha reached out a hand to cushion his fall upon the tiles. Stripped of their differing spears, both wearing the same uniform of blood, I could not tell which was which.

"I left them alive so they would kneel before you as they should have done in the military court."

The king nodded to the soldiers, who began yelling at the brothers to rise onto their knees. When yelling did not move Dalphon and Parsha, the soldiers began kicking them. I knew the sound would haunt me even more than the image of blood and whatever else it was that flew from them as they were kicked with such force that they moved along the tile like sacks of grain. A couple of cubits, then a couple more . . . but not as far as I wished. I wanted them as far as possible from me.

I had not expected that I might someday feel pity for Haman, but I could not help it when I saw that though he tried to hold his face rigid, his lips twitched and then began to tremble. It was a more sorrowful sight than if a river had flowed from his eyes and pooled on the tiles upon which his sons lay barely alive.

Xerxes was watching me closely. I knew it was not because he flinched from the sight and smell of men dying. He watched for my reaction. I realized that without knowing it I had stepped back — partly away from the king and partly away from the beating, as though I could not decide which was the greater threat.

I remembered the story Ruti had told me of King Saul's mistake in leaving Haman's ancestor, the Amalekite king Agag, alive. I knew Ruti would say we must work to correct King Saul's mistake. But bile rose up into my throat. I could not pretend indifference any longer or I might lose the contents of my stomach. The soldiers would spread word of my weakness and the whole palace would be laughing at me before long.

"I have seen as much as I want to," I said.

The king held up his hand. The look in his eyes was cruel, satisfied. "Enough," he said to the soldiers. "We must keep them alive until they are well enough to kneel to their queen. Only then will I allow them the mercy of death." He turned to me. "When you are ready, little Ishtar, I will allow you to slit their throats, drive spears into their hearts, or kill them by whatever other means you would like."

I would like one that does not include me.

391

He ordered the soldiers to drag the brothers away. I wish I had not looked into Parsha's eye first. I knew it was his, perhaps because Parsha's was the first strange face I had seen after being taken from my bed. The centers of his eyes then had looked like perfect round drops of honey that had begun to melt in the sun. They had been beautiful. Now they were mostly hidden by swollen flesh. But yet I saw into the right one. It was trained upon my face with such intensity that I knew the life had not fled his body at all, it had all been concentrated in his hatred for me.

Haman was careful not to step in his sons' blood when he was dismissed. He did not allow himself to hurry from the room, as I am certain he would have liked. The king dismissed even the servants who had come to clean the floor. "Leave it," he told them, waving them away with a small movement of his massive arm. And then we were alone with the blood on the tiles.

The king seemed content to study me in silence. I did not know what to do. I wanted both for him to see me standing tall and for him to see me peeking up at him through my eyelashes. I could not do both. I stretched my spine and looked at my husband with all the strength I wished to give him.

"I still do not know who you are," he said.

"My king —"

"But I know that during our first night together, when I spoke of war, your flinch was sincere. You do not like bloodshed, and you did not misrepresent yourself to me. I am glad of this. I have enough trouble knowing who to trust, little queen, and trouble is one thing I do not need any more of."

If the brothers' beating had been a test for me, it seemed I had passed. Or perhaps Xerxes had paraded them in front of me so I might see that I was only a woman after all, not strong enough to watch men being beaten.

"I had a dream in which you were standing in front of a target in the military court. I thought it meant only that you would put yourself in danger, which I do not doubt you will do again if given the chance. And so I wonder, how shall I keep you safe, child?"

Had he truly had such a dream? I disliked that he had called me child.

"If you are not afraid to walk among men who wish you dead, and in fact you speak of death as a victory, perhaps the thing you do not fear is your own death. I hope seeing it up close has convinced you it is not as easy or graceful as it seems."

"I could not wait idly in my chambers. I cannot let the men who will try to kill me think they are anything but cowards. I had to show them my face and force them to hear my voice."

"You think very highly of courage, particularly your own. This is a dangerous attribute in a woman."

"Do not worry for me, my love. It does not matter how much courage I have — I do not want to die; I do not wish to leave you. But if I must, then at least I will leave you with a legend of me that will make you proud."

As soon as the words flew from my lips I knew they had been the wrong ones.

"Women are not made to *be* legends. They are made to *raise* them and then stand aside and hold back their tears when they are taken away. Women do not live on through legends, they live on through sons."

Perhaps he could see by my face that he had wounded me. His tone softened. "I have already lost a courageous queen, little Ishtar."

He spoke as though he had misplaced her. As though one day she was gone and he did

394

not know why. I looked down so he would not see my thoughts.

"And I do not wish to see another great queen's heart filled with sorrow."

Did he truly think me great? I looked up to see if he mocked me. "They say the arrows that would have hit you changed course at the last second, and instead formed the shape of a throne-back behind you. They say that you plucked the arrow that would have killed you out of the air."

Now that I knew he saw nothing wrong in testing me I also knew I must be careful. Was he trying to see if I would take the opportunity to be proud? I lowered my head and peeked at him through my eyelashes. "I wished to be a legend only if I could be nothing else, my king. I wanted you to remember me well, and for mention of me to bring you pride and happiness, so that I could be with you always."

He was looking at me too carefully. I wished I did not have to be on display. I remembered my parents, at ease in each other's company, laughing, leaning into each other, completely unguarded.

"Do you know what you are doing?" he asked. There was no hint of disapproval, anger, or awe. He truly wished to know.

And so, because I knew it would be unwise

to lie unless I could do so with complete confidence, I answered him truly, "Sometimes."

"You may have temporarily shamed our enemies out of attempting another attack upon you. Perhaps for a few days, perhaps a whole month. But we will be prepared in any case. Earlier today I wondered if my finest soldier should guard you, and now I see that he must. He was the first to lay his bow and arrow at your feet. He is not susceptible to bribes or flattery — I have checked — and he will not hesitate to do what is right, even if it means turning his back to a room full of men with arrows quivering in their bows."

I tried not to show any emotion and to keep my breath steady in case the king knew anything of my short history with Erez and was watching for some reaction.

"He will protect you not only from assassins," Xerxes continued, "but also from yourself. Erez would have made a good officer, but this task is more important. He will watch over the wildest and most valuable of all my possessions."

Why, if I hated Erez, did my heart drop all the way from my chest to my sandals for him? I did not know how he would endure being confined to the palace, where there was no real glory to be had, just a duty that would only be noticed if he failed in it and I was harmed.

"He or another of your guard will always enter a room before you, and check to make certain there is no danger within. You will never be unguarded, not even in your chambers." He leaned toward me. "Little queen, know that he is my most loyal servant and will do exactly as I command."

Erez would not only be relegated to palace life, he would have to perform a task not so unlike that of a common servant. It pained me to think of how Erez had told me he wished to be an officer, and I had told him he would make a good one.

"Right now I am having your chambers searched for hiding places and secret passageways. First by one set of soldiers, then another. If the first missed anything, they will each sway upon a gallows high enough for all to see. This is the fate of your two Immortal guards who were not killed in the attack upon you."

I sucked in my breath. I remembered Erez telling me: "It is the number ten thousand that is immortal, not any of us. As quick as a man dies, he is replaced." I now saw how true this was. *I am sorry, Erez. I did not wish this dangerous and inglorious task upon you.*

"My queen," Xerxes said. His eyes bored into mine. "You will never again enter the military court."

I hope I will never again need to. I did not like the way Xerxes so easily spent lives convincing me he would watch over me, but these killings were likely as close as I was going to get to a declaration of love from him.

"Yes, my king." That morning I had hoped he would embrace me. Now I wished only to be dismissed.

"I will send the new members of your escort to you after I have spoken to them myself."

"Thank you, Majesty."

"Never fear that we are apart, my queen. I am watching over you at every moment."

I did not bother to avoid the brothers' blood on the way out. I would track it through the palace, from the throne room to my chambers. A few servants would clean it, but all servants would spread word of it, perhaps they would weave an entire tale. Hopefully one in which I beat the brothers myself. A tale was, as Mordecai had told me, more important than what actually happened.

The king had said women leave their legacy in a son, but I would be a legend yet.

CHAPTER THIRTY-THREE:
THE KING'S SOLDIER

My chambers felt empty without Ruti. The musicians could not cover the great silence beneath their songs. The day after my trip into the military court I sent for my handmaids. When I heard high-pitched chatter outside my receiving room, I rose from my satin cushions and hurried past a servant to open the door. All six girls dropped to their knees so quickly it was as though they had fallen.

"Rise," I said to their bowed heads. They stood and looked back at me, but also, I noticed, they looked past me, at my new chambers. We had not seen each other since I had become queen.

"Come in and see how Ahura Mazda has rained his blessings down upon me."

As the girls passed near me I was overwhelmed by the scent of the harem: a combination of roses, cloves, and mimosa mixed with essence of musk, sandalwood, myrrh, and balsam. I remembered standing outside the harem for the first time, foolishly thinking that inside I would find safety. My own chamber smelled only of the fragrant cypress and fruit trees in the Women's Courtyard below my balcony, and the rosewater my servants bathed me in.

Utanah was still kept away from the harem, but she visited me with my other handmaidens. She stopped and smiled at me. "One of the four Immortals standing guard outside of your chambers is more handsome than any man I have seen." She reeked as though she had swum in wine. She quickly added, "Any man besides the king, of course."

I could not ask aloud if Erez was the Immortal she spoke of, but I hoped if I stared at her, the wine she had drunk would move her tongue.

"I did not mean to upset you, Your Majesty. His blackened eyes are a little frightening, but they do not hide his beauty. I am so excited you are queen that I cannot help but see the beauty of all that surrounds you."

"You have not upset me," I said, uncertain if this was true.

After the heavy wooden doors had closed, I could not keep from staring at them for a moment.

I did not turn back toward my chambers until I heard Utanah exclaim, "It is richer and more beautiful than a field of shaded grass." She had dropped to her knees again and was running her hands over the rug in my reception hall, her fingers stretched wide.

Even Opi, who had no trouble holding her wine, could not hide her awe. She stared at the silk curtains hanging from golden rods and at the griffins and other reliefs along the walls, before going out to the balcony to stand with the other girls admiring the courtyard below.

I called the girls in to show them my wardrobe. At first no one touched anything. Then Bhagwanti sneaked a quick caress of one of the scarves. "It matches your lips," I said. She jumped and seemed ready to plead for forgiveness. Now that I was queen there was no trace of the girl who had put me in my place by merely raising one eyebrow. Would I become like the king, so used to flattery and peoples' fear that anything else would appear strange?

Before Bhagwanti had a chance to speak, I said, "I would like you to have it." Then I called out loudly, so all could hear, "I would like each of you to have a scarf."

Their shyness fell away. They set upon my wardrobe so frantically I wondered if they feared I would change my mind.

When each of my handmaidens had found a scarf, I invited everyone to retire upon cushions in the receiving hall. I called upon the musicians to play for us. This time as I listened with my handmaids I did not hear the silence beneath the notes. The girls did not stop marveling at their new head scarves, sometimes calling out to each other over the music. I tried not to look at the door behind which Erez stood.

"R-R-Ruti . . . ," the handmaiden who stuttered asked.

"Ruti has saved my life. Unlike Crier she has survived it. She will return to me shortly."

The girls were happy to hear this, but their happiness faded when I asked about the harem.

"Halannah does not ease her attacks upon us," the girl who had first looked like a boy when she came to the harem said. "But at least we are no longer concerned that she will take something from us that we cannot get back."

"Does she ask of me?"

I studied each girl's face, wondering if Halannah had enlisted another spy among my handmaidens.

Only Opi spoke without hesitation. "She says you will not be queen for long. She was called in to the king last night."

I willed the flush of anger creeping up my neck to stop before reaching my face. Even as queen I was only one of hundreds of women who belonged to the king. I could quietly suffer the indignity of it if only Halannah was not the woman the king preferred.

I could not keep from asking, "And the night before that?"

"Another virgin," Opi said. "One who did not come back with even the jeweled veil she wore into his bedchamber."

"I heard she did not make it to his bedchamber," Bhagwanti said.

"The king did not wish to lie with her?" I was ashamed at having to ask my handmaidens for news of my husband, and for the hopefulness in my voice when I asked of another woman's misfortune.

"He did not want her in his bedchamber. He had her in his reception hall and quickly dismissed her."

While the musicians played I could not help thinking of Erez standing on the other side of the doors to my chambers. Not more than twenty cubits from me.

After a while I noticed Opi watching me stare at the doors. She smiled. "Your Highness, the guard outside your chambers looks like he has taken many blows protecting you, and yet he is still as pleasurable to look upon as a Greek god."

Every handmaiden's eyes were upon my face. "Is he the one who first laid his bow and arrow at your feet after you walked between the other archers' arrows?" Bhagwanti asked.

"I do not remember," I said. I was glad news of my journey into the military court was already spreading through the harem, but I did not wish to draw any more attention to Erez. I clapped my hands and called for the twenty jugglers I had arranged. The girls had seen jugglers before, but they had not seen so many at once, throwing torches high overhead and catching them in bare hands. I wanted to impress the girls with the spectacle. The jugglers spread out, throwing torches back and forth to each other. They began to fan around us.

Do they plan to throw fire over our heads?

I heard the girls shifting around on their cushions and the nervous laughter of the girl who stuttered. Utanah cried out in delight.

The jugglers were forming a circle around us.

The two Immortals who stood guard at the doors inside my chambers watched carefully. I hoped they were thinking of my safety, and therefore their own, but I would not wait for them. I stood. A torch flew not more than a couple of cubits above my head. I did not allow myself to cringe from the hot rush of air. "Thank you. You are dismissed."

The juggler who must have been the leader called out, "Hold in three!"

The youngest was not more than eight years old. The boy held his torches too soon, and then tried to catch the torch thrown to him. He caught the third torch against his chest and began screaming as the flame touched his chin. But he did not drop it.

As I went toward the boy to take one of the torches, I heard the doors to my chambers open and footsteps rushing up behind me. Arms wrapped around me and it was as though I were still the girl I had been over a year ago, struggling against an unseen Immortal. Now it was me who screamed.

"Forgive me, Your Majesty, the king has charged me with keeping you safe, against your will if necessary." Erez spoke quietly, but still I heard him. The boy dropped the torch. As Erez dragged me away I watched my rug catch fire.

He did not release me until we were in my wardrobe. I turned and raised my hand to slap him across the face. I saw the bruises already there and lowered my hand.

"How dare you drag me from my own reception hall in front of my handmaidens?"

"You can hit me if you wish, Your Majesty. But I will still have to do as the king has commanded." His eyes were calm, and the confidence with which he spoke enraged me.

"How does it appear for me to be hauled away from my own reception hall in front of my handmaidens, servants, and all of the palace jugglers?"

"It appears as though your safety is being tended to and you are alive. You will remain so as long as I watch over you, despite your best efforts to place yourself in harm's way."

"The king allows you to place your hands on me?"

"I am to do whatever is necessary to see to your safety."

"I must return to my reception hall and calm my handmaidens. They are surely horrified by this ridiculous, chaotic spectacle."

"Your Highness, they are being dismissed and your chamber cleared of all but your guard and servants."

"How can that be? By whose authority are they dismissed?"

"Your new head eunuch Hathach, who the king has instructed to always be at the ready to step in for you when you are ushered to safety."

For a moment I was speechless. "Am I a child? Did not you lay your bow and arrow at my feet only this very day?"

"When I laid my bow and arrow at your feet, I was seeking to protect you. That is what I am doing now. I have been instructed not to heed those of your commands which compromise your safety. In disobeying you, I am again laying all I have at your feet, my queen. There is only one thing I can do for you and I will do it with all my heart, and with my life if necessary."

His heart. Did he mean it the way I could not help but want him to? It was once what I had wanted more than anything, but it was no longer enough. "And what of respect? Is that not what I saw upon your face as you knelt? My servants' and handmaidens' respect for me is diminishing each second I remain hidden away like a coward."

I did not wait for an answer. I tried to walk around him, out of the wardrobe, but he blocked me. "We will wait here."

I would not beg or be gentle. I had said please when he had kidnapped me and it had not moved him. This time I did not have to say please. "Am I queen in name only? If my handmaidens do not see that I am unharmed and all is well, there will be much talk in the harem and servants quarters."

"Your Majesty, I take my orders from the king."

I lifted my left hand. He caught it against his face as I struck him. I felt his sharp cheekbone, the short hard hair where he was supposed to have a beard, his lips, and his hand pressing against mine. His cheeks were flushed with emotion as he moved my hand across his lips and then back onto the tender bruised skin of his cheek so that I was cradling it. This was, I realized, what I truly wished to do.

I could no longer maintain the anger that was shielding me from something worse: fear. I knew he was telling me something he could not say aloud. He cared for me as much as I had wished him to, except, because I cared for him too, I could not welcome his feelings. He might die from them, one way or another. And I had the girls of the harem and my people to think of.

He stepped closer to me, so close our bodies touched. My fears became more muddled and then faded altogether. I pressed my face against his neck. I wanted to kiss him and taste the salt on his skin.

One of the doors to my wardrobe began to open, and Erez released my hand. I stepped back and let out a breath I did not know I had been holding. The heat of his skin still warmed my palm. I made a tight fist around it. I wanted to keep something of him with me, and the heat, for however long it lasted, was all I could have. I was the king's.

Erez looked stricken. His confidence and calm had fled from him as easily as my fears had fled from me. We had made a mistake, one I hoped he would forgive himself for.

A voice came from the entrance to the wardrobe. The Immortal from my guard did not address me. "The queen's chambers are secure."

I walked past Erez. "Soldier!" I called.

"Yes, Your Majesty?"

"Next time you speak about me as though I am not here, I had better not be."

I ignored his stammered plea for forgiveness and went to kneel over my rug. How would Utanah describe it now? The richest red, the deepest green, the most majestic blue and gold, were interrupted by patches of black, and in one spot the rug had burned away completely leaving the tile visible.

Even as I stared at the rug it was not the reason for the ache in my chest. I could never have Erez, not as I wanted. *I must think of him no more.*

I wished Ruti were with me. I wanted to tell her of what had happened with the jugglers and how the eunuch Hathach's command would override mine if ever my life were thought to be in danger. I wanted to hold her hands and see her face. I missed her so badly it was as though she had been torn from my body.

Please, God, send her back to me. However mangled her face is, I will be happy to look upon it.

CHAPTER THIRTY-FOUR: RETURNS

Though I knelt upon the rug, when Hathach came to introduce himself to me, he managed to bow so deeply that his head was lower than mine. I could hardly bear to look at the eunuch who was going to be a constant reminder of the limits to my power.

"Your Majesty, shall I present the Immortals of your new guard?" he asked.

"No." I stood up and faced him. Or I would have had he stood to his full height. I could not clearly see his face. Ruddy patches on his otherwise fair cheeks caused me to wonder if he drank more than a man that small should. Over his stooped frame I could see that Erez had not left me in order to resume his post outside my chambers. He had recovered his composure and was waiting for his next order. I took my gaze from him.

"Have this rug removed, Hathach, and arrange for another."

"Shall I have several brought for you to choose from, Your Highness?"

"No." I was certain that no matter how many times I said "no" to this new eunuch it would never become any less satisfying. "I will have whichever is least likely to remind me of this one."

I did not want Hathach to witness any emotion that might come into my eyes when I looked at Erez. "You may both resume your duties," I said as I turned away.

Ruti still had not returned by that evening. I paced back and forth. Where was she? Could the physicians still be tending her? Or had the king changed his mind and assigned her some other duty in the palace?

The two guards who stood inside the door of my chamber did not move a hair in any direction, but I knew they were watching me. Would they tell the other Immortals how I paced, how I seemed agitated, uncertain?

Finally I could take it no more. I would send Hathach for word of Ruti. "Open the doors," I ordered the guards. Hathach was not outside my chambers. Perhaps he was still finding a new rug. Erez and another Immortal were standing guard on the right side of the doors, and without meaning to I looked directly into Erez's eyes. Because it would appear strange to remain silent, I stupidly asked, "Are you the new members of my escort, the ones the king has chosen for me?"

Erez and the other Immortal knelt. "Yes, Your Majesty," the man said, "the king has given us the great honor of serving you. We will protect you from any threat great or small."

"No threat is small. Can I truly trust you — trust your eyes, your daggers, trust each of your words — trust you with my life?" I was too full of emotion.

"Yes, Your Majesty," he said. "We will guard your life with our own."

"What is your name?"

"Jangi," he said.

I stepped closer, so I stood over him. "I want to see your face."

Though he was older than Erez, perhaps twenty-two or more, his eyes were younger. They were wide and clear and seemed, like a child's, to go directly into his thoughts. His face was nearly flat, like a platter upon which something was being offered to me.

"Thank you in advance for your service," I told them. "Your task will not be an easy one. Rise." Erez rose slowly, using a hand to help push himself to his feet. For an instant

413

I wished that I had waved away their obligation to kneel, as I had seen the king do once before. But I could not pass up any opportunity to make men lower themselves to the floor before me. Especially now that I knew the commands of my head eunuch took precedence over mine.

I did not know what to say to gracefully end our introduction. "Thank you," I said again. "Good night." I turned and walked back into my chambers without acknowledging the pair of Immortals who had dropped to their knees on the left side of the doors.

The two guards inside my chambers shut the doors behind me, and once more I was alone with people I did not trust. Unlike Erez, my guards and servants were always careful not to look directly at me. If we sometimes gazed into each other's eyes surely I would better know if I could trust each of them, but for the moment I was grateful for their show of respect. I did not want anyone to look into my eyes and know how frustrated I was.

When the eunuch who bore the wine approached, I waved him away before I could give in to my craving.

The next morning, as my servants bathed

and dressed me and as they applied my cosmetics, I thought of Erez so near, perhaps too near, and of Ruti, who was too far away. If she returned to me I did not ever again want her to be out of my sight.

When I walked into my reception hall, the same two new Immortals were still at the doors. Hathach had joined them. They knelt, leaving a woman standing by herself. A scarf circled the lower half of her face and was tied behind her hair. The slightly crooked bridge of her nose and hooded eyes were visible. I started to rush toward her but abruptly stopped. *You are queen,* she would chastise me later if I embraced her in front of anyone. She quickly knelt.

It is I who should kneel before you, I thought.

"Your Majesty," Hathach said, "the king is happy to return such a loyal and brave servant to his most treasured queen, and he requests the pleasure of your company this evening."

"Thank you. I cherish the great love my king bears me and I will have my servants prepare me so that I am as pleasing and beautiful as Ishtar herself. You are dismissed."

When I brought Ruti to sit with me upon my cushions, the other servants suddenly seemed too intent upon their tasks. Their interest was so rapt it was surely feigned. I waved away a servant who was plumping my cushions and had the servant who bore the wine taste it in front of us and leave it. "You are dismissed from my chambers until tonight."

Once they left, I considered the two Immortals at the door. "We must be within sight of my guards," I told Ruti quietly, "but we do not need to be so near that they can hear us."

I led her from my reception hall into my bedchamber. Her sandals whispered along the marble tile as she shuffled after me. When we were seated on my bed I looked at her. Her eyes were guarded. "The debt I owe you is greater than I can ever repay," I said. "But that will not stop me from trying."

"You owe me nothing, Your Majesty."

"I will not carry an unpaid debt upon my shoulders. I will find a way to set it down, one good deed at a time. Now tell me, are you badly harmed?"

No. She did not look me in the eye.

"I wish you would take your scarf off, at least for a moment. I want to hear your voice more clearly and see your face."

"You should not worry about my face."

"Every time I look at it I will be reminded of your loyalty." I leaned closer and Ruti's hand shot up to press the scarf more tightly to her face. She shifted away. "Forgive me," I said.

"You are always forgiven everything, my queen. You do not need to ask; to do so is beneath you."

I pulled the royal purple scarf from my head, causing the gold coins to rustle against each other, and held it out to her.

She looked away.

"All should see how loyalty is rewarded," I urged.

After a moment she turned her head back and looked at it. A little spark came into her eyes. "I will hold on to this scarf better than I held the assassin's dagger, Your Majesty." The silk caressed my fingertips as she gently pulled it from my hand.

She wandered to the far corner of the room and kept her back to me as she switched scarves.

When she turned around, the royal purple scarf was tied around her head and over the bottom of her face. Her spine was straighter as she came toward where I sat upon my bed. "Tell me, Your Majesty, everything I have missed. You are to be watched at all times?"

She has returned, body and spirit. I was so relieved that I almost forgot to answer her question. "Yes, I am to be watched each moment. The king thinks I am reckless."

"I have heard how you walked between the archers' arrows, plucking one from the air." I could not tell from her tone whether she approved of this. "Perhaps Xerxes wishes not only to look after your safety but also to remind you that you are not a king. However humble and grateful you appeared the last time you saw him, you must appear more so tonight. Then he will not have to teach you of your own unimportance. You must seem already to know it."

"Vashti was not humble."

"And where is she now?"

"In his thoughts sometimes when he looks at me."

"It is commonly believed that people can put whatever thoughts they would like in his head. It is why everyone wishes to be as close to him as possible." She still had not rejoined me on my bed. "It is you who decides what he will see when he looks at you. Surely you know this?" Her eyes narrowed slightly — so slightly I might not have noticed if not for the scarf, which covered most of the rest of her face, emphasizing the movements of her eyes. "Did you not convince the king to assign an injured soldier to your escort?"

I fought to keep my voice even. "No, of course not. He is the one who kidnapped me so that I was made to march here with the other girls. He is the one from my nightmares."

"It is better that soldier pulled you from your bed, than a soldier who would have done worse."

"I had vowed to find out which soldier kidnapped me and kill him."

"You were a girl when you made such a foolish vow. You have too many real enemies to concern yourself with men who follow orders."

"I know you speak true, Ruti. I am grateful for your counsel." Hoping I had convinced her that I had not asked for Erez to be among my guard, I returned to the topic of the king. "I will heed your advice tonight. The king will have the most humble girl in his empire."

"Then perhaps tomorrow *you* will have the future of the empire in your womb."

As my servants applied more kohl around my eyes, more pomegranate to my cheeks and lips, and more powder to my face, the butterflies fluttering in my stomach seemed to grow teeth. I remembered the night I had already spent with him and how he had not called me back for many nights since.

Though it was my face the cosmetics were being applied to, it was Ruti they seemed to bring to life. "It is good you are shaking slightly, Your Majesty. The king will like that you are afraid, and perhaps he will not take it upon himself to make you more so. Perhaps he will be gentler."

When I finally stood in front of the doors that led from my chambers, my face was a mask of cosmetics, my skin was soft and perfumed beneath the crimson gown I wore, and my crown was pinned so tightly to my head that it pulled upon the skin beside my eyes. Around my neck I wore the chain with the eight-pointed star of Ishtar that he had given me. The king had allowed me only one night in which to conceive a son so far. I could not afford to disappoint him. Because I wanted to be fully alert, I had not had even a drop of wine.

I nodded to my guards to open the doors and suddenly I was looking at Erez.

In the torchlight I could see the bruises on his face. Tender, angry bruises. Or perhaps I was seeing with too much emotion. He did not look at me directly, but I knew he looked at me nonetheless.

I did not give him or the other members of my escort any orders. The king had issued a command from afar that made anything I said inconsequential. As we made our way to the king's chambers, I was glad Erez could not see me staring at him, pretending he was the man with whom I would spend the night. I knew I should not imagine such things. I should think of nothing except putting one foot in front of the other and trying not to frown. If I thought of the king — would I do something to anger him, was he angry at me already, would he use this night to try to humble me so I would never again do something as bold as enter the military court — the corners of my mouth grew heavy.

All too soon we arrived at the chamber doors. Before anyone had even raised a fist to knock, the king said, "Send in my bride."

I did not allow myself to glance at Erez as I entered my husband's chambers.

CHAPTER THIRTY-FIVE: THE KING'S BED

The king, seeing how my hand shook, smiled. "My little bird has returned."

Though we were only in his reception hall, as soon as someone pulled the doors closed behind me, he yanked my robe from my body and pushed me down onto the rug. I landed hard, feeling the roughness of the wool against my backside. With his foot, he moved one of my knees away from the other. Even my legs were trembling now. *Think only of the son that you will make,* I told myself.

He stepped back and lifted his tunic over his head. A shoulder rippled with muscle as he tossed it aside.

I could not summon an image of a son or anything else to ease my mind while Xerxes loomed over me. I squeezed my eyes shut as he came close. Nothing happened. I peeked up and saw him staring down at me, waiting.

A sudden rush of anger made me brave or perhaps foolish. I reached for the chain around my neck and held the eight-pointed star of Ishtar that he had given me up toward him. "Must I witness a king taking me — his *queen* — on the floor as though I were a common harem girl? Is that what you wish for your Ishtar, mother of your future sons?"

I scrambled back away from him and stood up. Though I was careful to look only at his face, still I could not help but see his arousal.

He was not so careful with his own gaze. He looked at my neck, then the highest part of my chest, and then his eyes moved lower.

I did not allow myself to step back as he came toward me again. He bent and carefully collected me in his arms before rising to his full height. I liked being raised so high in the air.

"You are not common at all," he said as he brought me deeper into his chambers. He set me on his bed. "It is both what draws me to you and the reason I worry — I do not know what you will do next." The gentleness fell away from his voice. "But I do not plan to worry tonight. Unpin your crown."

With trembling hands I did as he commanded. He took the crown from me and placed it on the table beside the bed. Then he held his hand out for the pins. I hesitated. I did not want to hurt him. "I have stretched my hand wide so that the pins will not catch in my skin," he said. "Look." I did not really look. I was afraid of seeing his arousal again. I dropped the pins into his palm and he put them beside the crown.

He pushed me back. "I have never before wished that a girl would come to me without first being scrubbed in rosewater and covered in oil of myrrh. I want to know who you are beneath your robes and perfumes; I want to truly taste you." His breath was humid on my skin. He kissed the inside of my knee, a kiss that began as only the press of his lips against my flesh and became something more.

My fear was falling away, being replaced by something else. He made his way up my body, his breathing becoming heavier and his hands tightening on my legs. An inarticulate insistence arose within me, causing me to press my hips up against him.

"Now, my queen, you are ready."

This time was more pleasurable than the last. I heard moans that seemed as if they came from someone else — not a girl, but a woman. A queen.

I am queen. I am the wife of one ruler and will be the mother of another.

When we were done I did not stir from where I lay with my knees pulled into my chest. The king held a goblet of wine to my lips so that I would not have to move. With his other hand he lifted my head so I could drink. "Each time I see you I am more grateful to Ahura Mazda for delivering you to me."

He drank what remained in the goblet, kissed both my lips and the star of Ishtar that lay in a pool of sweat upon my neck, and then rolled gently onto his back, being careful not to disturb me. After a while he began to snore. Still I did not move. I lay with my knees pulled into my chest until I fell asleep, wondering if Erez had heard me moaning, and begging God to give me a son.

In the morning I pulled my knees back into my chest and squeezed them tightly together. When the king opened his eyes he smiled and I felt a slight flush come over me, but I did not move. As he continued to look at me the smile fell from his face. His gaze became as intent as it had been the night before. I moved my legs to make way for him and we embraced as though we had been waiting a long time to touch.

Afterward he refilled our goblets. I did not want wine, and I did not want to leave the king's chambers until as many people as possible had seen me in the king's bed. "Might I have some water, Your Majesty?"

He looked alarmed. "Are you ill?"

"No, I have just developed a particular thirst for it."

"Whatever you would like, my queen, it shall be granted you."

The king placed his own purple and white robe over me and called the attendants into his chambers. As the Immortals, eunuchs, serving women, musicians, dancers, and the girl with a fan of date palm leaves entered, I shifted my legs slightly to draw their eyes to me. I hoped they would all recognize that the robe that covered me was the king's.

When the servants approached us with trays of different breads and all variety and textures of sheep and goat cheeses, I looked to Xerxes. Would he hold my head and bring the food to my lips as he had done with the wine? After the tasters had sampled the food, juices, and wine, the king beckoned to a servant girl. Without further command she brought a goblet of pomegranate juice to his lips, and then a goblet of wine. Between sips she fed him dates from her own fingers. No words were spoken. I could see that this was not the first time she had fed the king. Perhaps he sometimes did the same things to her that he had done to me. In fact, he could have done these things not just to her but to any other woman in this palace or his other three.

I straightened my legs as inconspicuously as I could and sat up slightly so I could eat. I tried to look as though I did not care that the king was being touched by another girl in front of me.

After the servant who bore the wine refilled the king's goblet, the king said, "My queen requires only water."

The attendants looked around. There was only one source of water, the heated water that filled the golden basin. One of the servant women started to move toward it.

"Do you think my queen drinks bath-water?"

The woman turned to the king and bowed her head so low it was as though the apology she stammered was incredibly heavy and would not come loose from her mouth. I had wanted the king to dote on me in front of his attendants, but not at their expense.

"Majesty," I whispered, squeezing my thighs together in an attempt not to lose the king's seed as I rose up to put my lips near his ear, "I would be honored to drink some of the very same water that will be used to cleanse your splendid flesh."

Without looking at me, he said to the servant, "You are lucky for my queen's compassion."

This time he did not ask me to bathe for him. He told me to return to my chambers and my servant's herbs. He kissed me goodbye and then pulled back to look at me. He was breathing rapidly. Abruptly he turned to the attendants and announced, "You are dismissed." When a servant began to wheel the basin out the king said, "Leave everything you cannot quickly bring with you. Wait outside."

We coupled once more. I knew I would be thinking of the king the next day, and perhaps for days to come. I would be thinking of him while over and over I begged God: *a son. Please. A son.*

The king's kiss goodbye did not leave me wondering if it would be long before he called for me again. He did not want to take his lips from mine. I hoped he was going to send the attendants away again. Instead he took a deep breath and released me.

The last touch I received from him that morning was his hand upon my stomach. He could reach all the way across the front of my body, his thumb easily touching one hip bone and his little finger the other. I thought, *We will fill this space.*

As I stepped from the king's chambers, I both prepared to see Erez and willed my body to pull the king's seed as deep as possible. So deep no one could ever again imply that I was not a true queen. Not without losing his life.

CHAPTER THIRTY-SIX: TRAPPED

Erez's jaw was so tight that I was afraid he had heard me moaning. He turned away from me. Fearing that he might begin to walk before I gave the command, I quickly said, "My chambers."

We moved through the greatest palace in the world as we would do many mornings in the coming months, without seeming to notice any of the treasures that surrounded us. Of all the things I pretended not to care about, Erez was the one that took the most effort. I knew I would walk behind him as often as the king called for me and as often as he sent me away. And yet I could not help studying him as intently as though I might never see him again.

Though he had not gone through a year of purification as I had, the palace had cleaned him just as thoroughly. More perhaps. He had been a true soldier, most comfortable with a cloak of desert dust. The bright saffron of his tunic was no longer dulled by a thin layer of grime, nor the bottoms of his legs by a thick layer. The muscles of his calves no longer looked like little boulders, as they had when I first saw him lashing the waterskin to the saddle of his horse.

Because of his honor, and because of me, he was trapped inside the massive walls of the palace for as long as the king desired. Perhaps he would not get to see any more of the world. I remembered what he had said on the march when I told him that it did not look like herding girls was all he did: "I have not trained to be an Immortal since I was seven for *this.*"

I am sorry that my life has suddenly become so much more valuable than yours. I am beginning a new life, and you will have to watch it getting bigger while your own shrinks.

When we arrived at my chambers and the two Immortals standing guard opened the doors, Erez moved to go first and inspect them.

"No," I said. *I need you.* "Jangi, it is your duty from now on to inspect my chambers before I enter them." If someone was to die inspecting my chambers, I was determined it would not be Erez.

Erez looked at me only briefly before

averting his gaze when I looked back at him. I did not know what he was thinking. Perhaps that we should be careful, even with our eyes.

When Jangi came out and reported that it was safe for me to enter, Erez stepped aside to let me pass. I walked slowly, silently finishing my apology: *And I am most sorry I can never tell you I am sorry.*

CHAPTER THIRTY-SEVEN: THE ROUTINE

We fell into a rhythm. It began in my body. Men moved through the palace, taking me to the king, or stayed stationed around my chambers, because I did or did not bleed.

Ruti, my guard, and I — all of us — seemed in league, as though we were all trying to make a son.

The routine was the same each month: one, I stop bleeding. Two, I am bathed. Three, I receive perfume treatments. Four, cosmetics are applied to my face. Five, I order my escort to take me to the king. Six, I spend the night with the king. Seven, I order my escort to return me to my chambers. Eight, I do not want to bleed.

But I do.

"Do not count the days, Your Majesty. It will fill you with worry and you cannot conceive when you are already full. You must make room for something else inside yourself."

"But we must know —"

"Do not count, let me." Her voice was clear, even with the scarf she wore over most of her face. "Time moves faster as you get older, and I am so old that you will conceive in what seems only the blink of an eye to me."

"Thank you," I said. But I could not stop. Not while I was bathed, not while I ate, not while I read, not even while I slept.

During the third cycle of the routine, a few days after I had stopped bleeding and had spent the night with the king, he said, "Sometimes, upon parting, you seem so full of anticipation that I wonder if you have taken another lover and are going to meet him."

My heart began to race. If I often appeared more eager to leave than I should have, it was because I did not like seeing Xerxes eat fruit from the fingers of other women and because I wanted to see Erez. "Your Majesty, no woman could want for another man after being with you. I am only eager for the herbs Ruti gives me, which might hasten the gift I want to give you. A son who will be as big and powerful as his father, and as worshipful of him as I am."

He looked carefully at me for a moment. Then he said, "Hathach, the servant I have assigned you, is my most faithful eunuch. There are few men I trust as much as a eunuch. My wise grandfather Cyrus understood their value and made great use of them during his reign.

"Cyrus died twelve years before I was born, but first he passed along his wisdom about eunuchs to my father, and my father passed it on to me. People are most vulnerable to attack when going about the simple tasks of daily life — eating, drinking, washing, sleeping — and this is why eunuchs are ideal servants. Who else do they have to be loyal to besides their masters? A man who has a wife and children will love them more than all others. A woman or girl, especially, is prone to love — love for a husband, for mothers and fathers, for children. But a eunuch is dependent upon and indebted to his masters, because most men — even a eunuch's own family — will consider him a shameful creature. A eunuch will be beaten, or worse, if caught alone. A eunuch needs protection and will pay his master with unwavering devotion." Xerxes nonchalantly ran his hand over his rings. "He will not fall prey to a bribe. He will see to his king's safety and do anything his king asks of him.

"And this is not the only benefit. A eunuch thinks more clearly than a man, because a man may lust for women or a crown. A eunuch can have neither. He can have only his position, and therefore all his thoughts are upon the same goal: pleasing his master."

I understood the king's warning. The eunuch had been assigned to watch me. Still, I said, "Thank you, my generous husband, for giving me your most trusted servant. I will make good use of him."

I had assigned Hathach to stand outside the doors to the reception hall so he could announce visitors. When I returned to my chambers he bowed to me as I walked past him. *Does he truly have nothing else in all the world but his service to the king? And does aligning himself with the king mean he has aligned himself against me?* I would tell him nothing I did not also want the king to know.

Both my head and heart were heavy. I hoped Hegai and Ruti had chosen wisely in aligning themselves with me. It was not only for myself that I wished to conceive a son. It was for them, and also, strangely, for Erez. He had risked his life to kneel before me in the military court; he would rise or fall with me.

■ ■ ■ ■

All of us continued carefully going through the routine determined by my body, as if the routine itself was our purpose. But really, we were waiting. Our destinies hung upon my womb.

The routine repeated itself four times. Then, one day, I woke up with Ruti staring down into my face. "It has been —"

"A whole month," I said. I sat up as though the new life propelled me. The servant who bore the pitcher of water I requested each morning hurried toward me.

"Careful!" Ruti said, putting her hand on my shoulder and urging me to lay back. "You must be careful not to move too quickly."

There was still water in my goblet from the night before, so I gently waved the servant away.

"Do not drink from anything that has not been tasted," Ruti said.

"He tasted it last night, as did I." As soon as the words left my mouth I realized how foolish it was to have waved the servant away. "But I have not watched it each moment since." I called to him, "Servant!" I had been advised never to learn this eunuch's name and to look only closely enough at him to know if someone else was sent in his place. I watched as he poured some of the water into a goblet and drank it. Though I was thirsty, I had the eunuch stand at the other end of my chambers while Ruti and I talked. I would not drink until I was certain he would not be sick.

"From now on, you must be gentle and happy and move slowly," Ruti said. "This is your only care, but do not let it be a care. Do not think on it too much." She put her hand on my stomach. "And do not tell anyone but the king. You must tell him or he will continue trying to plant his seed, damaging the seed he has planted already."

I remembered what Hegai had once told me: "Do not tell anyone what you plan to do, that way they cannot stop you." I would guard my belly, my future, and my heir by guarding my tongue. I finally called for the eunuch to bring me a goblet of water and then I dismissed him. "I am going to have the king's child, Ruti. The king's, and ours."

I often lay with my left hand upon my stomach, hoping the life inside me would reach up and move against my palm, reassure me that I was truly carrying a child. One day I asked Ruti, "Should I feel something?" I only saw the cruelty of my question after it had escaped my lips. She had never carried a child in her belly, or, if she had, she never mentioned it.

She came closer to where I lay upon my bed. I could not tell from her eyes whether I had hurt her. "I have heard that many women do not feel anything within their wombs until they get sick, Your Majesty."

"I am sick with hope, Ruti. I want to feel this child inside me and I want to do all I can for him. I will not allow any harm to come to our child."

CHAPTER THIRTY-EIGHT: DAGGER TRAINING

"Do you know how to use your daggers?" I asked Ruti the next day.

She was bathing me and she did not look up or take the cloth from my leg. "Yes. Plunge them into anyone who tries to harm you. I am old, but not so old I cannot thrust a dagger all the way through a man's back, into his heart."

I laughed. "I am glad you are a soldier in my army and not my enemy's. But me. Should not I also have a dagger?"

"Two. You should have as many daggers as you have hands. But also, you must be taught how to use them to defend yourself. When I defended you, I attacked someone who was rushing past me. Next time I will better know where to stab a man who, because he must go about his work in silence, is not wearing armor. My blade will enter his side and slide into his ribs. He will be dead before he even comes close to you.

You though must know how to stab someone who is rushing toward you. That is different, and I cannot teach you how to do
it."

"There is someone here who could teach
me." Erez and I had not come close since
we had stood together in my wardrobe
months before. I was confident we would
not give in to foolishness again. I had too
much to lose.

She looked sharply at me. "We must make
certain your training does not bring about
something even more dangerous than that
which you are training to defend against."

When my cosmetics were like a mask
upon my face and I was dressed in my most
commanding crimson robe, I had Erez and
Jangi called in from where they were posted
outside the doors.

Erez entered my chambers stiffly, perhaps
tired from standing for so long. As hard as
it was for me to rest, it must have been as
hard for him to spend his days and sometimes nights standing in one place when he
had spent his life traveling the empire. I was
happy to provide him a break from his
routine.

I dismissed all but Erez, Jangi, and Ruti.
Ruti was giving me such a foul look that I
could hear it as clearly as though it were

words: *Do not make it easier for people to spread lies about you. Especially the most dangerous lies — those with tiny pieces of truth inside them.*

"I know that I have the best guard around me" — I moved my gaze over all three of them — "and I would like to be part of it." I looked at Erez. "I must be trained in the use of a dagger."

Color drained from his face so quickly that I suspected I was not the only one who had nightmares about the night he kidnapped me. What in particular haunted him? Being bitten, my cry, how he had ignored my pleas, how he had dragged me toward the other girls' cries — one of his arms around my ribs and elbows, the other around my neck?

"Jangi, you will remain at the door." I could see by the slight rise of his cheeks that he was flattered I had addressed him by name. "With Ruti."

I walked toward the screen behind which musicians sometimes played and Erez followed. "Have you already forgotten that using a dagger is not as easy as it looks, Your Majesty?" he asked quietly.

Do not use that night when I was still a girl against me. I had not forgotten how I slipped the dagger from his belt and tried

442

to plunge it up the inside of his tunic sleeve and how it had been no match for his flesh. I had not forgotten how it had flown from my hand as if he had knocked it away.

I did not answer. When we were safely behind the screen I turned to face him. His eyes looked dry and tired. This did not make him any less beautiful. He had been standing guard for me a long time, and unlike other guards, he never closed his eyes.

"You would be better off if your plan was to stay as far from any danger as possible," he said.

My feelings for him did not dampen my anger. Rather, they seemed to increase it. "As *you* especially know, danger has always come to me."

He winced. "Will you be forever angry? Angry because you wanted me to care for you before I had a chance to, while you were just a shape in the dark — a tiny part of a task I was carrying out for the king? Can you not see that it is too late to change that?"

"My anger comes and goes with my nightmares. But my concern is no longer only for myself. You must have noticed that we have not gone to the king's chambers in over a month."

"Congratulations." Was he thinking of

those children he might have somewhere far away, and those that may have been flushed from their mothers' wombs with herbs or worse? Or was he thinking of me lying with the king?

The plate over my right palm had weakened my hand and made it difficult to reach into the leather pouch sewn inside my robe. I knew Erez was too good a soldier not to notice both the awkwardness of my movement and my slight fluster, but he did not comment upon them. "Is it better for men to know I carry this," I asked, "or should I keep it in the pocket sewn into the sleeve of my robe?"

"If they want to kill you the sight of it will not stop them. It will only make them prepare more carefully."

He stood as far from me as he could without leaving the area behind the screen. He seemed to enjoy our training even less than standing like a statue outside my doors. If he were not bound to do as I said, I was certain that he would exit my chambers as fast as his stiff legs could carry him.

"Your Highness, you will not help yourself this way."

"Not until you help me will I be able to help myself. We both witnessed all I know of using a dagger."

"Your teeth served you better."

"They did not serve me well enough, or I would not be standing here. Do not argue with me any longer. I do not *ask* for your help, I *command* it."

"Very well. Please sheathe the dagger, Your Majesty."

I slid it back in. Before I could fully withdraw my hand from the sleeve of my gown, Erez said, "No, that is not necessary."

I looked at him. Did he think telling me to sheathe the dagger would be the end of our lesson? "We are not done."

"No, we are not," he agreed. "Unsheathe it."

I had not even tightened my grip on the dagger in order to pull it from my sleeve when a shadow fell upon me. Suddenly dust, horses, and the cries of a hundred girls surrounded me. Though it was hard to speak with the dust rising off the road, I could not stop the pleas from flooding out my mouth and onto my lips. *Please, please, ple—*

"Esther! It is only me." He stepped back. He had my dagger in his hand and he held it away from us. His dark eyes were full of concern; he leaned his head forward slightly so they were more level with mine. "You are safe. We are in the palace in which you are queen."

I took a jagged breath. "Yes, it was 'only you,' *again*. Being attacked without warning once was one time too many. I did not think it was an offense you would want to repeat. I wish my hands were not trembling so I could slap you."

"If there is a dagger in your hand, your hand will be a target. I needed to show you this."

"You could have told me instead."

He opened his mouth and then seemed to decide against whatever he was going to say. "Forgive me," he said.

"That is the sound you make that I like least."

"Esther," he said so quietly that at first I did not know if I had heard him or read his lips, "I have done terrible things, things for which I do not know if I can ever forgive myself. But this is not one of them. I have been assigned to protect you. I knew no better way to show you that you should not carry a dagger, than to wrest it from you. Let nothing — no imagined defense and no sharp words — stop you from running away. If any man makes it past me, a woman with a dagger will be no match for him." He held it out to me.

I did not take it. "Kneel."

There was a cracking sound as he bent his knee to place it upon the tile. I pushed away any sympathy I felt for him. Keeping my right hand behind my back so he would not see the plate more clearly than I wished him to, I got as close as I could without touching him. Half a step more and his head would be against my stomach; but he did not lean away.

I took a long breath. I inhaled so deeply my lungs pressed against my ribs. He did not smell like the road. He did not smell like he had labored beneath the sun. He did not smell of old stale sweat, and he did not even smell of the sweat that shone upon his brow. He did not smell like a soldier but he withstood my anger with the calm strength of one. "Look up."

His gaze was steady as he did as I commanded. Though he was on his knee before me, and though he had not been able to hide his feelings for me when we embraced in my wardrobe, he was not at my mercy. He had only one master: duty. This angered me more than his reticence to teach me to handle a dagger. "I have heard all you have said to caution me. You do not need to say it again."

"Yes, Your Majesty."

I could not help but think that his dark eyes were even more beautiful against the purple hollows beneath them.

"The dagger," I said. His knuckles lightly brushed my leg as he handed it up to me. I grasped the handle, but he did not release it. I tried to breathe steadily and not shake as we just barely touched. When he let go I stepped back.

"Now stand and do as I have commanded: instruct me in how to defend the king's heir with a dagger."

He rose stiffly to his feet and once again it was me who had to look up.

"Your Majesty, your eyes are your most important weapon. You must always see the danger before it is on top of you."

Heat flared in my chest. "I did not imagine you would pounce upon me." I lowered my voice. "What if an informant were to tell the king?"

"The king assigned me to protect you. I must carry out my duty, even if one day he decides to put me upon the gallows for it."

"Do not assault me physically and then assault me again with the image of you swaying upon the gallows."

"I am ready for whatever is coming. I see the danger all around me and I know there are many ways someone could attack me. I fear you do not. You must learn to see more clearly or you will not have time to draw your dagger. Do not look only to where you expect the danger to come from; danger that comes from where you expect it is hardly danger. True danger is that which you cannot see coming."

Now there was enough sweat upon his brow that a bead formed and began to roll down his face. I suppressed the urge to wipe it away before it ran into his eye. He shook his head slightly, sending it toward the side of his face. "When the only weapon you think you have is a dagger," he said, "I fear you will only see danger that can be met with a blade."

"I did not ask for a lecture. Is your memory so short that already you have forgotten what I have commanded you to do?"

"Do you see how you are holding the dagger, Your Majesty?"

I was holding it in my left hand because it was uncomfortable to hold it against the plate over my right one. The dagger pointed from the little-finger side of my hand.

"I am holding it so that I can bring the back of it up against my shoulder and stab a man in the face."

"You have little leverage or reach in that position. Hold it so the point comes from the front of your hand. Stab any man who comes close. This may not kill him, but it will weaken him so you can do the safest thing of all — run away.

"Please sheathe your dagger again, Majesty. I will not touch you this time. I will tell you I am going to approach, and then you will try to draw your dagger before I reach you."

My hand shook as I sheathed the dagger. Perhaps this is what caused Erez to stare more closely at the plate over my palm. "Forget all I have said, Your Highness. There is no need for you to sheathe anything, and there will be no need for you to draw a weapon when you could carry one in your hand. One you would not even need to hold on to."

"I thought of having a small blade affixed to the center of the plate, but I use this hand just as I use the other. I do not want to leave a trail of blood every time I scratch my nose or reach to brush a stray hair out of my eyes."

"You will quickly learn not to do those things. The blade will help you to remember that you must always be ready. That may be its true value."

"I take it off at night."

"But I do not set down my weapons,

Majesty."

I felt tears forming in the corners of my eyes. I put the dagger upon the floor, then stood and extended my right palm. I could not keep from holding out that ugly, secret part of myself to him. If he gazed upon it without flinching, and if he looked at me the same afterward, then I would know he loved me.

He came close enough to cradle my hand in one of his own. With the fingers of his other hand he pressed my fingers back to better expose the plate. It felt as though a flame was creeping up my neck, into my cheeks. "There is plenty of room, perhaps even room enough for some sort of hinge, so that the blade can be safely tucked against the plate until you want to open it. But these chains will have to be tightened if you are to have a steady blade. Do they hurt?" He pushed one aside and gently moved his fingertip over the chapped skin beneath it. I almost began to cry from the pleasure.

"I caught Halannah's knife in my flesh."

He looked into my eyes. "I am glad you did, Majesty. But why is there no cloth beneath the plate to comfort your palm?"

"Because the plate is *jewelry.*"

He gently let go of my hand. I left it palm

up to him for a breath, as though he might take it again.

"Perhaps it is time for you to start a new fashion."

As I lowered my hand I did not allow any expression to come over my face. Not one of relief, nor sadness, nor longing. "I do not want to draw attention to this flaw or any other."

"Flaw? No one trusts a soldier without scars. No one wants to stand by him in battle for fear he cares more for his skin than anyone else's."

I could not keep my gaze from his arm. Though I could not see the teeth marks, I knew they were there. It gave me more satisfaction than it should have that one of his scars was from me. Without meaning to, I had marked him.

"It is different for men," I said. "In the harem women are sent to the soldiers for less."

"You are no longer in the harem, Your Majesty. And the king did not choose you because you are without flaws. He chose you because you are alive in a way the other girls are not."

I was so stunned by his words that I could not speak. He turned his attention back to the plate.

"If it hurts as much as I imagine, Your Majesty, you endure pain as well as a soldier. But you blush like a girl."

Something fell loudly upon the tiles and I turned to find Ruti standing unbent over a pitcher that lay on its side at her feet. "Your *Majesty,*" she said, as though reminding me of something I had forgotten.

"My training is done for the day," I told her. I turned slightly in Erez's direction and without looking at him, said, "Thank you. That is all."

"Send one of the servants to fetch Hegai," I told Ruti in a tone meant to convey that it did not matter whether she approved of anything I did.

"I hope he can help, Your Highness." She gave me a meaningful look before going to order one of the servants outside to summon Hegai.

CHAPTER THIRTY-NINE: HERE LIES THE EMPIRE

When Hegai arrived I drew him deep into my chambers where the guards could not overhear us. He gazed at me with such fervent adulation that I did something a queen should never do. I took a step back. He dropped to his knees. "My Queen, Great Ishtar. You are so beautiful to me now in the bright flush of full womanhood that I would be content to kneel here gazing upon your splendor for whatever remains of my little life. You are like a great bird who has finally mastered the wind. You are —"

Fearing he would profess his love for me if I allowed him to continue, I interrupted, "I am not yours."

He did not bristle at having to apologize the way he once would have. "Please forgive me, Your Majesty," he said. "I am only happy to think of all the good you can do now that you have proven that you are indeed Ishtar. If you can cause arrows to alter their course, and compel men to lay down their bows at your feet, then surely now you can have Halannah removed from the harem."

I was relieved; he had most likely exaggerated his adulation to convince me of my powers so that I might do as he wished. I placed my hand upon my belly. "I have not gone to see the king for over three months and I hope I will not be called to his bed for at least six more."

"Then you will rise even higher in his esteem. You will rule beside him." His face took on the sternness I had grown used to shortly after arriving in the harem. "*If* you give birth to a son and can keep him alive."

"It is a relief that you have not changed," I said, "except that your words cause something within me to clench." I hoped it was not the life in my belly. I wanted to shield my child from any knowledge that he was in danger for as long as possible.

"If I have given offense it is only that I have thought of you so often and seen you so little that I do not yet know if I am dreaming or if it is really you who is before me."

"It is you who is before me."

"Of course, Your Majesty."

I walked over to where he knelt. "Put your

hand on my stomach." A tiny piece of ruthless, unbridled greed from the king seemed to have entered me with his seed. "Here lies the empire."

"Your dreams have enlarged, Your Majesty."

"Yes, use both hands." I pressed them gently to my stomach. "There is some of the king inside me now."

"Be careful. I was once a man, and his desires have not left me."

I let go of his hands. He took them from my body carefully, making sure not to touch any other part of me.

"Do not let your dreams get so big that you do not see what is around you, Your Highness. You must be awake to defend yourself. Your fate wrestles inside you now."

"That is why I am going to carry a blade in the center of my right hand, a blade I do not have to hold. Hopefully a hinge can fasten it against the plate until I need to defend myself."

"I will take care of this. I am happy to see that I do not need to worry for you as much as I do."

"Do not completely abandon your worry. I would miss it." His eyes lit up as though I had given him something precious. "Have you heard anything in the harem?"

"Halannah is not happy about her cousins' beatings and confinement. But she is also somewhat checked."

"Checked in her behavior or her schemes?"

"Her schemes cannot be checked. But she has fewer willing allies since you walked unharmed through the military court and the king had Dalphon and Parsha beaten for not bowing to you."

"When I last saw Utanah she was overfull with wine. I cannot tell if she is truly happy. How does she fare wherever you are keeping her?"

"Neither so poorly nor so well that I am concerned."

"And her sister? Has her back been decorated like Utanah's?"

"No, Your Majesty. I assure you, if she has any injuries they are not where anyone can see them."

"You have a strange way of trying to reassure me."

"Perhaps you will better like what I have to say next. I have seen to it that the tale of your immortality, and of Dalphon's and Parsha's treason and subsequent downfall, was passed round and round the harem until it was so vivid women were talking about it as though they had witnessed it themselves."

"Thank you, Hegai. When I see the king again" — I touched my stomach — "hopefully I will be in a position to ask for the sun, the moon, and all the stars."

"He may now think Halannah one of the brightest of them, but her light will dim beside the mother of his heir."

When he left with the plate I felt naked. I had always taken it off at night, but it had never been out of reach. I became aware of my heartbeat, my breathing, and a tremor that was fighting to overtake my body.

"Do you need anything, Your Highness?" Ruti asked before I retired.

I had the urge to call Erez back in from where he stood guard outside my chambers and order him to stand watch directly over me and my child. But I knew that after the suspicion I had already raised that day, he could not be the closest guard to me for some time to come.

"No," I said lying on my back and wrapping my hands around my stomach, "this is all I need."

CHAPTER FORTY:
THE PLOT ON THE KING'S LIFE

Four months after I had conceived I awoke to Ruti shaking me. "You have a visitor."

I did not ask who visited in the dead of night. Hegai might once have had the audacity to call upon me at such a time for a matter less pressing than life or death, but no longer. Whoever stood outside my chamber was going to tell me of something too dangerous to keep secret until morning.

I often felt sick when I awoke, but my body seemed to know there was not time for me to kneel over a chamber pot. When I rushed into my reception hall I was startled to see that the visitor had not been made to wait outside. He stood just inside the entrance to my chambers with a mantle covering his head and torso. I could see by the slight rise and fall of the mantle that he was breathing heavily. As my eyes adjusted to the torchlight I better saw the stoop of the man's back. *Mordecai.*

I ordered my servants from my chambers. When I did not see or hear anyone hurrying from my chambers I looked around.

"Your Highness," Ruti said, "it is only the four of us."

I saw that what Ruti said was true. Besides her and my cousin there was only the Immortal who held the torch. Erez.

Mordecai stood taller and the mantle fell away from his face. I ran and threw my arms around him. My right hand was wrapped in a scarf, which I was careful not to get tangled in his mantle lest it come loose and reveal the wound beneath.

Whatever pressing matter had brought him to my chambers in the middle of the night had not made him any less awkward. He patted my back and then stepped away from me. "Majesty," he said, "my kind and courageous cousin, you have risen by the strength of your wit and beauty to the highest place a woman can occupy. But that place is threatened." As though he had already said what he needed to, he stopped to catch his breath.

"Yes?" I prodded.

"I know something that the king should also know if he is to save himself."

And therefore, if I am to remain queen.

"It is best if it is you who tells him of the

plot I have overheard," he said. "That way we will both be in his good graces, because together we will have saved his life."

"Cousin, do not hold back. Who is plotting against the king?"

"Two eunuchs, Bigthan and Teresh, who guard the palace gate."

My stomach turned. It was partly my fault that Bigthan had been sent from the harem.

"Last night," Mordecai continued, "I did not leave the palace until long after the sun had set. In fact it had been so long since it had set that soon it would rise. I did not know if I should return to my hut for what little time remained before I would have to be at the palace once again. My back ached and my eyes were tired. I was as weary as I had been since . . ." He looked at me. "Since you were taken from the hut I so foolishly sent you to."

I was careful not to look at Erez as I said, "Cousin, I regret if I have made you weary. How were you to know the king's soldiers would so thoroughly scour not only Shushan itself but also the surrounding countryside?"

"I console myself that it is all for the best now. Your parents would be proud. And now you are in a position to do great things, especially after I tell you what I have heard."

Yes, please do.

461

He took a deep breath. "Before I got to the palace gate I sat down. I do not know how long I sat there until I heard people walking toward me. One of them was speaking, and his high-pitched tone was that of a eunuch. I recognized his voice from the day he came upon you and me speaking in the women's court, when he demanded of me, 'What does an accountant want with a girl of the king's harem?' and threatened me with the gallows.

"He complained to Teresh that he was meant to serve in the harem, and should not have had to trade the smell of incense and perfume for the heat and toil of being always outside the palace. Then he said, 'I am only eyes now — two eyes — none of the rest of me matters. I could be a head without a body, a head without a mouth. I have been cast out. The way the palace looks down upon me now makes me want to hang my head in shame. It is as though all the eyes within it stare upon me in judgment; and for what, I do not know.'

" 'So then you are finally willing to part with your trinkets, bracelets, necklaces, and sigloi, to pay for the job that must be done to rid us of this king in exchange for a new one, one who will not set us outside the palace like common soldiers?' Teresh asked."

I did not believe Mordecai had memorized each word the eunuchs spoke but I did not want to check him in front of Ruti and Erez.

" 'When we must guard the threshold during the day,' Bigthan said, 'I cannot bear watching the sun pass above us, moving over the rest of the palace, where I cannot follow. There is no relief for me when it finally disappears each night, taking yet another day of my life, but not taking it quickly enough. Xerxes is no longer my king. I have exiled him from my heart. As he has exiled me from my palace, so shall I exile him from his throne. Yes, Teresh, I am willing.'

" 'Later then, this evening when the nobles come bearing gifts, I shall make certain one of the gifts is a golden goblet fit only for a king, and some red wine so sweet he will begin getting drunk at the first whiff. After the taster has drunk some of the wine, the king will greedily see to his own golden goblet. As soon as he touches the goblet to his lips, before he has even tasted the wine, he will be closer to the dakhma. The king will be dead before he knows it, and the new king, after we have helped clear a path for him, will generously reward us with all we have been without these last few months, and more.'

"As soon as they had passed me, and their voices had faded into the distance, I hurried back to the palace." Mordecai seemed to awaken from his own tale. His eyes were suddenly so wide that he no longer looked older than he was. He looked more like a brother than a man who had been my guardian. "The sun is rising, Your Highness. There is no time to delay."

Then let us not delay, cousin. "Was there any mention of how the goblet was poisoned and how it would make its way into the gifts, or who they think the new king will be?"

"No, Your Majesty. I have told you all I overheard."

And more, no doubt. "Then I will inform the king at once."

CHAPTER FORTY-ONE: WARNING THE KING

This was not easy to do. I sent Hathach to the king's chambers to tell him that I wanted to speak to him about an urgent matter. While I waited, Ruti hastily bathed me and rubbed oil of myrrh into my skin. She had not yet finished applying my cosmetics when Hathach returned with the message that the king was not to be disturbed.

I should not have sent a servant. I will go myself.

As no one, not even the queen, was to go to the king without being invited, I had to stand outside the doors to the throne room with Erez, the other members of my escort, and all the other people who wished to speak to the king. The king's advisers decided who could petition for an audience with the king, and as Haman was among them, I feared I would not get to speak to my husband in time to save his life.

Haman's eyes went immediately to my stomach. He jerked his gaze away as a child jerks his hand from a flame. He could not bear to be any more aware of me than he must. Me, and the king's heir.

After each petitioner was dismissed Haman admitted someone else to the throne room. I began to suspect that Haman would not allow me to speak to the king before the king decided he had heard enough requests for the day.

When the king was done listening to a relay rider from Egypt reporting on a minor insurrection, Haman admitted a Babylonian merchant in a turban and long white tunic who presented one hundred jars of "the highest quality sesame oil in all the world." I walked ahead of my escort to peek into the throne room. Haman glared at me but he did not tell me to step away from the doorway. I was hoping the king might see me and call me to him.

As the merchant spoke the king sighed and took larger and larger sips of wine. I flinched each time he reached for his goblet. Even the palace scribe could not suppress a yawn. The king did not allow the merchant to finish speaking. "Thank you," he said, "I will not forget your loyalty when assessing how much tribute is to be collected." He waved his scepter to dismiss him.

Before Haman could choose someone other than me to go next, I cried out, "Husband, I have news that cannot wait." The king turned toward me and before any look could pass between us he lowered his gaze to my stomach. I was glad I had allowed Ruti to dress me in three layers of robes. One might easily imagine a great bulk beneath my clothes, a bulk large enough to be the son of Xerxes.

He held out his golden scepter and I hurried toward him, passing by Haman, who knew enough to step from the path of a woman who carries the king's child. Before I knelt I put my hand under my stomach as though to cushion the life within, and Xerxes again waved his scepter. This time it was my kneeling he dismissed.

"My queen. What is the urgent news you bring?"

"Your Majesty, I request a private audience. It is a matter of great importance."

His eyes were as intent upon me as they were the first time he had seen me after ripping off my head scarf

"Leave us," the king said. "All but the royal guards."

I did not allow myself to glance at Haman as he and the other advisers filed out.

When everyone besides us, the servant who bore the wine, and the guards had left, the king said, "Come to me."

I took a few steps forward until I stood not more than ten hands' lengths from him.

"No," he said, "come all the way."

When I moved closer, he reached for my stomach. I feared he would realize my size was due to my robes and not his seed growing in my belly, but I did not let any emotion show upon my face.

I soon realized that I needn't have worried about my face. It was not my face with which he was concerned.

Four of his six guards stood near us — two behind him and one on either side. Though their heads did not move I was certain their eyes were upon us as the king handed his goblet to the servant who bore the wine and then spread his hands from one hip to the other across my stomach. He gently pressed upon me. I knew by the way his hands loosened and then groped again that he did not feel what he wished to. He leaned so far forward that his forehead almost touched my breasts. He took his hands from my belly and then suddenly I heard rustling and felt a rush of air where usually I was covered. I was unaccustomed to feeling anything upon my legs other than the cloths my servants used when they bathed me. I felt little bumps rise from my flesh as though I were suddenly cold. The king pushed all three robes up over my stomach.

Erez was still with the rest of my guard at the door. I did not allow myself to look at him or down at my body to see how much was visible from where he stood. The king's hands fastened upon my hips to keep me steady as he moved his knees apart and pulled me to stand between his legs, against the seat of his throne. He placed his ear upon my stomach, and then his lips. He did not move from me right away and his breath began to stir something inside me. I felt pressure in my belly and even in my sex. The feelings of tenderness for him that were arising within me made the news I must tell him feel all the more urgent.

I slid my fingers between his hands and my hips and freed myself. I pushed my robes down and took a step back. I did not wait for permission to speak. "Your life, my dearest husband and king, is in grave danger."

"I hope you do not mean my new life — the one which resides within you and which you are guardian of."

"The one within you, Your Majesty."

Though this was what he had said he would prefer, still his brow furrowed and he motioned the servant to hand back his goblet. "Your Majesty," I said as he grasped it, "if you take another sip it may be your last."

"How could you know this?"

"The palace accountant, Mordecai, heard Bigthan and Teresh speaking of it at the King's Gate. They plan to somehow poison you. I do not think your goblet is poisoned yet, but I also do not think it is a chance worth taking."

"Bigthan, the eunuch who was causing trouble in the harem? The one I removed at your request, seeks to poison me?"

It hurt me to say it but I knew it would hurt me more if I did not say it: "Yes, Your Majesty." I could not risk the king forgetting that it was Mordecai who had saved him. I looked about for a palace scribe. "My wise king, should we summon the scribe to come back and record what I know?"

He threw his goblet upon the floor. Wine splashed over my feet. *"My concern is for my life.* We can record this in the book of annals later. Tell me what Mordecai overheard, and *offer no more suggestions."*

Though the king was angry, I was happy that he had used Mordecai's name. I would

470

say it so many times that hopefully he would not forget who had saved his life, even if it were not recorded in the book of annals.

I told him that the eunuchs planned to kill him when he met with some nobles that evening. "Teresh said something about a gift you would be given — a golden goblet fit only for a king, and some sweet red wine. He said when you touched the goblet to your lips, before you even tasted the wine, you would be closer to death."

He stood up as though his throne had caught fire. I took a step back. "I must send soldiers to seize these eunuchs and any other servant who might know the details of their plot," he said. He towered over me. The concentrated awe of a few moments before, when he had kissed the child in my belly, had vanished. His large chest rose and fell unevenly, as though a mound of boulders were lifting up inside him and then crashing back down upon each other.

He sent for Haman, and told his guard, "You are about to be allowed the chance to prove yourselves."

He looked to my guard. "Erez," he cried, "come and let me look upon the face of my most skilled and loyal soldier." I could not help thinking, *my most loyal soldier.* I did not like that the king had called for him by name and I did not like the sight of Erez kneeling before the king. As Xerxes looked at Erez he seemed to be contemplating something, and I did not doubt the something was his own safety. Would he take Erez from me?

Another woman might have been heartbroken when the king waved a hand to dismiss her. I was relieved. The king had left me Erez, at least for the time being. As Erez led my escort back to my chambers I could not take my eyes off him. I feared that if I did, he would no longer be there when I looked again.

A few days later, Mordecai came once more to my chambers to tell me what had transpired after I warned the king of the plot on his life. When the nobles came bearing gifts, an Indian magistrate had his servants present the king with red wine and a silk cushion upon which lay a golden goblet. The king insisted that the bearer of such a fine gift be the first to drink from it, and that this would make it an even more cherished possession once it was his. The Indian servants who bore the gifts approached the magistrate with them. Everyone watched, unmoving. The magistrate's hands began to shake. He dropped to his knees.

"I do not know what this is about, Your Majesty," he had cried, "but I sense that something is not right with the goblet. Surely you cannot think I knew of any plot, or I would not have presented it to you, knowing I could not escape unpunished. I am your most loyal subject and will do all I can to help you find and punish anyone who wishes harm upon you."

Without removing his eyes from the magistrate, the king had commanded the servants, "Fill the goblet the smallest amount possible."

"I will drink from the goblet," the man had cried. "But please, Your Majesty, if you are going to fill it at all, fill it all the way and do not make this go on any longer than it must."

The magistrate did not seem to know it was the goblet and not the wine which was poisoned, or perhaps he was pretending, Mordecai told me. *But the king does not use precision when cutting out an infection. He swings wildly with a great blade.*

"Only when you have answered our questions will you be allowed the mercy of a quick death," the king had told the magistrate. He had waved his hand and soldiers seized the magistrate and his servants and dragged them away.

■ ■ ■ ■

It was recorded in the book of annals that Mordecai, the king's accountant, had bravely come forward to warn the king of the threat upon His Majesty's life. The executions of Bigthan and Teresh were also recorded. But not the sight of them. Everyone in the palace was made to go to the central courtyard and look upon them. Fifty people hung upon gallows. I had not even considered that the king would have so many gallows. Had they just been built for the occasion or were they transported from somewhere beyond the palace?

Are they kept on hand, always at the ready?

Hathach must have sensed my dismay. "His life is worth many more than these, Your Majesty."

The traitors' heads hung like those of rag dolls. Their gray, terror-filled faces made it hard to look upon them. My heart ached when I noticed a narrow path through the grime on Bigthan's face, from his eye to the side of his chin, where a tear must have fallen. But I kept all emotion from my face. I knew I could show no pity.

CHAPTER FORTY-TWO:
THE FITFUL BLADE

I tried not to allow all of my emotion to show upon my face each time I looked at Erez.

Unlike the king, whom I rarely saw, I saw Erez every day, and I did not have to pretend anything when I was with him. Well, sometimes I had to pretend I was not overcome with the urge to be closer to him than I was. When he stood guard outside my chambers I wished he were inside. When he stood guard inside my chambers I wished he stood near me. When he stood near me, I wished he was nearer still.

I never knew what a fitful sleeper I was until Hegai finally returned with the plate that fastened over my palm. He apologized that it had taken so long to procure. "It was difficult to perfect it, and this is not something that can be any other way." A little blade was welded between my second and middle finger, like a tiny sixth finger that reached just past the lower knuckle of the middle one. The hinge the welder had tried did not open quickly enough to satisfy Hegai, and so he had ordered it removed. The blade would always be poised to defend me, he said. Unfortunately, it did not match the gold plate, because gold is too soft to cut a man cleanly. Instead it was silver. There was no way to hide it.

"Thank you, Hegai. With Xerxes in Persepolis, leaving the palace in the hands of his chamberlains, including the one we like least, I need this more than I would like to."

"Your Majesty, I am not without influence, and Haman is only one of many officials — he does not rule here. Not yet. But I had the blade sharpened nonetheless."

It was small, too small to drive all the way through a man's heart. I would have to ask Erez how I should use it to defend myself during an attack. It looked harmless. But the morning after wearing it to bed I awoke tangled in shredded silk.

"Your Majesty, perhaps a blade is not a good nighttime companion," Ruti said.

"I must wear the blade when I am most likely to need it. I wanted a weapon that someone who would come to kill me in the night would not think to look for, one he would not know of until it was too late."

"Well if I cannot dissuade you from wearing it, perhaps I can advise you to have happier dreams, ones that do not toss you about so violently. What did you dream last night, Your Majesty?"

"I cannot remember."

Sometimes I dreamed that instead of Erez breaking into the hut to kidnap me, the kidnapper was a shadow whose face I could not see. As it bent over me, something warm dripped onto my face and its bitter smell choked me. The drip became a stream. The shadow was gushing blood. "Your flinch is not enough, Hadassah," it whispered. "You will flinch with your whole body when I tell everyone who you truly are. The king himself will wrench his seed from your womb." And then I saw the shadow's eye. It was Parsha's, and it leered down at me with all the hatred I had seen in it as he was dragged from the throne room. I knew that this time, if I did not escape, I would not be taken to a palace, I would not drink wine. I would not see a kind face ever again. I knew I must make certain to die in the struggle. I knew also that Ruti had lied when she told me "Death is the only true harm." It was preferable to whatever Parsha would do to me.

"You cannot remember at all?" Ruti asked.

She lowered her voice. "Your sheets are ripped apart as though you have lain with a demon."

I also dreamed of Erez. In one dream he was riding away from me on a horse. I tried to run after him but my legs were no better than they had been over a year and a half ago when I first heard the Immortals riding closer through the night. *Please do not run away from me, Erez. I cannot chase you.*

I was not sure which of these dreams I'd had.

I could see by her eyes that she was frowning. "You are taking years off my life. That blade is doing little good — the only one it is hurting is me." She looked at my stomach. "I fear one day it will also hurt you."

The next morning I awoke to feel something warm and wet upon my arm. When I touched it my fingers came away bloody. I sat up and started screaming.

Erez rushed into my bedchambers. He took a cloth from the table near my bed and pressed it to my arm. I hit his hand away.

"Hurry!" I cried. "There is an intruder."

"I stood guard all night. No one entered your chambers."

Erez lifted my right hand and gently pulled torn pieces of silk from the blade.

The tip was covered in fresh blood. He kept it cradled between us, as though there was something he wanted me to see. I was sitting up in the robe I wore to bed, my face naked of cosmetics. This did not make me feel ugly the way it would have with the king.

"How am I to guard you from yourself, my queen? You have cut your left shoulder."

"The blade is so sharp I did not feel it."

"It is a shallow wound. You are lucky."

"If the wound I made is shallow, how will this blade protect me from my enemies?" I took my hand from his. "It was your idea for me to have a blade fixed to the plate. Did you want me to get a weapon that could not really hurt someone?"

"Something I have learned, Your Majesty: you cannot be dangerous to someone else without also being dangerous to yourself." He stared pointedly at my shoulder. "Especially in the dark. Yours is not the least nor the most dangerous blade."

"You do not think I can be trusted with a real weapon?"

For a moment I was so angry I could not even gather together the words with which to reprimand him. He gazed at the wound.

"I forbid you to look any more at my arm," I cried. "I have not forgotten I cut myself, you do not need to remind me by continually looking at it. A man should not resort to arguing with his gaze the way women and eunuchs do."

I regretted the words as soon as they left my mouth. They were not words I would have spoken, and yet I had. Where had they come from?

"Forgive me," Erez said. "I will be more particular about how I tell you what you must know."

"Do not mock me."

"Darkness obscures everything a man puts between himself and his soul. It makes some men cowards, some men foolish, and others brave. But it makes all men more dangerous."

"Then it is good I am not a man."

"If you want to become truly willing to take a life, you will have to leave parts of yourself behind. I would not wish this upon anybody I care for. I watch over you so you do not have to become someone else."

My anger wavered. I tried not to show it. I wanted to look deeper into his eyes to reassure myself that he really did not want me to be anyone other than who I was already.

"But, Your Majesty, do not mistake the blade you carry for a toy. You can harm and even kill someone if you must."

He took my left hand. I tried to keep my

480

breathing even as he placed two of my fingers at the back of my jaw below my ear. Our faces were so near I could see all the little lines in his skin and smell the saltiness of his sweat. He did not look into my eyes and so I felt comfortable looking into his. He gazed intently at the place where he pressed my fingers. "Do you feel that?" he said. His breath was warm against my cheek.

"Yes." I winced. "It does not like pressure. This is the place upon an attacker where I should aim my blade?"

He took his hand from mine. "Cut straight across it. You will know you have been successful when a river of blood gushes from your attacker's flesh. There are other places that are good — his eyes, or above his eyes so blood runs down and blinds him. The front of the throat will make it hard for him to breathe. But the place where your fingers are is the best, and even a short blade will work. Your blade is small enough that your attacker might not see it coming and even when he does he will have trouble turning it against you." Now he did look into my eyes. "Unless he comes from inside your dream again and gets you to do his work for him."

The concern in his gaze made me tell him the truth. "I have nightmares. I fear I might lose those things that are most valuable to me." I felt heat rise into my cheeks but I continued. "Even when I am asleep I am fighting for them."

"You are only fighting yourself for them, and for that you do not need a blade. I told you I would watch over you at night. If there were blood on my dagger in the morning it would not be yours."

I felt my blush deepen. I turned away and noticed Ruti standing only a short distance away. From the expression on her face I was certain she had heard too much.

"My queen," she said, "what are you doing keeping a blade you cannot control so near to your child?"

Ruti gave me a cloth to wrap around my hand at night. When I argued that the blade would do me little good if it were covered, Erez suggested that I could leave the blade uncovered and instead cover those places on my body where the blade might cut. I was not sure if he mocked me.

"Do you have a better idea?" I asked him.

"Yes, Your Majesty. Hide the blade before you go to sleep. If someone comes for you, run."

"Where is it I will run in my bed chambers?"

"Away. Did I not tell you, Majesty, that

the best defense is to never allow yourself to be cornered?"

I thought about this after he returned to his post and Ruti came to lie upon a pallet beside my bed. "If you so much as turn in your sleep, Majesty, I will wake you," she said.

In the morning I summoned Hathach and told him I wanted a great long screen fixed to the floor of my bedchamber, one end pointed to where Ruti would put down her pallet each night beside my bed and the other pointed toward the entrance. I did not tell him why I wanted the screen, only that it must be secret. If only one attacker made it into my chamber, I stood a chance of getting away. I could flee my bedchamber on whatever side of the screen he was not on.

As I gave Hathach his orders I carefully considered him. The king had as much as told me that Hathach would report to him. The eunuch kept his gaze respectfully low, and it looked as though his whole body ached to join his gaze upon the floor. He was developing a hump.

I told him to go at once and stared at the hump as he walked away. *I must not forget that most of that hump is from prostrating himself before the king, not me. And perhaps it is, above all, a disguise. He makes himself appear smaller than he is. But I am not fooled.*

Chapter Forty-Three: The Kick

"Your Majesty, this is beneath you," Ruti said. She did not like the way I had begun to spend my days since the king had gone to Persepolis two months before. I was writing. She thought writing a task for low-ranking officials.

"Atossa herself taught Xerxes and her other children to read and write," I replied from where I sat at a table in my reception hall. Ruti stood back from it, as though she could not bear to associate herself with a queen stooping to a servant's task. "Perhaps that is what she is doing now, and why my husband cannot return to the palace."

"Bitterness does not suit you, Your Majesty," Ruti said, and then lowered her voice so the servants nearby would not hear her, "and it will make your child's bones brittle."

I smiled at Ruti. "I am not unhappy. I have the king's son or daughter in my belly, and I have you."

485

"His *son,* Your Majesty."

I hoped the life in my belly was a son, but I had to prepare myself for the possibility that I might have a girl. I would not love her any less. I would love her with my whole heart, as my mother had loved me. "His child. His and ours. I cannot wait to gaze upon the child's face."

"Then you should not be bent over straining to put down words that may get us killed. You should be resting."

Perhaps that was Ruti's true qualm with my writing. Ruti could not read and was afraid of what I was revealing upon the scroll I had sent to Egypt for. I had no choice. I knew I could not trust the men who write history to write my story. I had to write it myself.

"I have not recorded anything that might put us in danger," I said, even though this was only true if none of my servants could read Aramaic — not even their own names. And if I could keep the scroll from being stolen. I had to guard it as carefully as a mother guards a child. During the day this was easy because I was poring over it. Night was where danger always seemed to lay. Three times I had been attacked in the night, and I knew this was also when the scroll was most vulnerable.

I considered keeping it in one of the gowns in my wardrobe, but even at night an attendant was often present to keep dust from settling and to kill any beetles or moths that tried to make a home for themselves.

I ended up allowing Ruti to sleep with her arms around it, as though she cherished it or was waiting until no one was looking so she could strangle it. I insisted she keep a blanket over her so nobody could see it.

One night as I lay in bed looking down at Ruti and the lump where she clutched the scroll beneath the blanket, I was suddenly terrified. I was not thinking of Halannah, Haman, or the soldiers they might send to kill me. I was terrified of myself and my urge to tell my story. I was endangering Ruti, Erez, myself, my unborn child, and worst of all, my people, who Mordecai and Ruti said I would one day have to save. Why did it hurt me that people did not know who I was, and why did I think I could lessen the pain by leaving a scroll so that someone else might know what the king never could?

Three months after we had first realized I carried the king's child, I felt a tiny kick. The next day there were two more kicks. When I told Ruti she rushed over and put her palm upon my belly, next to my own. Then she knelt and gently pressed her ear to me. I moved my hand out of her way. "Your Majesty, were they happy kicks?"

"Yes, I think so."

"Are these kicks the reason you have kept one hand on your belly even while you write?"

I looked down at my belly and smiled. "I had not realized I was doing this, but yes, I am certain it is."

After a moment I stepped back and Ruti rose to her feet. "This is wonderful news. Should you not call upon musicians to celebrate?"

Since the episode with the jugglers I rarely had company. "I cannot allow people who might be under the influence of my enemies to come near me and my child."

"Yes, but perhaps you could summon just a couple of your handmaidens, and a single juggler or musician?"

"I do not need to celebrate with anything other than what I already have. You and my child bring me more joy than anything in the world. I cannot wait to hold him in my arms."

CHAPTER FORTY-FOUR: A CRIME ONE WOMAN COMMITS AGAINST ANOTHER

The desire to hold my child in my arms grew along with the churning in my belly. The mint tea no longer calmed my stomach. I could not keep the food I ate from rising back up. I tried drinking more of the tea, but this only seemed to make it worse. I could not imagine my child finding any peace in such a storm. I wanted him to be free of my body.

"How long will this last?" I asked Ruti between bouts of coughing and spitting into the bowl she held.

I did not need to look up at her eyes to know she was frowning. "It usually does not get worse in a woman's fifth month, Majesty."

"It feels as though there is a great hand clenching within me."

Ruti brooded throughout the day, and when I woke in the night she was pacing back and forth on one side of the screen.

The next morning, after the eunuch who tasted my food took a sip of the mint tea and retreated to the corner of my receiving hall, Ruti suddenly came rushing toward me.

I knew, as soon as she knocked the cup away from my lips, that I would likely lose my child. She could not knock away all the tea I had already poured into my belly over the last few months. She could not suck it from my veins or wring it from my flesh the way you wring dirty water from a soiled cloth. Though I knew it was too late, I put my whole hand in my mouth and pressed down until my stomach rose into my throat. I doubled over and heaved onto the marble tiles. Then I stuffed a fistful of bread into my mouth. Perhaps it could absorb any poison that remained. But the bread too ended up on the tiles. I tried again, forcing myself to chew this time, clenching and unclenching my jaw, all the while thinking of my child and the terror he must have felt. I wanted, more than anything, to be able to reach my hand all the way down to my belly and lift him from my body, wash him off, look at his face, and, most of all, to hold him safely in my arms.

I looked to the eunuch who tasted my food. His eyes were wide with terror, but he did not seem to be feeling his belly clench. He stood perfectly rigid. "You," Ruti yelled at him. "Come! Drink the rest of this."

"No," I whispered. "No one is to drink the tea now."

"Should not we send for a physician?" one of the servants asked.

"No!" Ruti cried. She looked as though she might attack the girl. She bent to my ear. "Send for Hegai and then dismiss all but your taster." I nodded weakly. "Her Majesty wishes for you to fetch Hegai," Ruti told the girl.

I waved away all the servants from my chambers except the taster. I even waved away the Immortals who stood guard inside the doors. Surely Erez, who stood guard outside, would know something was wrong when he saw the parade of servants exiting my chambers. Worse, Hathach, and therefore the king, would know.

"Rest, Your Majesty," Ruti said when all the other servants were gone. "We will wait for Hegai. It is your own life that is important now. Hegai will know how to bring a physician here in secret."

"Surely there's still something we can do."

"Yes. We can wait for Hegai."

"Why did you knock the cup from my hands?"

491

"To preserve your life."

"But what of *my child's* life?"

"The child, Majesty, may survive, but not as you would like him to. He will be deformed, or slow, or both. The palace and then the entire city of Shushan and then every part of the empire will know you have given birth to a child who no god watched over. It would be better for you to never have any child at all than to have this one who will cause the king to send you away."

"Surely something can be done! We must save him, however damaged he might be." I began rocking back and forth. "Do something," I cried. *"I order you."*

Ruti tried to wrap her arms around me, but I pushed her away.

"*You have given up too easily.* I can see that already your thoughts have turned to how we will make it seem as though this never happened. I am not surprised you had me call upon Hegai. You are not unlike him." Immediately I was filled with shame. "Forgive me, Ruti. It is myself I am angry with. I was not as smart as I needed to be. Neither the blade nor the screen in my bedchamber protected my child."

"Your Majesty, you are still queen," Ruti said slowly, as though to make certain I did not miss a single word. "Do not ask forgiveness from anyone but the king."

Not asking for forgiveness was the hardest task I had ever been given. I wanted Ruti's forgiveness, Mordecai's forgiveness, even my escort's. I had jeopardized all of our positions. I thought of my people — what if I no longer held enough sway with the king to save them as Mordecai had said that one day I must? But most of all I wanted my child's forgiveness.

I ran into my bedchamber and began ripping down the ridiculous screen I had ordered Hathach to get for me. From the corner of my eye I saw Ruti watching. She did not interrupt as I tore through the layers of cloth with not only the blade between my fingers but also with my own flesh, until I was scratched and tangled in the tattered screen.

Ruti began to rub my back. After a moment, by the slight tremble in her touch, I knew that she too was crying.

Hegai was only shocked for half a breath. He gathered himself together so quickly I would have missed it if I had not been watching closely. "Pennyroyal," he said. He looked at me and spoke with even more firmness than usual. "It is time now to think of the girls you wish to save. Think of Utanah. Think of Ruti. You can no longer save the child, but you can still save many more."

"What do you suggest I do?"

"Keep drinking the tea until you bleed."

"Is not there a safer way?" Ruti cried.

Hegai glanced at Ruti as though a foul odor came from her. "A knife is more precise than poison, but also much sharper," he said. "It leaves marks."

"But whoever has poisoned the tea will surely not continue if he discovers that the queen knows."

"Whoever has made the tea does not own all the pennyroyal in the empire," Hegai replied. "Someone else will make the tea for us."

"What of secretly calling upon a physician?" Ruti asked.

"When the queen starts to bleed we will call upon the finest one that can be trusted. There is no use doing so now."

I tried, but I could not bring any more of the tea to my lips.

"What do you plan to do, Majesty?" Ruti asked.

"I do not know. I only know what I will not do."

I did not get long to think about what would happen once my child was born —

how I would keep him from being taken to the nursery and how I would protect him from the scorn of any who might see whatever deformity he would have. That very night, the hand that I sometimes felt clenching within my belly squeezed so hard I cried out.

"Dismiss all of your servants. *Quickly.*" Ruti said.

The violent wrenching pains in my belly worsened. Ruti gave me opium tea to drink and put blankets under my hips, but surely I bled through them. I could feel a warm sticky wetness pooling beneath me. It was not just blood. Some of it was thicker. I had the terrible thought that it was my child. My hands tried to grasp at the wetness beneath my hips and there was a new pain.

"Your Majesty, please give me your hand." It was Erez's voice. Despite the pain I could not stop clutching at the wetness beneath my hips. Someone grabbed my right wrist and I felt the plate being removed. Then my hand was naked. As naked as the inside of my womb. Ruti gave me more tea, and after a while I fell asleep.

When I awoke I knew that my child was gone. Carried away in blankets that were buried or burned. Ruti did not want me to get up, even to use the chamber pot. "You have already lost a lot of blood."

"I have lost more than blood."

"I know, Your Majesty."

I looked at her in the scarf, which only showed her eyes. "I know you have lost as much as I have." *We are all in danger now.*

"We must stop thinking of what we have lost or we will lose everything we still have. Do not forget that you are still queen."

"Where is my taster?" I asked Ruti after two new tasters — a eunuch and a woman my age — appeared with my breakfast of bread and honey. The woman was pregnant.

"Hegai took him."

"Certainly he could not have known anything."

"Nothing is certain."

Over the next few days I fought to keep from saying the sad, cowardly things that kept rising to my lips like bile. *I am not without a child. Sorrow is my child. He will be with me forever. I have ingested a poison that turns a womb to an empty space that can never be filled — not by food or love or wealth or power. I have lost what was most important to me in all the world.*

When Hegai returned to my chambers to

check on me, or perhaps to instruct me, I told him, "I must have Hathach dispatch a messenger to Persepolis. What message shall I send?"

"I was poisoned," Hegai dictated to me, as though it were me who would deliver the message, "and had a miscarriage. I am well now and cannot wait to behold my beloved king's face once again."

"What of the person or people behind this? If I do not find out who poisoned me, I fear I will always suspect everyone a little."

"As you should, Your Majesty, if it will make you more careful." Before I could say anything he went on, "A girl has confessed to making you pennyroyal tea instead of mint tea. But it does not matter who made it. It matters who ordered it made, and she does not know — she only knows who told her she must do it if she wished to keep her parents safe. None of those she named has implicated Halannah, but none needs to do so for me to know it was her. This is a crime one woman commits against another, and none has more reason to cast you from the king's favor than she does."

The loss of my child felt nearly too great for me to bear. I was not yet ready to think of the advantage Halannah would gain from my loss. But I could not help asking about the servant who had poisoned my tea. "What has become of the girl?"

"She is missing her hands now, the hands that dropped the pennyroyal into your tea. I thought it best to keep her around where she would be a reminder to others, but after more thought I decided the story left behind by her absence might be more advantageous. She is now useless for all but one task. When she heals, she, along with the others she has implicated, will be one of the now-handless girls who are paraded through the palace and then sent to follow in the train behind the Immortals with the camels, mules, and other concubines who attend them on long expeditions."

"This is ugly work," I said.

"Matters of life and death often are."

"I can hardly bear to look."

"But you must, and do so without flinching, Your Majesty."

Hegai drew out the words "Your Majesty." Like Ruti, he seemed to think I needed to be reminded that I was queen. "My eyes are open now," I told Hegai. "I will not look away from anything, no matter how ugly."

CHAPTER FORTY-FIVE: XERXES' HOMECOMING

Upon receiving my message about the miscarriage, the king returned from Persepolis. "He summons you to come to him as soon as you have stopped bleeding, Your Majesty," Hathach informed me.

I did not like to think of what words passed between Hathach and the king. I had always trusted Hegai to look out for my interests when he spoke to the king because my interests were the same as his own. I was still uncertain of Hathach's interests.

"How does he know I still bleed?"

"Do you clean your own chamber pot?"

I stood from my cushions and stepped closer. My voice was not as steady as I wanted it to be. "Do *you* remember that I am queen?"

Hathach bowed low, transferring so much of his weight that I was not sure he would be able to stand up without stumbling. "Forgive me, Your Majesty. In my concern for you I spoke to you as though you were a child and not the resplendent queen you so clearly are."

After I dismissed him, Ruti turned to me, "He spoke improperly, but he helped us. He was angry at us for not protecting our secret. For some reason he wishes to help us. I will clean the chamber pot from now on."

Before half a month had gone by I stopped bleeding. Afterward I felt an even greater sadness.

"There is nothing left of the child," Ruti said. "It is time to start again."

I did not tell her of the pain within my belly. I promised her I would seem as carefree and happy as any woman seeing her beloved husband again after a long absence.

"I know you will, Majesty."

Even with perfume, cosmetics, and a robe of red and gold I did not feel beautiful. *It does not matter how you feel,* I imagined Hegai telling me, *it matters only how you appear to feel.*

As my guard escorted me to the king's chambers, I kept my gaze upon Erez's back. I focused on how broad it was and how steadily he walked. I had never seen him falter or truly lose control, not even when he had gotten angry and told me not to talk back to *any* of the soldiers, or when he fought Parsha and the other Immortals at my wedding banquet. He was like a boulder that could roll slowly down a mountain without succumbing to the earth's pull.

When we arrived at the king's quarters and the doors were opened before us, I reminded myself that I had walked before a military court full of hostile soldiers without being harmed. I could surely walk into the chamber of a disappointed king. As I approached the doorway I brushed slightly against Erez. "Courage," he said quietly.

I stopped just inside the entrance and forced a smile. From across the room, the king studied me. I had forgotten how massive he was, how each of his hands could have wrapped halfway around my waist. How his torso was so huge that if he ever needed to be carried it would take several strong men to move him. I raised my head as high as possible and then bowed. "My king, I have missed you during your long absence."

"Sometime you will accompany me to Persepolis, and see what a masterpiece I have sculpted while I was away. I have completed the banquet hall."

I was grateful he did not wait for a reaction. It would have been difficult to feign excitement that he was completing his home away from me. "Come, my queen, you should not stand when there are cushions so near."

He held out his right hand and I walked across the room, my sandals whispering along the floor too loudly to my ears. I was surprised when he pulled me in and bent to press his lips to mine. Because of how tall he was he nearly had to bow to kiss me. He wrapped his left hand — the one that was not holding mine — around my back so I did not stumble from the force of his kiss.

My heart moved in my chest, a hopeful trembling.

Xerxes rubbed his thumbs against my hip bones, silently asking a question a king does not need to ask.

"Yes, I am ready," I answered.

He lifted me into his arms and carried me toward his bedchambers. The guards there threw open the doors and stepped out of the way just in time to avoid a collision. "You are dismissed," he told the servants.

He kissed me and I lay back on his bed and opened myself to him. He was gentler than usual. Afterward he continued to kiss me and lightly rubbed his hand over my

502

stomach, comforting my womb.

When we awoke the next morning he did not beckon the serving girl to hand-feed him. Instead he waited until all the servants were assembled and then announced, "I am finally home. Home is where my queen is, and all who are blessed enough to live in my home must treat it as a temple to my queen. If ever I find that anyone has tried to harm her, or has withheld any knowledge large or small that might keep my queen safe, he will experience the boats."

The Immortals, eunuchs, musicians, dancing girls, and servants with platters of bread, fruit, honey, and wine suddenly stood like statues, watching him.

"Have you heard of the boats?" he asked them. Without waiting for an answer he continued, "I will tell you. Listen carefully so you do not forget a single detail, as you will be asked to describe it many times during your service in the palace. If you forget any of what I am about to describe to you, you will spend your last days helping us perfect this technique.

"A man is laid in one boat, with his head, hands, and feet left outside. A second boat is placed over the first. Then the man is drenched in milk and honey. It is poured not only into his mouth but also over his whole face. Soon the man cannot even see the sun for all the flies that are biting him. They are a cloud layered one, two, three flies high. For the man, now, it will always be night. His face is kept turned toward the sun though, so that the milk and honey continue to bake. He has no chamber pot other than the boat he lies in, and soon he is no longer alone there. All manner of creeping things and vermin spring out of the mess he has made and they enter him through his bowels. The man does not die, not completely, for many days, and neither does his family."

Haman and Halannah will have trouble devising a better torture than this, I thought as I looked at the horror-stricken faces of Xerxes' servants.

And indeed, there would be no more attempts on my life for nearly five years.

Chapter Forty-Six:
The Only Place

Erez and my other guards escorted me back and forth to the king's chambers almost a hundred times over the next two years. The king and I were hopeful at first. But then, secretly, I lost two more children, and I was only pretending to be hopeful. I still drew my knees into my chest after lying with the king. But as soon as the king began to snore I gently lowered my legs to let his seed flow out of me. I did not want to lose any more children.

I lost another child in the third year of my reign. "That is not a child," Ruti said as she collected the bloody blankets. "It is only part of the home your body was preparing for one."

"I did not bleed last month, it is a child."

"A queen's people are her children," Ruti said.

That is when I realized that she knew it too: I would never have a child.

■ ■ ■ ■

Sometimes when the king was gone at Persepolis I wondered if that was where his son Artaxerxes was. He had begun looking at me differently, as though from a great distance. Sometimes he did not seem to see me at all. A few times this slowed my feet as we neared his chambers.

One day when the doors to the king's reception hall swung open before me, I walked forward a few steps and then stopped. I could not bring myself to walk past Erez. I wanted him between me and the empty look in the king's eyes. But I could not afford to bring suspicion upon myself and Erez so I pushed myself forward, into the king's chambers and into his bed.

When we were done the king did not bring a goblet to my lips and hold my head so I could drink. I did it myself, feeling his seed spilling out of me onto the bed where we had briefly coupled.

In the morning, one servant girl fed him dates from her own fingers and another massaged his shoulders with her tiny hands. I did not look at the girls' faces; I did not want to remember them. I tried to keep a serene expression upon my face between bites of bread, cheese, and fruit. The relief I felt when the king kissed me and sent me from his chambers was so great that the corners of my mouth lifted even higher than where I had forced them.

"You are even more eager to leave than usual," he said quietly.

"It is only that my servant's herbs await, Your Majesty."

"Perhaps your servant should try a new recipe."

My chest tightened. "I will make certain of it, my king," I said. I did not care that he was about to get into a golden tub behind a screen where two serving girls awaited him. I only wanted to get away from him and the disappointment that had grown between us more quickly than a child ever could have.

I was not completely certain that the king had lost all hope until the night when I arrived at his chambers just as another woman was leaving.

Halannah did not have her usual elaborate braid piled high on her head, but her skin was as white as ivory and the heavy lining of kohl around her huge brown eyes had not run so far down her face that I did not recognize her. Xerxes stood in his reception hall watching her leave. They seemed of a size, matching figures. How could I fill the large space she took up? She looked victorious as she emerged. She barely glanced at my face before dropping her gaze down to my belly. Her cheeks swelled with satisfaction.

As I walked past the protective shield of Erez and Jangi, my hand twitched with the desire to puncture Halannah's bloated cheeks with the blade between my fingers.

"Oh, are you still coming to my lover's chambers?" Halannah asked quietly, continuing to gaze at my belly for a moment before looking up at my face.

I forced a smile and touched the crown upon my head. "I am grateful that when I leave the king's chambers tomorrow morning, it will not be as a concubine returning to a harem full of them."

She laughed, and then dropped her gaze once again to my belly and her voice to a whisper. "I did not leave anything for you, but it is doubtful you could have made use of it even if I did. Perhaps one day you will only wish you were headed back to the harem, instead of the hovel you are certain to end up in if you survive."

"I promise I will not get there before you," I said, and walked past her into Xerxes' chambers.

"Your queen has arrived, my king," one of Xerxes' eunuchs announced. Reluctantly, the king took his eyes off Halannah. I bowed slightly, straining to keep the smile on my face.

Perhaps he saw my distress. "My queen, food cannot be truly savored when you are too hungry," he explained. "Come."

I knew I would not be savored. My feet were heavy as I followed him into his bedchambers.

The next morning I was too humiliated to look into Erez's eyes. But still, it was comforting to follow him back to my chambers, falling into the steady rhythm of his walk and losing my gaze in the, pattern of tiny stars that decorated his saffron tunic. His back was not as broad as Xerxes', but it was not so high above me either; it made a better shield.

"Your Majesty," Ruti said after my bath. "You look wooden. Are you unwell?"

"I am tired of hope," I told her. "To hope is to look around you and say, 'This is not enough.' " Before she could correct my youthful foolishness, I said, "And yet I know it isn't enough, and still it is disappearing even while it appears to be here every bit as much as it was yesterday."

"Your Majesty, we must find something to occupy your mind before you become strange."

I continued, "Think of how quickly I almost lost you."

I could see from her eyes that she frowned. She gestured to the screen behind which the musicians had just begun to play for me. "Would you like the musicians to play a faster melody, perhaps one that does not lend itself to so much musing?"

A faster tempo did not keep me from my thoughts. I thought of not just my own life but also those of the people around me. I thought of how one woman of the harem might grow wealthy from the king's gifts, another might be made drunk in front of the eunuchs or king and be sent immediately to the soldiers. Some might go back and forth to his bed enough to grow rich from his gifts, others might see him only once and never again. They would spend each day knowing they were one day closer to servitude. Did any of them even realize that Hegai's favor was more important than anyone else's? That it was usually Hegai, and not the king, who decided which woman went to the king's chambers each night? I regretted this thought, which led me to an even darker one. The only woman the king asked for besides me was my worst enemy. The woman who had taken my child from me and now wished to take my husband.

I could not halt the dark thoughts, or silence the cries that came from my body; only wine helped.

"You need entertainment, or fresh air, Your Majesty," Ruti insisted.

I remembered the Immortals who had explored my chambers after the last assassination attempt upon me. One of them had stopped to pick up the goblet that lay overturned and empty next to the cushions I had fallen asleep on, then smirked and said, "So it is as we have heard." If I were to sit in the courtyard, people might say that I drank more than a woman should. To make Ruti happy, I chose instead to have Hathach summon jugglers.

"No torches," I told him, "they will juggle fruit. And no children." Ruti and I had once agreed that children were least likely to harm me, but I no longer wished to see children.

Ruti looked sharply at me after he left. "Do you no longer value your life?"

"Halannah has taken what she wished from me," I told her, "and is probably enjoying the king's disappointment. Perhaps she is hoping he will get rid of me himself. I do not think any juggler or musician — adult or child — will drop his fruit or throw aside his harp to take up a knife and slit my throat."

Still, Ruti trained her eyes upon the jugglers as though her gaze was what kept the apples from falling to the floor. She did not even notice me staring at her. My heart lifted. I was thinking of how blessed I was to have such a loyal servant and friend, and of how much I loved her.

"Soldier," I called to Erez one day when he stood guard inside the entrance to my chambers. The king had gone to Persepolis the month before and had still not returned. I did not know how many goblets of wine I had drunk.

Erez came and stood before where I reclined upon some cushions, listening to the musicians. "Your Majesty," he said as he bowed. I could see some sort of pain in his eyes. Was it sadness, anger?

"Thank you," I said.

"For what, Your Highness?"

"For telling me I must see more clearly, and that danger which comes from where you expect it is hardly danger. You knew that if I had a dagger I would only see trouble that can be met with a blade. If I had listened more closely to you, all my children would not be dead."

He did not allow the stiffness in his legs to keep him from lowering himself until he was kneeling beside me, his face only a few hands' widths from mine. The wine and my sadness, added to all the time we spent near each other, allowed me to look at him for the first time without shyness. The lines in his skin had deepened. Not the lines that form around a person's eyes from smiling, but those that form in a brow that is too often tense or strained. His gaze upon me was so intense that without wine I would not have been able to return it. He looked at me as though he wanted to help me. And I wanted to let him. I knew I was the cause of the pain in his eyes.

If he were not a soldier, and I were not queen . . .

It was better he did not know my thoughts, but I did not want to completely take my eyes off him. I moved my gaze from his eyes to his sharp cheekbones and the short dark hair along his jaw where he was supposed to have a beard. I looked at the space between his chin and his neck. If I took off my crown I could bury my face there.

"Soldiers *train,* Your Majesty. The first time I shot an arrow you would not have been able to guess what I was aiming for. Some soldiers die in the military court when we practice."

"This was not a practice."

"*You* have survived. That is all that truly matters. And you can always try again."

"What if my womb is altered so that nothing can ever come of it?" *Would* you *want me if I were barren?*

"Then the king will still have a beautiful queen who is forceful when she needs to be and pleasing and sweet when that serves her better."

Did he truly think that would be enough, or did he only wish to warn or perhaps comfort me? "When the king returns I will put down my goblets and smile and blush like any wise girl knows she must."

"I hope so, Your Majesty."

I wanted to put down my goblet and touch his cheek, his jaw, his lips. Many nights I had thought of his mouth and how it would feel to press my own against it. As he knelt beside me I had to squeeze my goblet with all my might to keep from reaching for him. My hand began to shake. I had to dismiss him before any of the servants saw my desire, though perhaps it was already too late. "You may return to your post."

He bowed his head slightly, not taking his eyes from mine right away. "Yes, Your Majesty."

Ruti glared at his back as he walked toward my chamber doors.

As she took my hair down that evening, I reached up and grabbed her wrist so suddenly the comb fell from her hand. "Do you know why I love him?" I asked.

No one was within hearing distance, still Ruti did not respond.

I let go of her hand. "Because he knows I am barren, and, unlike the king, it does not change his feelings for me."

Ruti came to stand before me. I could not tell if it was terror or anger that widened her eyes. "Hush with this foolishness," she whispered. "He has the luxury of feeling no concern. He does not have anything to pass on."

"He does have something to pass on. His goodness, his courage, and his strength — strength that does not wish to overpower but only to protect. You do not need to rule the whole world to be worthy of admiration, only to be a good ruler of the small part that is yours."

She studied me a moment, a moment in which something was happening beneath her head scarf — perhaps she was biting back the words that came to her lips — before she finally spoke. "Your Majesty, be careful what you pray for. The only place the two of you could be together is upon the gallows."

Chapter Forty-Seven:
The Woman Who Walked Beside Me

477–474 BCE

The king prized the eunuchs because he believed they had nothing of value left to them except their service to him. He thought that he was more present to them than they were to themselves. But over the next few years I came to realize that surely there was another person who figured as large for them as the king: the person each of them could have been. I knew because I too had a person I could no longer be walking beside me.

What if I had guarded my womb more carefully? I would wonder, and suddenly she would appear next to me, wearing the same robe I wore. Her breasts and hips, heavy from childbirth, shifted from side to side as she walked. In each of her hands was a smaller hand, a child's hand.

I could not bear to see the faces of the children I might have had. Still I kept pace with her. Perhaps, if I did not ever completely lose sight of her, the children could somehow be mine.

I looked at Erez as often as I could without taking away all doubt that we were nothing more to each other than queen and guard. Looking at him quieted my dark thoughts. Twice, just in time to stop it, I even caught my mouth lifting into a smile as I gazed upon him. After this I tried to never gaze at him directly. Sometimes I pretended to take an interest in something near him, which was easiest when he stood guard inside the doors of my chambers. I looked at the doors as though I wished to venture out, perhaps to see the king. But I did not want to leave; I wanted everyone besides Erez to leave. And then I wanted him to come closer.

I became bolder about ordering him to do things for me. He too became bolder, perhaps because of boredom or anger at the king for confining him to a thankless task in the palace. One that caused his muscles to grow weaker and his body to become stiff from standing for most of each day. Or perhaps he desired me as I desired him. I ordered him to carry messages out to Hathach, ones he did not hesitate to come close to hear. I commanded him to rearrange the tables in my reception hall, and to check beneath my bed for assassins, though I knew there were none. I just wanted him near my bed, so I could feel his spirit near when I lay in it at night unable to sleep.

CHAPTER FORTY-EIGHT:
HAMAN'S VISIT TO
THE ROYAL TREASURY

474 BCE

"Queen, do not forget our people," Ruti said suddenly one day, as though she had been holding back for a long time. I was sitting at a table in my reception hall, writing upon a scroll. "I fear that since coming to the palace you have stopped thinking of them."

I could not tell her or Mordecai the truth: sometimes I could not bear to think of our people. I feared that I no longer held enough sway with the king to protect them.

"If you are called upon by God to stand against Haman and speak for our people, will you be ready?"

"I will have no choice but to be ready."

"It is not only when a crisis strikes that you must endeavor to be wise. You are making decisions every moment of your life, and they are not without consequence. If you choose to dote upon the soldier, you will lose your position with the king. Mordecai and I believe you will one day be called upon to stand up for our people. That day is near."

"Yes, I have heard this before. Is there news?"

"Majesty, clear your chambers."

My belly tightened; she was not just cautioning me out of habit, as I had hoped. I dismissed everyone from my hall and a few moments later Ruti opened the door to a visitor. A mantle covered his head and torso, just as it had on the night when he came to my chambers to warn me of the plot to kill the king.

I did not look forward to whatever news my cousin brought, but he himself was a welcome sight. I went to him and pushed his mantle back so I could look upon his face. Even though I had startled him, the tiredness did not leave his eyes. He looked to the scroll upon the table and half-smiled. "Are you writing history?"

"I am no songstress, and no tale I could fashion is more riveting than one involving a king and his friends and enemies, so I have little choice."

"I cannot fault you for this. But I hope the scroll is well kept even when you are not writing in it."

521

I inclined my head toward Ruti, and Mordecai nodded. "Then it is in strong, capable hands." He turned to her. "You have taken good care of our queen. Thank you. She will need you more than ever now. Haman is upon us."

I braced for whatever news Mordecai brought. Though he had never been capable of relaxing, I invited him to recline upon my cushions and have some wine. He chose instead to remain standing, with his mantle about his shoulders, as he told me of Haman.

"Two days ago he sent servants to collect the scrolls upon which I record the tributes collected from each province. I told the servants that the king has entrusted me to oversee the records and that they are a matter for only the king, the eunuchs he has assigned to help me, and me myself.

"Later that day, one of my eunuchs announced that Haman himself stood at the doors to the treasury office, demanding the scrolls.

" 'The guards are right not to allow him in,' I told the eunuch. 'I will go out to meet him.'

"His bottom lip was curled like that of a child as he looks at a smaller child from whom he is going to steal something. 'Turn over the scrolls, Jew, before you bring more suspicion upon yourself.'

" 'What need do you have of them?' I asked him.

" 'You are hiding something. Have you reached your own hand into the empire's riches?'

"I ignored his accusation. My hut and all my possessions are no greater than my salary affords me. I stepped back and signaled to my treasury guards to close the doors.

"Haman stepped in the way of the doors and yelled, 'What need do you have to keep them from outside eyes?'

" 'The need to perform my royal duty to the king,' I said, 'which I am certain is not what brings you here.' "

I interrupted Mordecai. "What *did* bring him, cousin? Did he wish to assess the subjects' taxes in order to see if he might convince the king to raise them?"

"My queen," Mordecai said, "how I wish that were the case. One of my eunuchs has informed me that Haman has been meeting with other advisers and with high-ranking military officials. He does not simply wish to raise taxes. If he gets hold of the scrolls he will share them with all those whose support he seeks for his campaign. He will tell them of the great wealth a campaign against the Jews will bring them. And then he will convince Xerxes to rid the empire of a dangerous people, a people more loyal to their God than to their king.

"He will avenge the death of the Amalekite king by killing every last one of us, and then he will take all that is ours, my queen."

"The king will surely not allow such a campaign against his own subjects!" I cried. But my words held more hope than confidence.

"That will depend upon you, Your Majesty," Mordecai said.

My heart felt as though it had fallen into my belly. "Did Haman say anything more of his plans?"

"He came closer, so close the olive oil in his hair left a stain upon my tunic. 'Next time my request will bear the seal of the king, and I will not have to ask before I enter.' "

Mordecai pulled his mantle over his head. "I do not want to be away long. I do not even return to my hut in the evenings. If Haman comes back when I am not there my guards may not withstand his threats and bribes." He had never initiated any touch before, but now he took my hand between his long bony fingers and squeezed it. "Unless you can stop Haman, he will destroy us."

Chapter Forty-Nine:
Desire

I needed someone to answer a question I had been carrying upon my shoulders since arriving in the palace. I found an excuse to send Ruti to the kitchens and dismissed all my other servants except Erez and Jangi. Ruti may have suspected my true motive but she could not disobey my command.

Then I beckoned to Erez.

He came and knelt beside the cushions I reclined upon. Jangi's eyes did not follow him. They never did when I called him to me.

Very quietly, I asked, "Do you think I am still Jewish?"

Erez unbowed his head and looked at me as he spoke. "I have seen you absently praying a few times, Your Majesty. Is your prayer still the one I heard as you tended Cyra on the march to the palace?"

I rarely prayed. But when I did, regardless of what I prayed for, my prayer was always the same. "Yes."

"What is the name of the prayer?" he asked.

"The Sh'ma."

"What does *sh'ma* mean?"

" 'Listen.' It is a call for our people to recognize the glory of God."

"And has not your God listened to you also?" When I did not answer right away he continued, "You have the loyalty of a powerful eunuch, a servant who is willing to die protecting you, your cousin is near, and" — his gaze upon me tightened, as though to make certain I took in his words — "you are queen."

"Why should He listen now? I am fattened not only by wine but also by foods that are not slaughtered according to His laws. I have lost the child He placed in my womb. Who am I to be a leader of my people? If they heard the morning silence in which my prayers go unsaid . . ."

"Your Majesty, we all skip our prayers sometimes."

"For years?"

"Sometimes for lifetimes."

"You do not pray."

"Perhaps I pray like you, without knowing it. I doubt you have gone more than a month without acknowledging the glory of your God."

"Even so, I tremble at the thought of my people knowing me as I have become. This is why I do not allow myself to think of them. Not when I neglect my prayers, not when I eat unclean foods, and most of all, not when the king's uncircumcised body is on top of mine."

Erez turned his head away as if I had slapped him.

I quickly went on. "And yet that was my peoples' last hope, that I might bear the king a son and secure my place in the empire and in his heart. Now that I have failed he rarely calls me to him, and each night he is not with me I know he might be with Halannah. The wine cannot rid me of this knowledge, but still I keep drinking it."

Erez turned back to me. "You have done what you had to, and the king is a fool."

I was shocked to hear him speak so callously of the king, but he did not take back his words. "He is more fool than king. He does not know who to keep around him, and someday he will die before his time without having truly loved you. It will be one of the many mistakes of his reign."

Erez came so close that I could see a tiny scar over his right eye that I had never seen before. "My queen, I would not ignore you or leave you because you drink too much, or because you are angry more often than you should be, or because you are sometimes rash and reckless. If you could not bear me a son, I would not love you any less for it."

I had longed to hear him say that and still it was both sweeter and sadder than I could have imagined. I wanted nothing more than to touch him — with my hands, my lips, my entire body — but I could not. I felt tears forming in my eyes and knew I could not let them fall. Erez moved his body to block Jangi's view and bowed so that his head touched my left hand.

I wanted to touch him with both hands. I drew my left hand away in order to take the plate off my right one. He saw what I was doing and rose up to help me. His touch was so pleasurable I wanted to lay back and close my eyes.

There was gentleness in his eyes as he gazed upon my scar.

"I will bless you," I said loudly so that Jangi would hear.

Erez lowered his head again and I placed my hands on either side of his head. It was the first time I had touched his hair. I did not spread my fingers and run them through it as I would have liked. I pressed lightly, bowed my own head, and said, "Let integrity and uprightness lead you. May you watch with eyes on all sides of your head — eyes that see perfectly for leagues in every direction. May Ahura Mazda himself guide your dagger and bow. May he guard you as faithfully as you guard me."

I took my hands away and he raised his head slowly. By the sadness upon his face I knew I would not like whatever he was going to tell me next. "There is talk among the soldiers of a new mission. One for which Haman believes he will soon have the king's approval. I told you once that I would do anything the king commanded. But, my queen, I will fall upon my own blade before using it against your people."

I felt my lips begin to tremble. Erez reached for my hand but suddenly I noticed Jangi's eyes upon us. I pulled my hand away. "That is all, soldier," I said.

He bowed his head. *"Courage,"* he whispered and then returned to his post.

I called Jangi to me for a blessing so that my blessing of Erez would not seem strange. His eyes were not as wide and clear as they had once been. They no longer seemed, like a child's, to go directly into his thoughts. Even as he lowered his head it seemed that he was watching me.

CHAPTER FIFTY: TIME IS SERVANT TO NO ONE

"You are too eager to leave, my queen," the king said one morning. It was not the first time he had said it, but this time when I stepped from his reception hall Erez and Jangi were not waiting to escort me back to my chambers. It took all of my restraint to walk calmly behind the two new Immortals and not command them to hasten their pace. I had to see that Erez was still in my chambers so I could breathe again.

He was not outside my chambers, and he was not inside them.

"Your Majesty," Ruti said, "you look as though you are possessed."

"Where is he?" I asked.

She did not have to ask who I meant. "Your Majesty, I do not know. The last I saw him he was escorting you to the king."

I went back to the doors of my chambers. It was agony to wait while two of my guard opened them. I had brushed past Hathach on my way in, hardly noticing him. Now I did not call him in but marched out to where he stood with the two new Immortals. "Hathach, where are the members of my escort who usually return me to my chambers after my nights with the king?"

"Your Majesty." He knelt, as he always did when he saw me. He never gave me time to wave away his prostrations.

I did not have the patience for this. *My escort?*

"The king replaced two of your Immortals."

I tried not to allow my face to move a hair's width in any direction. I imagined what Hegai might advise: *do not speak, and perhaps, to fill the silence, he will tell you all he knows.*

"They are training for a special expedition, Your Majesty."

I stepped closer to him. If I were not so desperate to know of Erez, I would not have revealed my ignorance. "Tell me all you know of the expedition."

"Unfortunately, the king did not tell me anything more than that, Your Majesty."

I wanted to ask him, *What was the king's expression when he told you this? Was there jealousy, cruelty in his eyes? Did he say the word expedition mockingly? Did he say Erez's name, and if so, did he say it as though he still cherished him, or as though he would crush him like a fly that has flown too close to a prized horse?*

I stared at Hathach so he might offer something further, but he remained silent.

I could not sleep. Fear and anger tossed me back and forth from one side of the bed to the other. I remembered my parents' gasps as a soldier took their lives. I thought of Cyra, and how I had not been able to save her. The many children I had lost moved in a circle around me.

I could not allow another voice to join the haunting chorus in my head.

It does not matter what lengths I must go to. I must figure out a way. I must save Erez and my people.

Over the next month, I came to realize how much thinking of Erez, looking at him, and knowing he was near had helped me through my days. Every fear and unhappiness had been lessened by his unwavering strength. Without him I felt like I was trapped inside a boulder falling faster and faster down a mountain. But it was not his absence that most upset me. What upset me most was not knowing if he was safe.

"Your Majesty, you have not risen to the

533

highest position a woman can in order to pine over a soldier who may have overstepped his bounds," Ruti told me.

"How would the king have known what he did or did not do?"

"It is hard to completely hide one's feelings, Your Majesty. Perhaps you yourself somehow told the king."

The look I gave her caused her to take a step back. "I love you like my own kin, Ruti, but do not forget your place or I will be forced to remind you."

"And do not forget yours. You are a barren queen who may be suspected of the gravest crime of all. One much worse than killing your husband: allowing another man to take what is his and give it back used and soiled."

"Surely the king must know this is untrue."

"The king knows only what those closest to him tell him."

"I am still thinking of how I might get close to him again."

"Think quickly, Your Majesty. Time is servant to no one."

CHAPTER FIFTY-ONE:
NEWS OF MORDECAI

All the king's courtiers in the palace gate knelt and bowed low to Haman, for such was the king's order concerning him; but Mordecai would not kneel.
— Book of Esther 3:2

Ruti was massaging my back with a cloth during my bath one morning when I heard her clear her throat. "Haman rises in the king's esteem, Your Majesty. Now all but you and the king must bow to him." Perhaps she had told me during my bath because she thought the hot water and massage of the cloth upon my back might help me to remain calm. "Parsha and Dalphon are still prisoners, but Haman and his other sons are amassing great wealth. The king allows it because some of this wealth ends up in the royal treasury."

"How has Haman come upon this wealth?"

"Through plunder, threats, and, according to some, promising favors."

I was silent.

"You have not figured out how to win back the king."

"Not yet."

The next day Hathach admitted Hegai and my handmaids to my chambers. The girl who stuttered did not even wait for me to dismiss Hathach and invite her and my other handmaidens to recline upon my cushions and partake of some refreshment. "The palace ac-c-c-ccountant is crying out in the c-courtyard, in the city square in front of the palace gate. Hegai said you would wish to know."

"And there is a certain air about the concubines," Opi said. "Halannah looks as though she might burst with happy news of some kind."

Hegai quickly assured me she was not with child. "The harem wine makes certain of it. But your handmaiden speaks true of Mordecai. He has torn his clothes and put on sackcloth and ashes."

My stomach tightened. My cousin had always feared drawing attention to himself, and he would not have abandoned his watch over the treasury for any but the gravest news.

Opi spoke again: "I heard that the accountant would not bow to Haman, and now he cries and has rent his clothes because of some revenge Haman wishes to enact." From the look upon her face I knew she believed what she had heard. Hathach too looked saddened to hear of the palace accountant's distress. *Perhaps I can trust him.*

When it was clear my handmaidens had no more information, I told them to watch Halannah closely and find out all they could in the harem, then I dismissed them.

"Your Majesty, we must get clothes to Mordecai," Hathach said, "before the king decides that he is a troublemaker."

The sense of time pressing down upon me caused me to be direct. "Can I trust you? The king said you were his trusted servant, and that you are unwaveringly loyal to only one master."

"The king is correct. I do serve only one master: Ahura Mazda. He is my king and he is against the killing and plundering of innocent people, even people who do not worship him. Haman has no god but greed. He must be stopped, and I will help however I can."

I looked to Hegai. He nodded slightly. He

believed Hathach, and so did I. "Have a servant bring clothes to Mordecai," I told Hathach. Then I put a finger under his chin and raised it so I could look into his eyes. I was surprised by their lightness. "Mordecai, my cousin."

"You honor me with your trust, my queen," Hathach said, and rushed away to carry out my orders.

CHAPTER FIFTY-TWO:
THE EDICT

There is a certain people, scattered and dispersed among the other peoples in all the provinces of your realm, whose laws are different from those of any other people and who do not obey the king's laws.

— Haman, Book of Esther 3:8

"Forgive me, Your Majesty," Hathach reported that evening, "but Mordecai refuses the clothes I sent him. What do you wish me to do?"

"Hathach, you yourself must go to him."

I could do nothing but pace while I awaited his return. When I beckoned to the servant who bore the wine, Ruti quickly said, "Your Majesty, remember that God has not yet put anything before you over which you could not triumph."

Nothing except pennyroyal. I fought back the dark thoughts about my womb, but I could not summon any confidence that the king valued me more than Haman. In fact I could not even be sure that he valued me half as much.

Hathach's eyes were heavy when he returned. Ruti stood close to me as he explained that Haman had offered the king a large payment into the royal treasury.

With a great, knowing dread, I asked, "What does he wish to buy?"

Ruti moved closer, as though she might have to catch me.

"For ten thousand talents of silver he has bought from the king an edict whose words I cannot bear to speak aloud," Hathach said.

Somehow I held out hope against what was already clear. "Why has my flesh and blood put on sackcloth and ashes? Has Haman bought someone's death?"

"Yes."

I took a deep breath. "Whose?"

"All Jews, Your Majesty, young and old. Even women and children."

"No." It was not me who had spoken but Ruti. Though she had known this day would come she refused to believe it had arrived. My legs felt weak beneath me.

"The edict for the destruction of your people was issued in the name of King Xerxes and sealed with the king's signet ring," Hathach said quietly.

Anger joined my fear. Haman had not even needed the treasury scrolls to secure whatever support he needed. My people's lives had been sold cheaply.

"No," Ruti said again.

I pulled her against my chest and wrapped my arms around her. I had forgotten how small she was. Her body was rigid, and for a moment she did not return my embrace.

"Jews in every province are fasting, weeping, and wailing," Hathach said. "They too are in sackcloth and ashes."

Ruti began to weep.

"Your Majesty," Hathach continued, "Mordecai says you must go to the king and appeal to him. You must plead with him for your people."

The king had not called for me since the morning I had walked out of his chambers to find Erez gone. Going to him without being called was a crime punishable by death. Perhaps he would seize upon the opportunity to rid himself of me. I had the terrible thought that if the king knew I was Jewish it might strengthen his support of the edict.

I could not tell him I was Jewish. I had to find another way.

"Tell Mordecai that if anyone enters the

king's inner court without having been summoned by him they risk death, and I have not been summoned to the king for the last thirty days."

When Hathach went to deliver my message to Mordecai, Ruti stepped away from me. "Your Majesty," she said, yanking off the purple head scarf I had given her, "I did not risk my life for a coward."

Her lips were not split only lower from upper, they were split diagonally across, so that they were in four parts of different sizes. Bulbous, grotesque. The outer part of her left nostril was gone. It seemed I was not looking at one surface, but many — a face made up of different pieces pressed together. Because she had believed I was worth defending, the pieces would never fit neatly back together again.

I did not allow myself to look away, even though I could not truthfully tell her anything she wished to hear. "You know my favor with the king runs low."

She spat upon the floor. "And what of your favor with all of the people who have helped you to your throne?" She turned and walked away without even bothering to secure her scarf.

Chapter Fifty-Three: Ghosts

It was not long before Hathach returned with another message from Mordecai: "Do not imagine that silence will save you. Surely you have not risen so high for yourself alone, but for all of our people throughout the empire who will be wiped from the face of the earth if you do not save them."

Mordecai is done hiding, and he wants me to follow in his footsteps. But he has not disappointed the king as I have.

I did not send back a message right away. I dismissed all my servants, even Ruti, and lay upon my bed in darkness.

As disappointing and full of heartbreak as life had sometimes been, I wanted to keep living. I thought through every possible way I might save my people, attempting to find one that would also preserve my life. I could come up with nothing. I knew of only one way to turn the king against Haman, and it would almost certainly result in my death.

Sobs overtook my body. They strained my lungs and the inside of my head. They shook the bed as though I suffered a terrible fever. For the first time, I saw the childishness of all I had expected from life: a mother and father who would live until I myself was old, a husband who loved me and only me, children, grandchildren that I would live long enough to hold in my arms.

Now that it was coming to an end, I longed for every bit of the life I'd had, even the troubles. I wished for what I already had as though it were a treasure, which I finally saw that it was. It was a treasure I had not realized I would have to return.

I needed time to think of exactly what I would do, so I sent Hathach to Mordecai with a message to assemble all the Jews in Shushan to fast on my behalf for three days, after which, though it is a crime punishable by death, I would go to my husband uninvited. "If I perish," I said, "I perish."

Hathach bowed low and did not immediately rise up.

"At once," I told him.

The night before I went to the king I dreamed of the woman who appeared whenever I wondered *What if I had guarded my womb more carefully?* The woman I could no longer be, walking beside me holding my dead children's hands.

She had always been unaware of me, but in the dream she turned her head and stared into my eyes. She looked like me, only larger and her face more creased from smiling. She knelt and spoke quietly to the children, then she let go of their hands and pushed them toward me. I held out my arms. They looked at me. My arms grew heavier as they stared but did not come closer. Finally the woman smiled sadly at me, took their hands, and turned back in the direction she was going, hurrying the children along beside her.

I watched the woman I could have been walk away, hips shifting side to side, children bounding along beside her, all of them getting smaller, smaller, until even when added together they were still smaller than I was.

Goodbye, I said, and let them go.

I thought of telling Ruti of this dream, but pretending that when I let the woman and children walk away I could see more people in the distance — *our* people, celebrating. I told myself it was not a sin to lie if it put her mind at ease. Selfishly, I did not want her to be anxious during what remained of our time together. I was still holding on, trying to wring life from my last days.

I knew I had to let go, even of the days ahead. My hands had to be free to perform the task before me: saving my people.

By the next morning I had devised a plan.

As Ruti bathed me, she observed, "I have never seen you look so sad or so strong."

I did not know if the dead missed the living, but if so I would miss Ruti terribly.

"Do not be gentle. My skin must glow from across the room."

If God could forgive me for eating meat that was not slaughtered according to His laws, for wearing a likeness of another god against my chest, and for lying with a gentile king, He could also forgive me for what I was going to do in order to win back the king's love long enough to turn him against Haman.

CHAPTER FIFTY-FOUR: THE GOLDEN SCEPTER

The servants, and even the guards — who were not supposed to move at all unless commanded to — turned their heads toward me as I approached the throne room in my royal apparel. A weight had been thrown from my chest and my heart lifted. I would leave my body soon and so it did not confine me. I no longer had to try to save myself, I was free to think only of my people, and for them I could do things I could not do for myself.

I walked ahead of my escort and stopped where the king could see me. Something lay before the throne and I saw that it was a map of the empire. The king gazed at it while Haman spoke quietly into his ear.

"My king," I cried. "Behold your queen." He looked up and I parted my royal robe; only my flesh and the star of Ishtar the king had given me lay beneath it. Even my scar lay bare. I hoped seeing it would remind

the king of our first night together, when he had traced it so gently my heart ached, and said, *The best soldiers bear scars.*

The king extended his golden scepter toward me so suddenly it nearly flew from his hand.

I walked through the path the servants and petitioners made, letting my robe billow out to either side. I was finally doing for my people what I had promised to do: whatever it took.

The king waved dismissively at the map in front of him without taking his gaze from my body. Out of the corner of my eye, I saw Haman glare at the servants who rushed to move the scroll from my path. I touched the tip of the king's scepter and then fell to my knees. I'd had Ruti pin my crown to the back of my head so I could press my forehead to the floor. When I did so, my robe blanketed me. The king bade me to rise. I remained kneeling but I raised my head from the floor and threw back my shoulders. The robe fell down around my legs, leaving me in only my veil and crown.

His gaze moved to my neck, my shoulders, and then my chest. "I had forgotten how beautiful you are. The looks of my servants and advisers have reminded me."

"I wanted to be naked but for your love

and the crown you placed upon my head."

His gaze traveled up my body to meet mine and his eyes softened. "The first time you came to me you did not adorn yourself with any jewels. You wore nothing but a robe and the plate over your palm. I will not forget that you wanted nothing but me, and how that made me want to give you everything."

He reached a hand out and I leaned forward so he could touch my face. I felt a whoosh of air against my lips and then my veil was no longer in front of my eyes.

"I still have no need of anything but the love I bear you, my king." I reminded him of all the things I had never asked for. "No bejeweled robes or head scarves, no fine leather sandals, no silver or gold. I have no need of all except one thing."

Still holding my veil away from my face, he dismissed everyone except his chamber servants. Haman's kohl-ringed eyes had narrowed so much I almost could not see it was me they gazed upon. *Do not worry, we will meet again soon,* I thought as he left.

When all but the king's closest servants had gone, he asked, "What troubles you, my queen? And what is your request?"

Hearing the warmth in the king's voice, I let out the breath I had been holding. "If it please Your Majesty, let Your Majesty and Haman come today to the feast that I have prepared."

The king studied my face. I thought he might ask me what game I was playing at, but instead he said, "If that is your request," and let my veil fall across my eyes once again. After one last look at my flesh he dismissed me and sent a servant to inform Haman.

It was a victory, but a bittersweet one, as along with it would come the end of my life.

I rushed to the Women's Courtyard, where the feast was to be held, to make certain everything would be ready in time.

CHAPTER FIFTY-FIVE: THE FIRST FEAST

As I waited in the courtyard for Haman and the king, I had more courage than I had ever had before, but still I knew it might not be enough to last through all that was to come. I absently ran my fingertips up over the plate on my right hand until they touched the sharp point of the blade. I dropped my hands to my sides and cast my gaze up to the sky. I began silently praying the Sh'ma. I did not stop until I heard footsteps.

Haman and the king approached side by side. Haman must have thought that the reason I had invited him was that I wished to win his love; his face was bloated with pride, not unlike that of his niece when she had emerged from Xerxes' chambers.

I bowed low before the king and invited them to recline upon the couches around the long table that was covered with breads, sweet orange and grape jellies, and every kind of nut. Haman did not bow to me or even wait for the king to first choose a place before lying down on his side and calling to a servant for wine. The king did not reprimand him. He had probably grown accustomed to Haman's impertinence long ago, or perhaps Haman's sacrifice of his sons had secured the king's trust.

I bent to plump the cushions that lay upon the couch the king stood before, then I rose and thanked him for coming. I turned to Haman. "And you as well, my handsome nobleman."

Haman's eyes widened and his lips came apart, as though he had a question, but he said nothing. Then he gathered himself back together and narrowed his eyes. Perhaps he thought I mocked him. I tried to maintain an air of adoration as I returned his gaze. From the corner of my eye I could see the king look from me to Haman and back. "Surely you have not invited us here to look upon my adviser," the king said. Then he laughed, as though realizing the ridiculousness of such a notion.

"Oh!" I said, hoping to sound like someone suddenly awakened from a dream. I bowed again so the king might think I was overwhelmed by guilt or fear, but his gaze had already moved to the food on the table.

Once the king was settled upon the couch, I did not allow servants to fill the king's or Haman's goblets or bring trays of food to them. I did these things myself. I filled a goblet for the king, and then refilled Haman's goblet. He held it out to me and I wrapped my fingers around his. I could feel his smooth skin and long nails — he did little work. I did not let go right away, not until I was certain the king was watching. I willed myself to blush. I do not know if my cheeks reddened, but as I let go of the goblet I cast my eyes down, feigning embarrassment at my own loss of control. The king was not laughing now. His huge lips were pressed together into a thin, angry line.

I was certain the only thing standing between the gallows and me and Haman was the confusion in the king's eyes. I had to rid the king of this confusion.

As I arrayed myself on the couch next to Haman's, across from the king, the king seemed to grow larger. His huge body dwarfed everything for cubits in all directions. His lips turned down at the corners, and suddenly something felt wrong. Up until that moment I had been so focused on planning what I would do at the feast that I had thought of nothing else. If I continued any further along the path I had set out on, things would start happening very quickly. The king would not sit idle upon a sense of betrayal. Though I was no longer afraid of death, I was not yet ready for it. I had not said thank you or goodbye to any of the people I loved.

"What is your wish?" Xerxes asked. "Even to half my kingdom it shall be fulfilled."

"If it please Your Majesty to grant my wish and accede to my request — let Your Majesty and Haman come to the feast which I will prepare for them again tomorrow."

The king looked carefully at me and his look was not warm. "As you wish." He set down his goblet and stood abruptly. Haman, perhaps seeing Xerxes' irritation, did not persist in his earlier impertinence, but he leered at me when the king turned away. Without even knowing my plans, he somehow thought I was acceding to his new position of power. To him I was just a desperate girl without anything of value. But I was certain I still had more than Haman did; I had something I cared about more than my own personal ambitions. I watched him walk away. My heart almost filled with pity for him. *No matter what he has, he will never be satisfied. He will never be free.*

Chapter Fifty-Six: Friends and Allies

That night I wrote four letters.

The first one was for Mordecai. He had taken me in and cared for me as though I were his own daughter. He had taught me to read even though that made me more independent of him. I would never again have to ask him to read something to me. I knew it was not a small thing to make me more independent. I could see everything more clearly now that my life was running out; Mordecai had liked having me near. He was not one to be loudly happy, but even through his exhaustion I had been able to see something like a little bird of happiness set free behind his eyes as soon as he had returned to his hut each evening and found me waiting for him. I told him I was grateful for all he had done for me, and that God could not have left me in better hands than his.

The second one was for Hegai. He was

not always easy to love, but I loved him anyway. I thanked him for his wisdom. It had helped save me from Halannah, so my life could be sacrificed for something better.

For a long time I pondered what words to place upon the scroll I would have Hathach read to Ruti. Finally I wrote, *My servant, the thanks I owe you is too heavy to carry into death so I am writing you this letter before I go. My spirit will not be free until I tell you what I should have said years ago: you are the most courageous person I have ever known. The bravest thing a person can do is survive when it would seem to most that little is left. You have survived to help someone, and I praise God that I am that someone. You have saved my life many times. If not for you I would have been too afraid to close my eyes at night, too alone to have gotten up each day.*

Erez's letter was the shortest. There were no words that would make it any easier to leave him. *I am going to use all the courage you have given me to save my people, and to save you too if I can. If I do not succeed, know that I have tried with all my heart.* That was as close as I could come to telling him I loved him.

I trusted Hathach to deliver Hegai's and Mordecai's letters and to read Ruti and Erez their letters. "If anything should happen to me," I said when I called him in and handed the scrolls to him.

His hand shook as he took them. He bowed his assent but did not leave when I dismissed him.

"I do not have much time, Hathach."

"I have news, Your Majesty, news that you may not like to hear. But I would be remiss in my duty if I did not tell you that after the feast, Mordecai was in the palace gate as Haman passed through it. Mordecai refused to bow. Your Majesty, I am sorry to tell you that Haman has had a gallows fifty cubits high built for Mordecai."

I felt as though the wind had been pressed from my lungs. "You should have told me at once."

Before I could panic, he hurried on. "As of a few moments ago, it still stood empty. The king is in his chambers for the evening, and Haman would not hold a public execution without speaking first to him."

I tried to think of what Hegai would do. "Have you friends in the king's chambers?"

"I have friends everywhere," he replied.

"Then I have an idea."

He listened with his head bowed as I told him how we could help Mordecai without seeming to. When I finished he looked up at me. "Your Great Majesty, I am blessed to be of service to you. I will go at once to talk to the king's eunuch."

Several times in the night I got up and went to look at the doors to my chambers. "Your Majesty," Ruti said, "the doors have not moved. What is it you are watching for?"

I would not tell her of my plan unless it was successful. I simply said, "Our fate."

"You cannot improve upon your fate by watching the doors." She coaxed me back to bed and rubbed my back as she told me she knew I had found my courage. "I can see it in your eyes. Now that you have done your part for the day, relax and trust that God will do His."

Sometime before dawn I fell asleep.

In the morning Hathach burst into my chambers and stood stooped before me. My heart beat harder as he struggled to catch his breath. I had a servant bring some water. After a moment, I said, "I have even less time than I did last night, Hathach. Even if you have to speak in small pieces, please tell me what news you bring."

"Forgive me." He took a deep breath and said, "When I received no news this morning, I ran to the king's chambers myself to speak with his head eunuch and I have just returned. Last night, the eunuch did as I asked and made certain the king did not sleep. Each time the king closed his eyes and his breathing began to deepen, there was" — Hathach smiled — "a noise of some sort that woke him. The eunuch suggested perhaps the king might fall asleep more quickly if he would allow him to read aloud from the book of records. Strangely" — Hathach's smile spread across his face — "he read an account from a few years ago, of how Mordecai the Jew had sent warning to the king about a plot on his life."

"The eunuch made certain to say 'Mordecai the Jew'?"

"Yes, Your Majesty. I am certain that he carried out the plan exactly as I asked. He is a very loyal, very well paid friend. He reports that the king sat up in bed and asked him to read it again. Then the king said, as though he had forgotten it up until that moment, *'Mordecai saved my life.'* He also remembered that *you* were the one who delivered Mordecai's message."

I knew hope could be deceptive, and that altering my plan with Haman might be dangerous, but I could not beat back the thought that surely I had been lifted again in the king's esteem. Lifted above my status as barren queen. Perhaps I did not have to pretend an affair with Haman. Perhaps I did not have to die. "I was right to trust you, Hathach. Thank you."

"Oh, but that is not all, Your Majesty. This very morning Haman was in the courtyard on his way to see the king, likely to speak against Mordecai. The king called him in and asked, 'What should be done for a man whom the king desires to honor?'

"Assuming the king spoke of him, Haman said, 'Let royal garb which the king has worn be brought, and a horse on which the king has ridden and on whose head a royal diadem has been set; and let the attire and the horse be put in the charge of one of the king's noble courtiers and paraded through the city square. The noble shall shout so all can hear, 'This is what is done for the man whom the king desires to honor!' "

I had not expected to laugh ever again, and certainly not as hard as I did as I guessed what came next.

"The king told him to make haste getting the garb and the horse and to go with them to Mordecai the Jew."

"The king himself said 'Jew'?"

Hathach raised his gaze up from the floor, and I saw that light shone in his eyes. "Yes, Your Majesty. The head throne room eunuch is also a friend of mine. Actually, all of

560

the king's attendant eunuchs are friends of mine."

Perhaps Mordecai was right, and I could turn the king against Haman by revealing that I was Jewish. "Thank you for all you have done, Hathach. If I do not return, I know you will do me the final service of making certain the letters I gave you get to my friends."

"Yes, Your Majesty," he said as he bowed to me, perhaps for the last time.

Chapter Fifty-Seven:
The Second Feast

Haman did not seem so sure of himself as he and the king approached on the second day of the feast. I was glad for his great pride. Surely it had made his task torturous. I could not help but smile as I imagined him leading a horse with my cousin upon it through the city square, yelling "This is what is done for the man whom the king desires to honor!"

He himself looked like a horse who has heard a loud noise in the distance. Bristling, angry with fear. I planned to press upon him until he lashed out or did something else that revealed his true nature to the king. I would welcome his unhappiness, though I knew that the more I angered him the more careful I would have to be. *He is dangerous, he will hurt someone. I hope it is only himself.*

As I bowed to the king I saw Haman's feet shifting in his sandals. He did not even wait until the king bade me to rise before he lay down upon one of the couches.

I thanked the king for honoring me once again by coming to the feast I had prepared for him. There was a tiny spark of warmth in his eyes, enough that I decided to trust in his gratitude more than his jealousy. I would finally tell the king who I was. Regardless of what happened afterward, at least I would not die a secret.

When the king had arrayed himself on some cushions that I had plumped for him, I lay upon the adjoining couch, my head close to his. From the corner of my eye I saw him raise his goblet and I smelled the sweetness before the wine spilled down his throat. I would not wait so long to make my request that the king was too drunk to understand it.

I looked at Haman lying upon the couch across from us. Though he reclined, I knew he was not truly resting but only affecting a pose of relaxation. Sweat from his face dripped onto the cushions he lay upon. The veins in his hands bulged from his skin, as though he were ready to grab or hit someone. His fingers were weighted with as many rings as Halannah's, and seeing them reminded me of how her rings had clinked together when she had slapped me. His chest was puffed out, and in his eyes I could

see he was already fighting for something —
most likely himself, or that part of himself
that wished, always, for more.

I turned to the king. "I have heard that
today a great man was honored, Your Majesty. I wish I had been there to hear Mordecai's loyalty declared throughout the city
square." I looked at Haman. "What is it you
said as you led his horse, Haman?"

"I said this is the man whom the king
desires to honor."

"And how did you say it? I so would have
loved to be there. Please say it just as you
did today."

Haman pressed his lips together, then
muttered through his teeth, "This is what is
done for the man whom the king desires to
honor."

"You said it so quietly?"

"My queen," the king said, "surely his
voice is tired. He can say it for you another
time. Let us partake of some wine."

"Yes, Your Majesty. Let us drink to the
man without whom you might not have
lived to celebrate this day. To Mordecai!"

Haman held his full goblet in his hand
but did not raise it to his lips even though
the king and I drank. I had ordered a special
pennyroyal wine prepared for Haman, one
that I told the servant who bore the wine

not to serve to the king or me. I had allowed Ruti to add some bathwater that she'd used to wash her feet. *No matter what happens,* she had said, *at least I will know he drank dirt from my feet.*

Haman continued to hold his goblet without drinking from it. His eyes sharpened upon everything before him, moving carefully from one thing to another, as though looking for a hidden threat. He finally took a sip from his goblet. He made a choking sound and spat wine over the fruits and nuts before him. He beckoned to a servant to take his goblet.

"The wine which I have procured for the king is not good enough for you, Haman?"

His mouth was still twisted in disgust. "This is not a king's wine."

I gasped. "Is not my husband a king? Is not any wine he has drunk a 'king's wine'?"

Haman glared at me for an instant before catching himself and smiling. He forced himself to take another sip, and the victorious look from the day before returned to his face as he managed not to twist his mouth in disgust this time. "The king is most dear to me, and to the empire. I only said 'this is not a king's wine' to make certain of your loyalty."

I was going to say "You insult the king,"

565

in the hope that the king would see that he should be insulted. But I did not have to. The king's voice was that of a man who owns the world and everyone in it. "I chose this woman, with the help of Ahura Mazda, from among hundreds. She has helped save my life. Yet you dare to test her, and therefore also to test my judgment?"

Haman's eyes bulged so much from their kohl outlines that I could see little red lines in the whites surrounding his large pupils. He bowed his head and said, "Your Highness, I am your most devoted and loyal servant. You are more dear to me than all else in this world. I would give you the lives of my other eight sons if it would prove my devotion to you."

The king had not yet taken the lives of Parsha and Dalphon, yet Haman so easily counted them among the dead? *Thank you for ridding me of any pity for you,* I thought.

The king laughed. "Perhaps I am only testing you too. You are still my wisest adviser. The one who is best at enriching the royal treasury."

Do not wait, a voice inside my head commanded. It was not my mother's voice, nor Ruti's, nor Hegai's. It was my own.

I fell upon my knees before the king. "My most beloved king, there is someone who would take from the empire a greater treasure than the wealth that comes from coins. He would take from you some of your most loyal subjects, including Mordecai."

The king looked as alarmed as I had hoped. "Mordecai, whom I honored only today for saving my life?"

"Yes, Your Majesty. This evil man I speak of wishes to kill the devoted subject without whom you might not have survived. If his wish had been granted when he first desired it, he would right now be pouring money into his own coffers, not yours."

The king stared at me with something held back in his huge eyes. Did he hold out hope that I would start laughing and declare it all a jest so he would not have to consider giving up the wealth Haman had promised him?

Haman said, "Your Maj—"

"Quiet," Xerxes said to him, and then turned to me. "Do not speak in riddles."

"Your Majesty, the people he wishes to destroy, I am among them." The king's grip upon his goblet tightened with a jerk, sending wine splashing over the rim. Haman gasped. "He has sold my people to be destroyed, massacred, and exterminated."

In a voice that shook the ground, the king commanded the servants, "Leave us! Every one of you." He turned back to me. *"Whom do you speak of? Where is the man who dares insult me by endangering my queen?"*

"He is right here, Your Majesty," I said, pointing at Haman. "He is the man who does not wait for you to choose your place before choosing his own. He is the man who insults the palace wine. He is the man who walks beside his king instead of behind him."

Haman's voice trembled as violently as the hands he held out to the king. "I thought only of my love for you, Your Majesty, when I devised a way to enlarge the royal treasury. If I had known your queen was —"

"Only a fool would threaten what is mine," Xerxes cried. "I am the most powerful king in the world. No man should insult my wine. No man should walk beside me, or seek to stand shoulder to shoulder with me as you have done so often, or choose a place at the table before I have chosen mine."

Haman was on his knees now. "Please —"

"Silence!" The king threw his goblet upon the table and came to his feet.

Haman cowered in the shadow the king had thrown over him. He began moving backward on his knees. "I beg of you —"

"Be silent before I cut out your tongue.

Your voice hurts my head and the sight of you blinds me with rage. I cannot think here. I must clear my head before my rage overtakes me."

The king stalked off toward the palace gardens, leaving me alone with Haman.

Haman leaned toward me. "Please, my queen, please forgive me. We will be more powerful as allies than enemies. I will find another people to enrich the royal treasury. I will pour the spoils not only into the royal treasury but also into your own personal coffers."

I placed a hand over my empty womb. "You have murdered the king's heir and the descendants he would have had. Only God can forgive you."

"Your Majesty, it was Halannah who ordered the pennyroyal for your tea and bribed the servants with the king's gifts to her." His voice rose nearly as high as a eunuch's. "It is *she* who threatened them with long, agonizing deaths."

"Then we will put her upon the gallows beside yours."

"Please, my queen, I hold much sway and will do you any favor, procure anything you desire" — he swept his arm to one side — *"wipe out your enemies."*

"You can rid me of my enemies by climb-

ing onto the gallows you built for Mordecai."

He stood and came to throw himself at
my feet. "Anything, *everything* I have, my
queen, it is yours."

"I want nothing from you except your
life."

He was crying now and he moved from
my feet to my legs, sobbing his way up my
body as he pled for his life. When he pressed
his head into my lap, my heart began to beat
as loudly as anything he was saying.

"There is nothing you can say or do to
win back your life, Haman. It is gone. The
only choice that remains to you is whether
you will die as a coward or a man."

He looked up at me and his eyes darkened.
He squeezed my thighs through my robe —
squeezed them as hard as Halannah had
done my first night in the palace. *"Jew."* The
wine smelled much worse on his breath
than it had in the pitcher. "If you do not
convince the king to save me, I will tell him
of our love, the seeds of which you foolishly
planted in his head yesterday. I will tell him
Mordecai arranged everything for us —
Mordecai came to your chambers with a
message for you and found us together, then
came up with a plan to keep our secret.
When the king returns he will see how you

offered yourself to me one last time."

He threw his whole body on top of mine, crushing the wind from my lungs. His face was so close to mine I could see only his eyes. I saw not only the little red lines in them but also the dark lines beneath, where kohl had seeped into the creases of his skin. I tried to yell for help, but my cry was muffled by his beard filling my mouth and then by his hand across my lips.

"I will die either way," he said, "but this is the way you will die."

My left hand was trapped beneath his body, but that was not the hand I wanted. I brought my right hand up and slashed his face. He cried out.

Heavy footsteps rushed toward us. There was only one man whose footfalls were heavy enough to be heard over another man's cries.

"What goes on here?" the king demanded.

Haman lifted himself from my body and, without turning to face the king, said, "It is she who invited me to lie on top of her."

Blood was falling from Haman's cheek onto my robe. "My king," I said. "I tried to drive him from me. Look how I cut him."

The king's face was nearly as red as Haman's blood. "Turn around," he commanded.

The hatred in Haman's eyes as he stared at me did not fall away completely but receded enough to allow something else to enter: respect. *Little, barren peasant queen, you win.* He took a deep breath and turned toward Xerxes.

The king waited for Haman to face him completely before he spoke. "Oh, my doomed adviser. Blood is falling from your face where soon tears will follow. My queen would not have cut you if she wanted you near. What lack of wit could compel a man to try to ravish my queen in my own palace?" When Haman tried to stammer a reply the king silenced him. "You have uttered the last lie you ever will."

Behind the king were more guards than I could count. Two of them grabbed Haman and pulled a black hood over his face. One of the eunuchs beside the king said, "This traitor has erected a gallows at his house, fifty cubits high, which he made for Mordecai the Jew, the man who saved your life."

Beneath the hood I saw Haman struggling to say something or perhaps simply to scream.

"Hang him on it," the king commanded.

CHAPTER FIFTY-EIGHT: THE KING'S DREAM

I went to see Haman and his ten sons —
Parsha, Dalphon, and their eight younger
brothers — upon the gallows. To look at
them I had to stare up into the sun. They
were just tiny dark spots, the opposite of
stars. All the ugliness we had been through
illuminated the beauty that lay over us.
Where the gallows ended the sky began.

Haman's lands were given to me. I knew
they were not only a gift but also a warning.
What had happened to the man whose lands
I owned could happen also to me. I had
seen a second black hood when the soldiers
came for Haman. The soldier who held it
had carried it back with him as Haman was
dragged from the courtyard.

When the king called me to him that
evening to give me Haman's lands, he did
not seem to sit as tall as usual upon his
throne. I fell at his feet and pressed my
forehead to the floor. "Thank you, my wise

and just king."

"I am not as wise as I once thought. I knew something plagued you. I thought it was someone. Now I see it was many people — your people, whose weight you carried with you into my chambers and could not set down, even when we were together. I wish I had known sooner. My queen, you should have come to me immediately, instead of fawning over the traitor in an attempt to win him over and save your people."

He reached down to where I knelt before him and jerked my chin so I looked up at him. "There is only one man's wrath you should fear."

I knew then that he was only going to warn me; I would not be punished in any way. Perhaps I was spared because of Mordecai's loyal service, or perhaps because if I were punished along with Haman, the empire might conclude that he had been cuckolded by his own adviser.

I looked up at him. "My king, please forgive me. I was desperate and did not want to trouble you." *You are moody and the truth alone could not be counted upon to sway you.*

"I summoned Mordecai after I had Haman taken away. Your cousin wears my signet ring now, the one Haman wore this morning. He is now my highest, most beloved official, and he has vouched for you. He revealed your relation and told me how you were an orphan when he took you in.

"Now we have something in common, my queen. He has saved both of our lives." His voice held no joy or relief.

"I am honored to share this good fortune with you, my king. But my peoples' fate is still uncertain. They are in great danger. The edict that went out calling for their deaths cannot be taken back, even with Haman gone, because it was sealed with your signet ring. And so I shall do as you command, and bring my plea directly to you." From where I knelt upon the floor, I tilted my head farther up to him, so he could see the tears rolling down my cheeks. "Their only chance of survival is that a dispatch be sent throughout the empire, declaring that the Jews shall be allowed to fight back if anyone takes up arms against them."

"My queen, did you not hear what I have told you?" He wiped the tears from my cheeks. "Mordecai wears my signet ring. He will write as he sees fit."

"Thank you, Your Majesty." I tried to keep my breathing steady so he would not know how afraid I was of what I must ask next.

"There is one more thing. Haman's niece, Halannah —"

"When Haman was tortured he named her and many others who have betrayed me in one way or another."

I saw the great sadness in the king's eyes. I wanted to tell him I understood the sacrifice he was making. "I know how you loved her."

"No, you do not. You only saw the worst of her. For a long time she was the only girl who seemed unafraid of me, the only girl who it brought me any pleasure to please. I did not feel alone when I was with her. I liked things exactly as they were and did not wish for anything to change between us, so I did not make her queen, even though I knew that was what she most longed for. I did not give her what she wanted so she took what was mine." He leaned down and put his hand upon my stomach. "Forgive me. I allowed my love for her to blind me to her cruelty and to the danger you were in."

"You do not need my forgiveness, my king."

"She was not half so beautiful nor so kind as you are." He moved his hands to either side of my head and pressed his face against mine. I thought he might kiss me but instead his great body shook and I felt wetness upon my cheek. "Forgive me that I did not love you as I should."

I waited for him to say that from now on he would love me, but for a moment he was quiet.

"My foolishness has cost us a son," he said. "Every time you lay beneath me, he is with us."

"I am sorry that instead of a child I have given you a ghost."

"There was a ghost here when you arrived. You and the other virgins were brought here to help me forget her."

Vashti. Her son was heir to the throne, but the king did not reveal whether she herself was alive or dead.

"The longer you live the more you live among ghosts," he said. "If I live much longer I will be surrounded by more ghosts than people: the men I have killed with my own hands, the men I have had killed, the people who died because I wanted, always, to rule more of the world than the world allowed."

"You no longer wish to enlarge the empire?"

"I have suffered defeats, and defeats only, for the last few years. I have learned that my most trusted adviser is an evil man, and

I have watched him assault my queen. In a dream, I have foreseen the hour of my own death."

I tried to pull back to look at him, but he held me tighter. "In fewer than ten years someone powerful will betray me," he said, "but I know it will not be you, because if I die, Mordecai will die too, and likely you and all your people along with him."

"Even if that were not so, Your Majesty, I would never harm you or allow anyone else to do so. I am your loyal servant."

"My little Ishtar, while I have not loved you as much as I should, I have loved you greatly. It just has not been constant. With us there have always been peaks and valleys. Added together and divided by the number of days we have known each other, I have loved you as much as I have loved any woman, perhaps more."

As his crying turned to sobs he slid from his throne and buried his head in my hair. I strained to hold him. He was so big that he could never be truly held the way other people could, feeling someone's arms wrapped all the way around him. But he gave me some of his weight and cried for a few moments while I held him as best I could.

Abruptly he pulled away and rose to sit

again on his throne. "You are dismissed,"
he said.

Chapter Fifty-Nine: Purim

In the coming days my people rose up against those who wished to destroy us and take all we had worked for. We killed seventy-five thousand men and did not lay hands on the treasures of even one. We wanted only our lives.

A holiday, Purim, was made of the two days that followed our victory. Mordecai ordered every Jew to observe Purim each year with feasting and merrymaking.

"*You* commanding people to partake of feasts and parties?" I teased.

He smiled briefly at me. His responsibilities had been increased tenfold. He did not attend the parties very long himself. He always had something else he needed to see to. But I did not let that, or anything else, concern me. I had let life go, and it had come back to me. I had decided I would hold it with more loving hands.

■ ■ ■ ■

The year following my peoples' victory, I
was approaching the banquet hall to join
the Purim celebration when I saw Erez. I
had not seen him since I had come out of
the king's chambers to find him gone. I had
so badly wished to see his face that sometimes it seemed if I just turned my head
surely I would find him standing guard
behind me, or if I would just open the doors
to my chambers, he would be on the other
side of them.

As I continued to walk toward where Erez
stood guard outside the banquet hall, my
legs felt strange beneath me; I wanted to
run but I could hardly walk. He looked as
he always had: calm, watchful, surer of
himself than he was of anyone else in the
world.

I did not want to quickly walk by and then
have to wait another year to see him. I
needed something — quiet words or at least
a look — to pass between us.

I slowed my pace, almost to a halt. What
could I say? *I have missed you with all my
senses, my soul has missed yours? I have
longed so deeply for you that sometimes I
have been certain you were with me?*

Besides the slight rise and fall of his chest, only his eyes moved. Without turning his head, I saw him glance in my direction. Then I saw his hand disappear inside his tunic and emerge clutching something so small I could not see what it was. I ordered the two Immortals beside me to move in front of me and continued at a snail's pace so Erez could transfer whatever was in his hand to mine unseen.

I tried not to look into his eyes but could not keep from glancing briefly at their dark centers. I knew that he was watching me in the way I had watched him when he was my guard — watching from the corner of one eye while seeming to stare straight ahead. As I came close I could see his pulse throbbing in his neck. He pressed something into my hand. It was hard not to tighten my fingers around his as soon as they brushed my palm, but I waited an instant and his hand was gone, leaving something in its place. I wrapped my own hand around it, being careful not to grasp it too tightly. I could feel that it was a tiny scroll.

All night I waited to open it. I felt it in the sleeve of my robe and imagined what it might say. He had told me more than once to be strong. That was how he said *I love you.* But surely he knew I no longer needed to be told to be strong.

The dancing, singing, and drinking went into the morning. When I left with my escort Erez had been replaced by another guard. I hurried back to my chambers, dismissed all my servants, and opened the scroll.

I had assumed Erez could not read or write. As I looked at the sureness of the handwriting, and read what was written, I knew I had been wrong. *I was not lying when I said I would have fallen on my own sword rather than raise it against any of your kin. By ending Haman's mission you have saved my life. I await the chance to return the favor.*

CHAPTER SIXTY:
LEAVE-TAKINGS

Ruti died a few years after our peoples' victory. "I thought that if a woman could not bear a child she was of little use in the world," she said. She was lying on her back with her eyes closed, her hand in mine. "But you taught me otherwise, my queen. You have made me more proud than a woman like me has a right to be, and now I can die at peace with the world."

Not long after Ruti died I summoned Hegai. I had never longed so desperately for a comforting embrace, but he was so formal I could not imagine calling him closer and putting my arms around him. I bid him to rise from where he bowed low before me. "The king told me once that he had foreseen the hour of his death," I told Hegai. "He said someone would betray him, but he did not know who."

"He doubts his judgment of character, as he should. You must keep your ear to the ground."

Artabanus, one of Xerxes' officials, had placed his seven sons in high positions and would surely not be satisfied until one of them, or he himself, sat upon the throne. Xerxes could not remove him from his post without losing the support of some of the most powerful people in Persia. Whenever I saw Mordecai, his brow was so deeply creased with worry that I had the urge to reach out and smooth it with my hand.

"Do you know something?" I asked Hegai.

"Nothing for certain, except that if Xerxes is assassinated, you must flee. If you do not, you will be killed, or worse. A queen's story ends with her son's, unless she has no son, and then it ends with her king's."

I did not argue aloud. The life I would make for myself would be argument enough. "Hegai, you are now my most trusted friend. We will flee together." *And Erez will be our guide.*

He laughed. "How I would love that, if I were not . . . as I am." I did not blush or look away as I once would have, and after a moment he sighed and continued. "My queen, I cannot leave. There is nothing for me outside these walls. I would not be satisfied to be merely a servant to a wealthy noble, and that is the most I could hope for if I fled. I am suited only to palace life. And, if you will forgive my lack of humility, I think, perhaps I could even come through a coup with my position intact."

What I had told him years ago was still true: I did not want to leave him. But if the king was assassinated, I would. "I do not doubt you, my friend. Thank you for all you have done for me."

He bowed to me, and I bowed back.

EPILOGUE

465 BCE

For eight years, Erez and I continued to pass little scrolls back and forth on Purim without speaking or looking at each other directly. In the morning, after I read the scroll he gave me, I forced myself to hold it over a flame. I kept the ashes in a tiny gold case I wore near my heart. Though we only saw each other once a year, and I was never able to ask him any of my questions — did he still have the king's favor, was there anything I could do to help him — somehow I still felt as though Erez and I were always together, getting older, wiser in each other's company. I felt closer to him than I had when he guarded me each day.

On the ninth year, Erez did not press anything into my hand as I passed him on my way to the Purim celebration. I tried not to look disappointed. It would appear strange for me to be sad on such a happy occasion. After I had gone a few more steps, Erez called out, "Your Majesty, you dropped this."

I turned around and walked past my escort so I could take the scroll directly from him. I had not looked openly at him since the last time he had walked me to the king's chambers nine years before. I was startled to see how much older he had gotten. Some of the hair near his temples was starting to turn silver and deep lines cupped his mouth on either side. But this was not as startling as seeing that he was looking at me directly. I tried to hide the pleasure I felt at having his dark eyes on mine. I knew from the intensity with which he gazed at me that something big was coming and that he was not afraid. I gazed back with equal force. *I am not afraid either.*

He pressed not only a scroll into my palm but something solid and sharp as well. I did not have to look at it to know what it was. It was as familiar as though I had just torn it from my neck and dropped it upon the banquet hall floor yesterday. He had gotten the Faravahar back. My heart swelled and I had the urge to press myself against him.

Perhaps my desire was written too plainly across my face. He bowed abruptly, but not before I noticed his smile.

"Thank you," I said, and forced myself to walk away.

I was surprised to see that Mordecai was at the Purim celebration. He had been so busy for the last few months that I had hardly seen him at all, and when I had, he could spare little time to talk. He approached with a brow even more tangled than usual. "What is it, cousin?"

"I have come to see you," he said quietly, "perhaps for the last time." Before I could protest, he went on. "I do not know if Artabanus will succeed in taking the crown, but I do not want you around while he tries. You will be welcome in any Jewish quarter in the empire."

"As will you. We will go together."

"For the sake of our people, I must try to retain my position here."

He was the one person I had known all my life. I had already lost Ruti, and when I fled I would lose Hegai. I did not want to lose Mordecai too. "Will you visit?"

"If doing so will not put you in any danger." He squeezed my left hand in his, then turned it over and kissed my palm. "May the God of Abraham and Sarah, Isaac and Rebecca, and Jacob, Rachael and Leah watch over you on your travels."

■ ■ ■ ■

When I returned to my chambers in the morning, I did not go more than two steps before dismissing my servants and opening the scroll Erez had pressed into my palm.

Next time we travel together, I will take you wherever you want to go.

I had not been outside the palace in fifteen years. Half my life. When I fled, my crown would not go with me. I unpinned it without a servant's help and stood feeling its weight upon my head one last time. I thought of all I had done to get it, how hard I had struggled to keep it, and the many people who had helped me.

Am I ready for another journey?

My hands were steady as I took off the crown and set it on a table beside the bed. *Yes, I am ready.*

AUTHOR'S NOTE

I've had a complicated relationship with the Old Testament since I was old enough to read it on my own. The one thing that always brings me back is the people God chose to carry out His tasks. He didn't call upon perfect people. He chose people who sometimes wished He'd chosen otherwise. When Esther isn't feeling up to the task of saving her people, Ruti tells her, "God chooses cowards to be brave, barren women to give birth to prophets, passionate men to be patient, and a man who stutters to command his people through the desert." Conflicted people. Ruti's line had been in the prologue to *Sinners and the Sea,* but I cut it before the book was published. The only way I could bring myself to cut it was to decide to use it in my next novel. I like the writers' adages *Only trouble is interesting* and *Hell is very story friendly.* Sometimes the worst trouble is that which one finds within herself.

Esther has a question many of us have at some point in our lives: *Am I worthy of the task I've been given?* This is one of the ways I sought to make her a human being, neither all-good nor all-bad. Ideals of perfection plague women and girls in a special way. We're encouraged to be "nice girls" and people pleasers. Which brings me to another of my favorite adages: *Well-behaved women seldom make history.* Hegai tells Esther "do not waste time trying to convince yourself that everything you do springs from pure and selfless goodness . . . I cannot tolerate girlish silliness." Esther must leave behind certain prized aspects of femininity to do what must be done.

Another area I wanted to explore in writing about Esther was her intelligence. Becoming queen is no easy task. I've never been satisfied with the assumption that many come away with after reading the Book of Esther: the king made Esther queen because she was beautiful. With hundreds of beautiful girls for the king to choose from, a girl would have been foolish to rely solely on her beauty. Esther is smart enough to quickly win the favor of Hegai, and smart enough to listen to him. In the novel, Hegai tells her, "You will have to learn to appear fierce and submissive at the same time. That is the task of womanhood, and you must master it while you are still a girl."

Liberties Taken

Those familiar with the Book of Esther may have noticed that I combined Haman and Memukhan into one character. Scholar Ilana Goldstein Saks notes the similarities between the two men in *Torah of the Mothers: Contemporary Jewish Women Read Classic Jewish Texts.* Both advisers manipulate the king in similar ways, and both generalize about the effects of a transgression on an entire population.

Another liberty I took was using the term "Immortal" to describe Xerxes' most elite force. Use of the term is thought to originate with Herodotus some years after Xerxes' reign. I also used Herodotus's exaggeration about the size of Xerxes' forces. Herodotus often blurred the line between historian and storyteller. Perhaps I was subconsciously thinking of him when I had Mordecai tell Esther, "The tale men fashion is as important as what really happened. Until many years have passed. And then it is more important."

ACKNOWLEDGMENTS

I'm so grateful for all the support I've received. Thank you to early supporters Amber McKenzie, Megan Atwood, and Heather Anastasiu, along with friends Inna Valin, Margie Newman, Alyssa Maizan, Jenny Updike, Michelle Meyers, Diane Grace, Dawn Frederick, Richard Nystrom, Tanya Pedersen-Barr, Karen Seashore, and Tom Remes. I couldn't have done it without the tireless members of my writing group, Sandy Stefenson and Richard Thompson, and my brilliant agent, Carolyn Jenks, who can light up a room from a thousand miles away, along with her well-chosen junior agents and editors, most especially Tildy Banker-Johnson and Caroline Pallotta. I'll be forever indebted to my unofficial and woefully underpaid local PR woman, Sue Stein. Becky Nesbitt and the other lovely folks at Howard have once again astonished me with their grace and insight; I can't thank them enough. Many thanks to super-hero Rabbi Morris Allen of Beth Jacob Congregation, my brother, Aaron Kanner, who is a champion in every way, my devoted father, Michael Kanner, and my mentor and friend Lynn Nelvik-Levitt, to whom this book is dedicated.

ABOUT THE AUTHOR

Rebecca Kanner's writing has won an Associated Writing Programs Award and a Loft Mentorship Award. Her stories have been published in numerous journals, including *The Kenyon Review* and *The Cincinnati Review.* She is a freelance writer and teaches writing at The Loft in Minneapolis.

The employees of Thorndike Press hope you have enjoyed this Large Print book. All our Thorndike, Wheeler, and Kennebec Large Print titles are designed for easy reading, and all our books are made to last. Other Thorndike Press Large Print books are available at your library, through selected bookstores, or directly from us.

For information about titles, please call:
  (800) 223-1244

or visit our Web site at:
  http://gale.cengage.com/thorndike

To share your comments, please write:
  Publisher
  Thorndike Press
  10 Water St., Suite 310
  Waterville, ME 04901